KISS THE BABIES

Hi Carol!,

From the Portsmouth Herald to Yankee Magazine to ... this? I hope you like it. Love,
Dean

KISS THE BABIES

Peter E. Randall Publisher
Portsmouth, New Hampshire 03801
2022

© 2022 by Dean Ludington.

No part of this book may be reproduced or transmitted in any form or by any means, electronic or mechanical, including photocopying, recording, or by any information storage and retrieval system without the written permission of the author, except where permitted by law.

Printed in the United States of America

Softcover ISBN: 978-1-937721-88-6
Ebook ISBN: 978-1-937721-89-3
Library of Congress Control Number: 2022909782

Peter E. Randall Publisher
5 Greenleaf Woods Drive, Suite 102
Portsmouth, NH 03801
www.perpublisher.com

Book design: Grace Peirce

Front cover illustration: Justin Hess.

This book is dedicated to Bryn Emily Taudvin and Molly Katherine Taudvin.

Acknowledgements

Endless thanks to: Sharon Ryan, Robert Marchewka, Jack Terrill, Steve Doonan, Jeremy LeClair, Dave Tulli, Bill Sexton, Shelly Cohen Konrad, Justin Hess

Prologue

I've never had terminal cancer yet.
But during the worst of it, this thing, I wake in the night, upright, bolt, feeling the diagnosis. Sick and afraid. How did this happen? What am I supposed to do now? Will I be OK? I'm not OK. Then, coming awake, think . . . take it easy, nobody is dead. Nobody is dying.
No. But it got pretty close. And then some did.

* * *

Bette was skinny towards the end. Impossibly skinny. Not enough meat on the bone to live.
Bette was tall, a six-footer, and always thin, but her eighty-year-old self was just bone and loose bruised skin and blue eyes.
Bette was a badass with raging intellect and bottomless, inexhaustible curiosity regarding all topics. Her loyalty to the principles and the people she loved was intimidating.
Like many of her badass ilk, Bette was a full-time contrarian and also very sure of herself.
Bette could be an enormous pain in the ass with her OCD schedulings for family gatherings and her black and white concepts of right and wrong, but at least her notions of what was right were right. Her notions of wrong were her own. She believed in the Golden Rule and believed that you should too.

Bette relentlessly came through for the people she loved. Never more so than on this day in question. Also, on this day, watching her work, I knew that I'd be losing her soon.

Bette loved Mae and Bea beyond measure. She hated the situation we found ourselves in, all four of us. All five of us actually. She hated this custodial tug-of-war. And because I was her son and she loved me too beyond measure, she knew I was in the right and that Mother of Twins was in the wrong. This making of heroes and villains was not helpful. We were all heroes. We were all villains. Except for Mae and Bea. They were and are innocent victims of adult manufactured malfeasance.

On this day, Mae was weeping, softly, confused and trying to be brave, belted in beside me in the truck. She was confused and frightened because her sister Bea didn't want to go to the farm this weekend and her mother was not going to make her go. Mae was given the option and, weeping, reached for my hand. Bea was also weeping when we left and I could not believe the strength shown by both of my daughters, making decisions that no child should have to make. As far as I knew, this would be the twins' first night apart since birth and before.

Instead of driving Mae the thirty long minutes to Serious Farm, I headed instead to Bette's, only seven minutes away from her mother's house.

Bette's blue reading chair faced the sliding glass doors to the porch deck so that she could keep an eye on all things: the bird feeder, the mailbox, the sunrise. Bette limped out to the porch when she saw my truck pull in, eschewing her cane, delight clearly registered on her face due to this unexpected visit by her beloved. Her look quickly changed when she saw that one of her beloveds was absent.

I walked around to the passenger side and helped Mae down. I dried her tears with my thumb and smiled. "Grammy's," I said.

At ten years old Mae was a little big to carry anymore, but I lifted her to my hip and carried her towards her grandmother. On the porch I set Mae down and she walked directly to Bette and hugged her leg, pushing her sad face into her grandmother's hip. Bette put her hand on Mae's head, stroked her hair and mouthed at me, "Where's Bea?"

I shook my head.

This was next-level stuff. An escalation of tactics. A malicious agenda in the works. This was serious.

Inside, Bette led Mae to the ancient plaid love seat. Bette lowered herself painfully and then patted the place next to her for Mae to sit. Mae climbed up and snuggled in close to her grandmother. Mae rested her head on Bette's side and Bette reached a scarecrow arm around Mae's shoulder. Mae's face was impossibly sad, but she'd stopped crying.

Love, I thought, looking at them. *Love will fix this somehow.*

But at that moment, it was losing. Love was losing. It was abundantly clear that I was losing them. My daughters and my mom. Losing my mom to time and nature and my daughters to a more horrible and unnatural thing. And because I myself am not so good at the love and not at all sure I could live without them I figured maybe it was time to go for a drive.

BOOK ONE
People Changes

— 1 —

Charleston, South Carolina.

We missed it. Drove right by it.

There was nothing to indicate, from the elevated roadway we were on and then bridge, that there was a large- or even medium-sized city or town anywhere below. No exit signs for downtown that I saw, or buildings taller than a church steeple. There were some shipyard cranes down there, and some houses. Trees. Water. An aircraft carrier parked off to the right on a river or ocean. Otherwise, not much.

As we descended the bridge there was a sign proclaiming a Mount Pleasant. We rolled off into heavy construction and large chain grocery stores on the left and right: your Harris Teeter, your Whole Foods, your Piggly Wiggly, your Trader Joe's. It wasn't overly pleasant here thus far, strip malls and torn up roads. Flat as Nebraska, there was no Mount and nothing that looked like it might be the city of Charleston. I told her, "I think we missed it."

She may have responded. If so, I did not hear.

Earlier that morning in hilly Virginia, over motel lobby coffee in tiny paper cups and motel lobby cellophane pastries and motel lobby miniature yogurts in sickly pastel colors, I asked if she'd ever been to Charleston, South Carolina.

"No," she said, not looking up from her thimble of pink.

"Wanna go? Get lunch? Look around?"

"Sounds good," she might have said in her whispery mousebreath of a voice. Low, shy, and in a decibel range I found nearly impossible to pick up with my damaged hearing.

"Did you say, *Sounds good?*"

"I did." She would not look up at me so I could not read her lips. I did not know at the time that I could read lips, but why else would it help me to hear by looking at lips? I should have been able to put two and two together.

"You did?"

"Yes!" she said, looking at me. Annoyed?

"OK," I said. "Charleston."

"OK," she said, still looking at me, showing me her lips, maybe getting the hang of it, both of us, getting the hang of this.

OK. We were in no particular hurry, so we were in no danger of losing time or screwing some sort of itinerary because we had none. It was early December and turning icy and dark back in Maine, where we had come from.

We had the windows halfway down as we drove along and then turned around to take another try at finding Charleston. The air was warm and thick here. The digital thermometer on the dashboard of my boring car read sixty-eight degrees. The sun was out. I felt pretty good, all things considered. Considering what we had both left behind, back in Maine.

We were running, but not even away because we had to go back. We were both quite lost. Quite hurt. Only I did not know that she was hurt and she did not know that I was lost. The conversations we'd had to date had been a little awkward and fairly thin in scope and depth. We didn't know much at all, regarding one another.

I took a quick right on a street called Anna Knapp and got us turned around. Charleston had to be back there somewhere.

— 2 —

In the cold drizzle, in the dooryard of her daddy's house in Freedom, New Hampshire, I told her if she wanted to go for a drive to be at my place, Serious Farm, at six the next morning and we'd go. She said, "'Kay."

Her face gave nothing away, yea or nay.

It was an irresponsible Hail Mary on my part, this invitation to drive away. We'd be quitting our jobs with no notice. It was a half-hearted but heartfelt pitch for company because I'd been lonely. I was going on this drive either way, but, it felt all right to ask. There was not a lot to lose, it seemed. Not for me.

The next morning, when I looked out of my east-facing bedroom window at five-thirty, I saw headlights bouncing down my long and unpaved excuse for a driveway, the lights smashing against the dense row of pine trees which lined the drive. When her car hit the particularly deep hole and bottomed out about halfway down the drive, her headlights lit up the lower trunks of the trees and then shone all the way upward, into the morning dark sky and back again as her shocks decompressed.

Hers was a Nissan Something: old, formerly sliver, rusted, reliable maybe. With my bedroom dark I watched as she exited her car wearing a bulky full-length down coat and knit winter cap. I guessed that her car heater did not work. She stood in my driveway and surveyed the yard, the apple trees front lit by the motion-activated spotlight over Serious Garage. The apple trees with December naked limbs but black and withered apples still hanging on like Tim Burton Christmas ornaments.

She stepped out into the crunchy frozen grass of the lawn to take in the hulk of the barn, Serious Barn, which presided over all. I liked very much that she was curious about

Serious Farm, looking around patiently before coming to the mudroom door.

She looked at her watch. She stood still long enough for the spotlight to go out. I knocked on the window glass. She looked up to the sound. I knew she could not see me as she gave a tiny and shy wave, on faith that someone, that I, was there somewhere. Amazing faith, this girl must have. Or something else. Nothing, perhaps, to lose.

She was coming along.

Damn. She was coming along.

I really hadn't thought this through.

— 3 —

Here's what I knew:

Her name was Bojean. It was pronounced Bo with a long O and jean as in the French kind . . . shon with a short O, emphasis on Bo. Bojean. She told me she was named after Bojan Križaj, a Slovenian alpine skier. Her daddy, she said, had heard the name on the TV at some time in the 1970s when Križaj was at the top of his game, liked the name and altered it only a little to bestow upon his baby girl. I told her I liked the name too. I did. I do.

She was a peculiar beauty.

It was difficult not to notice her in our little group of new hires at the neuro-rehabilitation facility up there near Freedom, New Hampshire. There were eight of us, the new hires. There were two female kitchen staff, a maintenance guy, a female RN, two female technicians of which Bojean was one, and me, a case manager. I did not know what any of these jobs specifically entailed, including my own.

All persons in this group were significantly younger than me, including the administration lady in charge of our orientation, including the HR guy who had hired me after a suspiciously short interview. There may have been only one or two upon this hill older than me, but I felt like the new kid in school.

The new hires appeared to be local mountain folk: not too yappy, weatherbeaten, outfitted in work clothes purchased at Marden's or Big Lots or Reny's, DIY haircuts, missing and misbegotten teeth, hard New Hampshire and Maine accents like you'd figure. They were the working poor, like me.

Bojean stood out from us. She looked to be sixteen, unblemished and pure while the rest of us were the opposite. I would not have been surprised if she identified as Amish or Shaker. She bore some sort of a halo.

As we went around the room introducing ourselves there in a windowless basement room of the security building of the campus, the others spoke in smoky dog barks, guttural mumbles and blue-collar confidence. Her voice was a hint of a foggy mist upon a bog on a warming July early morning—barely there and then gone. I did not come close to catching her name or the brief biography we were all asked to give. But as she spoke, she looked directly at me and I looked directly back.

Her face was an oval and her eyes too. Her skin was milk white on this day in early September, meaning she had not spent much of her time this past summer sunning. Her eyes were honey-colored, but dark honey, farmer's market honey. There may have been flecks of gold in there . . . she was only three feet from me and she kept looking at me. I guessed her to be five-foot-four or five-foot-three but not five- feet-five. Her hair was a story unto itself.

There was so much of it, her hair. Grain colored, amber, ripe grain not the dried-out wheatfield kind, with short radius waves, not quite kinked or curly but crimped kind of, crinkled. It tumbled over her shoulders and halfway down her back. Later, when she learned that her "clients" would identify her hair as a target to be entwined in dirty fingers, to be yanked and ripped from her skull, bloody sometimes, she would bunch those amber waves of ripe grain into a bun and keep them hidden under a ball cap.

Her nose was straight, narrow, and proportional upon her oval face. Her lips were pale but full enough that you'd notice. Sparkling teeth. On the first day of our orientation she wore grey corduroy Levis and clean Nike running shoes. On top she wore a soft-looking navy-blue V-neck sweater with a grey t-shirt underneath. Her sweater and her Levis were loose fitting enough as to not give away many secrets, but it was clear that she was healthy and well established. She had a very pronounced cleft in her strong chin, a chin dimple. I resolutely focused on that dimple when she looked at me and later when we knew each other well enough to converse. I focused on that dimple so as not to consider all the rest of her, her lovely face, her fuselage. It was all there, lurking on the periphery. But I refused to notice, much less acknowledge. I kept reminding myself, *You are a professional now, act like one.*

— 4 —

The first day's drive was somewhat wooden.

Bojean was not a natural conversationalist. I would ask her a question to try and get the ball rolling and she would give a one word answer that 70 percent of the time I could not hear. She sat with her back wedged between her passenger seat and the door of my lame Volvo S60. I've regretted a car or two in my life but none more so than this particular assemblage of nada. I'd been fooled by the black-on-black leather interior and heated seats and heated steering wheel. Fooled by the rare (the dealer said) six-speed manual transmission. It was a Volvo but it may as well have been a Toyota Yaris or a Geo Prism. No go. No guts. No character. I couldn't wait to wear it out and move on to the next. The S60 was the most lackluster car I'd ever owned but my recall of this trip is of her in it, all suspicious, quiet, and softly coiled in the corner, thereby making this car memorable forever.

I took the hard left out of Serious Driveway onto Route 9 East and made a beeline for 95 South. She never asked where we were going or for how long. I liked that. I liked that because I didn't know where we were going or for how long. I assumed we'd be back for Christmas. My family would be expecting me. I did not know what Bojean's Christmas obligations were.

An hour down the road, taking 128 to circumvent Boston, I asked her, "Does your family do Christmas?"

She smiled, a very welcome sight, and said, "We certainly do. Does yours?"

"Yes."

I felt her looking at the right side of my face, expecting more. This time it was my turn to be silent. I thought of my daughters, Mae and Bea. They'd made it clear they did not wish to come up to either Serious Farm or Grammy's for Christmas this year. We negotiated an overnight at a Cambridge hotel on the twenty-sixth, to be returned to their mom's house in Lexington by noon of the twenty-seventh. *On the Twelve hours of Christmas my true loves gave to me . . .*

. . . as opposed to the grand Christmas extravaganza each year until this year at their grandmother's house in Rye, New Hampshire. These holiday annuals were indeed a warm and wonderful gathering of a clan: my brothers and their wives and their children; two of my mom's favored husband-and-wife combos: Everett and Elizabeth, Pat and Steve; and the occasional stray friend of the family with no place to go that year. For many years Christmas at Bette's was something to very much look forward to. In hindsight, those days were the best days when most folks were getting along and the babies were babies. Christmas at Bette's was a hoot. It was a bray.

Of course, Mae and Bea were part of the Christmas Eve bash every other year, as was the shared-custody norm for a large segment of the child population in modern America. On the years they spent Christmas Eve and morning with their mother, Mae and Bea were allowed time with me on Christmas Day afternoon, where they met up with sleepy but still present cousins, hung over from Bette's Yule-O-Rama.

Yes, Bojean, my family did Christmas for many, many years. All of the years. But this year would be a challenge because of strained marriages, children getting older and on to their own agendas, collapsing custody agreements, and Bette's accumulating health issues. This year's gathering would most likely be the last of its kind. Change was in the air.

People changes.

Instead of talking about it, I asked of hers.

She smiled over at me, warmly. "Maybe later," she said. We were already in the run-up traffic funneling south toward the George Washington Bridge. I'd made this drive many times before, blasting through NYC, making sure not to get sucked unwilling onto an off ramp for the Cross Bronx Expressway or the West Side Highway. Even with enormous overhead green signs pointing the way, sometimes centrifugal forces pulled the car into the maw of commerce and fuckery.

She looked out the windshield, across my face and out, taking in the skyline as we ascended the GWB. She was giving off some kind of alien visitor vibe as if she were cool and acclimated to these surroundings, this low cloud ceiling, this mad traffic with horns blasting for no particular reason, as if she were cool and acclimated but in reality was a spy attempting to assimilate these sights and smells including mine and not give away her astonishment and fear. She looked out the windshield across my face while clutching a metallic and glass rectangle. I stole glances at her while pretending to be monitoring traffic flow.

"What is that?" I asked.

"What is what?"

"That thing in your hand."

She looked down at her hands and then held it up to me, to see. I looked at it, a flat black rectangle. "What is it?"

"iTouch."

I waited for more. There was no more.

"What is iTouch?"

"Music," she said. And then, "We need to find an adapter for it." This was my introduction to i stuff—Pod, Pad, Phone. Later on in the drive she would reveal a GPS she'd brought along. Initially, I scoffed, at both the touch thing and the global positioning device. By the time we made it back to Serious Farm I was sold. For a while.

It was only just past noon when we cleared the NYC bird's nest tangle of deceiving off ramps, on ramps, and other exits. At the apex of the GWB I looked down at Manhattan to my left. Just then I began a new symptom of dissociation. Hallucination, maybe. Not the safest thing to be doing while city driving.

The Raven, my college love, my first love, my most intense love was down in there somewhere; maybe downtown where she worked, maybe at her present apartment with her husband in Park Slope, maybe at her mom's at Rockaway Beach. She would never again leave the confines of the boroughs. I'd lured her out somehow, when we were but children, with promises of everlasting devotion some thirty years earlier, barely in our twenties. I'd lured her out to come live with me in San Francisco and then I left her there. She's never quite forgiven me. I know this because I check in with her from time to time to this day. She has not forgiven me. *YOU TOLD ME YOU'D LOVE ME FOREVER!* I could hear her as if she were in the backseat of the car.

I yelled back, *I DO! I LOVE YOU STILL AND FOREVER IS CLOSER THAN EVER!!*

I glanced at Bojean. She did not react to the yelling. The yelling was in my head. Good.

As we trundled along and I made the decision to veer west by southwest on 78 to avoid the Philly-Baltimore-D.C. traffic morass, I began to grow concerned over when and where to stop for the night and how *that* was going to play out. I had assumed that by now, seven hours into the drive, we'd be swapping stories and laughing uproariously, becoming friends. Not so. It turns out that Bojean was not the uproarious kind.

I've gone for many long drives in my life. Enough automobile travel to know that while I enjoy the pre-dawn darkness driving with hot coffee, the empty pre-dawn roads, and the adventure of the day's drive ahead, I know too that post-sunset driving is not for me. After ten to twelve hours of piloting, my nerves are needles and my vision is mush. When weary, I overreact and underreact to traffic around me. I like to be ensconced in my hotel room, or tent, or bed of pick-up truck as the day's darkness rolls in. Traveling so close to the winter solstice makes for a relatively short driving day. At 1 p.m., breaking into Pennsylvania, I aimed to make it onto Virginia 81 before scouting out billboards for cheap accommodations.

At a truck stop, she found a gizmo, a cassette tape thing with a wire and male adapter coming out of it which would then plug into her iThing and play her music through the Volvo stereo system. This seemed to please her. Her music was nothing I'd heard but not horrible. Mostly a succession of chick singers sounding like squealing dolphins along with a few rap selections, and even those were okay. A minute or so into each new song I would ask, who is this? She would patiently tell me.

When we crossed the state line from Pennsylvania to West Viriginia she asked, without looking at me, "How old are you?"

"I'm fifty-two," I said. "How old are you?"

"I'm twenty-four."

I meditated on that. She let a minute go by before stating, "My father is fifty-two too."

That makes complete sense, I thought, before answering, "I don't know anyone who is twenty-four."

Turning her head toward me, and with laughter in her eyes, she said, "You do now."

— 5 —

Not long after our orientation was complete and I saw how it was, I began to refer to our place of employment as Mayhem Mountain.

The mountainside into which Mayhem was dug was a one-hour serpentine drive north from Serious Farm. A beautiful drive. A mesmerizing drive filled with anticipation and some dread on the way to work in the morning and beer-cooled relief on the way back in the evening.

Physically, the place, Mayhem, was staggeringly lovely.

The facility had to be one hundred acres anyway, housing 150 clients. It had clearly been a farm at one time as there were ancient apple orchards all up and down the property. It was encouraging to me that the decision makers for Mayhem Mountain decided to keep these orchards, to maintain an aesthetic. The evenly spaced trees lent an order, a calm, to a disorderly environment. I later learned that none of the fruit could be consumed due to the amount of anti-psychotic medications dumped into the facility's septic system, which then leached out into the orchards.

It was a gated campus, or rather, a fenced-in campus. A prison, really.

Our employment began in early September. Famous New England September and the weather was crystalline, the light throughout the day brilliant and clean. The temperatures were cool fifties in the morning with mists covering the low-lying bogs, in the mid-seventies at mid-day with a whiff of chill settling in at the end of our work day at 5 p.m. We were first shift, Bojean and me. Naturally, there were three shifts at Mayhem Mountain, as the helpless yet reckless clients couldn't very well be left alone overnight.

I came to learn through gossip and tall tales that as violent and bloody as things were daily on our first shift, the second was a combat zone, with sunsetting behaviors and the normal thankless and often pointless chore of trying to put a kid to bed, or a middle-aged person with the mind of a kid. Bedtime struggles were epic, with black eyes the norm for both staff and clients. Restraints, physical and chemical, were against the law, but the law rarely ventured onto these haunted grounds.

Third shift was purportedly quiet, but when things went sideways on third shift, they went very sideways: 3 a.m. escapes over barbed-wire-topped fences and into the wooded hillsides; attempted suicides by borderline personalities swallowing batteries, razors, or bars of soap; attempted sexual hookups and rampant, chronic, facility-wide masturbation. Brain injury and autism, it turns out, do not dull the human libido. They may, in fact, sharpen it.

Here at Mayhem the boys longed for the girls, the girls longed for the boys, the boys humped the boys and the girls humped the girls. And humans being humans, the staff partook in their own nocturnal shenanigans, sometimes keeping to their own and sometimes sampling the client base. Third shift at Mayhem Mountain, as lore had it, was a never-ceasing fuck fest: brain trauma as an aphrodisiac for both the traumatized and their keepers.

She, Bojean, was a client technician for the student aged population, ages eight to eighteen. Translation: spoon-feeder, nose-wiper, tear-dryer, escorter to and fro, wheelchair-roller, shower-er, diaper-changer, mother, father, and, inevitably the target of vicious, spontaneous, violent freak-outs by the clients.

One would think a client technician would have his or her hands full with a one-on-one tech-to-client ratio. And they would. However, the actual ratio was five clients to one tech. The rustic and spartan cabins that housed the clients had beds for twenty. Four techs were assigned to these cabins each morning with the understanding that at least one tech each day would call out sick, sometimes two, sometimes three, and some days all four. In these instances, senior staff would be required to fill in, which was the equivalent of the hapless substitute public school teacher scenario—more mayhem than the norm. These clients were brain damaged in some way but they were not stupid. They could manipulate with the best.

Bojean told me, when we began to have conversations after work, that she was too shocked to even register pain the first time she was punched in the face by one of her charges. She waited until she got to her father's house in Freedom after work to cry and apply ice to the swelling in her jaw.

Being a client technician required no formal education, no college degree. The vast majority of the techs were young women in their teens or barely out. The wage was minimum.

I watched it all from above. I was given an office in another cabin housing another group of twenty student-aged kids. My cabin was all male. Bojean's cabin was co-ed. I had no idea what the therapeutic rationale was for one or the other. My cabin, my office, was situated uphill from the majority of the campus buildings so that I could peer down upon the schoolhouse, the medical building, the admin building, and the largest structure of all, which housed the adult population along with the cafeteria and gymnasium. I also had an astonishing view of Mount Chocorua due north, Mount Washington to the northeast, and all in between. Looking almost straight down this mountain I watched as the September shadows altered and diamonded the surface waters of the larger Ossipee and Silver Lakes. Unnamed bogs on just the northern side of Highway 25, the Ossipee Trail, appeared in sharp relief through this early autumn atmosphere that made me feel as though I'd gotten a long overdue update on my glasses prescription.

This was my first professional gig out of grad school. I was a freshly minted MSW and had taken the first job I was offered. Why wouldn't I?

I'd interviewed for two other jobs just after graduation and never heard back from the panels who'd grilled me. I'd been utterly unprepared for entry into agency type work, as I'd been my own boss for the better part of thirty years and was accustomed to being the one asking the questions, not answering them.

During the interview at Mayhem, I have to admit that I wasn't really listening to the job description, as I was more focused on not saying anything disqualifying or looking out the window. The White Mountains were so close and vivid I wanted to eat them.

As a result, I missed the extremely subtle references made during the interview to the nature of the population being served . . . unpredictable and dangerous. When HR called me less than six hours after the interview to offer me the position, I accepted. When they emailed me the specs on salary, holidays, PTO, sick days, health insurance, and the rest, I stared at the starting salary of just under 40K and I did not know what it meant.

I'd run a stonemasonry concern for decades. I was used to money coming in for stone work and money going out for materials and contract labor and insurance and such. I really had no idea how much, exactly, wound up in my pocket over the course of the work year. I left that to my buddy Doc, the accountant. Doc had been a pretty good college basketball player but his nickname came from his surgical skills with the books and the numbers.

As I stared at the email and the figure they proposed, it seemed low. Like, really low. I knew coming into my new occupation, my new profession, what the ballpark pay scale was for an MSW grad, but again, I didn't really know what it meant . . . what a bi-monthly paycheck would look like and what the buying power of that paycheck would bring. Would it even cover child support? It turns out that what it meant was that I would barely be scratching the lower rung of middle class in the second decade of the twenty-first century. This new job was my entré into the world of the working poor.

Good thing I never really cared much about money.

I did, however, reach for my phone in Serious Office and called HR at Mayhem Mountain. I identified myself and asked if this salary were negotiable. The woman at the other end said, "Sure." I asked to whom I should direct my negotiations and she said, "Me." She said, "Go for it."

I got her up to 40K exactly and agreed to show up for work the following Monday. I felt uneasy about my decision and I thought the unease was due to the crappy pay. It turns out my instincts were being nudged into their extreme danger zones by something far more depressing and dangerous than the evil that is the dollar bill.

— 6 —

An hour or so past sunset I took an exit for Harrisonburg, Virginia. I was severely underfunded for this journey. I had about six hundred dollars in my checking account and a credit card and no job to return to. I was not trying to impress Bojean but I also didn't want to frighten her with absolute bottom-of-the-barrel overnight accommodations. I can sleep anywhere, and have, but had a hunch that her sensibilities may not be the same. I found a mid-level econo-shelter and pulled in. Under the carport thing in front of the "lobby," I asked if this was okay.

"Yeah," she said.

"Pardon?"

"Yeah!" she said.

"You want to come in?" I asked, not knowing if being left alone in the car while I checked in might make her nervous. She shook her head, no.

Inside, I glanced at the obligatory motel pamphlet display rack and saw that this Harrisonburg was home to James Madison University. I asked the desk clerk lady how far we were from the campus and she pointed toward the lobby window and said, "right over there." I tried to peer out the window to where she had gestured but could only see the reflection of a haggard man in need of a haircut squinting back at me.

I got back behind the wheel and pulled around the building to where our room for the night was situated. First floor, near the ice and vending machines. Parking lot half full with out-of-state plates upon out-of-state cars pulled off 81 for the night. Snowbirds, perhaps, headed for Naples, Florida. Parents, perhaps, visiting homesick freshmen at JMU. Lovers, perhaps. And us.

"Here we are," I said.

"'Kay."

So, so, so very awkward.

— 7 —

Case manager. I was a case manager, it turns out.

I discovered this when I pulled aside the administrative lady who was conducting our weeklong orientation.

I identified myself and asked her if she had any idea of what my job description might be. She knew who I was and knew I was a case manager.

I admitted my embarrassment for not knowing. I also admitted that somehow I'd not been listening to that particular part of my job interview, hoping she would find the humor, and told her I could not find my job description in the information packet I'd been emailed.

She found no humor in this, or in me.

She looked me up and down, this mountain lady, this wiry specimen. It felt vaguely sexually threatening. "It will become clear," she said. *Clee-uh.*

— 8 —

After we were dismissed for lunch and warned not to interact, yet, with the clients, I made my way out of the windowless basement room where we were being oriented and made my way over to the administration building where my interview had been conducted. There was a paved lane between the security building where I'd been and the admin building. I passed several clients going the other way. Some were accompanied by staff and some not. They looked me over and I looked them over. They bore the hint of *somewhat off* but did not appear to be overtly damaged. They might have thought the same of me.

I could not recall the name of the man who had interviewed me and did not want to randomly ask for the office of "the bald guy," so I approached a friendly-looking woman typing away at a computer at a desk out in the open in an almost foyer type area with floor to ceiling windows looking north toward the White Mountains and was once again stopped agog by the vista. I stood very close to her desk, staring out.

"May I help you?"

"What a view!" I said.

She smiled and looked over her shoulder. She stopped typing. "Isn't it though?"

I explained my dilemma. She knew who I was and why I'd been hired. She laughed and generously told me the things I did not know.

My interpretation of her interpretation of my job description was such: I would be assigned a caseload of twenty to twenty-five clients. I was assigned the youth group, the kids.

My main responsibility was one of data entry on the daily activities of my caseload and reporting weekly to the insurance concerns that footed the bills for this very expensive operation. I was also to facilitate weekly conference calls with these insurance concerns and with the parents or legal guardians of the kids on my caseload.

Whatever time I had remaining after these administrative duties was to be spent interacting with the actual clients: visiting them in their cabins or classrooms, walking them to the dining hall, participating in afterschool activities.

"How much time is that, generally?" I asked.

She shrugged her shoulders and said, "That depends on how quick you are with the data entry. Data is primary. No data, no income. Actual contact with the clients is generally left to the techs. If you need specific information about a child, the techs will be your best resource."

"Better than the actual kids?"

"Usually, yes. Many of these children are nonverbal."

Data entry. Good lord.

When I returned to the basement room in the security compound, I was late.

A dangerous-looking man with an old-school Johnny Unitas flat-top haircut, Popeye forearms, and spectacular beer gut was in front of our group.

"All right with you if we start?" he asked. *staaaht?*

"Yes," I said. I sat down and for some vague reason a wave of emotion crashed over me. A loneliness. This loneliness moved from wherever it originated and settled into my throat. I wanted to cry. I did not, but really wanted to.

Bojean, four seats to my left, studied my face. This only made my loneliness worse. I believe I blushed, then smiled at her and nodded. I did not want to be in this basement room. Not at all.

— 9 —

"Would you like to go for a walk?" I asked Bojean as she sat on the edge of her bed, her feet barely scraping the carpeting of our room.

"Where to?" she asked.

I anticipated her question and though she whispered it, I was able to answer, "We're right at the edge of the James Madison University campus. Want to take a look around?"

"'Kay," she said.

Okay.

It was cold out, early evening, but not freezing. We walked side by side on the sidewalk, but she was following my lead. I saw a clocktower two blocks down and assumed it was part of the campus. We headed that way. It was good to move, to stretch, to breathe real air. Come to think of it, this was mountain air. What mountains? Blue Ridge? Allegheny? Are Allegheny mountains, or a river? The air was delicious. Shenandoah?

I took a large, deep breath. I took another, all the way down into my belly. "I came here once, these mountains, when I was in college. We camped somewhere off Skyline Drive. It was spring break, I think. Buds were out on the trees. I remember thinking I wouldn't mind living around here. We were somewhere closer to Charlottesville."

Bojean didn't respond. It wasn't really a question.

"Have you ever been around here before?"

"Oh yes," she said.

"Really? Vacation?"

"Nope." We walked on and found ourselves on the JMU campus. It was early enough that students were still crossing from classrooms to dormitories, dormitories to dining halls. "My stepfather got a job in Love."

Got a job in Love? What in hell did that mean? "What do you mean?"

"He got a job, at a church, in Love, Virginia."

"So, you presently live in Freedom. And you once lived in Love."

"Yes."

"I don't believe that you have mentioned your stepfather."

"Nope." We walked on. I was suddenly very hungry. Hungry and getting tired. "He was a pastor of the Nazarene Church." I noticed that she was speaking up, and enunciating.

"Really?" I said. "How long were you in Love?" That sounded funny, coming out of my mouth and embarrassed me a little. I was also stalling, trying to think if I knew anything, anything at all, about the Nazarene Church. I did not.

"About three months," she said. We walked on.

"That doesn't seem like a long time. Is it standard for a pastor to move on after three months?"

"Nope," she said, "not at all." We were walking down a hill towards a street of commerce. I could see neon and traffic. "We were asked, he was asked, to leave." She didn't give me the opportunity to ask a follow-up question. "A story for another day," she said. "But it wasn't the first time we were asked to leave and not the last."

I looked at her face and kept looking. She did not take the bait. She did not look back, only straight ahead. Then, without looking at me, she took my elbow as we walked.

We found a diner, a real diner, and had grilled cheese and tomato soup, both of us, because it was perfect. We conversed a little, mostly quietly speculating on customers of the diner and the Elvis (young) lookalike cook who was visible through a cutout in the diner wall. I could see that she was weary and the silence between us had become comfortable, to me at least.

We trudged back up the hill to the motel; again, she took my elbow. We entered our room and then things got weird.

— 10 —

The dangerous-looking man with the dangerously close-cut flat top told us tales of danger.

For two hours he regaled us with war stories. Again, I felt somewhat sexually threatened watching and listening as this man's eyes glazed over and as he tossed spittle recounting the specifics of his recently broken nose and busted knuckles as a result of going up against the enemy.

He slipped at one point in his soliloquy and actually called the clients the enemy. I assumed he was retired military.

When he finished romanticizing war—the concussions, contusions, and broken bones both given and received—he cynically began a three-day hands-on seminar on peaceful physical solutions to escalated client behaviors.

The concept behind this phase of our orientation was to learn the kung fu skills required to fend off murderous attacks from spun clients while keeping the invisible corporation that owned and operated this for-profit-clusterfuck and our own selves safe from litigation.

Our first lesson was in verbal de-escalation. Flat Top, actually chuckling, demonstrated how to calmly sidle up to an agitated client and, without touching them and using a slow and sweeping palms-up hand gesture à la Vanna White or The Temptations to suggest to the client, "walk with me, talk with me." We all laughed, us trainees.

"It works!" the danger man said, while his facial expression and body language in an easy-to-decipher code said, "Yeah, this never works."

For an hour he had us practice this pointless technique on one another. A sidling up, a sweeping Motown hand gesture and a calming, nearly whispered entreaty to "walk with me, talk with me." When it was Bojean's turn to whisper to me, I swear that if I were an angry client, I might have calmed and complied. Too bad for her that I was not one of her clients.

For three days we were taught a perverse square dance with increasingly complicated grips and physical maneuverings. We were shown gentle takedowns. We were shown pain-free finger locks and arm bars (there are no such things as pain-free finger locks or arm bars). We were taught safe words to be spoken to alert the hopefully nearby staff that we were losing control of a situation and required backup. The ultimate alert was "Dr. Grey!" If we were losing the battle, we were to ask whomever was in the area, firmly, for Dr. Grey. When the name Dr. Grey was spoken, it was a free for all. All hands on deck. Alert security. Extreme sublimation.

For each new move, we practiced on one another. Wrestling mats were spread across the basement floor to lessen the chances of us accidentally concussing one another. I asked Flat Top if nearby staff would hustle a wrestling mat to us in the event we had to take a client down. He looked at me and said, with menace, "I see you."

The only person in my orientation class, other than Flat Top, to remotely register my incredulity regarding these days of hand-to-hand combat basic training was Bojean. She too took on the slack-jawed expression of *Surely you jest* with each addition to our self-defense arsenal. The remainder of the working poor bore down to the tasks of memorizing their moves and their lines of this insane kabuki.

Bojean and I paired up for practicing the technique of helping the client to their feet after they have been sufficiently calmed by being pinned flat on their backs until morale was sufficiently improved. The move required the helper upper to support the downed individual's lower back with one hand while hooking an armpit with the other hand and, while using our legs, lift the fallen to their feet.

I knew enough about leverage from my many years as a stonemason to recognize that this was a shit technique for lifting anything. This was a potential back killer, but I was not going to point this out to Flat Top because Flat Top was on to me.

I was kneeling next to supine Bojean, listening to instructions. When we were told to go ahead and practice, I slid my left hand under the small of her back. She lifted herself down there a tiny bit to help me. I thought, Lord help me.

Next, as I reached for her armpit with my right hand, I tickled her. On purpose. I don't know why. I may have been rattled by the subtle pelvic lift. I may just be an idiot. I tickled her pit and she shrieked! Loudly!! I heard *that* clearly!!! As did the rest of the class and maybe half of the campus. Flat Top squattled over. "What in the hell? What did you do? Are you all right, Miss?"

Bojean was now giggling.

I apologized to her and she said, "I'm extremely ticklish."

I apologized again. *For fuck's sake, you're a professional now. Act like one!*

— 11 —

I pointedly avoided Bojean for the remainder of the week.

I pointedly, diligently, followed instruction and went through my paces.

My deviations from doing as told were not working out for me.

I had not seen my daughters in a month.

— 12 —

Climbing up the basement stairs and stepping out into the September afternoon lifted my spirits some. There is no better air that I have inhaled than the New England September mountain variety. Unless it is the New England September ocean variety.

The security building egress spilled out onto the narrow blacktopped lane that connected the main buildings at Mayhem: the schoolhouse way down there close to the cabins, the infirmary, the administration building, security, and the main house that quartered the dining hall and the residences for the adult population.

The kids were shuffling from their cabins to the dining hall as I stood breathing. I was free for the day and looking forward to the scenic drive back to Serious Farm. My attention was drawn to a particular kid coming my way. He looked like an aged teen, his affliction having worn hard miles upon his Civil War face. He was boney and concave with dark circles under his eyes and greasy dark bangs almost to his nose. I don't know what it was about him that caught my eye, but it became clear that he noticed and he did not like it. I stood off to the side of the lane to let him pass, but he came toward me and kicked at my ankle.

I was wearing work boots. I always wear work boots. And though he kicked me hard, the angle of the kick was wrong and I could feel and hear his toes crunch. The kick did not hurt me at all. He stood, looking at me, and said, with no inflection, "Ouch." We squared off for one moment and then he walked away, limping.

Serves you right, was what I thought.

The ride home was a slip off the mountain and a merge onto Route 25 (The Ossipee Trail) East. The Maine state line was only two miles along and over into Porter, Maine. A quick right off 25 onto 160 south and its cratered surface serpentine to Limerick. On this day, I pulled into the Porter General Store for a depth-charge-sized can of Foster's Lager. It was cold against the insides of my legs as it was too large for a Volvo cup holder.

I loved this drive. These were the most horribly maintained and beautiful roads north of San Cristobal de Las Casas; potholed, cracked, frost hoven and narrow with hardwood trees and pines lining the no-shouldered blacktop. Maine was a poor state with few discretionary funds to spare for infrastructure. No one complained much as this was how it had always been.

After thirty carefree minutes of only me and my Foster's on 160, I decided to stop in Limerick for a fresh roadie, this time a 16oz Budweiser. I make sure to discreetly toss the dead Foster's can into the mini dumpster at the side of the country store before going in. The light is fading now as I go in and past the cooler with live bait, the counter with homemade whoopie pies the size of manhole covers, a shelf with plastic wrapped Fruit of the Loom white t-shirts and row upon row of salty snacks and cheesy dips and Hormel canned meats. I decide to get two tall Buds, one for the remaining miles and one for home and the Red Sox game.

There is a bit more evident civilization and traffic now as I continue through Limerick and connect to Route 5 and then 202 and on down to Alfred. Past the jailhouse where I picked up my buddy Lancaster some years back after a two-day stint for some indiscretion or another and the Hannaford and south on 4, which will take me all the way into North Berwick, almost dark now.

The speed limit on Route 4 in North Berwick drops from fifty-five to thirty at the town line. Only locals know this and the police generate revenues on the perfect rural speed trap. It is best not to make any careless mistakes to rouse the interest of a bored country cop, especially with an open beer cradled in the crotch. The lights at Route 9, a left and the last mile to the farm. Down the long dirt drive and there she be. Serious.

This is Thursday. Thursday used to be the first night of my time with the girls. Thursday to Sunday every week but that went away over a year ago and I have not seen my girls at all, not even for dinner out, in a month. I have asked and have been turned down.

I make my meal; I watch four innings of pointless September Red Sox, playing dogass baseball, solidly in third place behind the Rays and the Yankees, and fall asleep by nine fifteen in Mae and Bea's bed.

My life.

— 13 —

Awake well before dawn. Like, well before dawn. Like 4 a.m. These were my favorite hours at Serious Farm, no matter the season. When the girls lived there, it was a quiet two hours of coffee and ambient music before the storm of twin engines roaring to life at six. When they woke I made them breakfasts of blueberry pancakes or American cheese omelet with their initials in melted cheese on top or oatmeal, which they enunciated "moatmeal."

Before the school years, life was about finding ways to burn their bottomless energy, either by playing outside on the farm or drives to the beach. During winter it was snow suits and boots and VHS movies and reading books aloud. They loved *The Sound of Music* and *Willie Wonka* on film. They loved *The Old Man and the Sea*.

Once they reached the age of five, it was the Friday morning get-them-to-school-on-time routine. Up early, quick feed, into the truck, and drop them at their school in Portsmouth. Put in a short day of stone work and pick them up at two to either head back to Serious or a visit with Grammy Bette in Rye or a hang at the mall in Newington with bags of candy from the candy shop.

Even later, when the custody terms were trod upon and the visits dried up, the dark pre-dawn with chores of feeding the chickens or just walking the floodlit property with coffee and memories was something I enjoyed. But the joy of late has faded. I've never in my life, before now, not been pleasantly surprised to awaken and be thrilled by the notions of coffee and life. It concerned me, this new and joyless era.

This job, this mayhem, though, made something stir. I don't think it was joy, but it was Something anyway. Sometimes Something is enough, enough to keep putting one foot in front of the other.

It was the drive to Mayhem:

It took me over hill and by God dale. It steered me through some of the most desolately magnificent townships Maine has to offer: New Englander homes gone paint-free for decades with clotheslines full and big cars on blocks; yard appliances, rusted and ruined in dooryards, just like you read about; mobile homes in skewed formation, some barely off the roadway and some deeper in the woods barely seen when the leaves are on the trees; rushing streams running parallel to my travel and then breaking quickly underneath while the C60 rattled cheap over wooden planked and sturdy thirty-foot-long bridges with no railings; kids at bus stops with camo book bags and camo ball caps; moms on front stoops in housecoats, camo PJs, coffee cups, and languorous cigarettes watching and waiting till school bus #23 driven by a down-the-road neighbor comes and swallows the kids whole; dads driving twenty-three-year- old F-250s like madmen up my tailpipe and then around me with curses on curved roads with solid painted center do-not-pass lines down the middle when you could actually still see the lines through the decades' fade of no town or state dollars available for infrastructure.

The way to work in the morning could be hectic somewhat with those harried men going off to whatever occupations occupied their days. I enjoyed being one of them. It had only been months since I was hauling stone and tools in the back of my truck. I was one. My Volvo embarrassed me, a little.

As soon as I tumbled downhill from Parsonsfield to Porter and the Ossipee Trail, my focus returned to Mayhem. Today, Friday, was the final day of orientation. On Monday, we entered the fray.

— 14 —

We finished early on our final Friday. It was a day of filling out paperwork for payroll, for insurances (I had been living without health insurance for three years, so this was a triumph), for meal vouchers, calendars indicating national holidays, PTO explanations, dress code expectations, and a hearty congratulations for now being a part of the Mayhem Mountain Staff. I guessed that this serving of red tape was saved until the last day so that these efforts might not be wasted on dropouts. We'd had three.

Stepping out of the basement into a brilliant September early afternoon, seventy-three degrees, cloudless, still, the White Mountains sitting patiently across the northern horizon, late summer insects whirring and chirping in the surrounding grasses and orchards . . . I did not know what to do with myself. I did not want to go home. Not yet. Although there was plenty to do there at Serious Farm: the ridiculous two-acre lawn needed mowing. Wood always needed splitting. I was working on hauling crushed stone into the dirt-floored basement one wheelbarrow load at a time down a plank, through the bulkhead. I had a twenty-yard pile of stone to distribute down there. The thought of toiling, alone, at Serious did not appeal. It was Friday. I was now an official professional. I wanted to celebrate but had no one at the moment to celebrate with.

"Whatcha doing?"

Bojean. How long had she been standing there, there next to me?

I shook my head, still looking north. "Nuffin," I said. "You?"

"Nuffin," she said. Then nothing. A quiet minute passed with the atmosphere on the mountain becoming even more still. Where was everyone? In school? Napping? The crickets sang.

"You ready for this?" she asked.

"Not sure," I said.

"Wanna come over to my house?" She said. "Talk?"

I turned my head to look at her. She was looking north.

"Sure," I said. "Where do you live?"

She pointed out and down, down to where a white church steeple poked its pointy head above turning hardwood foliage. "There," she said. "A town called Freedom."

The road off the mountain was like a bobsled run . . . narrow, steep and twisty. I could not help but imagine these mountain roads in snowy icy February and the treachery. If my drive time was an hour each way in pristine late summer and fall, I could easily imagine two hours, at least, through a nor'easter. Maybe this Volvo would pay off then, but I doubted it. In those conditions I would be driving my 4x4, eight-miles-to-the-gallon Silverado, most likely.

I followed her Nissan as we bottomed out at Route 25, crossed over and headed into Freedom proper. We drove past a scattering of '50s ranches, '30s New Englanders, Capes of all eras, and '80s Colonial kits. We hung a right and meandered through the Freedom flats: a family-run gas station with two teeming and open-doored mechanical bays stuffed to the brim with greasy, rusty, and ongoing reclamation projects; a mobile home enclave; the dog-eared library and second-thought historical society building. A sweeping left and we rode straight into Oz. Downtown Freedom at first glance appeared as a mockingly ornate bedroom community for a reclusive subsidiary of the One Percent.

The main street was barely a quarter mile long, you could see where it T-ed off at the northern end by a road running east/west, but architectural abundance was packed in cheek to jowl. Granite-curbed concrete sidewalks defined the borders of the freshly paved lane (the Freedom road agent either lived here or was indebted to someone for something). Sugar maples thick at the trunk with hundreds of rings beneath the bark stood sentry on both sides, planted some century ago, showing off at nearing peak foliage.

But it was the dozen or so homes plotted side by each on the main that gave the street its movie-set feel of cartoonish displacement.

Five- to ten-thousand square-foot homes with period piece gardens replicating the seasons lived by the gentry who founded this confounding compound. There were three-story Federals with gabled ends and hipped roofs and secondary L's larger than the average worker's homes grafted onto the main frame. There were Georgians with mansard tops. There were oversized Colonials with what quickly counted out at twelve rooms atop twelve rooms atop twelve rooms. The Federals had pilasters supporting elliptically arched entryways. First-floor curved bay windows sat bulging below second-story triple windows with smaller pilasters under octagonal cupolas with copper domes and copper downspouts. Some roofs were of slate. Massive chimneys of ingenious ornate design (Gothic arches and overhangs and contrarian basket-weave recesses built into the façades) and meticulous construction dwarfed the rooflines and made these homes look like miniature replicas of the Titanic or landlocked Mississippi riverboats. Shutters to windows were painted black or hunter's green or arrest-me red. Some had candy-striped canvas awnings.

I could see a fast-moving river about twenty feet wide running behind the houses on the east side of the main street tumbling through retaining walls made of fieldstone bigger than Buick Roadmasters and laid tight by craftsmen laborers using who-knew-what methods of locomotion to move them into place.

Oxen? Indians? Aliens? Offspring?

The exposed foundations were of enormous and expertly quarried granite monoliths jimmied so tightly by farmer masons that a paper envelope might not slide between the joints. The exposed exterior craftsmanship of these houses was so blatantly above the standards and means of the surrounding Yankee hoi polloi that it was difficult to enjoy the artistry. I wondered how the original subsidizers of these sore thumbs were not ultimately dragged from the velvet interiors and hung from much younger-than-now maples. And I wondered what sort of pretentious riff raff lived in them now.

Throughout my New England years, which were piling up but definitely winding down, I'd done my fair share of slow touring along many New England back roads and through tucked-away townships and never seen anything resembling this, this elegant monstrosity of a village.

Relics of these types of homes could be found, rotting usually, here and there and all across New England, the remainder of booms and inevitable busts come and gone. Mill owners and sea captains had these monuments to success built when they were flush and with no end in sight. Less ambitious family members or clever villagers took them over when the principals died or the money ran out and did not have the wherewithal or the gravitas to invest in meticulous upkeep. To stumble upon this Freedom fleet of updated and freshly polished symbols of prosperity from both bygone and modern times was somehow unsettling and somewhat absurd.

I assumed Bojean would lead me through this section of Freedom and on to the place she lived: a trailer, a duplex with roommates, a miniature apartment complex. Instead, she nosed her Nissan into a graveled circular drive offering itself to the grandest of the grand.

She pulled up nose-first to a service entrance and without looking at me or waiting for me walked up to and unlocked the red painted door and stepped inside. She left the door open a crack, the only acknowledgement given that I had been invited and was right behind her. I sized up the house as I walked the short bluestone path to the red door. There had to be thirty rooms. A boarding house like the ones in Provincetown, I figured, or a very well-maintained, upscale apartment building or perhaps even a condo conversion situation. I estimated the structure to be at least ten thousand square feet.

She was at the sink, her back to me, in a large and low-ceilinged kitchen, drawing two glasses of water. Through the window over the sink I could see the fast-moving river that I'd noticed on the approach. It appeared as though the stream were running right up against the eastern wall of the kitchen, giving the impression, looking out the window, that the house and its foundation were set in or hovering over the moving water almost like a mill, and there should be a mill wheel attached and turning somewhere on this peculiar and enormous house.

"You live here," I said, not a question but a declaration of passive-aggressive disbelief.

"Yup," she said, still not looking at me, "I do."

"Nice place."

"Thank you."

"Is this a shared kitchen?"

She turned, finally, to look at me. "What do you mean?"

"I mean does the rest of the house all use this kitchen?" Looking around some more, it did not appear to have that shared kitchen look of clutter or duplicate toast-r-ovens or stacked dishes in the sink that someone would get to later on.

"What rest of the house? I don't know what you mean."

"I mean, I guess I mean, who else lives here?"

"Me. Nobody. I live here."

I finished my scan of the kitchen and noted the four doorless doorways opening to dark and narrow hallways.

"This is your house?" Now and truly a question as opposed to an accusation.

"Yes," she said. "Well. It's my dad's. He's not here. He's hardly ever here."

"Holy smokes and Jesus!" I couldn't help it. I couldn't remember if we had established a cursing relationship. I laughed, "What yo daddy do?"

She laughed too, but ignored the question. She set the glasses of water on the kitchen island and sat down at one of the six vintage speakeasy barstools surrounding it. The kitchen was not particularly modern or ostentatious . . . no Viking range or built-into-the-wall refrigerator or granite countertops. The appliances were twenty years old but the furniture, the narrow farm table against the wainscoted wall and the stools, were country craftsmanship, maybe Shaker.

"Do you live here by yourself?"

"Right now I do." I sat down at the island and discreetly scooted as close to Bojean as I could without being obvious. I was picking up every other or every third word with my for-shit hearing and making semi-coherent conversation through context. I didn't even realize I was getting good at this method. I may even have been learning to read lips without knowing it. "My dad comes and goes. He travels a lot. My sister and her husband visit occasionally."

"Your dad travels for his work?"

She looked straight into my eyes and did not answer.

"Is this the house you grew up in?"

"For a while."

"Where did you grow up?"

Bojean looked down at her hands. She appeared somewhat pained that the conversation was starting out this way . . . about her. Very quietly, too quietly for me to discern, she said, "Something something something wagon." I definitely heard the word *wagon*.

"Pardon?"

"I said, mostly in a station wagon. Why can't you hear me?"

I felt myself blush. It happens more than I care to admit, the blushing. "I'm sorry," I said. My mother had been progressively losing her hearing over the past several years so I knew how aggravating it could be to try and carry on a conversation with someone continually saying "pardon," or in my mom's case, "HAH?!!!," like it were the listeners' fault that *she* was deaf as a haddock.

"Seriously, what's up with your hearing? I noticed in orientation that you'd lean toward whoever was speaking and then you'd get a kind of a blank look. It's pretty obvious you can't hear for shit."

We *were* establishing a cursing relationship. Excellent!

"Well, yeah, I'm pretty sure there's some hearing loss. Also, you have a very tiny voice, don't you think?" She, I think, glared at me. At least her eyebrows furrowed toward the middle and her eyes bored in. Hickory-colored eyes.

"I do have a tiny voice," she said, the glare softening, maybe, somewhat, "but I can project when I want to. Any time I want to." She was projecting just now. "But it would make sense for you to have your hearing checked, wouldn't it? You are in the listening business, after all." I hadn't really thought about it that way. She had a point.

"It would. Indeed."

I took a sip from my glass. The water was cold and delicious, well water. Her hazel eyes were still softening and switching maybe back to the beseeching that I was more familiar with. I took another look around the private kitchen in this private house. There was some green in her eyes. Some amber. Hickory. Hazel.

— 15 —

When we got back to the hotel room, I went into the bathroom to urinate, running the water in the sink so as not to offend her or frighten her with stream sounds. When I re-entered the room, she was under her covers, up to her neck.

"Did you want to use the bathroom first?" I asked.

"'Kay," she whispered. But she didn't get out of her bed right away. I lay down on top of my bed and used the flinker to turn on the TV. I made a point of seeming extra engrossed in *SportsCenter*.

She took the opportunity to slide out from under the covers, fully clothed, with coat still on, find her travel bag and quickly slip into the bathroom. I heard the bathroom door lock. She was in there for a while before I heard the shower running.

I was almost asleep when I heard the bathroom door open and out of my peripherals saw her, with her back to me, untie the cord of her very heavy-looking and floor-length white bathrobe and lay it on the bed. She wore flannel pajamas and, without me really looking, while trying not to look, what appeared to be her heavily wired brassiere underneath. And socks. I tried to think . . . do women usually or ever wear their bras to bed? None that I knew. It would seem to be an unnecessarily uncomfortable accommodation to modesty.

Never looking over in my direction, she slipped under the covers and lay with her back to me, face to the wall.

We'd just walked together, her arm in mine. Hadn't we? I lay there for a moment, wondering if I'd transgressed. It is no picnic, being clueless. This feeling of stumbling screwing up, clueless screwing up, had been following me since the birth of my daughters. The feeling of *What did I did?* I turned off the TV and rolled off the bed as befits a man with essentially fused vertebrae. I barely even thought about the pain anymore, it was just a thing to live with. As I stood up as straight as possible to make the walk to the bathroom, I had to smile: deaf, crippled, and clueless. Sounds about right. What do you want to be when you grow up, son? I'd like to be deaf, crippled, and clueless.

I brushed my teeth and I took my shower. All I'd brought to sleep in were my boxer-briefs and t-shirt. I could creep from bathroom to bed in darkness tonight, but how would I conceal my relative nakedness, compared to Bojean's propriety, in the morning light?

I'd worry about that in the morning light.

I was under the covers and I think asleep when I heard Bojean's voice, eerily low but as clearly audible as though she were sitting in a chair right next to my head.

"When I was six, on Christmas morning, my father came out to us, my mother, my sister, and me, as homosexual.

"Of course, I did not know what that meant. But my mother took my sister and me out of the house immediately. She packed one suitcase and walked us, through the cold—I remember it being very, very cold—walked us to our pastor's house. It was not a house. It was a trailer.

"The trailer was only a mile or so from our house, from my father's house. But it seemed like a very long walk. My memory is of a very long walk. And not knowing why we were suddenly walking on Christmas morning. I remember my father crying as we left his house. I remember looking at him over my shoulder, crying, in his bathrobe, in the red doorway. I remember he didn't try to stop us.

"Homosexuality is forbidden in the Nazarene faith. For-bid-den. We walked to our pastor's trailer and I remember sitting in the tiny living room of the trailer, with my sister, while my mother and our pastor talked in his bedroom. We stayed in the pastor's trailer, sleeping on a pullout sofa, for a few days. Then we left. We left in our pastor's station wagon.

"I did not see my father again until I was sixteen years old."

I felt prickly heat, goosebumps, on my skin as she spoke. The way she spoke. I'd heard multiple variations of her speaking voice, from the mousebreath to the annoyed to accommodatingly clear. This was different. So very low and, somehow, spoken to someone other than me. She spoke as if before an audience. She spoke as if trying to reach the back corners of a large room but without shouting. She was projecting. She was projecting as if she had been taught how to project. She sounded like another human being besides the Bojean I knew. Lying there, under the covers at a mid-level chain motel, in Harrisonburg, Virginia, on the road to nowhere, goosebumped, it became abundantly evident to me that I did not know this person, at all. I did not know her but wanted to. This may have been the beginning of trust. This felt important.

The silence, after her last sentence, lay upon me like one too many heavy quilts. I labored to breathe.

Finally, not knowing if she was done, or asleep, I asked, "Where did you go?"

She answered immediately, "Only," she said. "Only, Tennessee."

I laughed. Freedom, Love, and now Only. "Only, Tennessee," I repeated. I loved the way it sounded. I loved the notion of Only, Tennessee. Love, Virginia. Freedom, New Hampshire.

"My grandparents live in Only."

"My mom got her marriage annulled by the church. By February she was married to our pastor."

I waited for more. In the dark, I waited for more. Five minutes passed. Ten. The clock radio clock flipped to midnight. No idea why, I asked Bojean, "Do you love your father?"

"Very much."

"Is your pastor, is your stepfather, is he a good man?"

Immediately, with the voice sounding right next to my head, she said, "No."

Another long pause followed. The clock radio clock flipped to 12:15. I heard Bojean laugh. It was a giggle, like the giggle when she told me she was ticklish. Bojean said, "I have daddy issues."

In my head, I thought, that sounds about right.

In my head, I thought, I have daughter issues.

Then, apparently, we slept.

— 16 —

We slept, but not well and not for long.

I heard her, restless in her bed. The clock radio clock flipped to 3:36. I heard her get up and go to the bathroom. I was awake.

When she returned to the bed and continued her restless rolling, I asked her, "You awake?"

"Yes," she said, whispered.

"Wanna go?" I asked.

"Yes," she said, projected.

Over motel lobby coffee in tiny paper cups and motel lobby cellophane pastries and motel lobby miniature yogurts in sickly pastel colors, I asked if she'd ever been to Charleston, South Carolina.

"No," she said.

"Wanna go? Get lunch? Look around?"

"Sounds good."

"OK," I said. "Charleston."

As we settled into the Volvo and headed south out of dark Harrisonburg, I asked Bojean, "Is your father a good man?"

"Yes," she said, projected. "He is a very, very good man."

With the sunrise in our eyes as we banked east towards the coast, she said, "He is the best man."

We were turning around on Anna Knapp Boulevard in Mount Pleasant, South Carolina at a little past 1 p.m.

— 17 —

She took her beatings like a pro.

The Monday of our introduction to live fire arrived. I was told to attend a staff meeting of case managers and team supervisors in a building that housed classrooms. From my seat at a conference table, I watched through the window as a group of four young women, technicians, a group that included my Bojean, walked past my building and disappeared into Roosevelt Cabin. The six residential cabins for the kid population were named after presidents. Later that week, sitting alone in my office of Eisenhower Cabin, I realized that all six of the cabins were named after wartime presidents. Was this a coincidence or no? They were: FDR, Eisenhower, Lincoln, Truman, Johnson, and I swear to God, Nixon.

I was told by my team leader that it would take me several weeks to master the data entry proficiency required to satisfy administration. I was told to focus solely on learning this function.

"When do I meet the kids on my caseload?"

The four other case managers smiled at me. They were kids, three dudes and a girl, in their twenties. I wanted to like them, but I didn't like the way they were smiling at me. Unkind smiles like know-it-all postgraduate dicks.

"Don't worry about your kids," Team Leader said. "They're fine. All you need to know about them right now are their names, their guardians' names, and the insurance company covering their tuition."

As the team went over the week's agenda, which was a series of meetings like this one to get ready for the weekly conference calls with insurance providers and guardians to justify payments, I saw Bojean and her squad of technicians come out of their cabin leading the twenty residents. Bojean trailed the pack, watching. She was wearing a thin smile while walking next to a bean pole female patient. The patient/client was at least six feet tall with spider limbs, long, and a herky-jerky gait. She was sticking close to Bojean's side. Just as the pack crossed in front of my window, I watched helplessly as the client, Beanpole, reached out to Bojean and grabbed her hair with both hands and yanked Bojean straight to the ground, hard. The Beanpole began to shriek while standing over her and ripping at Bojean's hair.

"Jesus!" I stood up and headed for the door.

The three dude case managers were quicker and were out the door and on the client in seconds. They had Beanpole subdued, with her crazy long arms pinned to her side while I helped Bojean to her feet. She had not cried out. She appeared more confused than hurt.

"You okay?"

"Okay."

"Holy shit," I said.

"Yeah," she said.

One of the case manager dudes came over to us and addressing Bojean said, "You're going to want to wear a hat. Your hair is a target."

"'Kay," Bojean said.

"That information would have been helpful, like, yesterday," I said.

"That information should be, like, self-evident," Dude said.

I wanted to slap the dude and say, *There's some self-evidence.* But I did not. I've never slapped anyone. The two other case manager bros had calmed Beanpole who was now laughing delightedly and covering her mouth with her hands as in *Whoopsie, did I do something wrong?* And just like that, it was over. The gaggle of patients and their keepers headed down the lane to wherever they were going and us case managers went back inside.

Settling back down, self-evident case manager dude said to the other dudes, "Who's the new tech?"

"Don't know," one of the other dudes said, "but she is fine."

"She looks familiar," Self-Evident said. "I've seen her someplace before."

The other of the other dudes said, "I'd like to see her someplace." The dudes laughed. They seemed to relish this sort of violent interlude. I was utterly invisible to them.

I was given an enormous binder with data entry protocols and procedures and told to make myself at home in my office in Eisenhower and practice.

Each new day for the first two weeks I was told to go practice.

My office faced north and a little east toward Mount Chocorua. There was a big window with my desk situated at its sill, so I could look up from my data entry work and look out. I could also look down upon the activities here at

Mayhem. I could see it all. The view of the lane connecting the kids' cabins to the schoolhouse and the infirmary and the dining hall was unobstructed. Only a tree limb with quickly dissipating leaves blocked a small section of my view. In a week the leaves would be down.

I marveled at the patience and toughness of not only Bojean but also her technician cohort. They were young women, all of them. Each morning they disappeared into the narrow doorways of war president cabins to care for these damaged children. They woke them from their afflicted slumbers, fed them as best they could their breakfasts of toast with peanut butter and juice. They showered and clothed them and walked by their sides to classrooms where probably nothing sunk in. How could it? They sat with them while the lessons droned on and stood with them outside during recess, where more often than not the children either cried with loneliness and confusion or stared out toward the mountains, like me.

Toward mid-morning I would venture out of my office and stand, breathing this razor air and watch. I was a voyeur, an unarmed sniper watching and trying to will peace below. I cringed whenever I saw a child go off, either standing, screaming with clenched fists, or attacking their caregivers. I recoiled for the kids with their unholy tinctures of seething anger and mute terror mixed with seasick confusion and abject longing for the place they lived before here. For home. Whatever home meant or felt like in their roiling minds.

So strange, this vantage from my office or just outside, all of this macabre theatre of the woods playing out below, the characters miniature and cartoonish in movement and scale from my view.

But it was real. The assaults upon staff were real with screams emanating from actual lungs through chapped lips. The assaults and then the counter-assaults by staff and by fast-arriving security with their latest battle-tested choke holds and calming measures were real. All real. I saw blood sometimes and it was real. And across the valley below, the foliage on the mountains committed toward winter, hinting hard at the colorful bombast of Columbus Day just around the corner. Me, watching, invisible, as usual.

On one particularly clear blue morning during my second week of protocol practice, I was standing outside looking down as Bojean, with Red Sox hat, escorted her ticking, wild-eyed Beanpole to her classroom. This morning, Bojean looked up, straight to me, straight into my eyes, somehow knowing I was there all along, and her face, beautiful, poker, giving nothing away, broke a little and it begged, *Help me. Help me, Holmes.* While the mountains beyond bespoke serenity and calm.

I had to go down there.

— 18 —

I waited until I saw them coming back mid-morning, a parade of wheelchairs and the raucous ambulatory. They looked like an ambushed platoon coming in from night patrol. I watched and waited until they were all inside. I considered devising some pretext for entering Roosevelt Cabin but decided no one would ask what I wanted and no one would care why I was there.

I left my office and descended the railroad tie steps that connected my upper-level cabin to the down-below level. I pulled open the front door to FDR and was confronted by blackness. Blackness and body odor. I stood blinking, waiting for my eyes to acclimate from the overwrought sunshine and clarity to the murk within. While acclimating, I listened as best I could. It was quiet. Probably too quiet. I imagined twenty-five sets of subterranean eyes fixed upon my fresh meat. Easing into the foyer of the cabin, I was not far from wrong.

The cabin brimmed with humanity, a full silent house. The cabins presented as smaller on the inside than out due to low low ceilings designed to hold in the canned heat during winter months. I waded through the mob, scanning for kickers or biters, staff outnumbered today nine to one. I looked around for Bojean.

I saw the Beanpole before I saw Bojean. She was butt naked. The Beanpole. Up close, rather than a fiction from hundreds of yards away, the Beanpole was lovely of the face with magazine-cover, heroin-chic cheekbones, enormously round backlit blue eyes and long, those crazy long spider legs and arms striated with sinew under unblemished skin. The girl was uncomfortably stunning to look at. I tried not to look.

She was staring at me, jabbering, and in marionette style began to advance toward me. Here came Bojean, out of the crowd, out of the gloom, to intercept her. Bo took Beanpole lightly by the elbow and tried to steer her away from me. Beanpole glanced at Bojean and Bojean cringed just a little, but held tight. The two of them were still six feet away from me, it seemed, but the Pole reached across that distance to me and ran her hand down my chest, my belly and further south. She had very long arms. I stepped back, just out of her reach.

She could not speak. Not English anyway. She was grunts, squeaks, and ejaculations, pointing at nothing in particular and pushing Bojean around. But Bo managed to body this elongated human being down a hallway and into what I presumed was the girl's bedroom. In a moment, Bojean came back alone.

"She prefers to be nekkid," Bo said. I was surprised by her pronunciation of the word. The word *naked*.

"Ah ha," I said. "What's her name?"

"Patricia."

"Ah ha. Are you okay?" I asked Bojean.

"Yep."

"Say what?"

"Yah! Good!"

It wasn't my imagination, before, watching from above and thinking her eyes were beseeching. They were, unquestionably, at this moment, pleading, *Help. Me.*

"Hey. Maybe we should get together after work," I said.

"Yes!"

"Maybe do some processing?"

"Okay! Yes, okay! Processing!!"

"Okay. I'll follow you off the hill after."

"Okay!!!" I could hear her very well.

"I like your hat."

During this brief exchange, a Black kid had somehow and stealthily gotten up very close to me and grabbed hold of my ID badge, which was clipped to a lanyard, which was hanging loose around my neck.

There were very few African Americans living in New Hampshire at all and even fewer up here in the mountains. This facility drew from Boston, Philadelphia, Baltimore, and NYC systems. It was a for-profit business and marketed itself throughout the land. There was someone with an office in the administration building responsible for recruiting in far-off locales and I'd bet she made a lot more than 40K per annum.

The kid may have been eight, he may have been eighteen, it was hard to tell. I'd seen him, from above. The top of his head came to about the bottom of my chin. His hair was cut close and he smelled good, like soap. When he grabbed my lanyard and I looked down to see what was the what, I figured, okay, kid's being playful, and so I laughed and put my hand on his shoulder. His shoulder was a knob of muscle, tense, hard, a little sweaty through his t-shirt. I asked, politely, for him to release me. "Let go, please."

"What's this guy's name?" I asked Bo.

"That's Rueben," she said, looking concerned. But then her attention was taken by the return of the Beanpole, still naked, hair wet for some reason.

"Okay, Rueben," I said, gently, "Let go. C'mon, man. Leggo my eggo. Ha ha." He cranked down another turn on my lanyard. Rueben did not take to my kind of humor. My forced jokes and my touching his shoulder seemed to make his muscles go tighter.

Rueben was staring up, deep and weird, into my eyes. His black autistic irises completely devouring my watery and waspy blue ones. He clamped down a bit harder again and started to twist the lanyard.

"Okay, okay. Time to let go. *Now.*" I could feel a miniature pocket of panic developing in my solar plexus, the whispery genesis of fight or flight reaction to a potentially dangerous situation. Just for the hell of it, I whispered at him, "Walk with me, talk with me."

Yeah, nothing.

I put my right hand over his with the idea of gently but firmly removing it from my personal property. He had no intention of letting go. I slid my hand down his and tried to get my fingertips between his fingers and the palm of his hand. It was like trying to shuck an oyster without an oyster knife.

The fight or flight acid was making its way to my throat area. Here it was, the sort of a situation we had been trained to expect and I knew I would truly detest. The concept of violence terrifies me. Not so much that I might get hurt but rather what I might be capable of if I were to ever completely lose my shit on another human. Rather than ever find out, I'd avoided violence my entire life. But also, I didn't relish the idea of getting hurt.

I've mentioned, I believe, that I was a stonemason for most of my working life, so, while not being the overly aggressive type, I'm also neither a physical weakling nor a complete beta. Still, I couldn't just cold cock the kid.

I looked around to see if assistance from staff might be in the offing. Bojean had her hands full with Beanpole. Otherwise, I saw no immediate help available. I decided that this was actually a good thing because I didn't want any witnesses to what I was about to do. There were a few clients watching us, but what were they going to say? And if they could actually speak, who would believe them? Their word against mine.

I wanted to give Rueben one last chance, so I bent my face down so that our eyes were an inch or two apart and I spoke slowly and lowly: "You need to let go now. You're going to let go. Let go right now. Please!"

There may have been a safe word or a magic phrase to use with this particular kid in a situation like this, but "let go" wasn't it. Nor was "now." He just stared and mouth breathed in, mouth breathed out . . . his breath was surprisingly okay.

While talking to him, I managed to get a pretty good purchase on his pinky. Rueben's little finger was thicker than one would imagine belonging to a lithe teen or preteen and stiff like the spring on a shock absorber, but I began to get some traction.

I had both of my hands wrapped around his, and with our faces so close, it may have appeared as though we were praying together or I was giving some fatherly advice or going in for a kiss. As I managed to get his pinky separated from his knot of a fist, he continued to wind down on the lanyard so that his knuckles were right up under my chin and into my throat. I glanced sideways to see if the coast was clear before I attempted to snap Rueben's finger like a crab leg. Bojean was watching all of this while still being pushed hither and yon by her tall client.

I got the pinky bent back almost parallel to Rueben's wrist before his mouth opened. He had good teeth. His mouth opened and I was afraid he was going to scream or suddenly articulate, loudly and clearly, that he was being hurt by this bad case manager man here. I didn't give a shit. I was being choked by my own lanyard and not enjoying the experience. I was prepared to go all the way and rip the pinky out by the root. I recall thinking, what if he's like the Terminator or a lizard and doesn't know or care that he's being de-fingered because another will grow back? But then his mouth closed and he let go of me. Or he let go of me and his mouth closed. So I let go of him.

Compromise!

Success!

Then he quietly walked away. I stood there wondering where he was going. Bojean was busy blocking the continuous attempts of her long-limbed client to wind serpent fingers under her cap but she was also looking at me. She may have seen the whole thing. I could not read her face. This would remain a theme.

"So, meet you in the parking lot after?"

"Okay," she said.

The day passed, as they somehow did, and I stood leaning against the Volvo out in the staff parking lot at quitting time. It was a beautiful late afternoon in late September.

I watched her walk toward me: odd little creature, head down, ball cap, hands in jeans pockets, short stridden and quick steps like a plover chasing something in the surf, not looking up once even though I knew that she knew that I was standing there waiting for her. She went straight to her car, her shitty little formerly silver and now peeling Nissan that was a dozen parking spaces away from the Volvo. She put the key in the door and just before ducking in behind the wheel, gave me a quick glance which I guessed meant *Follow me.*

That afternoon, in her kitchen, she served us vodka. Not well water. No ice. No mixer. Vodka.

— 19 —

I blew it again.

I prematurely ejected off Highway 17 before we even made it to the bridge to Charleston. Cognitive decline? Maybe. Maybe, but this had been going on years, this weird inattention while driving. The good news is that this inattention has led me to some places far more interesting than the intended destination.

The exit I took led us to a stoplight and then into a placid little park called Patriots Point. This was very different from being shoveled off the Mystic River Bridge before being swallowed by Storrow Drive in Boston or taking the death plunge into and onto the West Side Highway of Manhattan. We were the only vehicle on this little lane leading up to a pavilion that presided over a green space under the bridge we were trying to re-cross. I thought maybe it was closed for business, it was so quiet, but then we saw two parked cars in a large lot and three children frolicking on a playset with guardians standing around smoking. There was a river behind them and a long pier running out into it. Bojean and I walked past the people and out onto the deserted pier.

"I think that's it over there," I pointed towards some cranes on the other side of the river.

"I see lots of churches. Church steeples," she said. And she was right. Beyond the cranes and above the treeline were a dozen church steeples with the occasional apartment-looking building mixed in, none taller than ten floors it seemed. Low country indeed. I'm not sure what I was expecting out of the city of Charleston, not much really, but I assumed there would be buildings.

We went into the pavilion to use the rest rooms. While waiting for Bo I grabbed one of those tourist maps of the area. Sure enough, across the river was the town, the peninsula of Charleston. Its streets, according to the map, were laid out in an easy grid. I looked to see if the river separating us from downtown had a name.

Not on this map it didn't.

We wandered out onto the pier, enjoying the warmth compared to December in Maine. The current of the river was strong and the hum of traffic above was hypnotic, but it was the milky humidity that had me happy at this moment. This softness of the air was something we might get for a grand total of three days per year in New England and I savored them when they came. The act of sleeping on top of summer sheets with windows open and a fan providing sleepy white noise is one of my fondest environments—the closest feeling to an opioid high without the niggling guilt of misusing an opioid.

The sky here above Patriots Point had now turned quickly grey and smelled of rain. I filled my lungs with the aroma of river and rain and a hint of paper factory somewhere out of sight. I wanted to throw an arm across Bojean's shoulder and share this sense of confounding well-being, but I did not dare. Her cloistered reticence was intimidating, and I was in no position to take any sort of chances with any sort of woman, of any age, not with my track record of late.

She was standing close to me as we leaned upon the pier's railing, looking down into the whorling (whirling?) eddies and across to the waiting town. "I'm hungry," I said.

"Me too," she said.

"I feel good," I said.

"Me too," she said.

"And I don't know why," I said.

She said nothing. I'd tried multiple times over the past months to address the obvious malaise present in both of our lives and she never ever rose to the bait. I'm not sure why I kept trying. "Let's go see if there are restaurants over there across this river with no name."

"'Kay."

We walked back to the Volvo and easily re-entered traffic headed over the bridge and toward the town. The first exit at the bottom of the bridge was for East Bay Street so I took it, not wanting to get caught up in traffic and whiffing on downtown again. We took a left onto East Bay and were met with our first visual of Charleston, which was, kind of, nothing.

We were greeted by sporadic shuttered and abandoned houses with weeded lots under and near the beautiful bridge. Foot traffic was light and consisted of a few roughed-up African Americans with shopping carts and limps. A huge, two-block-long brick shell of a factory on the right promised lofts for sale, eventually. At this moment it was movie prop walls held upright with sketchy-looking dunnage, rusty staging, and zero construction activity at the moment of our drive-by. We crept along in the no traffic and I decided to hang a right on a cross street called Race.

We cruised a quick three blocks through blown-out residences and pitted blacktop much worse than post-winter Boston potholed side streets. This was a Black neighborhood for sure, and we were two of the whitest people on the planet looking lost in the whitest-people-car ever designed. I specifically wondered at that moment on Race Street if I had ever known or even seen a Black friend or person driving a Volvo. I came up empty. I felt conspicuous.

I didn't know much about Charleston but I did know this was the saddle of the South with fortunes gained and wars lost over issues of skin color and commerce. I hadn't a clue regarding present race relations here, but my guess was that they were tenuous, just like everywhere else in this country of united states.

We took a left on a street called Meeting, still looking for the center of something, a focal vanishing point to spread out from. We passed a Church's Chicken and then a church. An empty lot with a van parked and displaying tiger print rugs and tie dye somethings. Flags? Fabric? Racks of t-shirts. No one at this moment had come to this desolate marketplace to buy. We drove past a liquor store with smoked windows.

Suddenly, at Mary Street, the commercial enterprises began to appear more upscale and the buildings occupied. We sat for a while at a red light. To the right was an open green space park ringed with palm trees and traversed by young and white folk mostly. On the far side of the park was a tall brick building with an extra-large church next to it.

The top of the building and the top of the church steeple appeared to be almost exactly the same height with the steeple maybe winning out by a couple of feet. We seemed to be entering Charleston proper. I was curious as to how the entire feel of the town changed so radically in only four blocks from downtrodden to upscale. Bojean gazed out the open window. The cross street at this intersection was called Calhoun. The name sounded vaguely historical and perhaps political. A president? A loser general? I'd have to look into this Calhoun character when an opportunity arose. As if reading my mind, or the street sign, Bojean asked, "Didn't the Civil War start here?"

"I believe it did. Fort Sumter."

"Do you know much about the Civil War?" she asked.

"Not as a whole," I said. "But I know a disproportionate amount about the Battle of Gettysburg. Don't ask me why." We made it through the intersection and I decided to pull off and find a place to park. These sidewalks looked inviting and the air continued to caress. The clouds were thick now and the air seemed greenish and I wanted to be out in it. I took a left on Society Street and found an open spot at the corner of Society and Anson.

When I exited the Volvo, I could suddenly see colors once again.

— 20 —

I met and got to know a couple of kids from my Eisenhower Cabin even though they were not on my roster. They were sweet. Teenage boys with typical teenage boy energy, clumsy bravado, and shy curiosity about me. They asked lots of questions. Did I have a girlfriend? How old was I? Did I like it here? I asked if they liked it here and they harmonized, *NO!* One kid's name was Joey and another's name was Joey.

Mainly, they wanted me to hook them up with phone calls home. Joey in particular wanted to call home every day. I didn't see any problem letting them use my phone. Not at first. But then Joey wound up weeping horribly by the end of each call and begging his mother to let him come home and I felt very badly for him.

Joey was from just outside of Baltimore, he said. Joey was from Long Island.

Baltimore Joey and Long Island Joey didn't seem to have all that much wrong with them. In an earlier time they would have been classified as mildly retarded and that would be the end of it. Special ed classes and lifelong jobs as key makers at the Ace Hardware. Today they were inmates at a sketchy lockup. I had no idea what their futures held.

I'd been letting these guys use my phone for the better part of my first two weeks when I got a phone call from my Team Leader.

"Holmes!!" Team Leader's ongoing *thing*, it seemed, was relentless enthusiasm. "Mr. Holmes Jensen!!!"

"Yes!"

"It's Team Leader!!! (I cannot recall his actual name; Chip? Chad? Jeremy?)"

"Yes, Team Leader!"

"Would you have time to meet with me in half an hour?"

"I have literally nothing else to do!" I said.

"Is that true?"

"Yes!"

"Hmm. Okay. Do you know where my office is?"

"No!!" I was still trying to match his enthusiasm, completely sarcastically. I needed to stop.

"Room 217! The Big House!!"

"Okay!" I said. "What's the Big House?"

"The big building? With the dining hall?"

"I don't know!"

"No," he said. "It's the big building with the dining hall. Second floor. Room 217."

"Cool!" I said. "Thirty minutes?"

"Can you?!!"

"I can!" I'd just told him I could, two seconds previous.

Looking out the window, I could see the building he was calling from. I had twenty-eight minutes to kill. Time dies hard for everyone upon Mayhem Mountain. My goal was to try and stick it out here for one year, for the experience, for my ultra-thin resume, and then move on. I would come up considerably short of that goal, mainly because of what was about to transpire as a result of this meeting with Team Leader.

I killed ten minutes just by staring at Mount Washington when there was a rap on my office door. Baltimore Joey came in, looking miserable.

"What up, Baltimore?"

Baltimore Joey had tears pooling as he told me about his friend Sarah who was sent home today. Her parents just drove off with her, back to wherever it was they were from.

"But that's good news, right?"

"Yeah," he said, and then began to sob. Joey was sitting in the chair next to my desk. I scanned my desktop and made a mental note to track down some tissues. I put my hand on his shoulder and he sagged, grateful, unlike young Rueben, for the touch. "Um gonna miss her," he said. "She was muh friend."

Change is difficult for everyone here upon Mayhem Mountain. "Can I call muh mom?"

"I've got to go someplace right now, Joey. How about when I get back?"

"Okay," he said, standing up. I don't know how old Baltimore Joey was, but he stood nearly six feet tall and had some weight on him. I stood with him. Very gently, very carefully he reached out to me. He hugged me softly as he laid his head on my shoulder and finished his tears, for now, for his friend Sarah. "I want to go home." And with head hanging low he returned to his living quarters.

I'd visited the Big House during orientation. The first floor contained the cafeteria, a large common room for the clients with fireplace, sofas and TV. There was a north-facing deck off of the common room with patio furniture tables and chairs. This was where smokers smoked. The first floor was open with high ceilings and tiled floors. It smelled like the meat of humanity and institutional food, but was clean with decent furniture. A parent or guardian checking the place out might think, *This is OK.*

I could not find an obvious stairway to the second floor. The clients sitting in the common area looked at me silently as I looked high and low. There had to be a way up there. Finally, I nabbed a passing staffish-looking person and asked how to get upstairs. "Ah," she said, and walked me down a hallway to a closed door which could have been a closet or a dorm room or a bathroom. It had no signage indicating anything. It was a closed door in a hallway. She opened the door and there were some stairs, narrow and barely lit from a light source on the second floor.

"Is this the only way up?" I asked, curious.

"No," she said. "There are a dozen of these doorways here and there."

"Odd," I said.

"You bet," she said.

The number of stairs up to the second floor were way more numerous than most. A regulation stairway has what, seventeen, eighteen steps? Standing in the doorway at the bottom looking up, there looked like thirty. The math was off for getting to a second floor, which is normally only ten feet or so above the first. A regulation stair riser is seven inches. 7" x 30" = 210 inches, which divided by 12 is 17.5 feet. Too many feet. As I climbed the seriously narrow stairway with severely wobbly railing, I counted twenty-eight steps, which is still too many. There was something askew about this building. Spooky and askew. M.C. Escher askew.

At the top of the too many stairs there was a landing that sagged underfoot. It sagged uniformly like one piece of plywood with one or no joists underneath for support. The plywood was covered over with thin and gritty industrial carpeting of indeterminate color. It looked and felt like dark sand in the dim light.

There was a door at one end of the landing I'd just come through and then five steps down at the other end of the landing, which emptied into a hallway filled with closed doors. I descended the five stairs and saw that there were multiple hallways connecting to this hallway. I also noticed that the closed doors had no identifying numbers upon them. These hallways were so narrow that it would be impossible for two regulation-sized humans to pass without having to turn sideways. The hallway sagged underfoot, like the landing, with the same dirty and threadbare industrial carpeting.

It was quiet up here. Low ceilings and no windows and silent. How was I supposed to find room 217?

I walked along tentatively and came to a crossroads of hallways.

At the crossroads stood a shadowy man, or a man standing in the shadows. He was tall, fit, and handsome. He was standing absolutely still and appeared to have been waiting for me as I came to this hallway intersection.

"Hello," I said.

He said nothing, arms by his side, looking straight into my face. I could have kept rolling by but it would be pointless as I had no idea where I was going. "Do you by any chance know where room 217 is?"

He stood there, studying me. By his appearance and his dress, which was neat and clean, I could not tell if he was staff or client. His hair was short, black and gelled. His eyes were clear and also black. His blue oxford shirt was tucked into khaki chinos. He wore black brogans, thick-soled and polished. When he was done looking me over, he turned and walked down the hallway that connected from the left. I followed him. He never looked back at me or made any sort of sound. In the back pocket of his chinos was a reporter's notebook. He stopped in front of yet another unmarked door, paused, and then continued walking without a word.

This door was slightly ajar and I could hear muted conversation coming from inside the room. I poked the door gently with my index finger and looked inside. There was Team Leader and another guy, my age or older, whom I recognized but could not place.

"Holmes!! Come in! Come in!"

I could just barely. The room was no more than thirty square feet, enough room for a miniature desk and two classroom-type chairs. An interior room, there were no windows. Light was provided by a fluorescent tube buzzing at an octave I could clearly hear. Team Leader offered me a chair while he and the other guy stood. When I sat, Team Leader sat and the other guy perched wobbly on the edge of the tiny desk. Our knees could not help but touch parts of one another.

"Holmes! Holmes!" he was shouting almost right into my face. "Have you met Frank?"

"I have!" I had no recollection of his name being Frank, or anything, but now I knew. I had no idea in which context I had met him. "Nice to see you again, Frank! How are you?" We shook hands long and sincere.

"Finest kind, Holmes, finest kind! You?"

"Great! Just great! Well above average!"

"Above average! That's great! That's funny. Great!"

Team Leader wore an enormous grin. You could tell he was thinking, *This is great!* "Well listen you two, I'm going to leave you alone! You've got some things to discuss, I understand!"

"OK, great!" Frank said.

"Cool!" I said, "great!" And then handshakes all around.

Team Leader stood and squeezed sideways out of the room, closing the door firmly behind him. Frank dismounted the tiny desk and took Team Leader's chair. "Thank Christ," he said, "We can stop bellowing now."

I laughed. "Why do we bellow along?"

"I don't know," he said. "Some sort of Stockholm Syndrome shit or another."

"Ah ha," I said. "Frank?"

"Yes?"

"What do you do here, and is this your office?"

"Ah, well. I am the team leader of case managers for the adult population. And yes, this is my office."

"Who designed this place?" I asked. "The Oompa Loompa? Coal miners? Submariners?"

"It's a pretty fucked-up structure, isn't it? You should see the basement."

"What's down there?"

"You don't want to know." We sat looking at one another for a moment. "Just kidding," he said, chuckling. "Or am I?" I took a quick liking to Frank.

— 21 —

Thirty minutes later, Frank wrapped up his tale of a client named Everyday Ed and how I had been hired specifically to handle his case. Just like that, my good feelings toward Frank evaporated.

"So why did you guys assign me to the kid population in the first place?" I asked.

"That was a screwup."

"And the reason I was hired was to manage this unmanageable cat named Everyday Ed?"

"Well, not... exactly. Okay, kind of. Okay. Being honest . . . on your resumé you included your former occupation, stonemason."

"Yeah?"

And you also put down under other achievements that you played Division 1-A college football."

"Yeah?"

"You need to be careful what you put on your resumé."

"And, no shit, you hired me specifically as muscle?"

"Yes."

"Because everyone else is terrified of Everyday Ed."

"Yes."

"Well," I said. "Fuck me."

"C'mon Holmes, you've seen the other case managers here. Not one of them weighs more than 140 pounds soaking wet. And that includes me."

"What about all of those kung fu moves we were taught? Don't those work?"

"Not on Eddie."

"Well, Frank," I said. "Have I mentioned, fuck me?"

"Just think about it," he said.

"What do you think I'm doing?" I said.

— 22 —

Eddie had a Problem. Eddie was a Problem.

The man they called Everyday came to Mayhem from Bolduc Correctional Facility in Warren, Maine. In his life he was not always Everyday. In his life he'd been Only Ed, or V, for his last name Villeneuve. Or Crazy Eddie. Or Extra Ed.

Eddie was a problem for Bolduc even before his Problem. He was cranky, antisocial, not too bright, and ultraviolent.

Before his Problem he was Only Ed and doing ten years for aggravated assault reduced down from attempted murder. The Problem's genesis was Ed's ill-advised attempt at a less-than-clean self-administered tattoo. It was a painful operation, even for Ed, with fat dull safety pin and ballpoint pen ink and he made himself sick before he could complete the project.

He was going for block letters on his abdomen: F on his left side, facing up so he could read it, and U on his right. That's right, he was communicating FUCK YOU to himself. He only made it partway through filling in the F and a partial outline of the U before he came down with severe flu-like symptoms that landed him in the prison infirmary.

The flu cleared up after a week or so, but Only Ed, as a result of an infection, became very confused and disoriented with no memory regarding his reasons for being at Bolduc. Also he could not remember his cellmate's name or ever having met him. The memory loss became more and more acute as time passed. The prison doc's best guess was that Ed had infected himself and contracted encephalitis, wiping out his short-term memory.

Because Ed started each day asking his cellmate, "Who the fuck are you?" Only Ed became Everyday Ed.

"So why is he here?" I asked Frank.

"Well, he wasn't doing well within the prison population. He'd get frustrated over his memory loss, didn't understand why he was in prison, and become angry. Fights." Frank would not look at me as he gave me this information. He leafed through Ed's file.

"Are we able to help with that?"

"We do our best," Frank said, still looking deeply into the dossier.

"How long has he been here? Has he been fighting here?"

"Not really. Been here a year. Not too many. Not too many fights. They're not really fights. Assaults. Who the hell is gonna fight that guy?"

Frank handed me the dossier and said, "I'm going to be straight with you. There's no way this guy should be here. He's a time bomb. He's here because the state of

Maine is paying us $23,500 a month to take him off their hands."

I let that sink in for a moment.

"Technically," Frank went on, "way over half of the clients we have here shouldn't be here. Technically we are a rehabilitation facility. Autism cannot be rehabbed. Borderline personality with suicidal and homicidal ideation cannot be rehabbed. Sociopathy is very stubborn and hard to rehab. But where else can these people go? A cynic might think we're just in it for the money. A cynic might also say we're endangering the truly brain injured by integrating them here with the severely mentally ill. What about you?"

"I'm not severely mentally ill."

"Good," he said. "Are you a cynic?"

"Of course."

"Does it bother you that we're breaking laws from here to February?"

"Not particularly," I said. "But I hadn't given it much thought."

"Listen, Holmes. This place is the last stop for the utterly fucked. No place and nobody would even consider housing most of these folks. The parents of the kids either don't exist or don't have the stomach to care for their own children, and I don't particularly blame them. These older clients have been pawned off by hospitals and are either wards of the state or are brothers and sisters of the fabulously well-to-do who wouldn't dream of caring for poor Uncle Talmadge even if they knew how." Frank was pink with passion. "This is home, Holmes. This is it. Most of your adult caseload will get sick here and die here. We'll ship the bodies to wherever we're told to and someone else will bury them without knowing very much at all about them. End of story."

I wasn't sure what this was—a pep talk, a personal purging of pent-up frustration, or a heat check for my dedication to the cause. Whatever it was, I was back to liking Frank because of it and thinking perhaps I was just the man to help Everyday.

So, as of this moment, I was a case manager for the adult team.

Frank told me that the adult population had adult problems and would most likely require more of my time than the children's problems did. The kids spent most of their days in class while the adults marked time with occasional physical therapy sessions and scheduled outings into the community, but 75 percent of their waking hours they were idle: smoking, watching, moaning, complaining, screaming, bickering with one another, spitting, singing off key, staring at the TV in the day room, and inevitably getting into some level of trouble for offenses such as stealing food from the kitchen, teasing other clients to tears, groping themselves in public, making unauthorized phone calls, and of course, assaulting staff.

I was assigned a total of six men plus Ed. Frank told me they kept case managers and clients unisexual because when they'd experimented with co-ed client/clinician arrangements, clients invariably hit on the staff with little finesse and often, the staff would acquiesce. There were too many dark hallway assignments taking place under the co-ed client/clinician experiment.

There were four male case managers on the adult side and three female. I'd met them all in passing and would be interacting with them formally in monthly staff meetings. The average age of the adult case management team was much closer to my own than on the kid side, and one of the female staffers even had a few years on me or maybe just looked like she did. I was not going to miss the insufferable case manager bros from the kids' side.

On my way out of Frank's office, after taking wrong turns in the hallways, going up four stairs in the middle of an open hallway and then down six further down the hallway and somehow winding up in the basement where I found, believe it or not, a beautiful little gym and an elevator to take me up to the first floor and familiar territory, I saw the shadowy man who had directed me to Frank's office standing against the wall of the day room and he was watching people watch TV.

I was within three feet of the front door and I could have walked out into the cold October air and beat feet back to my little office to kill the remainder of the day. Instead I said, "screw it," out loud, and walked across the room to where the tall man stood. From Frank's description, I had no doubt that this was Ed.

"Hi," I said. I gave him appropriate personal space, standing two feet off from him. He was an exceptionally good-looking kid. Jaw. Symmetry. Arresting eyes. Straight nose. He could be an L.L. Bean model.

He wasn't glaring at me, exactly. He maintained a poker face and alternately glanced at me and looked over my shoulder at . . . something, somewhere in the middle distance. After about twenty seconds of this I thought about leaving, but didn't. Finally, still not looking at me, he said, "Who you be?"—baritone and strangely ghetto.

"I'm Holmes. I'm your new case manager."

Ed glanced at me quickly and then returned his gaze off into the room somewhere. His poker face, however, quickly slid into something else that I really did not like. Eddie did not look happy. He came off the wall a fraction and reached into his back pocket. My hackles went from semi to fully up. The not-looking-at-me thing was starting to spook me. The shifting of his facial muscles from non-committal to committal spooked me more.

"Spell it," he hissed. He was holding a reporter's narrow notebook in his left hand and a pen in his right. I could see that the notebook was crammed with scribbled data.

"Spell what?"

He turned his eyes now straight into mine. His were the purest and most purely unblemished sclera pocketing perfectly round, perfectly black, and perfectly angry irises. "Yo *NAME!*"

"Ah," I said. "Holmes," I said. "H.O.L.M.E.S. Holmes." He wrote it down.

"Case manager you say?"

"Yes."

"Phone number," he said, and then, surprisingly, "please." I gave him my office number and he scribbled it down under my name and circled it. He glanced at me again, face not quite as hard, and then resumed staring off, over my shoulder. He nodded, I think. Apparently I was dismissed.

The ride home to Serious Farm required four beers.

— 23 —

I could not decide whether to decorate for Halloween. There were pumpkins sitting alert and waiting in Serious Garden, but as of yet I hadn't the heart to pluck them and place them in strategic Halloween positions.

Daylight was scarce upon returning from Mayhem and weekends were weird, still, with the dissolution of the twinners coming around. We'd had a clockwork routine for over a decade of Thursday arrival and Sunday departure with Grammy Bette coming for exactly two hours each Saturday morning for pancakes and brief relief while I made dump runs and, in the early days, for actual running runs. The muscle memory of preparing mentally for the energy onslaught of those two bundles of gleeful chaos would not fade. I don't think I wanted it to fade. Not ever, as those were the best days of life.

Serious Farm had become cavernous. Too many rooms to choose from to sit and polish off an evening with either vapid TV or a book.

The Friday night after my reassignment to the adult team and Everyday Ed, I decided to plunk down in Serious Office with Serious Easy Chair, Sirius radio tuned to ambient music, book, and serious glass of red wine. I was asleep in my chair before the wine was half gone. Two hours into this doze, my cell phone rang. It was ten p.m.

It was Kat calling.

Kat was far and away the brightest human I had ever met. It wasn't close. The MDs I've known, the PhDs, the goofy MIT grads, or the general contractors who thought they were the smartest men on earth, could not hold a candle to Kat's raging intellect.

She was a painter of abstracts, no metaphor, she painted for real. Her shapes and her colors and her painterly plans of attack haunted her at all times. She taught me what I was looking at when we made trips to Chelsea galleries in NYC to look at paintings and other installations. I studied her as she studied her heroes and it made me profoundly happy to do so.

She was ridiculously well read. She had internet access to university libraries and she devoured peer-reviewed articles on all subjects: war history, psychology, psychiatry, physics, pornography, education systems, surgical procedures of sub-Sahara cultures, mysticism. She would talk on subjects for hours and make it compelling. She read regular shit too, fiction: Updike, David Foster Wallace, Gabriel Garcia Marquez, Junot Diaz.

I met her while she was separated from her husband. She had four absurdly photogenic children and we met at some sort of elementary school function. We began chatting, her with her knowledge and thirst for telling, and I fell desperately in love with her.

She was five-foot-three with soft and sad brown eyes and brown hair and olive brown skin. On the occasions, later, when she spent the night with me, I would look at her face while she slept and could not decide if her eyes were lovelier when they were opened or closed.

I fell desperately in love with her very quickly and she allowed this. But she could not love me in return as she was too deeply committed to her sadness.

She allowed me to be desperately in love with her for three years before she finally, mercifully, put me out of my misery.

When it came, I said, "So you really don't love me. It feels like love to me."

She said, "I do. I do, but not like I should. Not like you want me to."

Not like she loved her depression. She would not abandon her sadness for any man or any child.

Kat knew Serious Farm very well as we made love on nearly every square foot of its eleven acres. Countless times on the ridiculous two-acre lawn, amongst the trees, down by the railroad tracks, in the barn . . . once in the rafters, the garage, in the snow, in the twins' summertime pup tent, in the bushes, on or in the hammock, up against her car, up against my truck, in her car in my driveway . . . unable to wait, every room of the house, the attic, the hallways, standing, sitting, crawling.

She allowed me to love her and in that way, the physical way, she loved me back well enough. It was confusing because it felt like love to me, what she allowed. Only I could not compete with her tragic self.

The best thing she did for me, among so many best things, that felt like love to me was, during the worst of these days regarding my children, with the tactics, the accusations and the ensuing legalities related to the accusations, when she saw the helplessness in my face, she jotted a quick note once and pressed it into my hand as I left her house in Portsmouth.

In my truck I unfolded the note and read what she'd written in her artist's hand: *Be strong. I will help you.*

I loved her desperately for all she did in those years.

She called at 10 p.m. to say hello. We had not spoken in six months. We hung up at 1:15 a.m. I have no recollection of what she talked about. I loved every word.

On Saturday morning, early, 7 a.m., Bea called.

"Hi Dad."

"Hi sweety."

"How are you?"

"I'm good, kid. How are you?"

"I'm gooooood."

"What's up?"

"Not much."

"How's the new school?"

"It's OK."

"Making new friends?"

"Yup." Then she said, "Dad, we're not going to be able to make it up this weekend."

And though it was understood, as they had not been up in over two months, the words still made my heart and my throat tighten.

"That's OK, kid."

"But we'll be up soon."

"I'll be here, kiddo. How's your sister?"

"She's right here."

Mae must have been sitting right next to her sister as it was less than a second. "Hi Daddy."

"Hi Mae." These beautiful girls. It felt like love to me.

— 24 —

Besides my own, my caseload, there were others upon Mayhem worthy of consideration.

The truly unruly lived in the Nixon cabin. Nixon was the furthest from all occupied buildings, the highest on the hill, surrounded by trees and close to the chain-link fenced perimeter as if perhaps to encourage escape. This was a male-only cabin and we saw them rarely as they had their own kitchen and seldom participated in general Mayhem activities.

If it weren't for the All Star, one may not have noticed the Nixonians at all, they were so well segregated.

However. The All Star.

He was six-foot-nine, for one. For two he weighed a well-put-together three hundred pounds, anyway. For three he was profoundly hairy. His wirebrush blue-black hair grew out in straight cables at an inch per day. His beard the same. He looked a bit like a mutant Jerry Garcia. Lots of hairs, not much face. I could not imagine for the life of me who trimmed these areas for him on what had to be a weekly basis. When he walked, he lumbered, stiff most likely, with medication.

I'd seen him, impossible not to, around. I'd asked team leader Frank about him during our briefing, just out of curiosity and curiosity over who he was and his story.

As noted, his cabin was the furthest most distant from everything and was populated by the hyper-aggressive and watched over by the most battle-hardened and sociopathic of the staff, according to Frank.

The All Star was twenty-four years old with a diagnosis of severe autism. He was nonverbal, mostly docile, due to those strong medications . . . but the rumor was that when the bad electricity got hold of him it was spectacular. *Walk with me. Talk with me.* Right.

Frank told me that when the All Star went off, people got *destroyed*! Waves of staff were required to subdue this cat. "So why doesn't my man Eddie live up at Nixon?" I asked.

"Too unpredictable," Frank said, looking away from me. *More unpredictable than the All Star?*

On this, my inaugural Monday as Adult Team Case Manager, five days before Halloween and at 7 a.m., there was the Halloween Parade scheduled for all clients who wished to or could participate.

I had not even made it to my office yet, as the parade assembled in the small parking lot in front of the infirmary below. I may or may not have heard about this event. If I had heard, I'd forgotten, so the gathering I witnessed confused me.

The kid clients were in costume and all set to walk in a semi-organized bevy from the infirmary to the admin building to classrooms to the Main House and back to the infirmary for trick or treating. It was sweet. The kids looked excited. I was standing on my dirt path above the administration building looking down on this colorful pre-pageant and became aware that the man who had interviewed me and hired me was standing next to me, also watching. We nodded hello.

We watched in silence as the All Star, towering above the crowd, dressed in a canary yellow and blood red clown jumpsuit onesie type thing with ruffled-neck pleated collar, rainbow Afro wig and red nose, and grotesque red lipstick smile stood out and above the shorties like a severely hammered thumb in the midst of his cohort. Why this crosswired leviathan was allowed to march with children one quarter his size was an amazement to me.

We stood watching, side by side, this administrator and me. Him with his briefcase and me with my hands in my pants pocket. We were both staring at the All Star in his clown suit. How could we not? Without looking at the man who had lured me to this place, I said, "Because it's not weird enough around here."

To his credit, the administrator laughed, but not loudly. Then he said, "I wonder where they found a clown suit that size?" It was a good question.

As I approached my cabin, empty this morning as the boys were out parading, I thought I heard my phone ringing, which was odd. My phone rarely rang. It rang itself out and my answering machine thing picked up. As I dropped into my desk chair I looked at the phone and the voicemail indicator told me I had twenty-seven messages. These would have been the first and only voice messages I'd received since starting work upon Mayhem Mountain.

I got an immediate bad feeling.

As I scrolled through, after twelve identical messages, it was clear they were all from Ed.

In a clear voice: "My name is Ed Villeneuve. You are Holmes Jensen, my case manager. Call me at the Big House as soon as you get this message. Thank you."

All of them the same. Same words, exactly, same intonation.

Was I ready for this?

What choice did I have? This was my job. I called.

"Good morning, Big House."

"Hi, this is Holmes Jensen, case manager. I'm returning Ed Villeneuve's call."

The woman manning the phone said, "Yes, hello Holmes. He's right here. Hold please."

A brief snippet of "Sailing," by Christopher Cross, then, "'Lo?"

"Hi, Ed?"

"Yeah?"

"This is Holmes, returning your call."

"Who?"

"Holmes Jensen. I'm your case manager. I'm returning your phone call."

Ed didn't say anything for a minute, but he wasn't silent. I could hear him breathing. I could hear him flipping pages in his notebook. His breathing got louder and more rapid in a short matter of seconds. I sat listening. If you were looking at me I'll bet my brow was knitted or furrowed, maybe both.

"Ed?"

Ed growled, I swear, like I imagine a badger would and at the end of the growl Ed intoned, quietly, as though he wanted no one but me to hear, "Mo-ther-fuck-er." More breathing. A grunt from the throat.

"Ed?"

"I talk. You listen." He was seething. "You gots one fucking day to get me out chere. One day. Or they gon be a blood baf."

Ed was, this morning, sounding really interesting. Besides being, obviously, very upset and murderous, he was talking, what? Cajun? He sounded Louisiana African American at the moment: a bit French, a bit south, quite a bit Black. I wondered where he'd picked that up.

I had no reasonable response, but there was a heavy silence between us so I said, "Bloodbath."

"Blood baf," he said. "Blood. Start wif you."

Again, I had little in the way of constructive comment so I said, "Huh."

"What time it is?" he asked.

"What?"

"What *time* it is? What time!!?"

"Oh, uh, it's 7:15," I said, "a.m."

"Seven fifteen," he said. I heard the notebook pages again. "I have bowling at eight. Pottery at ten to twelve. Then lunch."

There was silence but I could hear him still on the line. My eyes were open, I'm pretty sure, but I wasn't looking at anything. "OK, Ed," I said. "Hey, Ed?"

"Yeah?"

"I'm still on the line."

"Name please." He was back to polite white Maine guy.

"Holmes. Holmes Jensen. Case manager." The sound of pages flipping.

"Can you meet me in the Big House after lunch? Let's say one fifteen?" I said yes, but immediately thought about not, just to see if he'd remember, which he wouldn't, and if I could get away with it.

Then I asked, "Ed, where are you from, man?"

He said, "LA," and he hung up. I put my receiver gently back in its cradle.

By LA, I'm pretty sure he meant Lewiston/Auburn. Maine.

— 25 —

I considered calling Team Leader Frank to let him know that I'd reconsidered. That I declined to be the sacrificial lamb at the altar of Everyday Ed's violence. I thought about it all weekend and as squeamish as I am at the possibility of bloodshed, I also saw my assignment as a backhanded compliment and a challenge. If I could not get through to Ed with empathy and kindness, part of me thought I could take him. Physically.

Part of me is delusional.

It was Monday and it seemed I had actual work to do. In addition to the Ed situation, I had others on my caseload to meet and greet. I decided to wander down to the Big

House and begin the process of acquainting myself with the gentlemen.

I would be looking for: A guy named Ty. Frank called him Ty the Weasel, affectionately maybe. Ty was inseparable from Jules, a wheelchair-bound hipster with full-sleeve tattoos and a doo rag. Frank told me Jules had paralyzed himself with a hot shot, an overdose of too clean heroin. He was a former commercial fisherman from Providence, Rhode Island, with a wife and young boy child back there.

Also I would be hunting for a man named Talmadge, a fifty-three-year-old former insurance exec who had jumped from his suburban Medford third-floor attic window, landed on his neck on his lawn and lived. He was ambulatory, oddly, but severely brain damaged. I had Burris from Brooklyn, a Black kid who got clipped in the temple during a drive-by shooting. Also stuck in a wheelchair, Frank said Burris was the horniest man upon Mayhem and perhaps the planet.

Then there was a bedbound guy named Russ who was in the late stages of dementia, probably Alzheimer's. He was only forty-three years old and had not been lucid in three years. His family had the coin to pay for his care here. Why here and not a regulation nursing home? No idea. The views? Frank said Russ would be no problem for me.

And Everyday Eddie.

The formal entrance to the Big House was clearly a build-on to the bizarrely ramshackle original structure . . . a marketing tool to impress visiting family and representatives of insurance companies or prisons. A large brick landing led to enormous sliding glass doors that opened automatically with motion sensors. There were potted shrubs upon the landing and cozy looking café-style tables and chairs. Just like Paris. This entrance did a fine job of distracting from the otherwise fire-trappy and subterranean nature of the 90 percent of the rest of the building.

The day room was a quick left off of the main foyer. At this hour of the morning, pre-breakfast, the room was mobbed with humanity both sitting and standing. The deck just off of the day room was populated by smokers smoking pre-meal smokes.

Nobody spoke.

As I entered the day room, many heads turned. I counted fourteen clients in wheelchairs but my guys were easy to spot. Only Jules wore a doo rag and only Jules had a valet. I walked over to Jules and Ty. Ty the Weasel.

"Word on the street is you're my new case manager," Ty said, walking toward me, two octaves too loudly.

"I am," I said. "What street?"

"What street?" Ty repeated.

"What word? What street?"

"What?" he said.

"Never mind. Yes, I'm the new case manager. Good to meet you gentlemen."

"Nice to meet you, Mr. Holmes. Do you by any chance have a cigarette? By any chance a Marlboro?"

"Sorry. I do not."

"Oh, oh, oh that's OK. But you'll get me some, right?"

"I don't think so."

"But, but, but, Mr. Holmes, you're my case manager. You're supposed to get me my Marlboros."

"Is that true?" I asked. It might have been true.

Ty the Weasel gave himself up. "No. It's not true. I'm manipulating you." He stood there, looking up at me, sadly. "I'm sorry."

"It's OK. Thanks for being honest." Ty's buddy Jules kept a silent close eye or ear on this disjointed back and forth.

"I seen you," Ty said, "I seen you with Miss. Bojean. Miss Bojean." Too loud.

"OK, "I said.

"She's, Mr. Holmes. She's. She's. She's *HUMID!*" Way too loud. Some heads in the day room turned. Not many. Jules laughed.

"Mot!" Jules said to Ty.

Ty looked at Jules. "What?"

"Mot! Mot, moomid. Mot!"

Ty looked at me. "Is that true?" I was lost. "Is the word hot? Not humid? Hot?"

"Oh," I said. "Usually, yeah. But humid works." I'd just discovered that Jules had trouble speaking. He sounded like a stroke victim. The too-pure heroin had done substantial damage to several areas of his brain.

"So," I said, "I just came by to say hello. Any idea where I might find Talmadge and Burris?"

"Right out there," Ty said, pointing to the smoke pit deck. Ty reached out to shake hands and we did. Jules reached out a shaking and softly folded fist. We fist bumped and I wondered if he was a quadriplegic or paraplegic and what specifically defined one or the other. I had a lot to learn.

Outside, Talmadge stood at the deck railing, back to the smoking humanity, gazing out on the now barren trees of the Mount Washington Valley. I took a place next to him and did the same. Somehow, impending November had a way of sucking the sound out of the land. I'd noticed during my stonemasoning years that a hush descended upon the land with the arrival of November. I kind of loved it. I kind of hated it. I did not know how Talmadge felt about November and would never know. I stood with him for five minutes and he never acknowledged my presence.

Burris sat vibrating in his wheelchair, his eyes darting about. His sweatpants were tented. You could plainly see where the drive-by bullet had entered the left side of his head. A male technician stood nearby and I asked him if Burris could speak.

"Yep."

So I introduced myself to him. "Burris? I'm Holmes."

He glanced at me for a brief second and then his eyes continued bouncing around the deck. No response.

"I'm your new case manager." More nothing from Burris. I turned to the tech and gave him a questioning look.

"Hey Burris," the technician said. He got no reply. "Hey, Burris, what's your favorite thing in the world?"

Without looking at either the attendant or me, Burris spat out, "Puuuuuuusssssssssy!" The technician looked at me.

"There you go," the technician said.

I nodded my thanks and went back inside. I only had to track down Russ. Russ was housed on the first floor, confined to his room and his hospital bed. I now had a general idea of how to find my way into and out of the catacombs that were the inner rooms and offices of the Big House.

On my way through the day room, I saw Everyday Ed at his usual station with back against the wall, his hands behind his back, scanning.

I looked at my watch. Ed was supposed to be at bowling.

I walked up to him, slowly. "Hi Ed."

"Hi," he said.

"Did bowling get cancelled?" He glanced at me and then continued scanning the room behind me as if on watch for secret assassins. He didn't answer me.

"Okay," I said, "Good to see you."

Ed glanced at me again. "Good to see you," he said. I turned to walk away but was quickly arrested by a clamp hand on my left shoulder. The clamp hand turned me, easily, around to face Ed. "Bowling?" he asked with more than a hint of annoyance in his voice. "I don't fucking bowl."

I smiled and said, "Okay. My mistake."

Ed's eyes, black, were now boring into mine. "Them kinds of mistakes will get you killed in here." And he began to really squeeze my shoulder. It hurt.

"Okay," I said.

"A word to the wise," he said.

"Okay," I said, wondering if I could drop him with a straight right. Then he let go. I didn't scurry away immediately. I gave it three seconds, staring back into his eyes. Then I scurried away. I wasn't going to ask him about his pottery class.

— 26 —

I decided going to see Russ could wait for another time.

I walked past the Admin Building along the bisecting lane and then headed uphill on the footpath leading towards the cabins and my office.

The footpath wound through an old apple orchard that had not been tended properly in decades but still produced rock-like crabapples that now littered the matted November grasses like lumpy snooker balls. Some still clung to the gnarled tree limbs. They were macabre pre-Christmas ornaments. They were shrunken heads. There were well over one hundred apple trees in this ancient orchard still producing their strange and forgotten fruit.

As I walked along I noticed in the depths of the orchard some sort of slow-motion commotion. From a distance the commotion appeared to be an interpretive dance piece performed by a dance troupe of a half dozen but that probably wasn't right. I stopped to watch.

The lead in this choreography was a female client. She was semi-encircled by five men.

She was clearly in distress as I could hear her crying and see her face twisted with despair.

The client was wearing a sun dress of sorts, too lightweight for the November air. It was a light sea or julep green and gauzy and came to her knees. She was barefoot. I could see that her feet were very dirty all the way up to her ankles.

She had a mane of electrified dark blonde hair sticking up and out like an unholy halo. Her arms reached out into the distance in front of her and her hands plucked at the strings of an invisible instrument. Her movements were mesmerizing. As I watched her dance the word *diaphanous* occurred to me. I had to look the word up later to see if it made any sense.

She twirled in and through the ghoulish apple orchard trees. A fog would have been appropriate but the morning was clear and sunny.

The lesser players in this dance commotion were a handful of men trying to encircle her and follow her movements at a slight or safe distance. They seemed to be trying to keep her within the circle without her noticing, like a snipe. In this dance piece they could have represented paramours or protectors or bad dreams. All parties were moving liquid and slow, following the lead of the Diaphanous.

This dance was simultaneously lovely and sinister. No one in the group of men spoke. I recognized one of my colleague case managers. I recognized the dangerous-looking man from security, the man with the buzz cut. The remaining three men were unfamiliar to me.

The girl's crying seemed to turn to singing. And then back again. Her arms continued to flail the cool air. She seemed to be trying to grab hold of the lower clouds in the sky and pull herself up. Her head back now and wailing, Nina Simone style, she twirled like a deadhead tripping hard.

Diaphanous stopped suddenly and suddenly stepped out of her dress. She stepped out of her dress and continued.

I became aware of the stillness of this early November morning. There was no bird song, as the songbirds had recently departed. There was no wind in the trees. The girl had ceased singing, ceased crying. This was a silent movie and my mind registered only black and white.

I then registered, suddenly, that the entire movement had been drifting toward me and was now only twenty feet from where I stood on the walking path. Buzz Cut decided it was time to put an end to this performance. He was smiling an awful smile of giant yellow teeth in a mouth sunken and surrounded by neck fat. He tried to ease in on Diaphanous and each time he tried she felt his heat and twirled away, singing, crying.

She navigated through the fallen apples easily while the men angrily kicked them out of their way after rolling their ankles. I felt this might be a good time to mosey along and get to my office. This was fascinating, but none of my business.

She read my mind. I have no doubt that the Diaphanous read my mind for just as I'd begun to form a notion of escape, she came at me, fast. She covered the remaining distance very quickly and was on top of me before I could duck, dodge, or run.

I braced for impact, not knowing what this was—an attack? an escape?—or if I should defend myself, and if so, how does one defend against a naked Diaphanous? I considered an ¡olé! move, a matador defense, but too late, she was on me, way up, up on tippy toe and gently, very gently, she reached up and put her arms around my neck and laid her very warm head on my chest, her wirebrush hair tickling my nose. She was whispering now. She said, "please, please, please." She whispered *please* like a ghost child stuck wandering the earth for too long. I put my right hand on her back, very gently, and we stood like this. Please.

Buzz Cut came in fast. I tried to look him off but he knew his job and clamped his meathook into the crook of her extended elbow and expertly removed her from around my neck.

Diaphanous seemed to take it all as a matter of course, but she continued to sing, "Please!"

The rest of the men came in now and like the curtain coming down they blocked her from my view and began walking her down the hill along the path and back to wherever was next for her.

And just like that, I was alone, standing in the matted cold grasses with apples underfoot, their cidery smell apparent now, now that they'd been mashed by booted and bare feet. I watched the circle, the experts, taking Diaphanous away and thought of my daughters. Where was the father of the Diaphanous? Had he done everything in his power to help his daughter? Could he imagine her life?

I turned my body to the north and the west to look at the summit of Mount Chocorua where my young daughters and I had stood, at the top, not so long ago. We'd made the hike together, them eager and fast. While we rested on top, I told them the legend of the ledges atop Chocorua being a last resort leap for a defiant Indian brave. I told them the legend of how the white men had cornered the renegade brave on the ledges, cornered him for some crime the brave no doubt did not understand. They chased him to the edge of the very high ledge and left him with a decision.

The brave chose death over capitulation, and he'd leapt, perhaps looking out to where I now stood upon Mayhem.

I had no idea if this legend were true or not. Another version of the legend I'd heard was that the brave had been rebuffed by a lovely maiden and, unlucky in love, he made the leap.

I'd chosen to tell my daughters the story of defiance.

— 27 —

There were twenty-six messages on my phone machine. Twenty-three from Ed and three from the Big House front desk lady telling me Everyday was looking for me. Those three messages from staff sounded like warnings. I decided to skip our after-lunch meeting. I needed a much stronger strategy for Ed than loving empathy or mortal combat. I didn't think he'd miss me this day.

— 28 —

"Every day?"

"Every day."

"You're joking," she said, peering at me over the rim of her glass.

"Every single day. Twenty-three times a day."

Bojean sat across her kitchen table from me. We had broken into her dad's booze, again. I was working on my second Dewar's on ice and she was drinking vodka and something. Sprite maybe.

"Every morning at eight there are twenty-three messages on my answering machine. Twenty-three. Never more than that and never less. No idea what the significance of twenty-three is. That's Michael Jordan's number, but that's probably not it. Or maybe it is. Every time he introduces himself and demands that I meet with him immediately. And every day I call him back and have to introduce myself all over again. Then he starts to get pissed off."

"And you meet with him? Every day?"

"Well," I said, taking a good long sip and speculating about the ride home and my blood alcohol content, "one day I didn't. I wanted to see if he'd notice."

"Did he?"

"I'm not sure. I don't think so. I thought he might have been double angry the next day, but it's hard to tell."

"Wow," she whispered.

"Pardon?"

"I said, wow."

"Yeah. Wow. I really appreciate you taking the time to listen to this. It's just so strange. He always wants to kill me at first. Every time. He keeps predicting a bloodbath and I'm assuming he means me. I just stand there, toe to toe with him, nodding. His whole body literally trembles with rage. Even his eyes bounce.

"He has absolutely no idea where he is or why he's here. When he stops shaking and unclenches his fists, I'll ask him a personal question and he'll answer, politely. He'll ask if I can authorize getting a couple of smokes from the day nurse so we can go outside for a while and talk.

"He's told me about prison and the reason he was in there. Some friends ripped him off on a meth deal of some sort and he beat one of them half to death. He's told me about his brutal childhood in Lewiston: junkie mom, drunk and abusive dad pimping Mom out to friends coming through the house at all hours of the day and night. His baby sister dead from some kind of an infection no one got around to noticing. He has about a twenty-minute limit on storytelling at which point he'll reach out to shake hands like we've really bonded and then walk back into the building. An hour later he calls me and it starts all over again."

"And he always talks like a Black guy?"

"Not always. That comes and goes. Usually when he's angry. 'Blood baf.'"

"Hmmm." She sets her drink on the table and looks at me. Skepticism? "Well, what do you think?"

"What do I think?" I can't hear her, but I think I'm definitely learning to read lips. "I'm not sure. So far he's been able to de-escalate after the initial rage, but it's damn spooky up until he does. And it's every day! It's like I'm getting ready for hand-to-hand combat every morning on the ride in."

"It's always getting ready for hand-to-hand combat," she pointed out.

"True," I said. "How's it going with you?"

Bojean brought her elbows up to the tabletop and rested her oval face in her hands, the universal sign for weary. "Um," she began. "do you know that little girl Angela?"

Angela was notorious: barely over four feet tall, severely autistic but very smart and very cunning and very, very mean. She had most recently kicked out a side window of a company van that was taking her to the dentist and scratched her case manager to the tune of stitches. I could not imagine being the dentist going into that tyrannosaurus mouth. She could gouge like a fisher cat with her nubby nails. She could be funny as hell, truly witty, and then slap your face while you laughed in appreciation of her wry observations. She required two staff members at all times or she would beat the bejesus out of any unlucky client standing around or in her way. She had the only private room on all of Mayhem Mountain and third shift posted a sentry outside her door at night. Angela had a history of escape attempts.

"Did you know she is allowed 'private time' whenever she wants?"

Studying Bojean's lips, I said, "No. What do you mean?"

"Private time. Whenever she wants to rub one out she says, 'private time', in that gangster voice of hers and we have to escort her to the bathroom so she can masturbate. This happens multiple times a day. She is a very horny little girl."

"Whaaaat? Are you serious?" It hadn't occurred to me that Bojean might even know what masturbation was.

"Yes. Serious. We don't mind because after she's done she's pretty mellow for a while." Bojean blinked heavily; I could see she was exhausted. "So, she called for private time today and the bathroom is just outside the classroom she was in, so I took her by myself. Her private time is usually pretty quick, a minute or two. Today, she was in there for quite a while. I thought maybe she had a good one going with Batman."

"Batman."

"Yes. Batman is her favorite fantasy. She also likes Hulk and Captain America, but Batman is her man. She has lots and lots of comic books. Her mom and dad send new ones every week."

"OK."

"So I wait a bit longer and finally knock on the door. She says, 'Come in'. Have you heard her voice?"

I have heard her voice. It's eerie. Almost a perfect imitation of Marlon Brando as the Godfather.

"So I crack the door slowly to give her a moment and I see her standing there with her pants around her ankles. There's shit everywhere. On the floor, the walls, her face. I've got the door all the way open now and Angela is standing there, staring at me, and does that gesture, like the old Italian men do when they talk, fingers pinched together kind of gesticulating at you. I'm standing there with my mouth hanging open and she says, 'My poop is yellow.'"

I couldn't help laughing. I tried to drown it in another sip from my scotch. "What did you do?"

"What do you think I did? I slipped in it."

I'm really laughing. "Did you go down?"

"I went down. I went down and I rolled. When I tried to get up, putting my hands in a splash of poo, she came at me. Her shitty little hands were about an inch from my throat when Mr. Winter pulled her off."

"Good Christ!"

"Yes."

"Bojean?"

"Yes?"

"Was the poop yellow?"

"Yes it was. It was yellow poop. Stinky. Bad."

On my scotch-buzzed ride home, all I could think about were the words "rub one out" and a "good one going" with Batman emanating from Bojean's mind and mouth. It was as though acknowledging a daughter may be turning into a sexual being: a little unsettling with a dollop of pride and mystery. I turned up the radio to NPR and tried to distract myself with worldly disaster, suffering and science.

— 29 —

We survived: Bojean, Ed, Jules, Ty and me. Burris and Talmadge survived. Russ continue to die but didn't. Everyone upon Mayhem survived right on through November.

Thanksgiving lurked.

My last day on Mayhem began in the dark of Serious Farm. I sat upright in bed awakened by a complicated tramadol dream involving my daughters and the Rochester Fair at 3:50 a.m. There was no sense in trying to get back to sleep or to interpret the dream. My breath hung in the bedroom air. Serious cold.

Just before the dawn is the coldest and darkest part of the day, so the story goes. Serious Farm lies in a bit of a hollow that collects the colder air and frosts the daylights out of the remaining goldenrod, which by now is brown rod, and the milkweed and the tall dead grasses of my unmowed fields.

Leaves remaining from the annual Big Rake crunch frozen underfoot as I walk from house to garage to Volvo. The landscape at Serious is sparkling lovely under floodlight on this cold and clear November morning. Constellations remain in the near but not yet dawn. The constellations have rotated in the sky since I found my bed. All seemed right with the universe except for those two missing stars, M and B.

The dawn came clear but shifted quickly from weak November sun to bleak overcast in the time it took me to get from North Berwick to Alfred, a fifteen-minute drive. The cloud cover seemed to hover an ominous fifteen feet overhead and the sky gave every indication it was about to start spitting up snow.

Pre-Thanksgiving snow is, to me, is one of the saddest weathers on earth, though I have never lived in climates featuring tornados or volcanoes, and only briefly in earthquake territory. When I see the first flakes of winter filtering down from the heavens, Vince Guaraldi "Christmas Time is Here" soundtrack plays mournful in my mind's ear and I sigh, like Charlie Brown, at the impending long slog of winter's cold and winter's grey days dead ahead. The Volvo's lame brain indicated via dashboard light that it was twenty-eight degrees on this nearly Thanksgiving morning.

The drive this day made me sleepy.

The kids waiting at the bus stops on my route now wore camo polyester down coats over baggy basketball shorts and Walmart hightop sneakers. No winter hats, not yet. The house-coated moms now watched over their flocks by morning from inside their duct-taped polyurethaned screen doors instead of outside with their cigarette smoke bouncing off the plastic in foggy waves and back into the mobile home interiors. The no-smoking inside rules do not apply on this route in rural Maine.

The F-250s on my ass billowed plumes of poorly processed N_2, CO_2, H_2O, and O_2 up into the cloud cover. The bleary and weekday hung over drivers swiping at windshield condensation that worn-out dash fans could not keep pace with.

This same quaint route north, which only weeks before, in its brief autumnal majesty, could convince affluent tourists from flatland anywhere to consider building or buying a vacation home here in rural Maine America, now looked like a dead-end lane through desolate Dogpatch. This was a depressing peek into my Maine, but one I was proud to be part of—this flinty, this carry-on, this tough-as-nails Maine.

I'd barely pulled into the staff parking lot at Mayhem and started the nearly half-mile trudge to my office when I was intercepted by Ty the Weasel. "Hi. Hi. Hi Mr. Holmes, Mr. Jensen."

"Hi Mr. Ty. What's up?"

"Road trip. Road trip. We're going on a road trip. You and me and Jules. Me and Jules."

"OK," I said. "Cool. Where we going?"

"Tattoo. Tattoo. Tattoo. Hurts. Call Mr. Frank. He said it's OK. Call Mr. Frank. He said it's OK."

"All right, Ty. I'll call Mr. Frank. I don't have any idea what you're talking about, but I'll call Mr. Frank."

"Tattoo time!"

"I know. You said that. But I don't know what it means." We were walking side by side, Ty and me, now splitting through groups of kid clients coming from the opposite direction headed to the dining hall. "Let me grab a coffee," I said, "and I'll call Mr. Frank. I'll meet you back at the Big House in an hour, OK?"

"OK. Yes. Yes. OK."

"All right, Ty. OK." I peeled off toward the Admin building where the staff coffee urn lived. I stopped and turned back to look at Ty. "How do you know so much?"

"I got. I got nothing else to do," he said.

In my office I hung up my coat, sat down, and reached for the phone. I was listening to the ring when I realized there was no red light flashing indicating voice messages. Nothing this morning from Eddie. Strange.

"A great good morning, this is Frank!"

"Wow," I said, amazed by Frank's continual enthusiasm, a Team Leader's enthusiasm. I would and could never be a Team Leader. I wondered who he was at home.

"Yes?" he said. "Hello?"

"Hey Frank, it's Holmes."

"Mr. Holmes! How are you on this glorious morning?"

"Um. Good. I'm good. I'm well. How are you?"

"Great! TGIF!"

"It is Friday, isn't it?" I'd completely lost track.

"So," Frank said, "are you up for a little drive into Conway this morning? We've given Jules the go ahead to see his tattoo artist. Have you ever driven a wheelchair van before?"

"Yes," I said, "I'm up. And no, I haven't. Van."

"Well, no worries. It's easy enough. I'll go over procedure with you. Jules is looking forward to it."

"And Ty."

"And who?"

"Ty. Ty said he was going as well."

"Oh no he isn't. I wouldn't do that to you."

Sure you would, I thought, thinking about how he slipped Eddie onto my roster.

"So how goes it? How are you and your new clients getting on, overall?"

"Overall? Well, we've circumvented a bloodbath thus far. Is that what you mean?"

"Ah. The bloodbath. That's been introduced, has it?"

"Every day."

"Yes. Well . . ."

"Anyway, yeah. Let's get the ball rolling on this field trip before it starts snowing," I said, letting my boss off the hook. "And I have no problems bringing Ty along."

"You don't have to. He wasn't scheduled to go on this trip. He does this. Insinuates himself. Really, your day with Jules will be a lot easier if Ty stays here. That kid is a phenomenal pain in the ass."

"Do we have any who aren't?"

"We have those three or four who are in comas." Frank was an interesting combination of optimist, pragmatist, and realist. I would miss him after today.

Frank met me at the motor pool, which consisted of the wheelchair van and a brown Mercury Sable. The van was a retrofitted and rusted 1983 Ford Econoline. White. Average White Van. No identifying signage on the doors or side panels, which I think was a wise move on the part of management. No need to freak out the local populations with forewarnings of Invasion. They'd know soon enough that the Afflicted were among them, no need to advertise. The van came equipped with an electric platform lift thing with welded on O-rings at four corners to strap the wheelchair down, a driver's seat, a passenger's seat, an ashtray spilling over with butts and candy wrappers, and a hole in the dash where the radio used to live. Automatic tranny, manual windows, manual locks, manual everything. Sweet ride. Frank said the electricity for the lift was sketchy and if it died there was a hand crank option.

"You have a valid license, right?" Frank asked, handing over the keys.

"Presently," I said. "But it's tenuous."

"Tenuous? Why?"

"I tend to quaff a lager sometimes behind the wheel. Not today, of course."

Frank laughed. "I wouldn't worry too much," he said. "When it comes to quaffing, here along the Ossipee Trail you are among friends."

On cue, Ty and Jules came wheeling out of the Big House. Jules was a big guy, well over 250 pounds, and little Ty was having a time pushing him up the incline toward the van. Jules wore a knit hat, black, pulled down to the tops of his shades, which were Oakley knock-offs, the Bono bug-eyed kind. He was wrapped up in a huge cloth overcoat, grey, and had a scarf triple wrapped around his neck. It was cold out, but not that cold. I wondered if his circulation wasn't probably skewed by his paralysis. Ty had on jeans, a jean jacket (the Canadian tuxedo), t-shirt, and B for Boston Red Sox ballcap. Ty parked the wheelchair almost right up against my leg and applied the hand brakes.

"Jules," I said. "Ty."

"W'up," Jules said with the mumbled remains of his voice. He extended a quavery right hand that was encased in a fingerless leather biker/rocker/BDSM glove. He could not straighten his fingers so we went with the fist bump. It passed muster with Jules, who smiled. Ty reached out for the same dap and then did the retracting hand explosion thing and made the accompanying explosion sound after we'd bumped fists.

"All right, boys," I said, "let's get this thing moving." The load-in was a bit more complicated than one would think, especially when the wheelchair passenger weighs as much as a linebacker and gives nonstop unintelligible instruction. He wanted to be turned to be able to look out the back window but the grommet and straps configuration wouldn't work that way. He wanted a cigarette, which took a while to fish out of his coat pocket, light, and put in his mouth. Ty wanted desperately to help but was more in the way and he annoyingly kept up a stream of suggestions regarding the load-in process. Twenty minutes later we were good to go. Ty jumped in the passenger seat and I got the vehicle to catch, start, and idle. I chunked the tranny into D and we were rolling. I had the directions to the tattoo studio and I was looking very much forward to a day spent away from the campus. Away from Ed.

From the back. "My oma tuka meek."

I looked back over my shoulder at Jules. "Say again?"

"My oma tuka meek!"

"That's what I thought you said." I looked at Ty. "Did you catch that?"

"He's gotta take a leak." We weren't even beyond the front gate of Mayhem.

I stopped the van and turned to look at Jules. He looked like an enormous wheelchaired Muppet looking back at me. I assumed he was looking back at me . . . hard to tell with the Bonos on. He appeared to be grinning or grimacing. "It's about twenty-five minutes to Conway," I said to the sunglasses. "It will take me forty-five minutes to unstrap your ass, probably hand crank you to the ground and get you to a bathroom. Do the math." Jules smiled at me, with teeth. "Can you hold it?"

"Mup."

"Is that a yup?"

"Mup."

I turned to look at Ty. "He's good, Mr. Holmes. Let's go."

I looked back at Jules. "If I have to stop this car one more time, young man . . ."

* * *

We took the back roads to Conway. Back road. Route 153 was the snake that wound down from the mountain to 25, the Ossipee Trail. Route 153 crossed over and into Freedom and then wound along through East Madison and Eaton right on into Conway. I'd never driven this neck of the woods. Since the leaves were down from the trees and the shrubberies one could see straight through the woods to homes formerly hidden back off the road and the way the homeowners kept their dooryards, either kempt or the other.

One could see grey waters of smallish bogs not quite frozen but soon. One could see stone walls running through the trees, former boundary lines or livestock corrals. I could plainly see the individual stones used to build the walls and whether they were any good for construction or if the farmers had to stack river-rounded bowling balls to clear the fields. Most of the walls were very old and very tumbled down but the stone stock looked lovely, featuring geometrically fractured granite broken in straight lines which made for amenable stacking several hundred years ago. We passed the occasional grand home in states of serious entropy. "How you doing back there?"

"Mwood."

Ty was as relaxed as I'd seen him to date, settled deep into his van seat and humming indecipherable tunes to himself, not bothering nobody. The heater in the van worked. Come to think of it, I was as relaxed as I'd been in weeks and weeks. We came into Conway and finding the tattoo joint was easy enough. It was only just before 10 a.m. and I was concerned that the artists would still be home in bed. Ty assured me that Frank had called ahead the day before and Jules' regular tattooer, tattooist, agreed to open early and meet us.

The place was called *DAMN RIGHT IT HURTS*. I pulled into the parking lot next to an early '60s parakeet green VW van in less than mint condition but beautiful. "Meek. Meek!" Jules was holding out a half-gallon-sized plastic urinal. I don't know where he got it. It must have been stashed in a pocket of his greatcoat. I noticed that the shop had a ramp and told Jules we'd have him to the bathroom in, hopefully, a couple of minutes.

"Mere! Mite mere!!"

"You want to take a leak right here?" I was catching on.

"Mup! Mick!!!"

"OK," I said, clambering between the front seats and into the back of the van. I assumed this was part of my duties as case manager guy. "Tell me what to do."

Jules handed me the urinal. "Mowd miss." I held it. Jules was able to unlatch his seat belt and wriggle forward in his wheelchair. "Mow, moo mip ott ma cak. Mip ott ma cak, n moke ut." I looked at Jules, reached out and took off his ridiculous sunglasses. His eyes were green and he was clearly enjoying himself.

"Do what?"

Ty, from the front seat and looking straight ahead out the windshield, said, "He said whip out his cock. Whip out his cock and stroke it." I stared at the back of Ty's head and then looked back at Jules. He was smiling, but I couldn't tell what the smile meant.

Jules started cracking up. It was a sandpapered and broken laugh but infectious and endearing. We all three of us were now laughing hard; Ty's laugh was a cross between a rhesus monkey and a majorette. Mine was with relief. Just three dudes laughing hard at stupid dude humor.

Still cough laughing, Jules said, "Merwous. Oma tuka meek. Mus met mippuh. Um gut ut." And he nodded down to his pant front. He wasn't wearing a belt. I'm pretty sure he wanted me to just get his zipper and he'd handle the rest, so to speak. I did so, Jules still chuckling and Ty now turned and watching. As I unbuttoned his jeans and lowered the zipper it occurred to me that this was somewhat familiar in a distant way. I'd helped Mae and Bea get in and out of clothing for years. Helpless babies getting into complicated jumpers and snowsuits. Booties and boots. Diapers and onesies. I got Jules' zipper lowered, conscious of not bumping or catching his junk on the journey down.

"Mo gun buh mik ed memus," Jules said as he wriggled his pants down, me still holding the urinal. I completely whiffed on what he was trying to say. I looked at him and shook my head: *Sorry man*. He continued to make progress on dropping his trousers and repeated, "Mo gun buh mik ed memus."

Ty said, "He says you're gonna be wicked jealous."

"Muh gut um donkey dick!" First I'd heard him be able to pronounce a D. His pants were low enough now and he was fishing around in his drawers for the aforementioned. I chose not to look. Jules and Ty were howling with laughter. I had the feeling I was not the first rookie case manager to be run through this drill. I handed the urinal to Jules, not looking at him, and I began to exit the van to give him his privacy. Him, his meek, and his donkey dick.

— 30 —

We—Ty and I—wheeled Jules up a long wooden ramp into a side door of the DAMN RIGHT IT HURTS tattoo studio.

The owner of the place was waiting for us. His name was Prufrock. That's right, Prufrock.

He and Jules knew each other well as Prufrock had inked somewhere north, he figured, of three thousand dollars' worth of art upon Jules' self over the past two years. "And that's with the gimp discount," he told me out the side of his mouth. Pretty much everything Prufrock said this day came from the side of his mouth. That's just the way he spoke.

He wasted no time getting ready and the steady buzz of the needle commenced and would not stop for four hours except to change colors and to wipe the blood away. Ty the Weasel could not sit still. His jerking around the good-sized studio; his alighting briefly in the barber chairs of the other absent artists, his picking up and putting down instruments; his speed reading of thousands of tat designs and photographs taped to the walls; his walking outside for a smoke unattended; his coming back in, were in wonderful concert with the sound of the tattoo needle buzzing like early June busy-as-hell honey bees.

"Should I be worried about him taking off?" I wondered aloud.

"Man ip mo aunt." I could if I wanted, according to Jules.

"Where the fuck is he gonna go?" pointed out Prufrock. Just then Ty ducked back into the studio bringing the smell of Marlboros with him. He walked over to a red Craftsman tool chest that one of the other tattoo artists used for his supplies. Ty slid open the top drawer and then closed it, slid open the second and then closed it, slid open the third . . . "If I find out anything is missing I will personally come and find you in the middle of that freak show you call home and stab you," Prufrock said, not even glancing at Ty.

"I know, I know," Ty answered. He'd heard it before.

Prufrock was working on some large lettering laid out in a half-ellipse, like the collar of a too-large t-shirt, right where the collar of a too-large t-shirt would sit on Jules, stretching from his far-left collar bone to his far-right but reading, I presumed, from left to right. I couldn't see what the letters were from my perch on a padded stool three feet away from Prufrock and Jules. The outline of the lettering was complete in about thirty minutes and the artist was now working on coloring them in.

"How's the pain?" I asked Jules.

He looked blankly at me with his smoky garnet eyes. He looked away.

Prufrock didn't look up from his work. "He's paralyzed, Einstein."

"Einstein? OK . . . ," I sat for a minute, " . . . *Prufrock.*"

Jules' eyes widened and he slowly brought his withered right hand up to his face, covered his mouth, and tried to suppress laughter. "*Yuh, Moomok.*"

Somewhere behind us, Ty started in with the gremlin laugh. Prufrock shut down the needle and turned toward me. He was not smiling. But he hadn't smiled since we'd gotten here. He was small and wiry, like a lot of tattoo artists seem to be. I had fifty pounds on him, but he was obviously a friend to pain, with his full sleeves and his neck work. He looked at me. Seemed to be sizing me up. He did not speak.

"Your parents T.S. Eliot fans?" I asked, breaking the silence.

"Fucking hippies," he said.

"Are you a love song, Prufrock?" I was pushing what little luck I had.

"Apparently."

"What the fuck are you talking about? Talking about?" Ty had wandered in close.

"'The Love Song of J. Alfred Prufrock,'" I said. "It's a good poem."

Prufrock turned the needle back on. "It's a long poem. And who the fuck names a baby after some guy who's growing old? I don't think they even read the fucking thing."

"White people . . . ," I said.

"Could be worse," Prufrock said. "They could have named me Alfred. Or J. Alfred."

"Or Annabelle Lee," I said, wondering if Alfred or J. Alfred were indeed worse than Prufrock.

"What? What? What?" Ty.

Still trying not to laugh out loud, Jules turned to Ty and said, "Muf eye maimed ufuh mome."

"You were named after a poem," Ty asked, incredulous, "tough guy?"

"Fuck off, Dead-From-The-Neck-Up."

The remains of the hours at DAMN RIGHT IT HURTS were spent listening to the Jules narrative about how he screwed up so badly and turned himself into a quadriplegic. Jules was an uninhibited storyteller and a good one. His yarn ate up the hours. The more he talked, the better I could follow his crippled syntax.

Jules is forty-two years old, has a son, three years old. The boy and his mother live in Rhode Island and visit a couple of time a year. Jules had been a commercial fisherman working mostly on long-trip scallop draggers out of New Bedford. He lived in Providence and lived the fishing life. Hard.

I'd done a fair share of carousing in Rhode Island once upon a time so we compared bars we'd spent hours in: Lupo's in Providence, The Twin Willows and the Mews down in Narragansett. He'd started fishing right out of high school and for a while was making a ton of cash. He only did the heroin occasionally. He really liked it but knew he was better off with the speedy varieties of drugs, better for working.

It was simple, he said. Two years ago he'd just gotten in from a two-week trip, rough as hell, hurricane season and very little to show for it. Fishing in New England was dying. The owners had indicated this might well be the last trip for the boat he was on. Screw it. He and a buddy went into town, to the bars over by Brown University where the sweet, smart co-eds drank and occasionally liked to slum it with fishermen as a part of their Ivy League educations. Bigger than fucking Dallas, they met a pair of hotshits from RISD who invited Jules and his buddy to their dive apartment to get high.

"Mupin ot sot. Mit muz moo leen. Moom! Mon!" The heroin was too clean, a hot shot, and Jules says the next thing he remembered was waking up at the hospital, paralyzed, boom, done. And now here in East Bumfuck, stuck. But not for long, he said, not forever.

"Oma mee mishm moon." Jules was adamant. He would be fishing again soon.

Prufrock was finishing up. He dabbed away the oozing blood and wiped his work down with an antiseptic baby wipe. He began to apply the Vaseline, so I stood up to have a look. The work wasn't the best I'd ever seen, the rainbow colors of the lettering looked like they were picked out by a third-grade girl and the font was some sort of urban tagging style shit that if the word carved into Jules' upper chest wasn't so plain and simple it would have been unreadable. The four-letter word he'd had added to his flesh palette was:

HOPE

— 31 —

We wheeled back through the campus gates in the early afternoon. We'd stopped on the way back to get Ty a carton of illicit Marlboros. He had the money and I still wasn't clear on the rules. All of the adult clients appeared to chain smoke but how they procured their product and how it was doled out was a mystery to me. Ty warned me that I could get in trouble by letting him smuggle in the smokes but I told him I'd just say I was manipulated by a man much smarter than me. He seemed fine with this cover. I was fine with it because it was true and I truly didn't care. The kid clearly enjoyed feeling autonomous, so, there you go.

"You guys hungry?" I was hungry. We'd not had lunch.

"Mup!"

"Yup!"

I downloaded Jules out of the van and Ty steered him over to the cafeteria while I dropped off the van keys at the security office. The majority of the offices throughout the campus were tiny and windowless and dark. I'm not sure what the institutional architectural fads or guidelines were back in the 1940s, but these offices the staff were given bordered on cruel.

Security was in the basement of the building where Bojean and I had gone through orientation. This building was right next to the Big House and directly across the little lane that bisected the campus. On the uphill side of the lane sat an abandoned greenhouse where nothing was green. The one building built to allow maximum light had been deserted. Dead stalks of past projects stuck up and out of cracked pots sitting on window sills.

"Those assholes give you any trouble?" The security boss never looked up from his computer screen as I hung the keys on the designated hook upon the designated wall for key hanging. The florescent lighting revealed copious dandruff in his buzz cut.

"What assholes?"

"The assholes you took out for a joyride." I looked down at the flaky skin of the skull of this guy who was the resident authority on all things secure. He'd been the man who had taken up the majority of orientation week teaching us the secrets of winning physical confrontations. This was the guy who came running when a client melted down and needed corralling. When his walkie talkie sparked off with a code blue, or a Dr. Grey, or whatever the term was for violent dementia on the hoof, he would bolt to his pickup and roll to the action. He always took his truck, even if the action was at the Big House, twenty feet away.

"They were no problem whatsoever." There may have been a hint of brass in my tone, I guess, because Buzz Cut looked up from his computer and gave me a head-to-toe-to-head twice over. If I were a woman I'd have felt violated. I felt violated anyway. Buzz grimaced what I suppose was a grin, which made his two chins into four. I left security feeling insecure.

Back at the cafeteria, a tiny worker in dingy white was standing behind the heat lamp steam table line with his arms folded. The serving pans were gone from the holes in the steam table and the three inches of steaming, fetid water could have passed as our soup of the day.

"Shit," Ty said, looking at me. "Shit, shit out of luck."

"Watch your language, little man," the tiny worker said.

"Look. Look. Look who's talking," Ty snapped.

Jules appeared to be nodding off in his chair, his chin resting on the taped-on Saran wrap protecting his H O P E tattoo.

"What's up?" I asked the worker.

"Nothin's up," he said. "Nothin' gonna be up till four thirty."

There was another industrial metal table at the end of the steam table, separate, and at ninety degrees, making an L. It was where the cafeteria staff put out the pre-made salads, desserts and sandwich makings. On the table, at this time, remained an institutional sized tub of peanut butter-like product, a gallon jar of generic jelly, and several plastic-wrapped loaves of the whitest of white breads.

There were clean utensils in bins in front of us and stacks of still warm-from-the-dishwasher plates.

I pointed at the Sysco foodstuffs, which looked damned good to me, and asked, "Do you mind? We haven't had lunch."

"I *do* mind." The tiny worker had puffed himself up like an adder. What the hell? Was everyone back here at Mayhem having a bad day?

"Noted," I said and picked up a butter knife, a big spoon and three plates. Me and my crew headed for the sandwich station.

"You better not," the worker said, voice hinting at hysterical.

Jules raised his head from his chest and said, "Mow me." Ty was pushing the squeaky chair towards the eats. "Yeah. Yeah. Blow me." The worker's arms came uncrossed and his eyes got cartoon round with tiny worker indignation. He was looking at me. "Yeah," I agreed. "Blow them."

Tiny stormed off into the guts of the kitchen and I made six fat PB&Js. We ate them, uncontested.

The Sysco was delicious. I asked the boys if personnel were always this uptight. They agreed that it seemed to depend on the time of day, or the phase of the moon, or the mood of the clients. "This, this place is pretty unpredictable," Ty figured. Jules nodded.

It was two thirty by the time we finished eating and cleaning up after ourselves. I had a couple of hours to kill before quitting time. Ty wandered off to the smoking pit and a young female technician was waiting for Jules to help him get cleaned up and get settled for a nap. She smiled at Jules and at me. As I was leaving the room, Jules said over his shoulder, "Mants, man."

"You're welcome, Jules. My pleasure." And it was.

— 32 —

Maybe this might work.

My dad always told me you can get used to anything except hanging.

Mayhem, at this moment, was growing on me.

This day thus far made it all seem possible.

As I walked parallel to long shadows of apple trees, I thought about the recent encounter with Diaphanous. Her melancholy dance had been beautiful to my eyes and the tiny dancer had come to me, trusting, reading my pure heart with the extra-sensorial radars of the afflicted. She knew that I knew. Gabba Gabba Hey, we accept you, we accept you, one of us.

Unlocking the door to my office, I could see through the glass panes that my phone was blinkering away. Stepping to the desk and checking my machine, twenty-three messages. Shit fuck. Fuck shit.

The apple orchard was late-November hushed as I retraced my steps back toward the Main House. The Sleepy Hollow branches were still life as the day's cold breezes had changed direction and now some warmth from a building southerly brushed my face.

I trod down the railroad tie steps chunked into uneven intervals and random riser heights set behind the Admin Building. Across the bisecting lane and feeling good on up to a narrower-than-building-code guidelines side door entering into the Big House, not really even preparing mentally for the Ed ahead because I can handle this, all of this.

As I entered into the day room, the usual suspects were lounging around, watching the TV sort of, somewhere between vigilance and a dream. Eyes upon me as I crossed the room to where Ed, sure enough, was standing against the wall with his hands behind his back and his usual concerned expression. I was within ten feet of Eddie and closing when I saw Ty across the way and he is looking at me, eyes wide, shaking his head, NO.

Why no? I smiled at Ty and kept rolling.

Ed had me on his sonar now and has locked me in. He was making strong eye-contact, digging in his back pocket for his reporter's notebook. Out of my peripheral I saw Ty leaving the room. This was beginning to feel like a scene from *The Sopranos* where someone is about to get whacked.

"Hey, Ed." Something felt wrong here. Or, extra wrong from the just normal wrong.

"Who you, mufuck?" Ed's right leg began to bounce. This was new.

"I'm Holmes. I'm your case manager," was how I begin. Was how I always began except now I'm using "case manager" instead of "*new* case manager." I felt it cut down on unnecessary detail, possible confusion.

Ed looked down at his notebook and bared his teeth, leg bouncing, both hands trembling with gruesome and terrible kinetic energy. He looked back up at me and appeared delighted, but delighted like a hyena at the moldering carcass of a wildebeest or some such meat.

He held the notebook up to where I could see it and pointed at something written there. The printed handwriting in the book was beautiful, close to calligraphy, and tiny, maximizing space on the page. There were three columns of information on the already narrow page. He pointed to a line of lovely lettering upon the page.

"Who this be?" I squinted in the shitty day room light. I was reluctant to lean my face in closer to the notebook like an invitation for a punch in the eye, but it was the only way. Ed had his fingertip indicating a name: Max Shure PO. 207-589-5595.

"It says," I said, "Max Shure, post office, but no box number, and then a phone number."

Ed's eyes narrowed, thinking. "It don't say post office."

"No, well, it says PO."

Ed looked hard at me. "Parole," he said. "Parole officer!"

"Ah," I said.

"He be *my* PO?"

"I don't know, Ed . . ."

"Why I got a parole officer?"

Ed was right up in my face. He was trembling all over. This was different and I felt I should maybe be afraid, but for some reason was not.

"Ed." I was calculating. "Ed, as far as I know . . ." I was calculating risk and I was calculating escape. I was calculating how to take this man down if need be because violence felt inevitable. I was calculating and trying to say Ed's name out loud as often as I could in order to humanize him. Humanize me.

I knew I had the element of surprise working for me because I was old and innocent and harmless looking. And I just had the feeling that if push came to shove, I could take him. " . . . as far as I know, you came here from prison."

"Not true!" he said, loudly. The day room was still, confused people looking on and looking frightened.

"OK, Ed."

"That is not true! I never been to prison!! Why would I been to prison?"

"The story you told me, Ed, is that you hurt a buddy of yours pretty bad." I was so lost just now. Was this a good idea? To remind Ed of the story of attempted murder. Fear was beginning to creep into my chest and I knew that was a bad thing. A thing Ed may feel or smell.

"That just ain't true!! I never hurt nobody! Never."

"OK, Ed."

"Never in my life!"

"I believe you, Ed."

"Can we call this phone number, this PO?" Ed was holding the reporter's notebook up to remind me of the name and the number written there.

"OK, Ed, c'mon," I said, and started to walk away from Ed, toward a side hallway that held an empty office with a phone that I'd used in the past. Something was telling me to get him away from the others in the room, the collateral.

"Where?" Ed's face was still hard with outrage but my compliance had thrown him off somewhat. He was maybe expecting resistance, excuse making. At this moment, though, how could anyone be anything but compliant with Eddie? How does one say "no" to this seething mass of damaged quarks?

"Let's go call your PO."

He caught up to me as we crossed the day room and was at my left elbow. I noticed others, both staff and client, watching us go.

I was walking Eddie to the empty office where I knew there was a live phone line. The door was open and I was about to escort Ed inside when one of my female case manager cohorts appeared from around a corner and professionally sized up my situation.

"What are you doing?" she asked, quietly, calmly.

"Oh, hey, hi," I said, "I'm going to help Ed here make a supervised call."

"In there?" She asked, nodding toward the open office.

"That's what I was thinking."

My colleague smiled at Eddie and said hello to him. Eddie stared at her, wheels spinning. She got up close to my right ear and whispered, "Not in there. It's too small. Only one door. If he goes off, you'll never get out."

I had not considered this. I wondered if this had been covered in orientation or if this was a more veteran understanding of potential disaster. I looked at my colleague with gratitude. "Good one," I said. "Any suggestions for a better place?"

"Do you have a cell phone?"

"I do."

"Outside is good," she said. Then she whispered to me, "I'll let security know you're out there." I nodded my thanks to her.

I turned back to Ed, who was still staring dark-eyed at my colleague whose name I did not know and whose name I would never find out. Ed was having trouble placing her, clearly, but he was trying. The tension Ed carried in his body was still vibrating, fists clenching and unclenching, right leg still bouncing. Usually, Ed would have been calmed by now, his frustration replaced by either a diverting conversation or a cigarette.

"Let's go outside and make the call, Ed. Do you want a smoke?"

"No." As we walked through the large glass automatic opening front doors of the Big House and out onto the bisecting lane, I saw Ty in my periphery. It occurred to me that it was Ty who'd alerted my colleague to the ongoing, unfolding situation. This, indeed, was about to become a situation. In the coming weeks, I would think about Ty often. He was about the only person I felt really guilty about leaving behind. I would have felt badly about leaving Bojean behind, but I took her with me.

I led Eddie across the lane to the concrete steps leading up to the abandoned greenhouse. There were eight steps with the risers at least a foot high, which made for awkward climbing. Mayhem was peppered with random and wrong construction.

"Okay," I said, sitting on a step and hoping Ed would follow suit and maybe relax a little, which he did not, looming over me and physically still coiled, "let's see that number."

Ed handed me his notebook, which I chose to interpret as a sign of trust. Squinting, I pecked out the number on my dumb phone and hoped sincerely that someone on the other end picked up.

"No way I was in prison," he said.

The phone did that shrieking sound indicating the number was no longer a number. I'm sure Ed heard it.

"No way I hurt anyone. I wouldn't do that. I would never do that!!"

I did not know what I was looking at, looking at Ed. Something immense was turning over in his poor brain. The look on his face was a sad anguish mixed with resignation and rage. His eyes had softened like I'd never seen them. Black. Softened. It looked as if he was going to cry, or was crying.

And just like that, it started and ended. He threw a right jab so quickly and sharp that I never saw it coming. I only heard the report as his fist snapped past my left ear and went crashing through the glass of the greenhouse door behind me.

His body was even closer to mine now, his face almost touching my own. I hadn't moved an inch. Ed pulled his right arm back, withdrawing it from the broken glass, squared up and threw a left. I don't recall flinching.

Again, his fist, which looked as big as a basketball whizzing by my head, missed my right ear I don't know how and took out another pane of glass in the front door. His left shoulder was pretty much in my right eye and I saw Eddie rolling his shoulder, rotating his arm while it was still within the frame of broken glass. I realized he was digging the meat of his forearm into the broken remains of glass. His right arm was hanging by his side and I glanced at it. It had not yet begun to bleed heavy, but the lacerations were wide and deep. I could see stuff, bio stuff, down inside the cuts, many distinct dots of red getting ready to unload. I saw white strings of something, very white, but did not care to understand precisely what I was looking at. He withdrew his left arm from the glass and leaned back so that his face was no longer within kissing distance.

"Jesus, Ed," I heard myself say, very quietly, more to myself than to him.

Quietly back, looking straight into my eyes, he said, "Get me home."

The blood was now filling in the deeply grooved cuts in his right arm and beginning to run down his wrists and fingers and drip big fat drops onto the concrete steps. I still hadn't moved. So much for my grand and delusional plans for self-defense. Buzz Cut the security guy was somehow now with us on the steps and very gently turning Ed by the shoulders and helping him into a sitting position on the stairs just below where I sat. Buzz Cut was simultaneously reaching for his fanny pack first aid kit and speaking into a walkie talkie, summoning help. All of the fight was out of Ed. He allowed himself to be manipulated into a sitting position. Buzz Cut took Ed's hands in his own and inspected the damage. The blood was now pulsing in geyser formation from several different locales and coming out at different angles. "We gotta get tourniquets on these," Buzz said, quietly, very calm.

"We gotta get tourniquets on these," Buzz repeated. He was talking to me. He took a roll of cloth gauze from his kit and took one end from its package and began to tightly wind the cloth around the crook of Ed's elbow. The lacerations stopped just short of the elbow. Buzz looked up from his work, patiently, to me and nodded toward his fanny pack. Moving, finally, I reached into the pack and found another roll of gauze. "You gotta go wicked tight," he informed me, calmly. I could hear the sound of a siren from two miles away, making its way up the hill. There was so much blood.

— 33 —

I could see colors again.

We made it through the congested intersection at Meeting and Calhoun and I decided to pull off and find a place to park. These sidewalks were nearly empty, inviting, and the air continued to caress. The clouds were thick now and the air smelled greenish and I wanted to be out in it, right now. I took a left on Society Street and found an open spot at the corner of Society and Anson.

We pulled up and parked under some sort of barkless tree, its trunk skinned looking and smooth. Next to that tree was an elegant palm with its intricately scaled shell and majestic green frond top. We were parked in front of a private residence that had oversized gas lamps on either side of its red-painted entrance door.

I came around the nose of the car to assist Bojean out and had to navigate a worn smooth block of granite, approximately eight inches high, three feet long and two feet wide, sitting embedded in the bluestone sidewalk.

As I took Bojean's elbow to help her out of the Volvo, she stepped up on the granite block and guessed, "For getting into a carriage? Onto a horse?"

"Makes sense," I said. I felt like I was yelling as the street held a feeling of hush. Perhaps the humid air muffled city sounds, if there were any. Maybe the vegetation that crowded every available negative space absorbed sound waves. It seemed a reverent quiet. A library quiet. A museum quiet.

I stood on the sidewalk, she on her perch, and we took it in. This isolated and lucky landing spot was regal and soft and lovely. The gas lamps on the street were burning, real gas, real fluttery gas flames at midday.

We walked up Society and around the corner onto Anson. The homes could not have been more in contrast to their neighboring structures: this house of brick, the next one of wood clapboards painted a salmony pink, the next an ivory stucco, the next of concrete painted a faint mint next door to the towering stained glass of a church. It all felt church, standing there, the vibe so holy, foreign, and safe.

To this point in our friendship, not a finger had touched skin of the other, but just now Bojean took my hand as we stood looking.

— 34 —

At the corner of Anson we turned right, away from the commercial bits we had passed through and into the heart of this harlequin neighborhood. The sidewalk materials I did not understand. This was bluestone. Pennsylvania bluestone. The pieces were dry laid and uneven due to tree roots growing and pushing up from underneath. What were they doing here? Who laid these sidewalks? How did the stone get here? Was there a trade agreement between South Carolina and Pennsylvania? Cotton in exchange for stone? They'd clearly been here for many years, the stones, trod upon by citizens come and long gone, judging by the smooth wear of the sandy stone like beach stone worn by waves.

I love bluestone, having laid tens of thousands of square footage, breathed in the dust of sawn pieces, leveled and pitched with exacting care for patios and walkways. But I know there are no indigenous South Carolinian bluestone quarries. If there were, I'd have used some of it. How did it get here? Why? We walked on.

The radical variations of architectural ideologies continued from house to house to church to house: grand four-storied structures with massively pillared piazzas stood side by each to brick ranch-style one-story units; ornate entrances with statuary populating expansive landings shared street space with tiny hobbit doorways built into brick arches; hurricane shutters the size of Cadillacs, painted pastels yellow, pink, and lilac guarded lead-paned windows while some designer with another vision outfitted downstairs rooms with small nautical round portals looking out onto Anson. The air, the air so thick and soft.

— 35 —

We walked along Anson, strolling, but hyper-alert to this strange place. A side alley with no name turned to cobble. A brick privacy wall was smothered by green growth of creeping vine. We saw manicured miniature urban gardens with miniature shrubs tucked into dooryards no bigger than a sandbox, fountains trickling. We walked under enormous live oaks presiding over porches with Spanish moss tendrils reaching down to make one wish to reach up and touch. Two-car garages that were clearly horse stables once upon a time constructed of sloppily laid brick. Stone pillars guarded a walkway heading toward a small carriage house or slave quarters tucked back behind a great and grand manse. Our heels clicked the bluestone.

We walked hand in hand. Quietly. Our footfalls the only sound besides our breathing, a complete lack of industrial noise from anywhere including traffic or construction. We crossed over Hassell Street with its name on a brass plaque embedded in the now concrete sidewalk. St.

Johannes Lutheran church, with black-and-white checkered outdoor-tiled vestibule, stained-glass windows and water-stained exterior walls sat quiet and waiting for Sunday.

We veered over to a Maiden Lane with a lichen-splotched knee-high brick wall along the sidewalk and the street paved with river stone. The sidewalk changed back to bluestone as we exited Maiden Lane and passed updated horse stalls with resting carriages and resting horses inside, still hushed, a horse person carefully brushing manes and horse bangs with accompanying barnyard-sweet waft as we tip-toed past the open barn doors.

The midday sky grew darker with increasing overcast only intensifying the colors of vegetation and the flamboyantly odd paint color choices of home and business owners. Over time, after moving to this painted town, I would come to understand that each walk along these streets would vary optically based on the degrees of light coming either from the sun or the moon or the gas lanterns or passing auto headlights. The same street, the same house, or church could be unrecognizable from the stroll before based on the variations in light. Even during this initial stroll, arm in arm now, the palette morphed from one step to the next as the overcast deepened.

We spilled out onto a street called Market. The street was divided by a median of open-air kiosks with a modicum of foot traffic on this early December midday. We ventured in through a side entrance to the Market, constructed very much like Faneuil Hall in Boston and selling gee gaws and hats and pipes and art and leather products, bracelets and wallets and maps of the city and gigantic lollipops and acres of hand-crafted jewelry.

We turned right on Market. I was ravenously hungry now. Clearly this was a tourist part of town as evidenced by both the Market itself and a sprawling patio restaurant called Bubba Gump's, which advertised recklessly with neon their endless shrimp menu. We walked past and I ducked into a gift shop. I found and bought a detailed street map of this Charleston peninsula.

We found a nearly normal-looking eatery on the corner of Market and Meeting. We were given a corner table next to a window where we could watch as the sky outside continuing its thickening and darkening. It looked as though we were in for some weather.

Our waiter was young and male and cheerful. He paid close attention to Bo and little to me. "You folks from out of town?" Bo told him yes.

"Are you staying downtown?" he asked.

"We don't have plans," Bojean told him, not directly answering his question. I was glad to see her deflecting the direct question of someone other than me.

"It floods bad here when it rains," he said. "You might want to get to where you're staying when it starts to come down." He continued to address Bojean solely.

"How bad of flooding are we talking?" I asked. "Like, biblical?"

"Sir?"

"Like, over our heads flooding?"

The sound of my voice simply was not registering. "Sir?"

"Do you think we'll survive lunch, or should we get out of here now?"

He finally looked at me and said, "Well, if it starts to come down now, it could be a foot deep within a few minutes. It don't generally get much deeper than a foot."

I looked at Bojean. "Do you want to risk it?"

"Yes," she said, deep into the menu.

"Me too." Something on the menu had already caught my attention. I asked the waiter, "How's the she-crab soup today? Is the he-crab out of season?" I was actually serious.

"He-crab?" he said.

"I'll go with a bowl of the she-crab and the oyster po'boy." Bo ordered a garden salad with shrimp. We watched out the window and waited. People on the street did not appear to be aware or concerned regarding impending floods.

"What do you think, Bo?"

"Sometimes I think," she said. "What do you think?"

"I think I like it here."

"This restaurant?"

"This Charleston. I'd kind of like to stick around for a bit if you don't mind."

"We may not have a choice," she said, "unless the Volvo floats." I studied the street map while Bo gazed, happily it seemed, out the window.

The food came and we ate it, not really hurrying. The she-crab was very good and very crabby with a little floater of brandy on top giving it an interesting tang. The po'boy was all right. Deep fried anything is almost always all right. We got the check, paid it, and I decided not to ask the waiter to recommend a hotel. We'd figure it out.

We retraced our steps back to Anson and to the car. I took a left on Anson because it was one way and it intersected with Calhoun. I took a left on Calhoun because a right would have put us into the Cooper River where the aircraft carrier was parked. Within a couple blocks we were back to the park we had passed on our way in.

At the far end of the park was a tallish building, maybe twelve stories, the only tallish building we'd seen thus far in all of the downtown area. It looked hotel-like. It could have been an apartment building. It could have been an office building.

The light was red at Calhoun and King which gave me time to read the building's grand marquee indicating it was the Francis Marion Hotel. I parked the car on Calhoun, fed the meter, and we went inside. We entered by the front entrance and were embarrassed by the razzmatazz of military-clad doormen.

The Francis Marion was old and grand with an ornately carpeted lobby with multiple chandeliers hanging where one might, later in the evening, sink into a leather armchair with a cocktail and newspaper and surreptitiously spy upon other guests traipsing to and from the elevator to front desk to piano bar to secluded corner settees hidden by enormous potted plants to the doorman-manned front door opening out onto King Street.

The desk girl was gorgeous, the rate was reasonable, the brass rails in the elevator were polished, and the room was perfect. We were on the seventh floor overlooking King Street and the park below, which turned out to be Marion Square. This hotel was an enormous departure from our econo-motel lodgings to date. The beds were wide and deep with duvets and far too many pillows for one man or woman to use for sleeping. The windows were floor to ceiling and I was happy to see that they could actually be opened. I was now wishing for the rain to begin and I wished to sit close to the open window and let the rain hit my face. The heavy air continued to be the best out of many wondrous and good first impressions of Charleston.

Bo went straight to her bed and flopped down, face first, and wriggled into the lux. I did not, did not, did *not* notice her squirming derriere.

"This is fabulous," she moaned into the pile of pillows.
"I concur."
"I'm exhausted," Bo said, face still deep in the down.
"How come?"
"Well," I said, "we've been driving for two days with no real plan. We just ran away from complete mayhem. You don't really know me. You just ate. These things add up."
"And this bed is soooo nice."
"And the beds are nice."

"What's next?" she muffled.

"Looks like you could use a nap. And I must walk," I decided. "See you in a couple hours?"

"'Kay," she sighed. "Don't drown, darling."

Darling?

— 36 —

I pocketed the room key. The hotel was so ancient or so hip as to have real keys, heavy metal keys as opposed to the credit card kind. I stopped at the front desk to bum an umbrella and then hit the bricks.

I exited the side door of the Francis Marion onto Calhoun, wanting to avoid the falderal of having doors held for me by the doormen dressed up in Sergeant Pepper. I stood on the sidewalk of Calhoun Street looking left and right, deciding which felt like the correct way to go.

I went right because over there was a steady flow of humanity looking like they were headed somewhere in particular. I was interested in what the somewhere might be, what might be going on in Charleston, South Carolina.

As I approached the biomass crossing Calhoun over and back, it was impossible not to notice that the individuals making up the mass were almost exclusively between the ages of eighteen and twenty-two, almost all of them female and 90 percent of those being flagrantly beautiful. Like, fashion model beautiful. Like, WTF beautiful. This was an objective, non-creepy, I swear, observation.

There appeared to be no end to them. Literally hundreds of these eighteen to twenty-two-year-old women slipping past my astounded eye sockets. I walked to the cross street where the migration was occurring, St. Phillip, and stood like an ornithologist in the midst of a once-a-century birding event involving a nearly extinct species.

Agog and yet studious, I was tempted to take notes. Where were the adults? Where were the suits heading off to peddle insurance—term and whole life, auto and home? Where were the tourist families with matching Tommy Bahamas and unfolded street maps? What in God's name was this cultural phenomenon?

I joined the biomass and crossed Calhoun, past a large art gallery/museum with tall windows and no people that I could see on the inside. The young people on the street were businesslike with backpacks and skateboards. And books. I wandered along, caught up in the flow and realized, duh, this had to be a school environment of some sort.

St. Phillip looked like any other city street with no obvious academic-looking buildings, until, that is, I came to an opening, a brick walkway on my right, which opened into a quadrangle of antebellum buildings both brick and timber much like down on Anson only arranged upon a square of sorts and available only to foot traffic.

This was indeed an enclave of learning, completely cordoned off from the hustle of regular Charleston. There were fountains and a statue of a mountain lion mascot and a density of more attractive young people, still mostly female, all under a canopy of live oaks spilling lush strands of Spanish moss from their brave and twisted branches. I'd seen city campuses before in Boston and New York, but this was beyond their scope for pure aesthetic pleasure, both architectural and human.

I had to sit down. Rows of park-style benches lining the walkways were empty as most pedestrians clearly had places to be. I looked at my watch: almost 2 p.m.

I'd stumbled into, onto, something, someplace magical, to me. Being here, sitting here, I felt a lightness, a regular glee for living that had been absent for months. I liked where I was, sitting here, wanting to be here as opposed to someplace else, anyplace else. Where was this? Looking around with the walking crowds thinning now, I noticed maroon banners hanging from lamp posts: College of Charleston.

Two young women came toward me from across this Gothic quadrangle. They were nearly identical with blonde hair of the same shade and nearly same length and cut. They were tall and fit and both wearing College of Charleston gym shorts with rain boots that accentuated their long and toned legs. Their faces were Anglo-fine, high and defined cheekbones and bright blue eyes. Both carried books on their hips and both wore too tight t-shirts. Without knowing it, they walked in unison, their steps in sync, left right left. They laughed easily in quiet conversation.

It dawned on me who they were.

These were children.

Somebody's children.

My children, only a short leap into their future.

— 37 —

Bea got ready for school in the dark. Her mom dropped her and her sister off in the dark. Second-period French class left her in the dark.

Bea looked up from her textbook, giving up for a moment on trying to follow her teacher's droning dialogue, and glanced out of the classroom windows at the dark morning sky, the overcast seeming ten feet overhead and now beginning to rain. It felt cold enough to snow. It smelled like snow. Bea was hoping for snow and a white Christmas.

Outside the window was the empty campus of Lexington High School.

Bea had been living in this Boston suburb for two years now but still had not made many close friends. Not like Mae had. Bea wondered, looking at the rain, what the plans were for Christmas this year. She didn't know if she and her sister would be going up to Dad's this year or not. When she'd probed her mom about it, Mom had told her it was up to them, Mae and Bea.

"You don't have to do anything you don't want to do," is what Bea was told.

That is what Bea was told every weekend that they were scheduled to go see Dad.

"You don't have to do anything you don't want to do."

Bea wanted to see her dad. But didn't. It was a long drive. It was a hassle. Bea definitely wanted to be part of Christmas Eve at Grammy Bette's. But didn't.

You don't have to do anything you don't want to do.
But can I also do what I want to do?
I want to.
I don't. It's too much trouble.

The class bell rang at Lexington High and Bea gathered her things. By the time she got home to Mom's this afternoon it would be dark.

In between classes, sister Mae slipped the pint of vodka from her backpack into her locker. After school she would grab it and head over to Amanda's to drink it mixed with Red Bull. Amanda had the entire basement of her parents' huge house as her bedroom and all to herself. Her parents never came down. Christmas was the furthest thing from Mae's mind. She was having so much fun doing what she wanted.

— 38 —

I walked until well past dark. I walked until my back ached like eight hours of stonework. I walked until my feet blistered and bled.

I got lost, doubled back, got found, got lost again but kept running into water, so knew I couldn't be too far afield. It never did rain, so I used the borrowed umbrella for a walking stick. I sang to myself. I stopped and stared at the immensity of certain homes. I watched streetlights and gaslights come on. I peeked in windows and a couple times was met with weary smiles of inhabitants used to this vulgar sort of tourista intrusion.

Before sunset, I gazed at plants and trees blooming in the pre-Christmas. The sounds of bird and insect life kept me company along with the ghosts. Oh yes, there were certainly ghosts. They were all around. This was not a question.

This was unlike lonely New England December, when all life becomes either folded in quiet or departed for the winter. In New England December, I feel utterly alone despite the impending family gatherings, the goodwill, the good cheer, and chirping of salvation bells on the streets.

Gazing this Charleston day at the immensity of certain waterfront homes and speculating upon upcoming Southern gatherings I felt most assuredly accompanied by good-humored spirits. Why they were good humored I have no idea given the bitter history here and the little I knew of it. All I know is that for the first time in months I felt content, safe, nearly joyous, and in good company walking this Dixie peninsula alone. I honestly considered that I was having a psychotic break.

I spent hours south of Broad, walking the entirety of Tradd Street, east to west from the Cooper River to the Ashley and back again. I walked the Battery and stood at parade rest as the sun sank over there beyond James Island.

I ambled along Broad Street, peering into art galleries and attorneys' offices. After dark, coming from the east, I came to King Street and hung a right, time to get back to my travel companion and either share my feelings of ghostly companionship here on these streets or probably not.

King Street, it turns out, is the Charleston equivalent to Newbury Street in Boston. A mile and then some of upscale commerce and wandering shoppers mixed liberally with the beauteous youth out looking for eats and drinks and each other. I was by now limping.

The lobby of the Francis Marion was roiling with early evening life. Groups of adults numbering four and six and eight were sitting, chatting with cocktails in hand or heading out into the Charleston evening. A percentage of the women in the groups were wearing red gowns and the men bowtied getups involving velvet and plaid. I stood at the edge taking it in and recalled, again, that it was coming onto Christmas. And it was the weekend or close to it, if I was not mistaken. Time, days, and dates were liquefying on me.

It felt holiday here, no matter the night. I desperately wanted a drink. I was thinking scotch, so I went ahead to the lounge and ordered one, signing the tab to my room and sat at the bar, sipping, smiling.

Chandeliers hovered over ridiculous fleur-de-lis carpeting with burgundy as its primary color, ridiculous but perfect. A piano with a piano man either hired or passerby played something fairly well, either an obscure Christmas carol or a piece by a composer I was unfamiliar with, which is just about all of them.

The lobby had levels so this was a multidimensional experience with an aural accompaniment of soft clinking ice of high balls and civilized "ha ha ho" punctuating muted merriment. The lobby was enormous, a football field at least. But way over there, as far as could be from anyone in the room, kitty corner and across from the lounge, in an armchair, red leather, the size of a Buick, was Bojean. And she was looking at me. She was holding an enormous wine glass and was looking at me.

Bojean, have I mentioned, is a beautiful girl. A beautiful woman. In a dress. She packed a dress?

She crossed her legs across the way and rhythmically bobbed her well-turned calf. My heart did an awkward somersault and I told it to relax. She did a little side tip of her head, subtle, inviting me over to her lobby quadrant. I stood still, squinting across the way, and pantomimed a wide-eyed *Who? Me? Gulp!* She pantomimed an exaggerated come hither nod. *Yes indeed, Sir. You!*

I tried to walk with a James Bondian debonair stride, but I'm afraid I might have been limping as a result of my four-hour promenade 'round the town. And I'm pretty sure I stunk. Nothing debonair going on here. I slalomed around and through the lobby crowd and made it to her side.

— 39 —

When I rolled off Mayhem that evening, after Eddie had mutilated himself, my clothes covered in sticky blood, copper smelling, it was over for me. Case manager closed.

That night was clear and cold. I did some drinking. Around midnight I went outside and sat upon Serious Deck and watched a UFO cavort for hours across the Maine skies. The lights I watched did impossible gymnastics, shooting from western horizon to eastern horizon in a blink. The lights would hover, the driver or drivers collecting data, I guess, and then blink across the sky and hover some more. I took a break from watching to go inside for a quilt my mother had made for me to put around my shoulders. I watched until 3 a.m., until I became bored with it. It did not appear that the UFO had come to abduct or destroy. I went inside and I got into bed but I did not sleep.

I called Team Leader at 7 a.m. "It's over for me."
"Yeah," he said. "Can you give us two weeks?"
"No," I said.

Five days later, in a steady drizzle, I drove on up to Freedom in the late afternoon hoping Bojean would be home. I drove straight to Bojean's door yard, knocked on her red kitchen door. She was home. She did not invite me in and stood looking at me with the door only opened a foot. It was dark inside. I asked did she want to go for a drive. I told her if she wanted to go for a drive to be at my place, Serious Farm, at seven the next morning and we'd go. She said, "'Kay."

Her face gave nothing away, yea or nay.

— 40 —

"Good evening, ma'am." I attempted the Charleston accent I'd been picking up on, a southern accent softer and with less cartoonish character than say, the Foghorn Leghorn redneck rooster country Tennessee type. This initial attempt came out closer to Cockney or Liverpudlian. Bojean was graceful enough to ignore it all together.

"Darling," she said, "join me for a drink?"

"Charmed," I said, pretty certain it was the wrong way to say yes. I tried again, "Yes. Delighted."

This young thing, nearly thirty years my junior, had me on my heels. Intimidated. I sat down upon the expanse of the arm of her armchair as there was no other place to sit. Her chair was an island in an ocean of lobby.

"Good walk?"

"Excellent walk. Good nap?"

"Exquisite nap," she purred and hugged herself, thereby creating décolletage for me to look away from. "You must be tired?"

"Oddly, not," I said, and I wasn't. I was happy to be here and ready to be around and awake for more of this peculiar feeling of relative content. "Don't the people in our little hotel look nice and truly festive?"

"I've noticed," she said. "Why do you suppose that is?"

"It's Christmas!"

"So it is," she said, "I'd almost forgotten. It doesn't feel like Christmas. Does it to you?"

Bojean took an elongated sip of her red wine, looking over the rim of her enormous glass into my eyes. When she finished the sip, her lips were stained burgundy and her eyes would not let me go. "Did I tell you that my father came out of the closet, at least to his wife and daughters, on a Freedom Christmas morn?"

She continued to stare me down. Was she drunk-ish? I answered, carefully, "You began to tell me this. Last night." I sipped my scotch and studied her eyes.

"Yes indeed. He did. I was six. My sister was seven. Mother fainted dead away and then woke up in hysterics. Weeping and yelling. Throwing stuff. Ignoring us, her kids, their kids." She was smiling at me as she spoke.

"Do you remember this?" I asked.

"Like it was yesterday."

"Do you remember what Santa brought you that year?"

"Hmmmm." Another long sip, still not letting go with her gaze. "What a strange question."

What Santa brought Bojean and her sister and her mother was a never-ending road trip that Christmas. There in the lobby of the Francis Marion, my young travel companion told me the complicated tale of the dissolution of her family of origin on that blessed morn and the sojourn that ensued: the quick romancing and marriage of her mom to a sketchy Nazarene church elder, to the excommunication of her dad from both the Nazarene church and his nuclear family. Literally. Both church and state gave the terrified gay man the heave ho with impunity. Six-year-old Bo was not old enough to vote.

While she spoke, a number of well-dressed revelers in the lobby walked, out their way it seemed, by us and tossed furtive glances our way. Odd.

Bojean had no reason, previous to the econo-lodge confession the night before, to share with me that she had been raised a staunch Nazarene. She explained, breezily, what that meant. It meant disaster for Dad, at least in regard to his relationship with the church and his immediate relationship with his kids. He got put out. By the New Year, Dad was forgotten and Mom was in the arms of the head Nazarene honcho of the Ossipee, New Hampshire outpost of the good church. The new daddy pastor had recently accepted a new Nazarene gig in New Mexico, so Bojean found herself in the way back seat of a station wagon that she has since associated with the smell of fear, loneliness and starting over in a new kindergarten by the end of Christmas vacation.

She told me that her new Naz Daddy had a 1979 Chrysler Town and Country station wagon in which he hauled the family from one short-lived pastor gig to the next. Sometimes they slept in the car while waiting for the next rectory to be readied.

I asked her why so many job changes and she just looked at me. I asked her if her replacement daddy and her mom were still together. "Yes." I asked her if she got along with her replacement daddy. "No." I repeated my question from the night previous if her replacement daddy was a good guy. "No. No. He is not a good guy." I told her that I knew less than zero about Nazarene-ism. "Google it," she said. I asked if she were a Nazarene still. "No," she said.

I left it at that. It had taken three months and 973 miles to elicit this much from her regarding her family. We still had some time on our hands and a return trip to make. She would release information on her schedule. I hoped to be around to receive it. Just then a woman in her thirties and in a deep blue party dress with dangerously plunging neckline came straight up to us and, looking straight at Bojean said, "Hello! Welcome to Charleston."

Bo said hello and thank you. When, with some reluctance on her part, the woman walked away, I jokingly said, "Know her?"

"Nope," Bojean said.

"So, the Freedom house," I said, "your daddy's house . . ."

"What about it?"

— 41 —

What about it indeed. What did I want to know? Would I be asking her about her house history if it were a three-bedroom ranch? Of course not. Why did it matter to me that Bojean drove her shitbox automobile to a thirteen thousand square foot manse each evening?

It mattered because there had to be a story. How this house? Who this house? When this house? I did not have the nerve to simply ask "who's got the money?"

"What about it?" She was smiling up at me, daring me.

"C'mon, Bojean. That's a several-million-dollar house."

"This has been bugging you since the minute you laid eyes."

"True."

"Nosey."

"True."

"Well," she said, "my queer daddy comes from money and knows how to make money."

"I know I've axed you this before," I said, the scotch swirling my mind, inducing me take on a weird persona, "but what your daddy do?"

Bo laughed, way down in her belly, strong and long. Everything about her in the past twenty-four hours seemed to be gaining strength. I could hear her better. She was making eye contact. She was drinking and she was laughing, hard. She said, "He and his partner produce theater." That was it, that was all she gave me. She was stronger, but she was still making me work.

"Partner," I said. "Bidness or romantic?"

No idea why I was talking this way. But she joined me.

"Bof," she said. "But more bidness. They gots a open relationship. Daddy always keeps a very younger dude onna side. It's a understanding they has."

"Theater? Like what? Like Broadway shits 'n shit?"

"Broadway shits. Exact."

"Like *Cats* 'n shit?"

"Exact."

"Did they produce *Cats*?"

"Tell me about your walk," she said. "What did you see?"

— 42 —

I related to Bojean what I saw and what I thought I saw. I tried to tell her what I felt. I told her about Tradd Street running from river to river and the quiet grace of the houses there. I spoke haltingly, inarticulate, trying to verbalize a feeling and failing.

"Remember I told you that for some reason I know about the battle of Gettysburg?"

"Yes," she said.

"OK," I said, "Imma fuck this quote up, but listen: *In great deeds, something abides. On great fields something stays. Forms change and pass; bodies disappear, but spirits linger, to consecrate the ground for the vision place of souls. And reverent men and women from afar and generations that know us not and that we not know of, heart drawn to see where and by whom great things were suffered and done for them.*

She sat in her lounge and stared up at me with the amber in her eyes. Glistening? She let out a long exhale, a sigh. Finally, "What is that?"

"That is a man from Maine who was at Gettysburg. Survived it. Dead now."

"What was his name?"

From across the great expanse of lobby came the bartender with a tray. Upon the tray was a glass of wine and a glass of scotch. He came to us and offering up the drinks, looking directly at Bojean and then at me, he said, "Compliments of the house."

I raised my eyebrows and looked at Bojean. Her face did not register any sort of expression, surprise or otherwise. "Thank you," we said. The bartender took our empties away and we sat, me looking at her, her looking out upon the lobby.

"Who was the man from Maine?" she asked.

"The man from Maine was Joshua Chamberlain. Basically, he won the war for the North."

Bojean took a sip, a good-sized sip, from her wine. "Do you believe this ground, this ground here, is consecrated?"

I took a sip, a good-sized sip, from my scotch. "Feels like it."

We drank on. We talked on. We became at least half inebriated.

It was barely past 9 p.m. and the revel was just beginning outside. I looked at my watch and at our empty glasses. "Want to go for a walk around the block?" I asked Bo.

"'Kay," she said.

We crossed Calhoun and bounced along King, side-stepping juiced pedestrians.

I walked us down a side street called George. It became immediately quieter here. I peered down the street toward the Cooper River and noticed a light fog had descended. Store lights were softer. Sound muffled. The fog swirled in lazy eddies, romantic, spooky. Or there was an even chance that this fog was my weary mind. My new-ish dissociation. I'd eaten enough hallucinogens back in the day to know that not all is what it seems sometimes and the mind is a mad artist with stockpiles of media at its disposal to create distinctly abstract palettes. This could well be fog art. This could be the elusive acid flashback. A minor stroke. To be sure, I asked Bo, "Fog?"

"Yes," Bo said, as if picking up on my confusion. "Fog. It's pretty."

I wasn't sure what I was looking for out here in the world, either for the next couple of hours or couple perhaps remaining decades. My feet, with blisters, were on auto. My eyes were on scan. My arm had a pretty girl attached to it. I felt all right. Above average. I felt all right not knowing what was next. I wanted to know what was next.

The pitted stomach of missing Mae and Bea was there, also in my throat, as always, but here on the street in a Southern city, I seemed to be accepting my powerlessness to do a damn thing about it except love them. Love them. All. Not only Mae and Bea but all of the others who navigated life with fear, confusion and malice.

What else in the world could I do but love them and try to let them know, without agenda, without desperation, that I loved them. My mistakes had been made, wrong moves, done and done, permanent records kept in court files and lawyers' correspondences of careless words from my lips repeated by manipulated children to hungry, angry ears of others.

But I loved my daughters hard and very real. I knew this. It was one of the few things I did know for certain. This love was real, and no circumstance could corrupt this love. Not in *my* mind. Not in *my* heart. The radioactive seeds of doubt had been deftly installed in the minds of my children, but there was nothing I could do about that. I'd tried to warn them, which was a mistake, and I'd tried to alert others who were in a position to help us, and I was not believable enough. I tried. Now all I could do was love. Love them and try to love me.

"Where are you?" Bojean looking up at me with concern, with question. "Where did you go?"

Apparently, I had stopped walking. I felt rigid. Other pedestrians had to detour, politely, around us while I blocked the sidewalk like a cigar store Indian.

"Just getting my bearings," I mumbled, "I guess."

"Seriously, where did you go? That was a little scary."

I looked at Bojean and decided to tell her the truth. "I was visiting with my girls," I told her, "I do that fairly often. I miss them. I love them quite a lot. Sometimes I become lost. Sometimes it hurts a lot."

Bo squeezed my arm. Laid her head on my shoulder for a brief moment. "Yes, you do," she said. "You love your daughters. That's why I love you."

— 43 —

Bojean put me to bed, I think. I slept until the early afternoon of the next day. I had not done such a thing since high school. When I came to she was there, in a chair, gazing out the window and down at Marion Square. We found a very comfortable coffee place called Kudu right around the corner on a street called Vanderhorst and whiled the day away there. Even Bo was flummoxed by the barely post-teen beauty pageantry that ebbed and flowed through and out of the shop throughout the day.

Bo picked up a flier from a countertop and brought it to our table out on the patio. The day was warm to us and humid to everyone. The flier advertised a College of Charleston theater department presentation scheduled for this particular early evening. One-act plays were to be presented by students of the theatre department as final projects for the fall semester.

"We should go," Bojean said.

"'Kay."

— 44 —

I have zero recollection of the one-act plays that piled up before.

They were pleasant enough, I suppose.

Some student actors fumbling over lines, some killing it.

We sat shoulder-to-shoulder in the tiny theater, which was a converted church.

We sat in bleacher seats with an audience of fifty or so, student aged. They were friends of the performers, most likely, or other actors awaiting their turns.

Between one-act plays there were five-minute intermissions, set changes, curtain, and then this:

Dimly lit, a wooden park bench at center stage with a cloth tarp draped over. Two trash cans covered with canvas tarps, one tarp for each can. Two window panes hung, ten feet off the floor, one stage left and one stage right. One shambling actor looking up at the stage-right window, then, shambling over to the stage-left window and looking up.

The shambling actor then limped offstage to return with a stepladder that he placed under the window at stage right. He climbed up the ladder and looked out the window, laughed, climbed down, and shamble dragged the ladder to stage-left window. He climbed up and looked out. Laughed. Climbed down, moved over to the side-by-side trash cans and pulled off tarps, letting the tarps fall in heaps on the floor. He looked in each trash can and laughed. Shambling actor moved to center stage, stood next to park bench and looked out into audience. He made direct eye contact with me, *me*, and said:

Finished. It's finished, nearly finished, it must be nearly finished.

The shambling actor was good. So good that I started to panic, panic rising in my throat. My throat was where my panic lived. My panic and my loneliness.

Me. No joke. He was looking at Me! This setting, this stage set, was Serious Farm! Bigger than fucking Dallas, it was. The lighting. The windows. The hardwood floor. The smell of an older structure. The lighting at 2:30 a.m. dark outside and feeble lighting within. Somehow they nailed it, the feel of latter-day and desperate Serious Farm. Somehow they perfectly replicated the hopeless and post-apocalyptic feeling of defeat of my downstairs office at Serious Farm. I felt cold.

What in holy hell?

I fumbled around in my bleacher perch and found Bo's hand and didn't necessarily mean to but squeezed pretty hard probably. I wanted to leave. Right now. Panic was making my face hot.

Bo looked at me in the dim light. *What?*

I looked at her and shook my head. *I don't know!*

The play continued, and I sat nailed to my bleacher seat. Gored. Terrified. Transfixed. Tripping hard. Disassociating. Out of body. Then back in body. Heart attack? Panic attack? As the play spooled out, I laughed at the wrong places and fought tears at the laugh lines. The whole time my throat tightening, the cords in my fat neck standing out, it felt, like a down-the-stretch racehorse. And the joke continued. The joke that college kids a thousand miles from the farm imagined and utterly replicated the macabre feel of Serious onto the Charleston playhouse stage.

What in the holy hell was I watching?

The shambling actor had long since pulled the cloth tarp off of the park bench to reveal a bum with sunglasses and horrible attitude. He also had no legs. Was the bum me? Or was the shambling actor me? In the other trash can was a legless mother, Nell.

Brutal chitter chatter between the bum, who was an asshole, and the shambling actor who was weary and somehow enslaved to the bum. Brutal chitter chatter regarding the nature of suffering and the futility of *all*. Nell remained silent.

What time is it, asked the bum.

Zero, says the shambling actor.

Zero? How many 3 a.m.s in the Serious Farm downstairs office trying to peer out of two windows only to see bounced reflection of dim lamplight and self, looking back, thinking, this is neither day nor night, this is just nothing, zero. Looking at the digital clocks of electronic devices and the 3 a.m.s registering nothing. Zero. And this shambling actor reading back to me my Serious Farm nights. Waiting for the sun. Waiting for a clue for as what to do. Sometimes in the dark thinking, *Finished, it's finished. Nearly finished, it must be finished.*

Have you had enough?
Yes! (Pause.) Of what?
Of this . . . this . . . thing.
I always had.

Shambling and bum kicking back my early a.m. internal and sometimes external office dialogue. *Have you had enough?* I was still okay, even with Mae and Bea disappeared. I was okay until Everyday Eddie ripped open his arm in an effort to go home even though he had no memory of that place.

Holding very tight right now to Bo's hand.
What is this?
Is it not time for my painkiller?
No.

What? How do they know? They couldn't know this. My daily downing of tramadol for my lower back and existential pain, feeling its opioid tingle now in this theater, holding tight to Bo's hand. I wanted to leave. I wanted to lie on my back in my hotel room and let the tramadol rock me to sleep.

Why don't you kill me?
I don't know the combination to the cupboard.
Go get the two bicycle-wheels.
There are no more bicycle-wheels.
What have you done with your bicycle?
I never had a bicycle.
The thing is impossible.

My mouth open mouthed-breathing watching this thing. I was the bum. I was the asshole. I was the servant. I was the trash-canned legless parent.

Dream interpreters, assholes in their own rights, say that we play, that we are *all* of the characters in our dreams. Our nightmares. This was a nightmare.

And hilarious.

It went on. I was crushing Bo's hand in the dark. She may or may not have squeezed back. She had not made any attempt to remove her hand from my claw.

I needed for this thing to end or I needed to walk out. I was nailed to my bleacher seat. My mouth. Open. Eyes. Riveted. My eyes went from bum to shambling actor to trash can to window to trash can to window to bum as the idiot words piled up. They were depicting Serious Farm, no question about that. What in holy hell was this? The legless mother in the trash bin died.

You know what she died of, Mother Nell? Of darkness.

Holy hell! My own mother, Mother Bette, back at home, now, old, dying of same. Darkness. She found no light, no grace, in her dying process. It only occurred to me then, in that church theatre, that Mother Bette was struggling horribly through her dying process.

A soliloquy. The bum summarizing. He made his last observations after long laments to darkness and absurdity and despair:

Since that's the way we're playing it . . .
. . . let's play it that way . . .
. . . and speak no more about it . . .
. . . speak no more.
Old stancher!
(pause)
You remain.

End. Curtain. Jesus. Christ!

Polite applause. More than half of the crowd had already left at some point during the evening, having seen whatever friend they had come to see. At the finish of this final abomination there were maybe fifteen people left in

Need Permission

the audience, getting up to leave while the trash can props, the windows, the bench, were removed from the stage.

I sat nailed to my seat. Bo was looking at me, patiently, with a smile. Did she know what had happened here? Did she know that this depiction of despair was an exact reading of lonely Serious Farm? She had not truly visited Serious. Not yet. I could not speak yet, could not let go of her hand.

Finally, "What *was* that?"

Bo was searching my face, my eyes, my eyes cannot focus, not yet. Smiling, Bo. "You don't know?"

"I feel like I know," I said and up came an urge to weep. I was exhausted. These children actors, these students had somehow stolen Serious Farm night and imported it to a Charleston stage. "I feel like I should know. No. I don't. What *was* that?"

"Beckett."

"What?"

"Beckett. Samuel Beckett."

"Beckett? *Godot* Beckett? *That* guy?"

"Yes."

In the quiet of the nearly empty theater I asked Bo, too loudly, "What the fuck is that guy's *problem*?"

Bo laughed very loud, delighted, and clapped her hands once. The students cleaning up the set looked out at us. We were now alone in the bleacher seats. The students cleaning up the set laughed as well for they had heard our exchange.

"We should go," Bojean said, as she stood, still holding my hand.

"Yes." We got up to leave, hand in hand. "What was that? What was it called?"

Endgame, she said.

"You've got to be shitting me."

— 45 —

Outside of the Chapel Theatre, standing in the fog that has appropriately returned. Standing, rooted again, next to the College of Charleston Treasurer's Office and Office of Instate Eligibility.

"What was the title again?" I felt emptied but full of quandary.

"*Endgame.*"

"Is that really the name of it?"

"Yes."

"How do you know this?"

Bo laughed.

"Seriously. Should I know this *Endgame*?"

"I don't see why."

"That was so fucking dark."

"Yes. Yes it is."

"Really good."

Bo, still laughing quietly, adorably, taking some of my fear away, "Yes."

"Holy hell!" I was rattled, thoroughly.

Standing there in the fog. Standing outside the College of Charleston Treasurer's Office and Office of Instate Eligibility, I fell in love with Bojean, thoroughly.

"I think," I said, "I think I need to process."

"Drink?" Bo asked.

"No drink," I said. "Can we just go to the room?" I felt tears trying to bully their way again. "I'm pretty shook up."

"I sense that."

— 46 —

I sat in the Queen Anne chair next to the open window overlooking Marion Square from seven flights up. Sitting as if smoking in a non-smoking room and blowing the offensive smoke out into the thick December air. My elbows on my knees, my head low. Bojean sat on the bed nearest the window. The bed nearest me.

"I thought we were watching plays written by students," I said. "The whole night. I couldn't understand how a college-age kid could come up with such complicated horror."

"Nope. Not a student."

"Tell me again how you know about this play."

"I didn't tell you."

"Tell me."

"I played Clov."

"You played Clov? What? When?"

"Once upon a time."

"Clov was which?"

"He was the boy attending to the rest. He was the boy going up and down the ladder. The one keeping the rest alive."

"What was it like being in that play?"

"Hard."

"I can imagine." I sat, thinking about a lot. "You've acted? You're an actor? Actress?"

"Actor. Yes, some."

"Did you tell me that already?"

"You never asked."

I felt embarrassed to look directly at Bojean anymore. I'd fallen head over heels. Ridiculous. "But how can college-aged kids inhabit these roles? The nihilism? The hopelessness?"

"What has college age got to do with it?"

"Well, what does a college-age kid know about such things?"

"Depends on the college-age kid I suppose."

"What entitled gringo college-age kid knows about such things?"

"Now you're being insulting."

"I am? Why?"

"What do you know about college-age kids?"

"I think I know the general demographic. I was one once. Several good friends were. White. Entitled. Pain free. Beer addled. Know nothing. Etcetera."

"Now you're just being an ass."

"I am?"

"You am." Bo turned her back to me. She unbuttoned her cardigan sweater and took it off, letting it drop to the floor. She undid her brassiere, letting it drop on top of her sweater. She got under the covers of the bed and she wiggled out of her pants. I don't know if the unders came off with the pants because she left all of that under the covers. I looked out the window while she undressed. She fluffed the pillows and put her bare arms on top of the comforter. "Ready?" she asked.

"I am," I said, and I was. I did not know for what, but I was ready. There was nothing left to be.

— 47 —

I was killed in a car wreck.

Before that I was serially abused by a man of God who insisted I call him Daddy.

I was happily dead and gone yet sent back.

You are the first and only to know about the man of God other than me and the man of God. I am certain that he can hear me right now, hiding in this hotel room closet, ready to hurt me like he promised if I should ever tell.

You ask how a college-age kid can know about such things as Samuel Beckett and his Endgame.

Fuck you.

You think you have co-opted misery with your sad separation from daughters Mae and Bea.

I am truly sorry for your pain Holmes but you did not invent pain.

I was killed in a horrible, horrible car wreck along with the love of my life. I was sent back and he was allowed to go on. I saw this as clearly as I can see you right now, see you not looking at me. Come here please.

I exhaled deeply. Did not want to. Go over there. My eyes remained fixed on the statue of the man John Calhoun atop his spire overlooking the Christmas-lit square seven stories below.

Please.

I stood up from my chair and looked at Bojean. She patted the bed, indicating I come and sit.

I went and sat. I didn't know what to do with my eyes, where to look. Did not know what to do with my hands, where to put them.

I sat and Bojean reached for my right hand. She took my hand, gently, and guided it under her covers. With her own fingers, gently, she unfisted mine and placed my hand upon her warm and flat belly. Kind of low. I tried to think of nothing. To only let her do what she had in mind, whatever that may be. I could panic in a moment or two if necessary. For now I would go with it.

She took the index finger of my right hand with the fingertips of both her hands. She placed it, my index finger, and guided it, south to north, starting perilously low and moved it upward past her bellybutton to my right, her left, and almost up to her ribcage. My mouth, I realized, was extraordinarily dry. She lifted my finger and started over, down low, and then up, tracing the same path. When we got to the top she had me trace back down, then back up until I realized the ridge of scar tissue she wanted me to feel. She had me acknowledging a long and serpentine scar running up her abdomen. When she was convinced that I understood, she placed my hand flat upon her belly, kind of low, and took her own hands away.

I was killed Holmes. My insides were out. I know this because I saw them. Trapped inside the car with the love of my life who'd come along somehow and saved me from the man of God.

I saw my insides out and we were dead and gone, the both of us. He was looking straight at me, our bloody faces only inches apart.

His name was Joao. He was looking straight at me and we were dead as dead can be. It was quiet and it was okay. Better than okay. Shoulder to shoulder. It was right. My insides out and Joao very well on his way. We were on our way. On our way to the next thing. It was fine, death. I was seventeen years old. I saw this! Please look at me!

I could hear every word she was saying. She was speaking loud and strong. My bad hearing gone away. The frequency just fine.

I turned my face from the window to look at her. She was calm and she was smiling, her white arms again on the top of the bed covers. My hand, surprisingly, still underneath and flat upon her warm belly, an electricity running through and up into me, a current.

I did see it. Do you believe me?
Yes.
Because I did.
Yes.
And I was sent back.
How?

I don't know. I don't know how. I might know why. There was something there with us, with me and Joao. Energy. An other. They kept going. Joao and the other. They never looked back. It was the only time I recall feeling afraid. Or alone. I didn't know if I was supposed to keep up. I didn't know what I was supposed to do.

And then I was back, in hospital. My injuries, they told me my injuries should have been fatal. My intestines were on the outside and they were perforated so that I was poisoned in addition to ripped apart. They put my insides back in and sewed me up and presumed I would die from infection and mass insult to the rest of my insides, my viscera. My viscera were pretty beat up.

They told me the love of my life, Joao, Didn't make it.

Oh, he made it all right, I told them.

No, *they said.* He didn't make it.

My mother found me. And the man of God. I was 1,723 miles away from where I had left them. Thank God, *my mother said.* Thank you, dear God.

Stop it, I told her.

The man of God would not approach my bed there in the hospital. He would not approach my bed with witness in the room. He stood across the floor with his dumb arms hanging dumb at his sides, his gaze upon nothing.

Bojean paused. Rested.

I saw it, Mr. Holmes. All of it. Do you believe me?

Yes.

I did, I do. I believed every word.

What happened to you? I asked.

I was killed in a car wreck.

Besides that.

I've told you. I don't think I can say it again.

Who was Joao?

Is Joao.

Who is Joao?

I met him at my high school. I did not tell him about the man of God. But he knew. He knew. He saved me.

And he was killed.

Yes.

And you were killed. Killed and sent back.

Yes.

And you were how old?

Seventeen. Bojean cleared her throat and pulled the covers up to her neck. *You've had a difficult night. Let's stop.*

Wait! You acted in *Endgame* before or after being sent back?

After.

My hands were out from under the covers. My hands were clutching one another. They were clutching each other, comforting one another, just like in a photo I have of Bea getting onto her first-day-of-school bus. Her little hands. Big backpack. That photo breaks my heart. Afraid, Bea, but brave. I am not brave. Never have been.

Tomorrow. Let's resume tomorrow, okay? I'm very tired. You look exhausted.

I don't think I'll sleep.

I think you will. Bojean reached out from her covers to turn off her bedside lamp.

In the dark, Bojean said to me, *I know you want to leave, Holmes. I saw it in your eyes the day we met. Why do you think I kept looking at you?* In the dark, she told me, *I know you want to leave. You will when it's time.* In the dark, she told me, *It's not time.*

In the dark, I felt saved.

— 48 —

She didn't come off as completely insane. Maybe she did die. The scar was certainly real. When did that Christmas tree get there?

Out in the middle of Marion Square was a tree shaped thing all lit up and resplendent. It hadn't been there the night before.

It was tall, fifty feet anyway. I squinched my eyes to try and focus as there was something not quite right about this tree. I squinched my eyes and ascertained there was no actual tree. No tree behind the lights. Only lights. I could make out a pole in the middle, holding up the lights. The lights, multicolored and waving gently in the breeze of this foggy night, were strung from the top of the pole and tumbled down, gown-like, tree-shape like, to the ground.

Each string of lights hung about a foot apart so they were close enough together to give the impression of being solid. From here though, from my window chair on the seventh floor of the Francis Marion Hotel, I could see through the lights and to the church behind the lights on Meeting Street. At the bottom of the gown, the tree-shape, there were door-like openings arched at the tops. There were four openings at equally spaced distances making a quadrant of door-like openings and I watched as a couple walked arm-in-arm into the opening facing the hotel and disappear from my sight. They had been swallowed by the big tree. The tree lights. I could not make out the couple on the inside of the lights. They had been swallowed by a Christmas vortex.

I wished to be swallowed.

All of the other trees in Marion Square, the real trees, had been draped, wrapped, and further festooned with white lights. Palms and oaks and what-have-you trees laced from trunk to frond. Had these been all here last night, all lit up like this? It was lovely, this display, whatever it may or may not represent, it was lovely. I wished to be swallowed, so I found my shoes and I found my jacket and I looked for my glasses that were already on my face and I turned toward Bojean to let her know I was stepping out.

She was asleep, her face utterly relaxed. My heart, again, melted, thinking about sleeping children leading up to Christmas mornings at Serious Farm. Thinking about the children hurt. It felt good too, for the children were alive, somewhere, and healthy and breathing in and breathing out. As was I. I was a father, their father, just apart for a while. No big deal. Like a soldier father. Like a businessman father. Like a professional athlete father. Away for a while. No big deal.

I stood and turned away from sleeping Bo and walked across the room to the desk to fetch the room key. Quietly opening the door to the hallway and quietly closing, the hallway was hushed and empty. I had no idea what time it was. It felt early morning-ish.

When the elevator door opened to the lobby, a lone disheveled woman in a red gown, ruined makeup, and blown-apart hair statement was waiting, wobbly and weepy, leaning against the lobby wall, for the elevator to take her to her floor and her room. "Hi," I said.

"Y'all go to hell," she said as she nearly fell into the elevator car.

"OK," I said. "Going."

— **49** —

The doormen were still working the big front door. "What time have you got?" I asked. Both young men checked their watches and the one on my right holding the door for me said, "Midnight, sir. Straight up."

"Thank you. Do you folks lock up at a certain time?"

The other doorman spoke up, "No sir. We here all night."

'Thank you. Very much. I won't be long."

"We here all night."

There was very little traffic on King Street. I was able to safely jaywalk over into Marion Square. There was a homeless person in a sleeping bag under a palmetto, his or her possessions piled near his or her head. Charleston, at this location, appeared to be rolling up the sidewalks for the night. A few blocks further up King Street, I could hear the drinkers coming down the homestretch on a liquid Friday night. But here, in the square, all was calm. All was bright.

I made a straight line for the Vortex Tree as the midnight church bells went off. Either the bells were muted intentionally so as to not disturb downtown sleeping residents or the fog muffled the pealing or my hearing loss contributed to the soft clack and clang of the more than several church towers out there in the damp night sounding the witching hour.

I followed the stone dust pathway that bisected the square. The one I was on led straight to and into the Vortex Tree. I stopped at the exterior wall of the tree, looking up. The gentle fog sifted through the gaps in the colored lights.

This Charleston fog differed from other fogs I have known. San Francisco fog was cold and hard and came in through the golden gate like a cold killer avalanche unexpected on a warm summer day, turning the air from warm and crystal clean to wet and dismal in zero time flat. Maine coastal fog is dense and salty and fish smelling, dangerous to boatmen and boatwomen, hiding shoals and other ships and entries to port.

This Charleston fog was wispy and damp without soaking the sleeves. This Charleston fog was sweet like a kiss. This Charleston fog, on this night, was welcoming somehow, like Bojean's vision of the afterlife. This Charleston fog may or may not have been composed of souls remaining and traipsing these cobbled and bluestoned streets. This Charleston fog, on this night, did not frighten me. I wanted in. I wished to be swallowed.

I was alone, it seemed, in the square.

I slipped inside the Vortex Tree and laughed out loud. It was fun in here! An amusement! A ride! I looked straight up and felt a fun form of vertigo, felt I was falling over backward but was not. I looked through the walls of light and altered my vision between staring at the strings of bulbs and switching to the long view of the church steeples over on Meeting and down Calhoun. So many steeples.

I sat down. Then I lay down on my back. Staring at the tip top of the Vortex Tree was intoxicating. I could hear myself laughing. And then I commenced talking to myself.

"No," I said. "I'm not buying it."

"No," I said. "To hell with Samuel Beckett. I do not accept his nihilistic premise."

My life, my life back in Maine, was falling like scales all around me, but I refused to sit blind or immobile in a grey room, trapped, waiting just to die. I did not accept this bleak person Beckett's notion of the cynical inevitable.

"Fuck him," I said. I may have been shouting.

"Fuck whom?" said someone.

Uh oh. Humanity had somehow snuck upon me. And close. I opened my eyes, which had gone closed at some point, and there stood the Law. Two Laws actually. A big man and a bigger woman.

"Oops," I said, still flat on my back. "Was I speaking out loud?"

"Yessir," said the man Law, "and distinct."

I sat up and brushed the pathway stone dust from my shoulders and as far down my back as I could reach.

"How much have you had to drink tonight, sir?" asked the lady Law.

"Zero," I said.

"Smoke?"

"Nope."

"Not impaired?"

"Well..."

The Law stood waiting, hands on hips, both.

"Well, what, sir?" asked lady Law, sounding somewhat impatient.

"No ma'am," I said, getting into the spirit of the South. "Not impaired. Just enjoying your fabulous Vortex Tree."

The Law both chuckled.

"You from out of town?" Man Law said.

"Yessir. Staying right over there." I pointed toward the Francis Marion.

"You be able to make it back okay?" Lady Law.

"I don't see why not."

"Okay sir." Lady Law.

"Thanks, officers." The Law began to walk back into the darkness of Outer Vortex from whence they had emerged. Lady Law stopped and turned.

"Who were you cussing out when we got here?"

"Ever heard of Samuel Beckett?"

"Yessir."

"Him."

Lady Law looked at Man Law. "Have you ever read Beckett?"

"Of course," Man Law said.

Lady Law looked back at me. "I'm inclined to agree with you," she said.

"Not so fast," said Man Law. "There's quite a bit more going on with Beckett than meets the eye." He looked at me. "Did you read him or did you go see a production?"

"Production," I said.

"I suggest you get the script. Read it. Read it twice at least."

"You think it's worth that kind of effort?" Lady Law asked her partner.

"I do."

The Lady looked at me and said, "There you have it." And they strolled off between the white-bulb-lit other trees of the square, the real trees. I wasn't done with the Vortex yet but felt I should get up off the ground.

— 50 —

As promised, the Francis Marion doormen were still at their posts, still dooring. "Merry Gentlemen," I said.

"Sir," they harmonized.

"God rest ye."

"And you, sir."

"Sir?" the doorman on the left asked.

"Sir?"

"You okay?"

"Indeed. Why?"

"We seen DP rollin' up on you out there by the tree."

"Eh. They were fine. They thought I might be impaired."

"True. DP do not take kind to the impaired here in Chucktown."

"Then why don't they move up King a little? I can still hear them up that a way."

"Oh, they up there all right. Plenty kids gonna end up in the tank tonight. Every night. Call Mama in the 3 a.m. to come get 'em out. It's a cottage industry."

"Chuck a drinking town is it?"

"Serious," said doorman on the right.

"More like a drunk town," said the doorman on the left. "They a difference."

"Are you gentlemen from here?"

"Yessir," said the man on the left door, "I'm from North Charleston. The Neck. Born and raised."

The man on the right door said, "I'm born in West Ashtray."

"West Ashtray?"

"Ashley. West Ashley. DP was on you fo' a good bit. What they wanted?"

"Ah. We got into a discussion about Samuel Beckett."

North Chuck doorman chuckled. West Ashtray doorman said, "Beckett? Dat bitch?"

I looked at the doormen closely. No more than twenty-one or so. Both African American. Both standing out here in the 2 a.m. holding doors. "Why does everybody but me," I asked, "know about Samuel Beckett?" The doormen shrugged in unison and in stereo pulled left and right doors for me.

I took three steps into the lobby and then came back. "What does DP stand for?"

North Charleston said, "Donut Patrol."

— 51 —

The competent girl behind the front desk was still there, still smiling. Working a twenty-four-hour shift? Or was it another, nearly identical competent girl in a form-fitting maroon blazer? I walked over and asked if it would be possible to retain our room on the seventh floor for one more day and night. Maybe two.

The competent girl did a quick computer scroll with efficient computer clickings and said yes. "And I can get you that for a reduced rate."

"OK," I said, "that's great. How come?"
"Sir?"
"How come reduced?"
She smiled wider, teeth impossibly straight, impossibly white, lips, impossible. "We appreciate you!"
"Huh," I said. "How do you like that?"
"I like it," she said.
"Me too."

— 52 —

For the second night in a row I slept for twelve hours. It sometimes took me a week to sleep twelve hours back at Serious Farm. We slept with the tall window open and the fog. The air here was a narcotic. My dreams were of happier level subconscious events than was the recent norm. I woke up in the early afternoon and I woke up naked. At least on this day I knew where I was.

Bojean was in the Queen Anne chair by the window, bare feet upon the sill reading *Gun and Garden* magazine. The window was open wide with a soft breeze of what felt like seventy at least degrees pushing through.

My eyes had popped open, as usual, at 5 a.m. I pleaded with the sandman to take me back, closed my eyes and hugged my pillow and listened for Bo's breathing across the street-lit room and hoped for the best. When I opened my eyes again it was 2 p.m. Unheard of.

"Whoa, goddam!" I sang, looking at the hotel digital bedside red numbered clock radio. "Whoa, buck an' gee, by the lamb! Who made the back-band, whoa, goddam!"

Bo looked over her shoulder at me and laughed. "What the . . . whoa, what?"

"Whoa. Whoa goddam. It's Lead Belly, I think. I just woke up. It's two in the afternoon!"

"Told you. Told you you'd sleep. Is there more to that song?"

"Indeed. It go:
Papa loved mama—mama loved men.
Mama in the graveyard papa in the pen.
I gee to the mule but mule won't gee,
So I hit him side the head with the single tree.
I haw to the mule but mule won't haw,
so I broke his back with my mother-in-law."

Bojean looked at me. She smiled. "Adorable," she said.

"How did you know I'd sleep? How do you know so much?"

"I don't."

"You do. You do know stuff. And I need to know what you know."

"Oh. No. I don't think so," she said, smiling.

"Yes indeed. I do. And I aim to know."

"Whatever."

"Avert your eyes for I am bathroom bound. Somehow I am butt naked."

"'Twas a night for naked, it seems."

"Now, avert your eyes," I said.

"Whatever."

"Last night..." I said.

"Later," she said.

Wrapping the bedspread around me, I made way for the bathroom, my old man bladder crying out. "I'll meet you in the park," Bo called to me through the bathroom door.

Between this sweet feeling of connection and safety, between the Beckett-knowledgeable Policia and Doormen, the appreciative desk lady . . . I didn't know what was real anymore and what was not. I chose not to worry about it. Not right now.

— 53 —

Showered and needing coffee horribly, I dressed in the same black jeans and black t-shirt getup I'd been wearing from the beginning of this drive. Not always the same T as I'd brought a dozen of the same model, black with pocket. The jeans were getting a little greasy.

I went to the nightstand to grab my wallet, phone, glasses and keys and noticed a book that was not there the night before. *Endgame*. Samuel Beckett. I picked it up and brought it with me.

Outside upon Marion Square I said to Bojean, "Where did you find *Endgame* on such short notice?"

"Bookstore."

"For me?"

"For you," she said. "A second and a third and a fourth reading are recommended."

"The DP recommended the same thing."

"The DP?"

"Donut patrol. The police. While you slept I became somewhat a suspect out here by the Vortex Tree."

"What's a Vortex Tree?"

"You'll see. Tonight, when it gets dark. That pole over there with the ropes of lights hanging down? When it gets dark it becomes a whole other thang."

"So, we're staying another night?"

"If you don't mind," I said.

"Holmes, I love it here. I want to move here."

Visions. I experienced more visions.

— 54 —

We made the short walk over to Kudu coffee and took a table on the patio. The outside air was impossibly soft this midday December day. Warm. The small and maybe rococo fountain presented a white noise that kept me in a state of drowse despite back-to-back double-shot lattes.

The questions of the previous day lay there between us and just below the sleepy surface, primarily her semi-working knowledge of the afterlife and how it dovetailed into my recognition of happily present Charleston spirits. On this December perfect day, we let it be.

I could have easily sat slurping latte until the light in the sky indicated it was time to switch over to booze. My feet were tender with new and squishy blisters from all of the walking during the past forty-eight hours. My back ached like a forty-hour stonemasonry end of the week. I had my feet up on the chair across from me. Bojean sat to my right. My back was to a five-foot brick wall that enclosed the patio and I watched the people come and go.

A male Kudu employee came to our patio table asking did we need anything? He smiled at Bo for an extra beat or two or three. The male employee was very pretty, a replica *Thelma and Louise*-era Brad Pitt, but perhaps we were both growing used to these beauties as neither of us commented.

"I'm really sleepy," I said.

"Then you should sleep." Bo was taking care of me. Caring for me. Perhaps this was the reason, a reason, for what felt like the lightening of my load, the heartsickness of being alienated from dear Mae and dear Bea. I'd been walking around with this seasick heaviness for so long with no help whatsoever that I'd begun to believe it was normal to carry that weight, alone. Bo was standing in, it seemed, for those people in my life who were fading away: my mother, my daughters, my friends who had heard enough of my forlorn. My forlorn may have been what ultimately drove Kat away as it was too much competition for her own.

And then, from the blue she said, "I think we should go looking for ghosts tonight."

"OK," I said. "What do you mean? Where?"

"Let's do one of these ghost tours." She was holding up a tourist brochure she'd most likely plucked from our hotel room.

"I'm in," I said, surprised that this was something she might be interested in.

"I'll find us a juicy one," she said. "Let's get you back to the room for your nap."

I told Bo I could probably find my way down King Street to the Francis Marion, one block away, if she wanted to remain. "'Kay," she said as two students with laptops and afternoon beers stole glances at us, at her.

I trudged the one block from Kudu back to the hotel in a fatigue haze, out on my feet. Five hours later, dark out the window, Bo was rocking my shoulder, waking me. I was utterly disoriented. Assumed it was morning. Changed my mind. Thought it was the night of the next day. Didn't know. Lost track of who Bo was for a moment. Scanned the hotel room, nothing was linking up. Good nap, dreamless and hard. It may have taken ten minutes to come around, but worth it. Bo sat patiently on her bed while my mind put one and one and one and one together. Finally I asked, "Ghost thirty?"

"How about food thirty and then ghost thirty?"

"Did you find us a juicy tour?"

"I did! The old city jail. The door bros say it's no joke."

The room was early evening shadowy with the perpetual soft streetlight coming in through our big and open window. I was cozy beneath the sheets. I didn't really want to get up, felt as though I could close my eyes and sleep through the night. Before drifting off into this much-needed nap sleep, I'd thought about the last three months of maximum four hours of sleep per night while trying to map a way back to my daughters; trying to understand how to help the poor souls living out their days at Mayhem Mountain; burning the midnight oil at Serious Farm wondering what to do with myself and how to do it now that relationships were ending, or changing. I felt at this moment that I could stay beneath these sheets for the remainder of the year, sleep off December and get a fresh start upon the New Year.

"Your hair looks amazing," Bo said.

I'd taken a second shower before slipping beneath the day's fresh sheets and was sporting, probably, an Einstein. "I'm glad you like it because I'm going out like this."

"That's fine. It looks like you've seen a ghost."

The weather had changed during my rest. I could hear the dripping of rainwater from ledges above and the hissing of cars on wet pavement below. How I could hear these phenomena with no problem and then struggle with the human voice was interesting. Different frequencies. The air through the window felt saturated and still warm. Looking out, the Vortex Tree was barely visible in the fog.

Ghost weather.

"So where is this old jail," I asked, "walking or driving distance?"

"Definitely walking. Maybe a half mile from here. It's on Magazine Street. It's close."

"Sweet! Let me collect myself and we go. What time does the tour begin?"

"They want us to be there by eight. The tour starts at eight thirty."

My stomach made a barking sound. My diminished soul craved charred cow parts. Burger. Steak. Blood. Please. Meat. We decided to eat at the hotel bar. Bojean was quiet. "Are you nervous?" I asked.

"A little," she said.

"Why are we doing this again?"

"I don't know," she said, shrugging. "It seems important. Or appropriate. Something."

"Maybe we should smoke some weed," I said, joking, as I had none and had no idea where to get some and would not have done it even if we had some.

"Do you smoke?" she asked.

"Not in many, many years. You?"

"Sometimes," she said.

We went downstairs to the hotel restaurant and ate the hotel food and it was good. Me an enormous and excellent cheeseburger with three pounds of tots accompanying. Bo tore into a green salad laden with grilled shrimp. We both powered our wine . . . me red, her white, and then we both had another. We were good to go.

Out on the street, the temperature had dropped. The rain was a steady drizzle and the fog this night was colder and denser than the past two evenings. The Christmas Vortex stood sentry off in the square with lights watery looking through the wet haze. We walked huddled together under the jumbo umbrella we had borrowed from the concierge. I could feel Bo's ambivalence. Before I could ask how she was doing, she said, "You should know that I take this very seriously. Ghosts, spirits, are real, very real, to me."

"OK."

"Have we discussed this?"

"I don't think so. Not beyond what we talked about last night. The afterlife."

"Spirits," she corrected me. "Energy. Do spirits mean anything to you, Holmes? Are ghosts real to you?"

It was a good question. These spirits and this energy in Charleston were definitely something. But ghosts? Real ghosts?

"I've never been in contact with one, to my knowledge. Well, I have, maybe, but that was more a hallucination, I think."

I told her this:

After my dad died, suddenly, unexpectedly at the age of fifty-four, I had a nocturnal chat with him that was real as that funeral day was long. I'd returned home from San Francisco for his services. I was sleeping fitfully in my childhood bedroom the night of Dad's burial and at some point in the night got up out of bed to sit in the chair next to the window, much like the setup in our hotel. It may have been sleepwalking. It may not have been.

As I sat looking out, out the open window, my dad appeared in the branches of the mulberry tree just outside. He was sitting there on a solid branch, right in front of me in his bathrobe, legs crossed, smoking a Benson and Hedges, just like in real life, only in a tree.

It did not shock me all that much and I began to pepper him with questions. I was so happy to see him. The questions were making him more and more uncomfortable, just like in real life. Finally, I asked him what it was like.

"What is what like?" he asked.

"Dead." I said. "Being dead."

He slowly shook his head, like so many times before in real life when he was surprised or disappointed by my lack of understanding a subject or a moment. He said, "It's against the rules."

"What is?" I asked.

"Asking that question," he said and he misted away from me. Smoke. I never saw him or communicated with him again. Not like that.

It must have been a major faux pas, that question. I was so disappointed in myself. I still am. I would love to talk with my father again. I'm still hoping to.

I told Bojean that sometimes I feel what seems like company, company when there's no one around. But I don't know what that is. She nodded her head. She looked worried.

We crossed over Calhoun at Coming and walked south until we hit Beufrain. Beufrain doglegged into Archdale and Magazine Street appeared, narrow and brick-walled on the right. We went two blocks down Magazine, walking in the middle of the road because it was dark, no streetlights here, and a little scary.

We emerged from the walled-in part of the street and found ourselves in front of an ominous stone building that could be nothing other than the old city jail with arched entranceways and narrow barred windows, dark and oily in the rain. A ground-floor room was illuminated by what appeared to be a single bare bulb. An ancient and black-painted wooden doorway with heavy metal hardware and no entrance light was the only way in. We walked up to the door and pulled back on the cold, cold handle.

"OK," Bojean said, tears running down her face. "Never mind. We can't do this. I can't."

I peered back over my shoulder down into the darkness of Magazine Street, from where we had come. "Okay," I said. We had taken this thing as far as possible.

Nearly finished.

— 55 —

Mae sat in the principal's office, busted. The unopened pint bottle of vodka sat on the principal's desk while he alternated between filling out some sort of paperwork and looking at Mae, disappointed and a little angry. Mae didn't even know the principal's name. *Mom's going to lose her shit.*

Mae wasn't looking forward to that confrontation. *I wonder where Dad is.*

All in all, Mae was not particularly worried about any of these things.

Sister Bea had already heard about Mae getting popped. She sat in algebra, wringing her hands worried. On the verge of tears worried.

— 56 —

The Charleston spell, the Lowcountry spell, was broken the absolute moment my budget Toyo tires on my rolling yawn of a car hit the blacktop of 95 South at Coosawhatchie.

We left reluctantly, lolling in our Francis Marion beds right up until checkout time. But it was time.

We found the road called the Crosstown that was also Route 17 South that was also the Savannah Highway. This road ran out through the stop-and-go commerce of West Ashley and quickly turned to a two-lane pathway through the swamp and by the town of Ravenel with only a gas station and a Dollar Store and an enormous car dealership. Chevy.

The Savannah Highway brought us quickly, very quickly, to lonesome December bayou stretching out on either side of the landfill roadway. Small road signs indicated townships called Ashepoo, Wiggins, Lobeco, and Dale down to the southeast, miles deep into the swamp between Highway 17 and the Atlantic Ocean.

These colonies would require further exploration at some later date. In the silence of our sliding further south I wondered, who lives down there? Do they speak English? Are they friendly? As we trundled along my mind's goofy eye created a 1960s model art deco silver Airstream up on blocks under a ring of enormous live oaks with curtains of cascading Spanish moss, the Airstream backed up to a tidal sluiceway and susceptible to lashing hurricanes, full moon tides, and alligators. My mind envisioned no internet and no TV, spotty cell phone service, a jury-rigged, screened-in porch. There would be a pirogue-type boat tied to a rotting pier. I wanted to live here someday, the oddball Yankee, hiding from some unspeakable sorrow, slowly accepted over time by the locals, bearded, bald, old, the Yankee. I hated to drive on past.

We saw a dead alligator, with the girth of a defensive tackle and longer, lying on his or her gunwale, rigored paws reached up to the southern sky as we rolled by, both of us staring and not speaking. I tried to imagine what other sorts of species of reptile and amphibian matriculated in and out of these slow-moving eddies with only eyes showing and waiting for something equal or lower on the food chain to falter by.

Once upon a time while hitchhiking through Arkansas trying to make my way to Paris, Texas, from Ruston, Louisiana, a man in a car pulled over not to offer me a ride but to warn me through his rolled down window, "Don't you let the sun set on your ass in Texarkana." There should have been ominous flute music playing as he gave his warning. It gave my eighteen-year-old soul a chill. What could he mean by this? I've never quite figured it out.

But. I was feeling the same regarding this stretch of highway on this long stretch of bayou, except I don't think they call it a bayou here. I was thinking this would be a poor place to let the sun set on one's ass if one did not have the shelter of an Airstream.

So long as the car was running and the radio connecting us to civilization and the light of day was upon us, this wilderness was a lovely experience. Were one, for whatever reason, to be on foot on this roadway in the wee hours, alone, no moon, with red eyes dotting the surface of black,

black waters, well . . . why was my mind going there? The odds were quite nearly zero of this oddball desperado scenario playing out. A more desperate and terrifying struggle was ongoing, a war already lost, the drafted cannon fodder already dead but not aware of it. Now was only how and where to bury the bodies. The body.

I looked over at Bojean and her eyes were wide taking in this Lowcountry scheme. I wondered what she was imagining. I could have asked.

— 57 —

This fairy tale of early winter swamp geography continued for miles, hardly any other cars on the road until Route 17 spilled its guts onto 95 and just like that it was over.

We joined the parade of northerners headed south and southerners headed north and license plates Ohio/Kentucky/Pennsylvania/New York/New York/New York/Massachusetts/Rhode Island and us/Maine. I felt Bojean go from heads up, neck straight, eyes scanning the swamp grasses and small hummocks with the solo lonely tree, leafless but laden with stilt-legged white birds with long yellow beaks, to slump shouldered and checking her electronic device, checked out. Welcome to US Route 95 South. USA.

We were on our way to Daytona, Florida to visit Famous Mac, my younger brother.

We both shut down, not speaking, barely conscious it seemed, until early afternoon. After we'd navigated Jacksonville, the roadways modernized and expanded significantly since I'd hitchhiked through there as an idiot undergrad headed for the winter warmth of Miami Beach during college winter break. I'd not thought about these hitchhiking experiences, Florida and Texas, in a long, long time. Talk about your bygone eras.

Wanting to get off 95 as quickly and permanently as possible, we angled east past St. Augustine and clipped into A1A south just north of Daytona. Brother Mac lived in a place called Ormond, his house snugged, best as I could recall, up to the Intercoastal Waterway. I had his address written down in an old-school address book. We'd use Bojean's magical GPS device to guide us in.

Brother Mac, Famous Mac, Big Mac, was an actual by-god icon in the funky subculture of professional motorcycle racing. He was a wrench, a crew chief renowned for being able to take his guy and beat yours or take your guy and beat his. He was a gearbox savant. Racing fans recognized him on the streets across the weird parts of America.

I'd been to my brother's house a time or two since he'd moved there from Orange County in California to be nearer to Daytona, the motorsport epicenter of the world, but I could not recall much of anything about the earlier visits.

Mac is a prodigious scotch drinker and is also perpetually injured and so there was plentiful booze and plentiful opioids, always, on hand. Our MO, whenever we saw one another, was to get fairly and then thoroughly wasted. Pleasant visits. Not much detail for me to recall. Mac loved to get sloppy and talk story regarding racing, racing, and racing. I needed to get sloppy to listen. I could give a flying fuck about motorsports. But in an oxycontin/Dewar's haze, it all sounded okay to me. Just not a lot of details remain.

Funny little aside about brother Mac's name. Brother Mac was the surprise second arrival of a surprise set of twins born to Bette and Dad. The proud parents had already decided on the name Andy if the baby child turned out to be a boy. They didn't have a second name prepared for a second boy and somehow my father convinced Bette to name him, it is on the by-god birth certificate . . . with exclamation point, Holy Mackerel!

So, Holy Mackerel and Andy. Get it? He quickly became Mac and the origin of his name was rarely spoken of again.

The GPS narrator lady, with her librarian diction, led us off A1A once we got to Ormond and through a maze of cement-block ranch houses. Most were shabby and sad with sandy lawns and cars on blocks in driveways.

Once we broke through these low-rent accommodations and found Mac's street, his street upon the intercoastal, the homes became fabulous, some more fabulous than others. Famous Mac did pretty well, salary wise. Also, he and his spouse, Ticky, had invested in California real estate while they'd lived there. They liquidated their properties in Cali after moving east and spent most of it on a big ass casa for $800K that would have been worth $3 million in Orange County and $75K in Gonic, New Hampshire.

— 58 —

Florida, USA. I don't get it.

I don't get it but I don't need to.

Along the last stretch of A1A before diving into the ranch house maze, we passed four functioning phone booths, holdout technology, with a desolate and tanned couple at each, all earthly belongings in pillowcases or shopping carts making what I imagined were last ditch phone calls to emotionally exhausted relatives or heartless junk connections. Presumptions, I know, but the Florida, USA roadways I've seen with liquor, donut, and auto part stores play out like the beginning of a documentary on cultural Armageddon. Two of the couples we saw had dogs with them, both beasts appearing considerably more healthy, hopeful and intelligent than their owners. I felt my Maine gloom returning.

Before leaving Maine I had warned brother Mackerel, I mean, Mac, that we might be stopping in, me and Bojean. From Charleston I let his voicemail know that it would be soon.

We found his house, green as fuck, some sort of lime variation, and pulled into the apron of the first of two three-car garages attached to his house . . . each car bay no doubt occupied by one or more of Mac's automotive projects.

Brother Mac was infatuated with buying any sort of used but classic sports car: Ford Mustang, Miata, Porsche, Dodge Challenger . . . and installing the latest crate LS Corvette engine into each. Big Mac told me once that a neighbor stopped to chat for a moment while walking her dog. Mac explained to her what he was doing with all of his cars and she asked, rightly, "Why don't you just get a Corvette?"

We got out of our not-a-Corvette, stretched, and hit the doorbell of Casa Mac y Ticky. As, mentioned, I'd warned brother Mac that we were coming but brother Mac possesses the tunnel vision of the hyperfocused successful person and if you or your concerns are not his concerns regarding the propagation of his race efforts, then more than likely your concerns will be deleted from his concern. In other words, I had no doubt at all that Mac had not alerted his wife or family that we were coming to visit.

Have I mentioned that I love my brother very much and have worried about him since we were little kids?

We rang the doorbell, waited, and then again. Eventually, a leatherette woman in her mid-fifties, sixties, or seventies opened the door and did a long forensic up and down of the two of us. We stood there and took it. I was not even close to confident that this was the right house.

I had no idea who this person unabashedly undressing us with her eyes might be. She stepped out of the shadows of the interior and joined us outside. She lit the smoke that was already out of the pack and between her fingers. When she had completed her inspection of us, she took an exaggerated drag from her Kool and blew the smoke directly into my face.

She then spoke from a voicebox demolished by something, the most obvious guess being the Kools, although it could have been radiation, undisciplined yodeling, or a hatchet accident.

She said, "Why is it that older men can bang little girls with impunity, but I get called a cougar or much worse whenever I hit on some teenage strange?"

Rhetorical?

And then she said with even more gravel, "I'm an entertainer. A cabaret singer. You've heard of me. I gave Sammy Davis oral before either of you assholes were ever gestated," and then laughed the drowned laugh of the lifetime smoker to let us know that all was in good fun. "Well, maybe not you," she said, looking at me.

I looked at Bo and Bo looked at me. "It's wrong," Bo offered.

"What is?" asked the cougar. "Blowing Sammy? You think you kids invented blowies? That's a laugh! Ha!!"

"It's wrong," Bo said, "that a beautiful and mature woman may not hit upon the teenage strange equally as a man."

The Coug gave Bo yet another complete visual and nodded. She flipped her cigarette into my brother's shrubbery and re-entered the house. We followed. I was now fairly certain this was the right place. It looked vaguely familiar.

"You must be Holmes." So Mac *had* told his family we were coming and this *was* the right house. But what part of his family was this woman?

"Yup. Yes. I am. I am Holmes."

"And who are you, sweetheart?" this stranger asked, once again and for the third time giving Bo a now lecherous once over with her heavily Maybellined eyes. "Ticky didn't tell me there was a broad coming too."

Ticky was my brother's wife of fifteenish years. She was a born and bred SoCal blonde, recovering alcoholic, not fully recovered shopaholic with torpedo-shaped store-bought breasts who wore high-heeled footwear at all times, even bedroom slippers, and consequently could be heard approaching by the ticky-ticky sound her footfalls made upon hard surfaces. To my knowledge, Ticky had never walked upon raw earth, dirt or grass, for if she tried . . . she would sink. I imagine it would difficult for her to sneak up on anyone, ever.

"I'm Bojean," Bojean said.

"Bo John? Spell it."

"B o j e a n."

"Fuck," the Cougar said. "Fuck you. You're fucking gorgeous. I know you from somewhere."

We, the three of us, stood in the rough shape of a scalene triangle at the edge of a large living room, beautifully furnished with very expensive looking sofas, overstuffed chairs, 127-inch flatscreen TV, oriental carpets over polished hardwood floors, several laptop computers sitting on several end tables and enormous houseplants placed beautifully and magnificently maintained by what I assumed was a houseplant maintenance concern. A crazily high-end Woodstock Soapstone woodstove was in the room for no apparent reason as temps rarely dipped below fifty in Daytona. None of this was of Mac's doing. Mac made pretty good coin at his profession, and Ticky lived to spend it, show it.

Mac, as noted, is a twin, fraternal. His brother, my brother Andy, lives with his wife and daughters back up in New Hampshire. I can hardly believe that they, or I, come from the same genetic Petri dish. I can't believe that my dad got away with naming them Holy Mackerel Andy.

Just then, out of the corridors of this avocado casa popped one of my two nieces, the younger one, a bit roly poly, her name escaping me. She took her place in the middle of our triangle and shouted up at me, "Are you Uncle Andy?"

"Nope," I said. "Close. I'm Uncle Holmes."

"Oh," she said, and abruptly padded back to wherever she had come from.

"She's a bit of a twat, that one," the Cougar explained. "Ticky's out shopping and Mac is who the fuck knows where. I know you're his brother but I cannot understand what my daughter sees in him.

"You get the room above the garage. You don't want to be down here in the middle of this shitshow when Ticky gets back, believe me. She's my daughter but I cannot understand what Mac sees in her. There are two beds up there, but you won't be needing them both, obviously." Coug reached into a pocket of her muumuu and came up with another smoke. She wandered across the living room and out a screen door leading to the pool area, leaving us to get settled in by ourselves, which was fine.

The room above the garage was fabulous. Big floor-to-ceiling windows that encouraged a lovely air flow of ocean scent. As Coug indicated, two king-sized beds, flatscreen TV, private bath, a door opening to a deck overlooking the neighbor's back yard and then beyond that the intercoastal, slowly rotating ceiling fans. We stood in the middle of the room, flummoxed, I suppose.

Bo set her bag down and sat at the edge of the nearest bed. I set my bag down and sat next to her, close. With zero pre-meditation, I leaned over and kissed her. Right on the mouth. I don't know if I was surprised or not that she kissed me back, but I was surprised that I'd kissed her. I didn't regret it right away, but still, what the fuck was I doing?

Just the one.

Then we sat there, looking straight ahead.

"What did you do that for?" Bo asked.

I had to look at her face to see that she was smiling.

"No idea. Whatsoever."

— 59 —

And then we heard a car pull into the compound and heard a car door open and slam shut and the distinct ticky-ticky sound of high heels on concrete and once inside the house the distinct ticky-ticky-ticky of high heels on tile and then hardwood floor and then coming up our stairs. I hadn't said a word to Bo about my sister-in-law. When Ticky entered the suite I think I heard Bo gasp a little. Ticky is an eyeful. Makeup. Lots. Lips so red. Tight tight very tight black pants with a hint of camel toe, tight silvery top with nipple, nails bright and long, heels of course, the SoCal works. Even for a well-traveled individual such as Bo with many friends, I supposed, in the theater, Ticky's look can be disorienting, overwhelming.

"Holllllmmmmsie!!"

I stood to meet her tippy toe charge.

Embrace. Cinder-block breasts crushing into my ribcage. Lipstick smears upon both of my cheeks.

Stepping back, almost staggering, I said, "This is my friend Bojean."

Ticky barely glanced at her, said, loudly, "Right on!!" emphasis on the ON, lofting upward like a question. "I've got to run my mom home. You met Mom?"

"Sure did."

"Right *on*!! Can you watch the girls? I shouldn't be too long and Mac will show up eventually. You're a doll. Buh bye." one-hundred-eighty-degree spin and gone, the sound of her descending the stairs fast like a Tito Puente timbale solo.

"Girls?" Bo asked. "More than one?"

"I guess. I mean, there are two nieces. I guess they're both in the house. I'll check."

I reached the ground floor in time to see Ticky's enormous Ford Explorer, contractor black, screaming out of the driveway. Downstairs was quiet now except for the hollow drone of TV show noise with laugh track.

I stuck my head into the room I'd seen the younger niece disappear. She was standing in the middle of a bedroom rammed full of horse dolls of all proportion. There must have easily been a thousand horse dolls piled on shelves, the floor, on a desk, the dresser. She, the niece—I was still trying to retrieve her name—stood facing a gigantic TV holding what appeared to be a quart-sized container of vanilla and chocolate chip yogurt in one hand and in the other, a spoon. She was staring at the television, no inclination or concern that a relative stranger was standing in her doorway.

"Is your sister around?"

Nothing.

"Is your sister around?"

"What?" Not turning from the strobing colors of her program.

"Is your sister in the house?" My niece, Rhonda (?), peeled the lid off of her bucket-o-yogurt, let the lid fall to the floor, landing yogurt side down, and commenced consuming, completely forgetting that she was engaged in a conversation, of sorts.

I ducked out of the room and moved down the hall. I opened another door into a pitch-black space. It was difficult to say for sure but the walls seemed to be painted black, the walls, the furniture, the bed. The windows were somehow letting in not a speck of light.

"Hello?"

"Get out!"

"Okay."

My job as babysitter complete, I retreated to the large and well-appointed living room and stood looking through large louvered windows out to the pool and hot tub portion of the compound. Either I hadn't noticed him drive up in the last minute or he had been out there all along, but my brother Holy Mackerel was sitting at a patio table in the corner of the fenced in yard/pool area, with a magazine and a water glass full of amber liquid and ice, and what appeared to be a jumbo Marley dangling from his lips. I walked over to the screen door and poked my head out. "Mac?"

My brother looked up from his phone that was resting on his magazine, smiled, and said, "Holmes!" He stood and we shook hands, hard. We, the Jensens, have never been huggers. "Get yourself a drink," is probably as close as we get to emotional. "In fact, bring the handle out here, and some ice. And there's beer in the shop fridge."

"Good to see you, brother." I was trying to remember the last time. Over two years was what I came up with.

"Good to be seen. Find your room okay?"

"Yes, man. We're all settled in."

"We? Oh, that's right, you did mention that you have a traveling companion." This would be the end of his curiosity regarding Bo, or me.

I fetched the handle of Dewars, a bowl of ice cubes, a too-tall glass, a beer to get myself rolling and joined my brother poolside. My brother and me sharing the Florida dream with petulant daughters inside watching TV, wife out shopping, and we the men getting slowly shitfaced next to a hundred-thousand-dollar swimming pool with hot tub at the edge of a neighborhood populated mostly by meth lab ranch houses and assorted other skylarks. This place made me so uncomfortable. I ate the first of the half dozen Percocet Mac poured into my hand from his bottomless prescription bottle. He must have been out of Oxy or was saving those for himself.

Brother Mac pointed out with a dreamy smile that on certain days you could hear the NASCAR vehicles twelve miles away at the famous Daytona International Speedway. He could not hear or did not notice the restless ocean a half mile to the east or the call of the lonely egret out over the surrounding swamps or the grunt of the gator.

For the next five hours brother Mac filled me in on the state of pro motorcycle grand prix, flat track, motocross and supercross racing. He told tales of the inner-circle gossip regarding riders, sponsors, and team owners. He spoke of the abysmal administration of all elements. He talked about his diet, his workout regimen, his business plans. Nothing about his wife or children. No questions about me or my kids or his ailing mother or his brothers or Bojean. It occurred to me that I couldn't recall the names of his children, so who was I to judge?

I sat and drank and listened. He was a compelling storyteller and I did enjoy hearing about his life. When I did speak up to ask a follow-up question to one of his tales, he would interrupt or over-talk me if my question was too long-winded, impatient to continue on. The night came on as he talked, darkness descending. We were close to the winter solstice. I saw no further signs of Ticky or either of my nieces. Bo never came down. No dinner was offered. We got increasingly blurry off the gallon of scotch, him more than me.

At 10 p.m. or so, Mac stopped talking, " . . . gotta work in the a.m." And he got up from his patio chair, stumbled, did not fall, laughed, and went off to bed. The Percocet he had given me had me cruising nicely. The air was warm and I was not sleepy and I had not thought about any of my worries or woes over the course of the evening. For this I was thankful. And at that moment, out on the Florida poolside, I understood why I loved my brother Mac.

When I was with him, his life took over all things. He demanded one's full attention. This, to me, was a blessing. And there at Florida poolside I realized that it had always been so with Brother Mac. I also knew, sitting there, that I could take no more of this Florida paradise and would sneak away sometime in the night without saying goodbye. I began to miss my brother.

As is the norm when I drink more than my aging liver can process, I passed out quickly but slept fitfully for three hours before becoming unquestionably wide awake with no chance of falling back to sleep.

I was in one bed and Bo, obviously, in the other. Awake indeed, my eyes adjusted to the dark and I saw that Bo was sitting up in her bed. No light on for reading, just sitting, awake.

"Hi," I said. "Did I wake you up?"

"Hello. Nope."

"I'm very hungry."

"OK," she said.

"Let's get out of here."

"OK."

"There's got to be a Denny's or something before we get to the highway."

"Yes," she said. "Are you OK to drive?"

"Probably not. Will you?"

"Of course."

We stealthed out, tippy-not-ticky toe, and after eating our glistening Waffle House waffles under brutal fluorescent lighting, we commenced to roll north and we kept on rolling.

Bo drove for three hours, me drinking gas station coffee. When I took over, I found a beautiful driving groove and it barely registered when we crossed over into South or North Carolina or Virginia. The sad December dawn made a milky appearance somewhere south of D.C., and even the bottleneck of the Beltway did not deter this relaxed and relentless push north.

We kept rolling. Mind off. Heater now on. Bojean had constructed a cocoon of coats and drifted between sleep and perhaps reverie. No more than twenty-three words between us from our departure to D.C. Here were three of those words as we burst out of the Beltway and into the grunge of the December eastern seaboard. Me: "Hungry?"

Her: "Not really." And then she fell asleep.

She fell asleep and I, irresponsibly, dug into my t-shirt pocket and fished out another medication. Soon I began to dream.

— 60 —

This road right here, this 95. My conduit out. My conduit in. How many times have I ridden or driven? At first in a southerly to escape home and then back again, northern, for home?

My first leaving, real leaving, not just hitchhiking around, was on a green motorcycle, the Minnow. What a farfetched and dangerous idea that was. Incredible no one tried to talk me out of it. No parent. No brother. No friend. Everyone seemed to think it was a perfectly reasonable sojourn. What would I say if Mae or Bea declared they were riding across the land, solo, on a two-stroke motorcycle with backpack and two hundred dollars?

I am leaving you, Raven. I am headed south in the fall, south and then west and never to return. Will you miss me then? Will you even think of me?

The letters I wrote to that girl, proclaiming everlasting love. *It matters not at all that you do not love me. I will love you for all time and forever. I love you. Please join me, Raven, please. Come to California. Leave the safety of your Rockaway. Leave for love! Come!*

She said no.

And so, I left for the first time. Brokenhearted and lonely, but not for the last time that way.

I'll show you, Raven. I am a man. I am a man upon a six-hundred-dollar third-owner Suzuki 550 GT motorcycle with backpack and Freudian imperatives to leave you and to leave my home, my mother, my father, and my brothers because I am a man.

I was ridiculous. I was twenty-one. I was afraid and brave. I can't believe I made it without a scratch, taking three months to make the Bay Area, running out of money, finding work on an oil rig in the Gulf of Mexico, alone across America, no cell phone, no GPS, no clue.

I returned home on an airplane, three years later, to bury my father. I returned home to find him sitting high up in the mulberry tree with smoke and as usual, little to say.

There is Baltimore, over there. Philly dead ahead. Do not take an exit here for food, rest, or fuel as these towns in the night are not welcoming to the traveler. I have learned this from my comings and goings. Maybe things are different now, but why take the chance? Keep rolling. North. Home.

Hireath. Have you heard of Hireath, Bojean? The poems to Hireath, the longing for a home that may or may not exist? The yearning. The Raven.

I loved you, Raven. It felt like love to me.

How many brokenhearted leavings? Not too many to count.

Why count?

What am I doing? On this road, this 95 North, yet again? This time with another broken heart and another beautiful girl curled up beside me.

Does it help, leaving?
Yes, it helps.
Does it help, returning?
Can't help it.
Will the circle be unbroken?

I left home again one year in the early spring, a lonely March, in my dead father's Toyota pickup truck. I went south and then west, stopping on the cold Natchez Trace to write a song for my father despite not knowing how to write a song. Sitting next to an Indian mound on the cold Natchez Trace with a notebook and the darkest tears I'd known in my twenty-five years of living. Longing to speak with my father somehow. Hireath. Never knowing until he was gone that my father was my home.

I drove west to San Francisco, the last forty hours non-stop as I desperately, brokenhearted, needed to get back to Sutter Street to my Raven. Raven who finally believed in my love and came along. She finally came along. She left her beloved Rockaway for love. It must have felt like love.

Then I left the Raven, unable to live a normal life after the loss of my father. I left her alone on Sutter Street. I left in a Volkswagen van. I returned east in a Volkswagen van someone named Creeping Jesus, leaving Raven with her own broken heart to make her own return home to Rockaway in a Renault LeCar she named Lee Car. We were broken, but will the circle be unbroken? I love her still.

Now at 11 p.m. on a cold December Route 95 in a Volvo I could call the Slug, north now of Philly and dead on to NYC. Mae and Bea in bed, a school night. Their dad, returning, but not to them, unwelcome, just returning because he cannot leave them. Not yet. This circle, as of yet unbroken. Returning again. Hireath.

I was standing by my window,
On one cold and cloudy day
When I saw that hearse come rolling
For to carry my mother away

Will the circle be unbroken
By and by, lord, by and by
There's a better home a-waiting
In the sky, lord, in the sky

I said to that undertaker
Undertaker please drive slow
For this lady you are carrying
Lord, I hate to see her go

Returning now to mother Bette who is dying. Strange thing. I've known her all my life. I hate to see her go. Next to me, Bojean stirs. She reaches her hand across and touches my cheek. I would not have known it was wet.

Leaving. Returning. Leaving. What a species we are! So restless! Bea tosses in her Lexington bed, fitful.

Straight up midnight on the George Washington Bridge looking east past the towers, east to Rockaway. I'm sorry, Miss Raven. I am truly sorry. I thought it was love. I think it is love. I get confused.

I have left home once for a divorce, the end of a marriage to a woman I can barely recall. I left to do a long lap around the country and to save my friends and family my awkward anger and my grieving for this gross failure. I do not recall her face well, this wife, but I recall her calling me out: *You do not love me, Holmes. Therefore, I am leaving you.*

She called me out. She was absolutely correct. I did not love her. I get confused. I was ashamed. I left home in a Ford F-150 in the summer. I returned six months later, skidding into Bette's driveway, snow piled high, in a Datsun 280-Z.

A raconteur I met in Austin, a friend of a friend, held me spellbound for the better part of a hot porch-sitting morning telling me about his near-death hallucinations brought on by some toxic blood disorder. When he finished he asked me how I liked my Ford. It's alright, *I said.* I asked him how he liked his Z. *It's okay, he said.* Wanna swap? *I asked.* Serious? *He asked.* Why not? *I asked. We swapped keys and the raconteur said,* All right, then. *We swapped titles and he said,* I'll tell you what.

I've left home in a VW bug and a VW Jetta, a Dodge 1500 pick-up and a Subaru XT (wedge thing), a lemon yellow Fiat and a Trailways bus. I've left and returned in the depth of hellacious winter. I've left and returned in glorious fall. A Saab 99-E. I remember a Saab. Creeping Jesus, the van. The Suzuki, the Minnow.

Everything turned out all right. vI did not die from these broken hearts. This is the lesson. I did not die from those broken hearts and I will not die from this one. Maybe. *Be strong,* Kat said, *I will help you.*

No. No you won't. Not for long. You cannot. These lessons are my own. It's okay. These broken hearts will not kill me. Maybe.

No one can help.

I looked to my right, to Bojean. She has helped. More than helped. Saved me, somehow. But how? I get confused.

Past New Haven. Passed New London and Groton. Past Kingston, Rhode Island in the 2 a.m., the Hireath bigger than Dallas. Returning for more home. One more time. One more try.

— 61 —

Bo was fast asleep when I pulled into a mini mart on Route 1 in North Hampton, New Hampshire, to fill up. I went inside and bought two bottles of red wine and a bag of barbecue chips the size of forty pounds of chicken feed. It was 3:05 a.m. and quiet on the Seacoast. The air outside of our heated tube of nothingness was brittle and frigid, maybe fifteen degrees. Another thirty minutes and we'd be back at Serious Farm, right where we started, only different. We'd been gone only a week but it felt much, much longer or even a quantum physics sort of displacement of time and energy or some such shit. I still felt oddly fresh after twenty-four straight-through hours of Interstate 95. The road dreams distracted me to a degree that felt I'd been exempted from physical laws of fatigue and hunger and thirst. I could not recall if we had even stopped to urinate anywhere along the way. I fished into my shirt pocket and found the last of the Percocet. I ate it.

Sweeping north along Route 1 until it merged once again with 95 and crossed the mighty Piscataqua into Maine. We made it without incident into South Berwick and linked onto Route 4, again, arriving home from the south onto Route 9, past Pratt and Whitney and down the horribly potholed driveway of Serious Farm. As soon as the first good snowfall hit, the driveway holes would be filled in with compacted ice and almost like a civilized human lived at the other end. The first good jolt woke Bojean. "Home?"

"Si."

"Is it good?"

"Remains to be seen."

Her car was where we'd left it, parked under the apple tree. Why wouldn't it be? I quickly trotted down to the barn to be sure the chickens were still alive. I'd left enough feed to last a month and unlike dogs or horses or the more intelligent mammals, chickens only eat when they're hungry as opposed to scarfing down all available foods and exploding from the inside. The chickens were fine, their red warming light hooked up to a timer glowing and the chickens roosting, looking at me with sleepy chicken eyes when I opened their coop door to say hello. "Hello ladies."

I trotted back up to the car and Bo was standing, stretching, looking up into the December constellations. The ones I knew were out and bright as well as the ones I didn't: Orion, Cassiopeia, dippers large and small appeared to be sitting one hundred feet above our heads in the clarity of this cold early morning. Her breath and my breath merged like thunderheads as we stood looking up.

I grabbed the plastic bag with the wine and the chips, leaving my travel clothes in the back seat of the Volvo. The Volvo. I now had a reason to respect this mundane contraption. It got us there and it got us back, which was commendable. Bo followed me onto the ground-floor deck and into the mudroom. She didn't bother to grab her travel gear either. Once inside I twisted the thermostat and was pleased to hear the muffled boom of the ancient furnace coming on.

Bo followed me upstairs to the kitchen. Yes, the Serious Kitchen at Serious Farm is upstairs with a backdoor leading out to a second floor deck which overlooks Serious Kingdom, which is a boggy field ringed by pines of multiple variety and more bog. The trees hide the Pratt and Whitney jet engine factory next door, so I pretend that the constant sound emanating from over there, a cross between a hum and a roar, is restless ocean.

Upstairs and we sat at the kitchen table with coats on while waiting for the house to warm. I de-corked the first bottle of red. Bo found glasses and we drank in the predawn. "Pretty impressive," Bo said.

"I know you're not talking about the wine."

"The driving. Almost exactly twenty-four hours straight."

"I'm inclined to agree. I don't recall ever having that kind of stamina before."

"I was watching you," she said, "clandestinely. You were driving the car, but you were somewhere else altogether."

"Mmm."

"You were laughing, grimacing. At one point the tears just rolled out of your eyes while your face seemed impassive, focused on the road. You thought I was asleep."

"You wiped my tears away," I said.

"I don't think I've ever met anyone like you before."

Uh oh. Something told me this wasn't going to be a complimentary observation. "Nor I, you," I said, trying to head this off at the pass.

"You know it's going to be all right, don't you?"

"What is?"

"All of it," she said. "I know your heart is broken right now, but it's going to be okay."

"Thank you," I said, "but I don't know how you can say that. How can you know that?"

"I know you love your daughters."

I waited for more. I needed to hear more. Bo only drank and heavily from her glass of wine. "Okay," I said.

"Okay," she said.

"It's a given," I said. "But loving them doesn't seem to matter. Or, it's not helping my situation any."

"It matters," she said. "It has to. It does."

I shook my head, not in disagreement so much as wonderment at how we had come to such a place, my daughters and me. The first bottle somehow already gone. "Okay," I said.

"I know you don't believe it."

"I've been told that they don't love me. I'm told that they feel obliged to me, but that they do not love me."

"Do you believe that?"

"Sometimes. After a while one begins to believe. I'm aware of my, um, unlovable aspects."

"Enough. Enough of that." Her words were slurred. Drunk? She had not gotten drunk the entirety of the drive. Mildly tipsed, but nothing like this.

"After a while, one begins to believe."

"Stop. I'm serious." She didn't look serious. Big cock-eyed grin. Eyes unfocused but sparkled. She had been trying to uncork the second bottle of bad red for minutes but was still trying to unfold the jackknife-style opener with no luck. I extended my palm across the farm table and she gave it over.

"Thank you, mister."

"You're welcome."

"Thank you for the driveaway. I needed it."

"Yeah you did. All of your lovely hairs may have been uprooted by now if we hadn't escaped Mayhem."

"Mmmm."

"You're welcome. I needed it too."

"I have to go now," she said.

"What?"

"Gotta go! It's time to go!"

I yanked the cork and said, evenly, "It's coming up on four in the morning and you've been, we've been, drinking."

"True. Both." Just the notion of her leaving hit me like a panic. We'd been in steady company for a week but it felt like considerably more. We may not have been communicating often or well. but we'd taken every meal together, walked side by side, bedded down in the same room each night. I was familiar now with her breathing and her silences. A surge of loneliness hit me like nausea. "Well then, let's drink this and sleep and then I gotta go." She said *gotta go* like a little kid late for class or late for supper.

"Okay."

She had become very quickly and very profoundly inebriated. No food, little sleep, bad red. I said, "Maybe we should save the second bottle for another time."

"You think there's going to be another time?" She wasn't being mean; she appeared genuinely surprised at the prospect that there might be another time. For us. "I assumed you'd have lost your little intrigue in me by now."

"I." I hadn't thought this through as I was hurrying ourselves up the Atlantic seaboard. Was this it? Why would this be it? Should this be it? Maybe. "I hope so. I hope there will be another time."

"Huh," she said, ignoring my suggestion to quit drinking and poured herself a solid one third of the bottle and drank it straight off. "Opportunity knocks," she said, looking me dead in the eye. I wasn't sure what that was supposed to mean. A wine-induced non sequitur? I thought for an ashamed moment that she was trying to seduce me.

"All right," I said. "Time to put you to bed."

"'tis," she said.

I got up with some difficulty, the wine and the drug and road exhaustion finally catching up and walked around to her side of the table and gently took her elbow. She allowed herself to be hoisted to her feet. I led her, very slowly, down the hallway, her full body weight nestled into my arms, down to Mae and Bea's room while she kept up a steady stream of low verbals. The sound coming from her was like that of bumblebees working a sunflower in Serious Garden in late August.

I got her to the big bed that my daughters still shared when they deigned to come around, which had now been several months past. Late August? Could it ever have been August once? Bo sat at the edge of the bed, coat still on.

She motioned for me to come sit with her, her index finger curling and then uncurling. "C'merec'merec'mere," she whispered. I sat.

"Opportunity knocks," she said, clearly now.

She touched my earlobe with the very tip of her tongue and giggled. She mumbled something, no idea what.

"Que?"

"Mmmm. Hmmmmm, I love you."

I laughed, astonished, frightened. "Whaaaaaat?" I stage whispered.

She very delicately belched and raised her hand to her mouth, the universal sign for excuse me and then distinctly said, "Please. Please Mr. Holmes. Please won't you consider hearing aids in the very near future? For you, sir, are quite very deaf. I said . . . ," and she said, clearly and loudly, "Opportunity knocks!"

"I know," I said. "I heard that." She couldn't have been clearer. I was petrified.

Bojean, seeing the fear in my face and understanding now that her message had been misconstrued, said, "*Opportunity Knocks*. It's a very popular TV show, dummy. I'm in it. Was a play. It won a Tony. Made into a TV show. Look it up." With that, she pulled off her coat, pulled the covers over herself, and was off to the land of nod. "I'm kind of a big deal," she giggled. I bent down to kiss the top of her head. I did not know what a Tony was. I would look it up. I laughed out loud when I thought of this: I did not know her last name.

"Love will fix this," were the last words she spoke to me.

In her sleep, she heard me laugh and she smiled.

When I woke up in my room at noon I knew she was gone. I sat up and looked out my north-facing window, out to the barn with the terminally leaking roof on a perfectly dank and dark Maine December day beginning to snit snow. I then looked out the eastern window to where the apple trees stood in an ancient row. Her little Nissan was no longer underneath.

"Hello misery," I said, "It's a brand new day."

And of course, looking at the empty yard, I died a little.

It wasn't so bad.

BOOK TWO

Learning to Die Lessons

LARRY

The job at hospice was a little bit more up my alley. I'd already interned for a New Hampshire hospice while in grad school, so I knew what I was getting into. I was oddly much more comfortable with the terminally ill than the mentally ill. The terminally ill are rarely violent and if that eventuality should take place, I was fairly certain I could handle them physically because most were old and all were dying.

I met an exception to that rule fairly early on in my hospice experience. His name was Larry. When I first met Larry, I assumed he was a family member of whomever was dying, as Larry looked as though he could easily bench-press me. He was a six-footer, 270 pounds, copiously tattooed and a sweet, sweet guy sitting in an easy chair in his super-nice mobile home welcoming me in with a crushing handshake.

Larry's entire family was there: his gorgeous and equally tattooed wife; his parents, his two daughters from his first marriage, his daughters' husbands, and a tiny little girl about six years old who was Larry's granddaughter. Larry was forty-six years old and carried colorectal cancer that swelled his genitals to the size of a volleyball. One could not help but notice this under his sweatpants.

He'd gathered his family this day, he said, because they wanted to do this thing right. Larry wanted everyone on board with what was happening to him and for everyone to ask any and all questions they may have about what hospice was and how this thing would play out.

"OK," he said to his assembled family. "The man is here to answer questions."

There was a long and uncomfortable silence.

Finally, the tiny girl raised her hand. Tiny face, big eyes, tiny mouth moving. She said something, this Cindy Lou Who said something and the room crumbled. Larry's daughters broke first, trying to muffle their sobs and failing, hands over mouths, sobbing. Then Larry's mom, then one son-in-law grimaced and hung his head, then Larry's wife, like dominoes, then the other son-in-law. Within seconds the entire living room full of people were weeping in their own fashion except for Larry and Larry's dad and me.

I learned in the coming month that Larry did not cry because he was a tough son of a bitch who did not cry. I learned that he inherited this toughness from his father, and that is why his father did not cry.

I did not cry because I had no idea what little Cindy Lou Who had asked, with her tiny hand in the air and her enormous eyes and tiny mouth.

I leaned over to Larry and whispered, "I couldn't hear. What did she say?"

Looking straight ahead but with a small wry smile he said, "She asked, is my Grampy gonna die?"

The next day I made an appointment with an audiologist. Within a week I was the proud owner of three thousand dollars' worth of hearing aid.

In two months, Grampy, Larry, did indeed die. They all died.

BOJEAN

So, by mid-January I had a new job.

By late January, Bojean emailed me to let me know she was pregnant. Opportunity, apparently, knocked. It hurt me somehow, as it might hurt any father kept in the dark about a daughter's new and seemingly important beau.

HERBIE

Herbie lived in a safe-enough-looking neighborhood situated a bit north of downtown Portland in a neighborhood called Pleasant Hill. His street was populated by newer construction homes of generic Colonial and ranch design. Perfectly nice. Perfectly pleasant. No hill. The neighborhoods of Portland, I was learning, were diverse in their spectrum of the perfectly nice to the perfectly awful. I liked the entire spectrum.

On the day I met Herb, the snowbanks were a frozen five feet tall and made the streets of his subdivision so narrow that parking the Volvo turned his particular street into a one-lane affair. People get used to this. Occasional unexplained dents and paint swaps were to be expected and if you dinged another vehicle while trying to squeeze past, no one really expected you to stop and leave a note with your particulars. If you cared about your car, you owned a garage. If you really cared about your car, you put it up for the winter. Most of the houses in this Pleasant Hill neighborhood seemed to have garages and mine was the only car parked on the snow-banked street.

I found Herb's particular ranch house with my newly acquired GPS that was pretty much mandatory for my position as a hospice social worker. My job was to go from patient house to patient house to nursing home to patient house to check on my caseload of the terminally ill and their justifiably stressed-out, overworked and anticipatorily grieving families. I thought it was interesting that at hospice, the customers were called patients while at

Mayhem they were called clients. They were all People with Problems.

The hospice home office was in Scarborough but I rarely had to go there but for the weekly interdisciplinary team meetings. Otherwise our team of social workers, we were four, were in our cars and on the twisty Maine roads hunting down all manner of dwellings: trailers, New Englanders, Victorians, many ranch styles and, once, a yurt. I got to know nearly all of the funky ghettos of Portland as well as farmhouses and mobile home parks settled upon the hill and the dale of southern coastal Maine.

Herb's walkway had been shoveled by someone with OCD, perfect edges cut down to the bare cement of sidewalk. When I got within five feet of his kitchen entrance door I heard someone yell, "It's open!" I was being watched.

I stepped into the small entryway/mudroom and it was as if I'd stepped into the smoked and smogged alleys of Calcutta. I involuntarily coughed after taking in the first lungful and the voice of the eyes that had been watching me said, "If you can't handle cigarette smoke you may as well turn around right now."

I coughed again and said, "Just give me a second." I stood there in the mudroom trying to breathe through my eyes. My eyes burned.

"Acclimating," I said.

I really don't mind. The smell of cigarettes reminds me of my father at home and the barrooms of my youth and the taste of closing time kisses before the world wised up to tobacco lies. My first trip on an airplane to check out Tulane University in New Orleans, I sat in the smoking section. Of an airplane.

I peered through the fog and could make out the shape of a man wearing a baseball cap sitting at the kitchen table, stubbing out a cigarette and then immediately lighting another. Fanning the so-called air with my arm might have been taken as passive aggression or a weakness so I carved a path to the table by steadily blowing out through my mouth while trying not to make a big production out of it.

Even when I found a chair across from the shape of a man, it was tough to tell what he looked like. But through the mist he appeared to be a miniature replica of Ernest Hemingway. He wore a snow-white beard, round face flushed reddish, and well, facial features just like Hemingway. You know what Hemingway looks like. He looked just like Hem, but in miniature. His head and shoulders—narrow with no meat upon them—were barely above the surface of the kitchen table. Unless his legs and ass were disproportionally thick, he could not have weighed more than 110.

Herb's left arm was strapped to his body with a tight sling and he held both a cigarette and a pen in the fingers of his right hand. In front of him were a coffee cup and a pad of sticky notes. I saw my name written at the top of the pad. His handwriting was legible. Either the fog was clearing or my eyes were adapting.

Herbie stared at me. "So," he said. "You're a clinical social worker, is that right?"

"Right."

"What, pray tell, is a clinical social worker?"

"Uhhh." Nobody had asked me that before. I did not have a stock reply for this yet.

"Okay, okay," he said, "let's start with an easy one. Jensen. Is that Swedish or Danish?" I coughed and said, Danish.

"Thought so," Herb said, "and I know what a clinical social worker is, don't worry about it."

I could now see that the hat on Herbie's head was a leather Harley-Davidson number, well worn, obviously not a prop. My guess was that there was an immaculately maintained soft tail in the garage, tarped for the winter. "Want a beer?" he asked.

"I'd love one," I said, "but I'm on the clock."

"That certainly never stopped me," he said, ruefully, I think. "Seriously, they're in the fridge if you want one."

"I'm good," I said. "Can I get you one?"

"No. I haven't been drinking for a while. I keep those in there for company." Herb took a long pull off his cigarette and shot the smoke out of the corner of his mouth as opposed to in my face. A good sign, maybe.

"So," I started, "I know virtually nothing about your situation. What can you tell me?"

"Well first of all, that's bullshit. If you knew *virtually*," he made a face at me when he said virtually, "nothing about my case, you wouldn't have found your way out here. Would you?" This was true. I also knew that Herb had melanoma of skin, secondary malignant neoplasm of bone and bone marrow, and malignant neoplasm of liver. He was lousy with cancer. I knew he was not long for this particular world, but I couldn't lead with that, could I?

"All right," I said.

"Want to start again, social worker?"

"Not really."

"You're off to a shaky start," he said, "but you're a big fucker, aren't you?"

"That's relative," I said, taking an unnecessary poke at his miniature stature. "I just came by to see how you're doing."

"Dying, apparently."

"Yup. If you're on hospice, you're definitely dying."

"Let's be clear," he said, "I've never been to a counselor in my life. I don't believe in it. But obviously, these are extenuating circumstances, so I haven't ruled it out. I'll tell you when I need counseling and when I need social work. Right now I need social work." I nodded. This was reasonable.

Herb told me he was troubled over whom to appoint as power of attorney regarding his material affairs, as well as end-of-life decision making if and when he was no longer capable. He had not established advance directives, and he knew it was time to do so.

Herb told me he had three children, two daughters and a son from two marriages and a dalliance. He was on tenuous terms with all three, he said, and hadn't seen the youngest daughter in years. He was fairly certain she lived in Connecticut, but not 100 percent. "They don't like me much," Herb said. "I've been a less than perfect parent.

"I own some fairly valuable artifacts," Herb explained, "and I don't want my offspring adding them to a fucking yard sale three days after I'm dead."

"So where do you want these artifacts to wind up?" I asked.

Herb chuckled. Took a long drag. Scribbled a note on his notepad. "Okay," he said, "you got me."

"How so?"

"I want the artifacts to wind up with my kids, numb-nuts. You do understand irony, don't you?"

"Sometimes," I said. "If it's really obvious." I was enjoying this barbed back and forth. So far.

Herb squinted at me through the smoke. His half smile disappeared. He stubbed out his butt and did not immediately go for another. He waved at the smoke between us with his good hand and then took another note. I'd known Herb for all of five minutes and was already way back on my heels. He was crusty. He was salty. He was, for a 110-pound man, intimidating.

"What sort of artifacts?" I asked.

Herb scooted his chair back from the table and with a grinding wince stood up. I stood up too, thinking that the chronic pain in my back was nothing compared to whatever this guy was carrying around. When he made it to his full height he could not have been more than five-foot-five. I thought, maybe he's more Picasso, with a beard.

He led me into his living room. It was barely furnished. The clean and polished hardwood floors had no rugs. An indistinct brown cloth sofa sat at an angle and pulled away from the wall. No throw pillows. Basic coffee table, basic floor lamp, both dusted clean. One free-standing wooden chair, straight backed, severe. There was an immaculately clean fireplace with immaculately clean fireplace tools leaning against the very clean hearth. Someone was keeping this place very neat and very clean.

On the fireplace mantel were some stone-carved figurines. An elephant and a tiger carved from green stone. A Buddha carved from white stone. There were some chess pieces, not an entire set, only the king, the queen and the two rooks. Hanging above the mantle was a rifle . . . a musket.

Herb stood in front of the fireplace looking at me with an expression of *Feast your eyes!*

"Nice," I said, looking closely at the carved pieces as if I could tell the difference between treasure and trash.

With great difficulty Herb lowered himself onto the sofa. I moved toward the straight-backed chair when Herb let out with a stream of *fuck fuck fuck FUCK ME* and tried to stand back up using his good arm to lever himself out of his seat.

"Your cigarettes?" I asked.

"Yeah."

"I got 'em." And I fetched his smokes, lighter, and ashtray from the kitchen table.

For the next ninety minutes Herb kept me riveted with just the beginning of his story.

It was evident that I was dealing with a very bright man, well-read based on his casual references to Aristotle, Kafka, Adam Smith, Kennedy (JF and William), Beckett, Samuel Fucking Beckett, and George Carlin. He was quite open about his alcoholism, slowed down lately only by daily nausea that had him down to a diet of saltines and soda water. Anything else, including Ensure, he said, made him gag.

He'd been a general contractor since his teens and had built hundreds of homes in the Portland neighborhoods both simple and grand, including the simple house we were sitting in. He told he'd built fourteen of the seventeen houses in this development. When I told him I'd been a stonemason for nearly thirty years he said, "No shit? You sure you don't want a beer?" I declined, again, and he said, "Jensen? Never heard of you. If you were any good, I would have heard of you."

"I went by Serious Stonework." Again, the peering through the newly formed tobacco fog.

"Seriously?" he said, and I assumed he was conjuring another degrading comment about what a stupid name for a company or some such.

"Seriously," I said.

"All right," he said. "I've heard of you. Why are you doing social work? You have a pretty good reputation as a stonemason."

"My back," I said, "is demolished."

"Imagine that," he said.

Herb told me about his son, a drunk, whom he had only just kicked out of this house this morning. The son lived with Herb off and on, with Herb giving him the heave ho whenever he got to be too irritating. "He's a good kid," Herb said, "but he can't get out of his own way."

His eldest daughter lived only a half hour north with her husband and her three children. Herb said he had yet to meet any of his grandchildren. "I don't even have a good reason," he said. "Just haven't gotten around to it."

"Who would be the more responsible out of those two?" I asked. When I met a hospice patient who lived alone, it was imperative to find a crew of people, besides the hospice team, to get on board with what would initially be checking in, but might quickly turn to caregiving. As the social worker, I would put the person living alone on my schedule two, three, four times a week so that if they took a header and couldn't get up, they hopefully wouldn't freeze to death on a linoleum floor before someone came along to check in. If I couldn't get anyone to live with Herb when his active dying process began, he'd have to go to the House. The Gosnell House. The last stop.

Herb ignored my question. "I guess I'm a pretty awful human being."

"How so?"

"Being estranged from my kids like this. Always one problem or indignation after another. I forget what I'm even fighting about with the eldest."

"Families fight. How does that make you awful?"

Herb glared at me. "I'm pretty sure I made myself clear. And if I didn't, I'll do so now. This visit is about social work. Power of attorney. Remember? Do not start with that analytical bullshit. Got it?"

"Yeah. Got it."

"You got kids, Holmesy?"

"Yes."

"How old?"

"Twins. Eleven years old."

"Boys? Girls?"

"Girls. Identical."

"Home to supper with them when you get out of here?"

"Nope."

Herb looked at me then, for a long moment. Whatever he was thinking, he didn't let on.

He stubbed out his cigarette and by reaching out for the ashtray his left arm shifted in the sling. Herb yelped, winced hard, and recoiled in pain. Looking at his arm, I noticed his left hand was fingerless. He had an intact thumb and four stubs, sawed off at the first knuckle. He saw me looking.

"Hey Ace, power of attorney."

"OK. So your kids are out of the question?"

"I didn't say that. I'm just trying to decide if my neighbor, a professor, would be a wiser choice."

"Does your neighbor know he's in the running?"

"Yes he does. He's on board."

"So your son drinks a bit. What about his sister?"

"No. She's a good kid. Great mom. She'll drink a beer, but she's no drinker."

"Have you asked her about being your POA?"

"No," Herb said, quickly.

I had a hunch. "Does she have any idea you're on hospice?"

"No."

"Do you want her to know?"

"Is this practical questioning or psychoanalysis?"

"The former."

"Plus some of the latter, right?"

"Jesus, Herb, relax. Try to let me do my job, how about?"

"Did you just tell me to relax, social worker?"

"Please. If you would."

"Go fuck yourself."

"If I could do that, I'd never leave the house. And fuck you too." I got up to leave.

"What did you just say to me?"

"We can try this another time, or not." I got to the door, half expecting an ashtray to bounce off the back of my head.

Herb started into an intense coughing fit that lasted a full minute or more and sounded like thirteen dogs drowning in the Saco River. I couldn't just leave while the man may very well have been actually dying. When he finished, he fished a butt out of the pack, which is not all that easy with only one hand, and fired up. He looked at me with his Hemingway face and said, "OK, wiseass, you can go. Maybe there's something to this clinical therapeutic bullshit. I feel better."

I left the house and minced my way over the icy sidewalk and past frozen snowbanks to the Volvo, smiling, stinking.

I called Herb's daughter the next morning, the next morning after not going home to supper with my twins. His daughter sounded like a perfectly reasonable person with no bone to pick with her dad and she had clearly inherited her father's intelligence. "Yeah, he thought he was keeping his cancer a secret. Narcissists have a tough time keeping secrets." She said this with no rancor.

"When was the last time you spoke?"

"A week or so. But I have a pipeline with the neighbors. They keep me abreast."

"Your father is a piece of work."

"Tell me about it."

I asked, "Will you be available to help him out, physically? When things start to move along, they tend to move fast."

"Of course."

"How about your brother?"

"Depends on what time of the day you ask, but yeah, I'll make sure he's available to help out."

This gave me a bit of peace, that the family appeared to be on board. "Did Herb tell you how he happened to acquire these lovely cancers?" his daughter asked.

"We didn't get that far."

"It's a hell of a yarn. You should ask him."

"I'll try. He's got some fairly stringent house rules dictating conversation."

"So you *have* met my dad."

GLORIA

Gloria and her husband lived in a dollhouse in a mill town west of Portland called Westbrook. They'd met as teenagers working in the S.D. Warren factory, walking distance from their respective childhood homes, married, and continued to work while raising a happy family in their dollhouse on a street of dollhouses filled with similar families. Now Gloria was eighty-one years old and dying and perfectly okay with it.

Gloria and her husband, whose name escapes me, were the sweetest people, the sweetest couple I'd ever met, ever. Deeply in love, still, sweet, and treasuring these last days together with a startling lack of panic, anger, or fear.

Before Gloria took permanently to the bed, she reliably had her makeup done, her hair done, her nails, and her jewelry on. Her husband, let's call him Ray, was relaxed and impossibly handsome for a man of eighty-one, or any age, tall, amazing head of hair, barely a face wrinkle. I don't think he knew how good looking he was. Maybe he did. Ray was clearly head over heels in love with Gloria, the way he spoke to her, held her hand, smiled at her. And she giggled at the attention, clearly so in love.

Before she took permanently to the bed, I would sit with Gloria and Ray in their spotless dollhouse kitchen and chat. My favorite part of these visits was when I would enter the home, cookies on a plate waiting for me, and I would ask Gloria how she was doing. Each time I asked, even after she took to the bed, she smiled beautifully, she was beautiful, and whispered, "Decent!" I don't know why this cracked me up, but it did.

I fell in love with this couple. I had the habit of falling in love with many of my hospice patients and their families. This is not a recommended habit.

Gloria had COPD and I learned rather quickly that when the decline came for COPD patients, it came in a hurry.

On my last visit with Gloria and Ray, my last visit before her funeral, Gloria was in the hospital bed that had been rolled into the kitchen. Gloria preferred the kitchen. There was a kitchen chair next to the bed and Ray indicated it was for me. Gloria's eyes were closed and she was sleeping with tiny shallow breathing. She was actively dying, a term that sounds redundant but I came to understand as a reliable progression toward death. She had one dainty foot in this plane of the living and one foot out.

The bed was cranked to a nearly 45-degree angle as it helped with the patient's breathing. Her oxygen was pumping and I put my mouth close to Gloria's ear and said, "Gloria, it's Holmes. How are you?"

She smiled thinly, totally not asleep, and mouthed, "Decent." I couldn't help it; I laughed.

Ray was standing behind me, watching, listening, "What did she say?"

"She said she's decent." Ray laughed too.

Gloria's ghost hand appeared from under her covers and found my ghost hand. With her eyes open, clear, looking at me she said, "I'm ready."

Then she said, "Right now." I very gently held her feather hand in my feather hand and didn't know what to say. She smiled.

"I'm going to count to three," she whispered into my ear. She closed her eyes and curled her bone fingers around my bone fingers. "One . . . two . . . three . . ."

She stopped breathing.

And then she breathed. She opened her eyes, smiling. "Let me try that again. One . . . two . . . three . . ."

"What's she saying?" Ray asked. I just shook my head, not taking my eyes off Gloria, my mouth probably hanging open.

Gloria, started again, "One . . . two . . ."

"Wait, Gloria, wait . . ." I whispered into her ear. She opened her eyes. I whispered into her ear. "Gloria," I said, "If this works, it is going to completely freak me out . . ." I said, "I don't know, but I don't think that's how this works . . ."

Gloria looked at me for a long moment. She looked at me and then giggled.

Over by the kitchen door as I was leaving, I told Ray what had happened. He shook his head, shook my hand, and laughed. I left, laughing. Later on, during the night of this day, Gloria figured it out.

BETTE

I was watching professional football in January with my brother Andy, my good friend Little Carrot, and Little Carrot's son. We were at Little Carrot's house in Portsmouth and it was a huge game, playoffs, our Patriotics against the San Diego Chargers who had an unstoppable running back named Tomlinson, as I recall. He was killing us. Ripping off huge chunks of yardage against our sketchy defense. We were behind by a lot lot, and it wasn't looking too good for the New England 11. We in the room were less than rowdy except for Carrot's kid who had ADHD. During the third quarter, my brother's cell phone went off. He ignored it.

It went off again.

Brother Andy listened, said "Okay," and put his phone back in his pocket. He let several plays go by before he said to me, "Your mother is being prepped for quintuple bypass surgery."

"Quintuple is how many," I said. "Five? Seems like a lot."

This was news. Bette's near lifetime consumption of kale and brown rice all for naught.

SAUL

Saul called.

In early February we had a three-day thaw with drenching rains that washed away nearly all of the snow cover that made us short-sighted and should-know-better New Englanders believe outdoor work was possible.

Saul called and said he finally had the scratch available for me to build his grand estate wall out in front of his grand estate. "Are you still in business?" he asked.

"For you? Today? Of course."

"Are you still pretending to be a social worker?"

"I am."

"Good Lord," he said. "Full time?"

"Yep."

"Doing what?"

"Hospice. Counseling the dying."

Saul muttered something under his breath.

* * *

Saul's Resumé:
- Saul was born and raised in Chicago. He retained that Chicago fish-slap-to-the-face of an accent with no intention of letting it go.
- Saul was the son of an alcoholic and abusive father. His father was a bricklayer. Saul was proud of the latter and matter of fact about the former. He wrote about these things.
- Saul was a Marine infantry commander at the age of twenty-one in 1967 during the height and the deadliest year of our Vietnam conflict. He led a company of 150 men into, and a smaller number, out of, unthinkable combat. Saul did not write or talk much about this but pointed me to objective literature chronicling his experiences. Historians considered his exploits so noteworthy as to be entered into historical ledger, like Joshua Chamberlain.
- Saul became an FBI agent after somehow surviving Vietnam.
- Saul's job for the FBI was to psychoanalyze, find, and then arrest serial killers. He was good at it.
- Saul became, after a while, a novelist. Saul's first novel made him semi-wealthy and got him kicked out of the FBI for writing about the FBI.
- Saul moved from Detroit, Michigan, where he'd done most of his FBI-ing to affluent Rye, New Hampshire, after becoming semi-wealthy.
- Saul was a Serious Stonework client initially who became a very good friend rather quickly.
- Saul, along with Herb, Gloria, Bette, Larry, and all the others, would be dead before this year was through.
- It was Saul's death, of them all, that prompted me to burn it all down. Or his death was the straw that broke the camel's back of my mind.
- Then I burned it all down.

* * *

"Before you get rolling on the wall," he said, "I'd like you to clear out a bunch of trees and all of the undergrowth on the right of the house. I think I want to turn that all into lawn."

"I can do that."

"When can you start?"

"Right away. This weekend."

"Good," he said.

"Good," I agreed. Sometimes with some of the jobs he called me about, I felt he was looking out for me more than needing the actual work done . . . providing me with a paycheck, although I had no idea why he might do this.

The Estate Wall, The Great Wall of Saul, however, he most steadfastly wanted done. He'd been talking about it for years. It was a grand vision and it was expensive and I'd been waiting to get my hands on this thing ever since Saul had brought up the notion some time ago.

HERB

Three days after our initial visit, Herb left a message at the hospice main office that he wanted to see me.

When I got to his house, Herb offered me a beer.

"No thanks," I said. It was 8:30 a.m. "What's going on?"

"A few things." Herb had his notepad in front of him and I could see the lines he had written, a punch list, and several of the items on the list were underlined multiple times. "First off, I spoke with my daughter. She's agreed to be my power of attorney."

"Good," I said.

"I hope so. We had a pretty good chat and I feel like I can trust her to carry out my wishes in regard to my estate."

"Good."

Herb glanced up from his punch list. "Second, I need you to speak to my nurse for me." I waited for him to tell me what about. "Don't you want to know what about?" he asked.

"Yes," I said.

"Jesus!" Herb said. "What's with the monosyllables? Are you mad at me for the last visit? If we can't exchange a healthy 'fuck you' with each other, then we're in trouble. Don't go all sensitive on me now. I've decided I need you, Holmes."

"I'm good, Herb. We're good. What's going on that I need to tell Becky?" Becky H. was Herb's case manager RN. She was a close-cropped, no-nonsense nurse who some people liked and some did not due to her brusque, butch approach. She wore a nosering and sleeve tattoo. She was an RN badass and I enjoyed working with her.

"She's recommending that I make a trip to your facility in Scarborough, the Gosnell House?"

"Really, what for?" The Gosnell was usually reserved for those definitively approaching their last mile.

The Gosnell was a low-key-looking one-story building with seventeen rooms wedged discreetly into a residential neighborhood in Scarborough. Our hospice MD had his headquarters in the building. It was an interesting place. Aside from the patients' rooms, there was a meditation room with an indoor waterfall, a chapel, a dining area with 24/7 chocolate chip cookies and coffee, soft ambient music over built-in speakers that sometimes creeped me out with its spectral overtones sounding like Hollywood notions of what moving on to the next plane sounds like. It was a place for the actively dying and Herb was not there yet.

Herb said, "She thinks it would be a good idea to install a port for a CADD pump?"

"Really?"

"Yes, really. Here's the problem, and I'm counting on your discretion and diplomatic skills even though you haven't displayed any so far. I'm, uh . . . I've, I've got a thing about needles."

CADD stands for Computer Assisted Drug Delivery and it's a little box that holds pain meds and electronically squirts it into a good vein of the patient at pre-determined intervals. The patient carries the CADD pump around with a little shoulder strap. The CADD also allows the patient to self-administer pre-ordained boluses of the medication for breakthrough pain management, which is when the regular computerized dose just doesn't cut it or when the patient just wants to get or remain high.

As most of us know, drugs' effects can be administered more quickly and effectively when they are shot straight into a vein as a liquid rather than in pill form where the grains have to be broken down in the stomach and delivered naturally like nutrition through the bloodstream. In order to access a vein, a port has to be installed, which requires what amounts to a minor surgery of going through the skin, clipping into a healthy vein and leaving a plastic portal that looks like a teeny tiny asshole on the skin's surface so the pump can feed directly into it. Makes sense? And the only way to do this is to give the patient a local anesthetic where the port will be going in and a local anesthetic requires a needle. Herb had this all figured out and he was not happy.

"What exactly do you want me to tell her?" I asked.

"I don't know. Tell her I'm fucking scared. Tell her I'm on the fence between doing this and just toughing it out until I croak. Tell her I'm a pussy, I don't care. I just don't want to do it."

"You didn't mention anything about this level of pain at my last visit."

"That's because you're a social worker and not a doctor or a nurse. No offense."

"None taken, but we work as a team. Any issues you're having you can tell me and I'll get the word to Becky H. immediately, rather than you having to wait for her next visit. And the other way around. If Becky's here and you've got some social worky shit going on, just tell her and she'll get a hold of me right away. Same with the doc. Same with the chaplain."

"Fuck a chaplain," he said.

Herb gazed down at his tabletop, his cigarette hand trembling noticeably. "Herb," I said, "this is a highly unusual way to get to know someone. I get the feeling that you don't let a lot of people into your life. But we kind of have to forgo the usual vetting processes and general paranoia. You're going to have to try and trust me. And trust Becky." Herb wouldn't look up. "Are you in pain right now?"

"Some," he said. Some meaning a lot.

"Becky left you with a box, right? The comfort pack?"

"Yeah."

"Have you gotten into it yet?"

"No."

"Where is it? I think we should explore its contents."

"It's in the fridge. Why did she tell me to keep it in the fridge?"

"It's so you don't just leave it in random places and lose track of it. Plus, if a junkie tries to break in and steal your stash, they usually won't look in the fridge."

Herb looked up at me. "Is that a thing?"

"It's a problem, Herb. Folks with opioid addictions have figured out when hospice is coming around and they'll walk right into a house and take the comfort pack. The hospice patients don't usually put up much of a fight."

"Nobody's breaking into this house. And if they do they're going out feet first," Herb said. "I'm righthanded, which is my gun hand, and my gun hand is still good."

"I believe you," I said as I got up and went to the refrigerator. In the fridge was a case of Bud Light on the bottom shelf and the comfort pack on the top. The innards of the fridge were as immaculately clean as they were nearly empty. "Bud and morphine," I said, "they're not just for breakfast anymore."

I brought the white plastic box over to the table. The box looked like the sort of first aid kit any contractor would have stashed behind the seat of his truck, only instead of bandages, tourniquet, and antibiotic ointment it held benzos, opioids, scopolamine, and stool softener. "You haven't even opened this yet."

"No. I've been trying to hold off," Herb said.

"I don't really understand why they want to install the pump. Usually that's for pain that the oral Roxanol can't handle."

"What's Roxanol?" Herb asked.

"Morphine."

"Oh. The nurse said that the putting in the pump is pre-emptive. I guess my special melanoma, once it gets into the bones, is renowned for pain."

I myself was crash coursing on various physical symptoms of terminal diseases such as COPD, Alzheimer's, and all sorts of cancer varieties. I learned that a pancreatic cancer was a very quick end; lung cancer symptoms were much like COPD and ugly; colorectal devastating with hardly believable physical side effects; prostate was slow and not necessarily fatal but sometimes; and now I knew that melanoma was off-the-charts painful and sometimes gruesome in presentation.

Later in my career, long after Herb was in the ground, I went on a visit with another nurse and helped her bandage a woman's melanoma tumors that were growing like veiny crabapples on the *outside* of her chest. Kinda fascinating. Kinda gross.

By the end of my five-year hospice run, I could pretty much ballpark how much time an individual had left to live based on what variety of cancer they had and how long they'd had it or by their physical appearance, mental attitude, food and water intake or sleep patterns. If someone was sleeping twenty-two out of twenty-four hours . . . nearly done with the living part of things.

Sometimes I'd enter into someone's house for the first time, meet the family, and then be escorted into the patient's bedroom and think, oops, this person is already nine-tenths gone. Every now and then we'd be fooled and think someone had a week or two remaining and by that afternoon they'd sneak away.

But for the most part it was not hard to predict when a body was coming down the home stretch. Herb had weeks or months to live, but things were changing and he knew it.

The patients get educated to their own illnesses by hospice nurses as their own oncologists will oftentimes simply drop patients once it is clear that their cancers cannot be arrested. Cancer docs seem to have disdain not only for the disease but also for anyone who dares succumb.

We make it clear to patients and families that pain can usually be managed. It's amazing how many people believe that their first taste of morphine signals the imminent end and will therefore avoid taking any or even talking about taking any. Some families believe we are actually trying to speed the dying process with morphine—actively trying to kill the patient. We are not.

"I'm assuming," Herb said, "that once I start taking these pain meds that I won't be coming off them." He was right. Whatever time remained would be in the foggy company of sweet sister morphine or brother fentanyl or cousin ketamine. Whatever cognitive baseline Herb had at this moment would end forever after the first big dose went down.

I took the bottle from the comfort pack and peeled the cellophane collar from the screw cap. I held the bottle up and raised my eyebrows at Herb as if offering another dripping cold beer from the cooler after a hot July work day. Herb blew a breath from puffed-out cheeks, pursed his lips, and tried to move his left arm within its sling. Herb gasped and winced. When the pain rush subsided, he nodded. The next level of dying was upon him. It was unavoidable.

I squeezed the dropper bulb and drew the normal fifteen milligrams of cerulean, raspberry-flavored Roxanol into the dropper. Then I squeezed a bit more because I knew Herb needed it. Technically, I wasn't supposed to be administering any sort of medication to anyone because I was not even remotely qualified to do so, but seeing as how Herb's face was as white as his beard and he'd hardly spoken because his lips were clenched with pain, I figured screw it. If this breach of protocol and law were ever questioned I would simply deny. It would be my word against a pain-addled former drunkard and dying guy. Plus, I didn't think Herb would rat me out. Now, were I to administer the meds to Herb and then take an additional pull for myself, then we'd be entering into a truly ethical gray area.

I reached the dropper across the table and rather than take it in his shaking hand, he, like a baby bird, like a baby human, leaned a bit toward my drug hand and opened wide. I resisted making a noise with my lips like an airplane coming into a hangar while my heart rose to my throat.

Two minutes later, after sitting in silence, Herb said, "It's changing. It still hurts like a fucker, but it's different." I nodded. Herb let out a long, long breath, as if he'd been holding it for days. "I haven't been able to lie down for four days. I've been sleeping in my recliner. Sleeping. Right. If I get an hour at a time it's a miracle."

"Is it the shoulder that won't let you lie down?" I asked.

"That and I'm half afraid that if I lie down I'll never get back up. OK, more than half afraid."

I nodded again.

"Mostly, I pace," he said. "It's fucking unsettling. It's almost like I'm a ghost in my own house, haunting myself. And I'm not even fucking dead yet. Am I?" This may have been the morphine talking, but probably not.

"No," I said, "you're not dead yet."

Herb lit a new cigarette off the fire of the last one. His hand was steady now. "You're going to think I'm crazy." Herb was having trouble keeping eye contact. He'd look at me and then quickly drop his eyes to the tabletop and his notebook. "It's like there's two of me. And we're engaged in some sort of crosstalk between conversation and argument. And I can't tell which is which."

"Do you mean which is conversation and which is argument?"

"No. No! Try to keep up, social worker. I can't tell which of the two Herbs is me. I can't tell if one is alive Herb and one is dead Herb. Or both dead. Or both alive. Or neither. I don't know. Am I asleep and dreaming? If so, I'm sleepwalking because when things straighten out I'm standing in the middle of the living room. Yeah. Unsettling. Jesus. It's like I'm slugging it out with myself all night long." Herb was now peering intently at me through the smoke, seeing if I might look away or show some sign that he was indeed off his rocker. "Have you ever heard of such a thing?" he asked.

I made sure to look straight at him. "Yeah," I said, "Yes I have." But this did not seem like the time to tell a dying man about my own nocturnal existential debates regarding to be or not to be. Not the time to tell him about the impossibly vivid dreams of my daughters, or the appearances of Kat the elusive artist of my fantasies that were neither argument nor conversation but pure hallucination. Instead, I asked him how he'd come to lose the fingers on his left hand.

"Long story," he said and then paused before adding, "Long story? Get it? It's a joke."

I said, "Good one."

"Ultimately it doesn't matter how it happened or who screwed up, even though it certainly wasn't me. My fingers though, my fault."

And then the entryway door burst open and I saw Herb nearly come out of his seat and then moan in pain. I turned all the way around and saw a man in the doorway: work clothes, big man, muddy boots. bearded, raw red hands, beer smell from ten feet away and bloodshot eyes. He stood there looking up at us. "For fuck's sake, ever heard of a doorbell?" Herb said, eyes watering from the adrenaline and pain.

"Door was wide open," the man said as he made his way up the three steps to kitchen level. He was staring at Herb to the point that I don't believe he even noticed I was in the room. He walked across the kitchen floor and went straight to Herb's side. "How you doin', old man?"

"The prodigal son returns," Herb said, grinning. "The drunken cavalry."

* * *

Days later, Herb left a message on my hospice voicemail.

Mr. Jensen, the message said, *this is Herbie. I would appreciate a house call at your convenience. This might be considered an emergency.* His voice on the machine sounded strange, high pitched and pinched.

I called him immediately. He did not pick up. I left a voice message telling him I'd be at his house in fifteen minutes. I was spooked as Herb would most likely not use the word emergency as a trifle.

When I arrived, Herb was not at the kitchen table and did not respond to my quiet knocking on the breezeway door. I checked the door and it was unlocked. I remembered what he'd said about his gun hand still being functional and when I stuck my head inside the door I said, "Herb? Herb, it's Holmes. Herb, it's Holmes, don't shoot me."

It was dead silent inside. There was a weird energy here. The energy of transition. It is a palpable electricity. Some can feel it. Most can't. I feared the worst. No. Death is not the worst. I feared I would not be speaking with Herb anymore.

"Herb?" I stepped inside and noticed there was no active smoke in the air. The place still smelled like an AA meeting, but the skies were clear.

I called for Herb, not too loudly, and still no answer. I'd only ventured beyond his kitchen once in these past two months, when Herb had given me the cook's tour to point out his eclectic treasured artifacts that he was terrified would end up in a yard sale. The musket. The chess pieces.

I poked my head into the living room and was greatly relieved to see Herb sitting, asleep, on his sofa, pillows propping him up, mouth open a bit and a low snore emanating.

He was wearing his Harley hat, which was slightly crooked and at this moment he looked fifteen years old, if a fifteen-year-old could grow a full white beard. He, at this moment, looked more like a mid-career Van Morrison than an old Hemingway. He looked peaceful. He looked beautiful.

I decided to sit with him for a few minutes but not wake him up. I was in no hurry to get to my next appointment . . . a young and former meth addict, former basketball player dying of COPD. We discovered we had some hoop acquaintances in common. Soon he would be simply former. The young guy's family was large and supportive and raging drunk at all hours of the day and yelling while Former tried to sleep . . . tried to die. It wasn't my favorite stop.

In less than five minutes, the snoring stopped and I looked over at Herb, who was staring at me with an expression I'd not seen on his face before or anyone's. His entire face was clenched except his eyes, which nearly bugged out of his skull with what looked like pure mind-bedlam panic.

His voice, when he spoke, was as least an octave higher than normal and loud and cracked. "Have we spoken yet?" My first reaction when faced with an open question such as this is to go for the joke, but not this time.

"No. I just got here."

He barely let me finish before yelling at me, "We've got a problem, Holmes! We've got a problem," and I saw the tears rolling down his cheeks, from both eyes, and into his beard.

"Herb! Herbie! What's going on, Herb?" I didn't know what the problem was yet, but he was on the verge of hysteria or collapse and he needed help grounding, needed to hear his name to let him know he was with a familiar and safe entity.

"Oh God," he moaned, loudly. "It's fucking killing me." I could see that either he could not move or was afraid to. It became clear to me now that Herb was at a cataclysmic level of pain.

"All right," I stood and pulled my phone and hit the number for Nurse Becky, his case manager, while moving closer to Herb and asking, "When's the last time you took your Roxanol? Where is it?" Herb was panting now, the whites of his eyes nearly maroon, which I hadn't noticed initially and somewhat freaked me out. I thought maybe he'd popped an aneurysm. I didn't know what the fuck, only that it was pretty much solely up to me to help my friend.

"I don't know when," Herb said. "But it doesn't help. Fuck, Holmes . . ." I thought I could hear his teeth crack as he ground down. I scanned his end table and the plastic bottle was sitting there, half empty, next to his cigarette pack, empty. I suctioned up a regular dose into the dropper and then kept squeezing until it was topped. I put the tip to Herb's lips and he opened his mouth wide like a baby bird. Like a baby for the bottle. I hoped the dose wouldn't kill him. I hoped it would. After he swallowed I looked for the bolus plunger for his CADD pump, found it stuck between the sofa cushions, and hit it. The pump made a little beep indicating that the morphine hit had been administered. The machine would not allow another hit for thirty minutes.

Nurse Becky called me back within a minute. If I have not mentioned my love and admiration for the overall competency of the hospice nurse: I informed her, as calmly as I could, that Herb was having a pain crisis, serious, and how soon could she get here. "I'm in Raymond," she said, which was halfway up Sebago Lake, "it'll be a half hour at least."

"Can you talk me through this?" I wasn't technically supposed to be administering any sort of medical aid, not only because it is illegal but also because I had no idea what I was doing. I was not aware of the urgency in my voice.

Herb said, through his teeth, "Holmes, calm the fuck down."

"*I am calm!*" Herb grinned, a little, I think.

"How many doses of Roxanol does he have left? I dropped off a new bottle yesterday."

I looked at the bottle in my hand. It was now less than half full. "About eight."

"OK, don't be afraid to give him a dose every five minutes. There should be enough until I get there. Do you think he needs to go to Gosnell?"

I hadn't even thought of that. It was becoming evident that I was not particularly graceful under pressure. "Absolutely," I said.

"I'm not going to Gosnell," Herb said.

"You can hear this?" I said.

"You're the deaf one, not me," he said. "I'm not going."

"We can have you there inside the hour, Herb, and get on top of this shit."

"You *are* deaf, aren't you? I'm not going."

Nurse Becky heard this exchange. "When I get there I can adjust the pump to give a bigger dose and a bigger bolus," she said. I could hear that she was already in her car and balling the jack. "Do your best, Holmes."

"Christ," I said.

"You're a comfort," Herb said.

"Sorry, man."

Herb looked at me. "No. I'm sorry. You're good. I'm glad you're here. This is really bad. Really bad."

I hit him with another double dose. And then in two minutes, another. I sat next to him on the sofa and recognized this as an amazingly intimate thing. Herb needing someone, me. And me so desperately hoping to help. Hoping my presence was some sort of comfort. Not knowing. Not knowing where his mind could possibly be right now.

After the fourth dose, Herb's face began to relax, just a little. I tried the bolus and it went through. "It's different," Herb said. "It's no better, but it's different. I'll fucking take it."

In fifteen minutes I was down to the final drops of hope and had no real plan B. I hit the bolus and it denied, not enough time having passed. Just then Nurse Becky hustled through the door after one polite knock. I looked at my watch. "Holy fuck," I said.

Her eyes were locked on Herb. "I know," she said. "I averaged ninety-three miles an hour on Route fucking 302. Both of you assholes owe me a drink." I grinned. Herb grinned, kind of. "Now!" she said. I stood up to go fetch Becky a beer. She shook her head. "I was kidding, Holmes. Nervous much?"

"This might be a good time to tell you that overall, you frighten me, Becky. Always have."

"Good." Nurse Becky took Herb's pulse, which was well into the tachycardic, and his blood pressure which was 275/195. He was in danger of exploding, basically. She stuffed her cuff into her bag of tricks and went to work on recalibrating the CADD pump. She nodded to her bag and said there were new bottles of Roxanol in there and go ahead. She then got on her phone with our medical director reading off vitals and particulars regarding Herbie. "Pain, Herbie, from one to ten?"

"Twenty-three," he said. "Down from a high of thirty-five."

"Impressive," Becky said and repeated this into the phone and raised her eyebrows at the guidance she received. She hung up and started pushing buttons on the pump with accompanying beeps and boops that reminded me of a pinball machine. She plungered the bolus button and Herb, essentially, unrolled like a skate tangled in a gill net after getting whacked in the skull with the fisherman's blackjack designed for this exact occurrence.

"Whew!" Herb said. "Damn."

"Right?" Nurse Becky said. She looked at me and said, "Another satisfied customer."

Just then a pickup truck rolled up to the ironweed snowbank outside the picture window of Herb's house. Right behind, a minivan. Out of the truck stepped the Son and Younger Daughter. From the van came Elder Daughter with Grandchildren.

Herb smiled as he watched his children and his grands through his living room window. "Company," Herb said, "is why I can't go to Gosnell. I'll go on Wednesday, I promise. But right now, I have company."

Becky nodded. "It's your call. I'll give your people instructions on overnight pain management. Your pump is topped off and I'll leave enough Roxanol in the fridge to sedate the neighborhood." I helped Nurse Becky pack up and clean up. Herb tried once to get up to greet his kids as they came into the kitchen. Failed.

"Help me, Holmes, please," he whispered, raspy and desperate. I looked at Nurse Becky and she nodded. I hooked my palm under his good armpit and cringing, both of us, helped Herb to his feet just as Elder, Younger, and Son entered the living room in their stocking feet. The grands were well behaved enough to hold back in the kitchen. It hadn't occurred to me that Herb's was a no-shoes household, but it made sense given his reputation for running an immaculate, if drunk, worksite back in his day.

All Herb wanted was to be standing when his kids came in. He introduced Nurse Becky all around, his voice steady, me still acting as an outrigger or a training wheel. Becky said we'd be out of their hair in a sec, but could she go over a couple of things? She told the family, calmly, that Herb had just had a blip on the pain scale and there were new instructions on pain management. "Are any of you going to stay the night?" she asked. All three nodded.

"Good," she said.

"Sit, sit," Herb said to one and all, mostly wanting to get off his own shaky feet. With her tutorial complete, Nurse Becky and I left the house.

Out in the street, Nurse Becky whispered to me, "I've never administered that much morphine to anyone. Not even a field amputee." Looking at her blankly, or maybe with a hint of question and horror, she explained, "a field amputation is when a limb is severed by a bomb. That's what we called it."

"Who called it?"

"Medics."

"You were a medic?"

"Navy. Two tours of Afghanistan."

"The Navy? In Afghanistan?"

"Navy medics and the Marines travel together."

"I did not know this." I let that fact roll around in my benumbed skull. I was not used to this sort of medical action. All I could think of to say was, "Herb is one tough bitch."

"He is," Becky agreed. "He's transitioning. Herb is actively dying."

"Aren't we all?" I asked.

* * *

Herb didn't make it through the planned two-day visit by his family. That first night he must have come face-to-face with himself at 3 a.m. and he had Son call our ambulance service, which took him to Gosnell. When I got there at 7 a.m., Elder Daughter and Son were sitting quietly in chairs pulled up to Herb's bed. The grandchildren were back home with Elder's husband. Herb was lying down, sleeping. He was linked to an IV that must have been dripping something good and strong into Herb's good arm. He was snoring lightly, as he'd been when I walked in on him the day before.

Elder and Son smiled at me and nodded. I pulled a chair up and sat. "I can't believe he's lying down. He looks comfortable," I said.

"Ketamine," Son said.

"That'll do it," I said.

The snoring came to a stuttering halt and we all looked at Herb. His eyes popped open and he scanned our faces with clear eyes. I like to think that he nodded at me. "Where's Younger?" he whispered.

"She had to go home," Elder said.

Herb looked at his daughter and then his son. "I miss her," he said. He died within the hour.

There was something going on in this room. Something incredibly moving and important. Yes, Herb was dying and dying very soon. There is an energy to this process, which I've mentioned, that is palpable. But more than that. In addition to that, this family was together, which is an energy unto itself. After decades of warfare and silence and offense and defense, this family was together. A difficult father with his difficult children coalescing at this most and last critical moment. I was so very proud of them. I pictured myself as the difficult father. I pictured my difficult daughters.

* * *

Herb's funeral afterparty was a sodden affair with a driving February winter rain bouncing off the frozen snow.

There were rough-looking men come up from Providence, and at least four of them named Vinnie hanging out in the unheated garage drinking cold beer in the early afternoon. There were dozens of Herb's neighbors along with former clients who spoke reverently about Herb's work ethic and fairness. Ahead of schedule and under budget, they all agreed.

Herb's grandchildren had taped crayon portraits they'd made to Herb's fridge of a man they'd mostly only heard about. I tried to be discreet as I peeled the DNR notice from the freezer door. I saw a woman standing alone in the living room. She was early middle aged and very pretty. She held a glass of wine and a photograph. I introduced myself and she told me she was Younger Daughter's mom. I should have guessed. We chatted a bit and I asked her about the photograph. She handed it over and it was an image of her and a much younger Herb, arms around each other's shoulder, smiling. As I looked at it, trying to imagine this man happy, she said, also looking at him, "My god, he was beautiful." I handed the photo back to her and nodded. "Yup," I said.

I slid out of the house knowing I would never be in contact with this family again. My ride home to the farm was the most hopeful I'd felt in many months. Herb had died with his children present and accounted for. Lucky guy.

HOLMES

The hallucinations were becoming too vivid to ignore. They were, perhaps, a variation of Herbie's nocturnal boxing matches with *self*. Sometimes the hallucinations would materialize while in the middle of a chore: changing the oil in the truck, winterizing the lawn mower, washing windows . . . and he, Holmes, would find himself standing with filter wrench in hand, staring out into nothing, no idea how much time had passed while the ghost scene played out in his mind. Other times he would be in Serious Easy Chair and the story from the novel he was reading would melt into his own dream and he would come to, look at the clock on the wall, see that forty-five minutes had passed and his face wet with tears.

It was getting bad.

KAT

Be strong, *you wrote on a Post-it note,* **Be strong, I will help you.**

Saturdays were a clockwork of scheduling filled with the chaos and curveballs that only twin toddlers could introduce into life's equation. Bette arrived each Saturday morning at precisely 9 a.m. and would stay until precisely 11 a.m., no ifs ands or buts. I would have enough pancake batter left over and blueberries to make her a stack of three, which she accepted along with coffee. The girls, from their room, would hear the commotion of conversation between my mother and me and run down the hallway to come say hello. Bette would greet them with her brittle notion of a hug and ask how their week was. The girls would jabber about what went on at their mom's house and watch as my mother self-consciously ate her late breakfast. By nine, the girls and I were almost ready for lunch.

Bette's arrival allowed me to go for a run, shower, and then transport trash to the transfer station. I could have made the dump run on any day, but the few minutes of liberation from tiny demands were welcome. The interesting part about this parenting arrangement was going from full-time part-time parenting to empty-time part-time parenting when they were with their mom. It was flood or drought, feast or famine, lonely or overloaded.

Friday nights were a carousel of nocturnal shenanigans. First one little girl would wake from her slumber anywhere between 9 p.m. and midnight to come padding down the hallway in footies to my room and asking into Big Blue the Bed. I would reach down and pull the baby in and curl up for a few minutes sleep before the other little girl would appear, eyes barely above mattress height and wanting in. When both would settle in and return to the Land of Nod, I would carry them one at time back to their room and tuck them back into their shared bed. After two or three cycles of these visits, I would give up and sleep on the floor of their room on a thin futon I kept rolled up there for this exact *eventuality. My presence there on the floor allowed the girls to sleep through what remained of the night. I did not care about what parenting books proposed to guide a child toward independent sleeping. I assumed they would eventually figure it out, and they did. By 5 a.m. when they were up for good, they were completely rested and energized while I awoke wasted and wounded. For a while I tried playing CDs of ambient music, Brian Eno and Pachelbel and Bach for Bedtime, and it worked for a while until Mae asked me to stop. "This music makes me sad," she said.*

Winter weekends were long, especially when twins were larval. Hours stacked upon hours of not taking eyes off rolling, twisting, crawling, toddling and them not taking eyes off Dad. Reading stacks of books aloud, some written expressly for them (Hungry Caterpillar, Good Night Moon, Clams All Year, Go Dog Go, Madeleine) *and some I snuck in to see if they'd notice* (Old Man and the Sea, A Wrinkle in Time)*, and them rapt and close and unaware of the topical switcheroo as we huddled under blankets upon sofa. They would reach up and touch my ear or my chin or hair while I read.*

Feedings started with bottles of course and moved on up to jarred, mashed veggies to pancakes and cheese omelets with the letters "M" and "B" in American cheese melted on top, to chicken nuggets and pools of sugary ketchup. Frozen pizza, homemade chili. Baked fresh flounder over brown rice au gratin and yogurt in a tube, applesauce. Broccoli, they loved them some broccoli. And thank God naps for all three of us, sometimes two hours and sometimes two minutes. Days of all routine and days all askew. One never knew.

Winter outdoors wading into and over drifts after forty-five minutes spent girding up with long johns and sweatshirts and snow bibs, coats, hats, gloves. Sometimes, upon setting foot outside, one flew east, straight for the ocean at a trot while the other flew west, back inside to blankie, not into nature this day and Dad standing watching not knowing who to corral because you can't just let 'em go it alone, not yet. One child would have to be miserable on this day being dragged back outside or back inside. If dad retrieved the inside kid and brought her outside, she would stand stock still up to her knees in snow, weeping until play time for the other was deemed over by daddy, at which time that child would weep at having her snow time cut short. Sometimes dad was patient with the politesse required to navigate these diametric desires and sometimes not.

All routine and all askew. One never knew.

Winter movies at the malls as the girls got a bit older. The hilarious first failed attempt when the previews played loud, explosive and long, and Mae hollering in excitement over the dialogue between cartoon fishes or dinosaurs or bugs, "Is this the movie?" and the other parents laughed out loud at the misunderstanding. The twins had had enough of this stimulation before the feature even came on and we were forced to bail due to the involuntary fidgets and fussing but later, within a year, them loving these movie matinees and looking forward to each and every new release by Disney and Pixar that came out bang bang due to desperately waiting parental dollars, not one title could I name now and every one where I fell asleep between my two beauties with Mae resting her head on my left arm and Bea resting hers on my right while I dreamed whatever dreams were in my head on those wintery matinee afternoons.

Later still, I bought a hot tub on credit and installed it in the doorway of the Serious Barn. We would make made dashes during Nor'easters from house to barn wearing bathrobes and barefoot through snowdrifts and horizontal blow knowing 100-degree bubbling waters awaited only thirty yards distant. After warming, and then becoming overheated, the girls would rampage, naked, out into the snow for a roll around white wash, giggling, screaming and then run back to the tub and plunge, headfirst, back into the bubbles. I sat stoic, smiles, snow swirling around my head, submerged to my nose like an alligator in a swamp keeping an eye upon his young. We had a little boombox with CD capacity and played "Moondance" and "Blitzkrieg

Bop" and Ry Cooder and sometimes Mahler to calm things down and sometimes War Pigs for a laugh and The Chieftains to Irish things up and sometimes Parliament to funk things down. We'd spend hours until the waters cooled and our skins pruned. Naps followed tub time as somehow the warm water to cold outside to back into warm house had narcotic effects.

Kat, when spring arrived, or even hinted, it was three winter convicts freed and nature became the best babysitter with so many options for activity. In the back field I mowed a long and serpentine oval at least a quarter mile long and we called it the Magic Path to make it more alluring. It wound in and out of a stand of pine trees and had wild field flowers within picking reach of the trail. By deep summer, the mowed grass of the path was soft and thick, protected from sunburn by the two-foot tall wall of grasses on each side. I would have them run the path and demand a bouquet of flowers upon return, which they would provide with alacrity. This would occupy them for thirty minutes while I sipped coffee or wine, depending not so much on the time of day but more so on how the day was going.

We learned the fundamentals of softball, first to throw and catch with mitt and swing little bats, followed by running bases consistently counterclockwise rather than wherever the spirit moved, to advanced concepts of double plays and infield fly rules. They could not get enough of playing pickle. They learned to pitch and later in a league, Bea underhurled her kid team to a playoff win over an undefeated and over-confident team coached by one of those cartoon intense parents who didn't think twice about getting into an Earl Weaver dirt-kicking disagreement with the poor overmatched volunteer umpire whose father never taught him the infield fly rule. It was exhausting work, those Thursday to Sunday weekends, Kat, and we would compare notes, you and me, single parenting notes, me with my two and you with your four.

Driving back to Portsmouth on Sunday morning in the Silverado I felt relief and heartache, missing my girls before they were gone and amazed I'd kept them alive for the duration. In the truck, playing their favorite on the stereo, the Jackson Five, "I Want You Back," they could harmonize, effortlessly, on the money, in key, with one another, switching back and forth from one taking the high and the other the low part, which occasionally led to arguments over timing but most times was savant. Me, driving and smiling. We swapped the lyrics of "I'll Be There" to "Elbow There" and when Michael Jackson came to the chorus, the girls would elbow me and each other, usually too hard, in the ribs. "Elbow There." Get it? We changed Ramones lyrics from "Rockaway Beach" to "Broccoli Beach." James Brown swapped out waking up in a cold sweat to waking up in a cold snit because sometimes after naps the girls would. We camped out back in the Serious Yard and then later we'd travel to Western Massachusetts and the New York Adirondacks for real campground camping and fishing. As the summer sun went down on our trips I would build up a fire and the girls would build s'mores with burnt marshmallow, chocolate squares and fresh raspberry and soon excuse themselves to put themselves to sleeping bag bed at their regular 9 p.m. sleepy time. In the morning, they would fish with five-dollar fishing rods. I did not fish, but I was designated hook baiter and releaser of little fishes pulled from the waters, the sunfishes or the mini basses or whatever finger fish were biting on summer mornings. The girls came to weekend gigs and helped the band set up, making relentless fun of the boys and especially Little Carrot, whom they inherently understood took himself way too seriously. On summer weekends they would stay at the venue until nine, when Grammy Bette would come and pick them up to take them back to her place. I would stagger into my mom's house post midnight and sleep on the floor next to the bed where the girls snored peaceful and secure.

We had a thing, my girls, my mom and me.

We had a thing, Kat, I thought was impenetrable. And then it became penetrable.

Be strong, you wrote on a post-it note, in your artist's hand, **Be strong, I will help you.**

Holy God I loved you.

LEE CLAIRE

After Saul called, I stood in the upstairs kitchen looking out across Serious Backyard Dawn and Serious Field. The coffee tasted like reflux. That was new. I'd not seen or spoken with Mae or Bea for weeks and I could feel myself beginning, or continuing, to deaden. To unspool. It felt supremely unnatural to have no contact with my offspring. The primal in me wanted to protect them at all times, to monitor their well-being. It was difficult to feed the primal with lack of proximity to the offspring.

I called in sick to hospice, called in pre-dawn to be certain I could leave my lie on a voicemail recording rather than lie to an actual human.

I knew I needed to get rolling on Saul's project right now. I was slipping badly. I needed to get outdoors to freeze and ache and feel. To feel something besides what I was feeling, which was nothing.

I waited until 8 a.m. and then I called Lee Claire. "Hey," I said.

"Holmes," he said, "the early riser. What's up?"

"What have you got going for work just now?" Lee Claire had just completed his MFA at Bard College. He was the most gifted musician I'd ever known. He played saxophone like the white reincarnation or the white son of John Coltrane. He showed the best bass players in town how to play bass better. Trumpet, guitar, marimba, piano, motherfucker. French fucking horn.

He was a sound artist, if that is what it's called, making weirdo installations here and there at some of the more liberal galleries in the area. I'd talked him into playing drums in Little Carrot's hideous musical effort called Clown. Drums were Lee Claire's eleventh most accomplished instrument, but he played for us as though his life depended on it. Perhaps his life did. I also used him as a laborer from time to time for Serious Stonework. Lee Claire was blond and artist-skinny, but strong enough for stonework.

"I'm dishwashing in Kittery."

"Sounds great," I said. "I've got a project. Thirty bucks an hour. You in?"

"Thirty? That's a significant improvement upon my present financial situation. I'm in. When?"

"Soon. Like. Soon. This weekend? Maybe today?"

"I'm in," he said. "What day is today?"

"Is it Friday?" I asked.

"Could be," he said.

"Let's get coffee and I'll give you all the details. This is a good one."

"Cool," he said. "Where? When?"

"Caffe Kilim? In an hour?" I was feeling more stable already.

RALPHIE BOY

Then I called Ralphie Boy. He picked up immediately. "Holmes away from Holmes," he said. He always answered my calls this way. I liked it.

"Ralphie Boy."

Ralph had worked with me, for me, off and on for over twenty years. Mostly on. He was a talented stonemason, probably better than me, but he had issues. The two biggest issues were alcohol and depression. Or depression and alcohol. It was a chicken or egg situation. His dependability fluctuated depending upon his symptoms. His third biggest issue was a hatred for the monied class we worked for and was our bread and our butter. It was a dilemma. The poor people, our people, could not afford us. Hell, I couldn't afford us.

I loved Ralphie as much as or more than a brother. I also fired him multiple times over the years. When his depression hit, he would medicate with scotch and become deeply unreliable until his depression subsided. He refused to get any sort of help and he was useless to me as a worker during these phases. So I would let him go and wait until he pulled out of it and we'd carry on. I didn't know how to help him, plus I had my own shit to deal with.

Ralphie was aware of the ongoing flirtation with this Great Wall of Saul. We'd talked about it, planned it, salivated over it. It was to be our dream job: dry-laid fieldstone, double-faced with entrance and end pillars, four hundred lineal feet total. Sigh.

I would use Ralphie for the stonework only. Lee Claire and I would handle the brush clearing and the rudimentaries such as breaking down the existing wall, footing digging, material gathering, all planning and estimating.

It was best to let Ralphie focus on stone. He had defined notions of what was beneath him and brush clearing would be one. Plus, he was almost always busy with other work. Since I'd gone off to grad school, Ralphie had built several spec houses as well as updating his underwater construction work resumé. He was a licensed diver in addition to having a strong handle on nearly all the building trades: roofing, plumbing, electric, foundation work. He was probably the most competent human I knew when he wasn't drinking and depressed or depressed and drinking.

"To what do I owe this?" he asked.

"It would seem the Saul Wall has been greenlighted. Greenlit."

"Seriously?"

"Yessir."

"You do realize it's February."

"I do. He's got some extemporaneous shit for me to do before we start on the wall. I'll try to deal with that for however long this break in the weather lasts. And then it's wall ball."

"I thought you were a shrink now."

"Yeah. I'm going to have to do some job juggling."

"What is the pay scale these days for stonework, same as before?" I was a notorious overpayer. The other stonemasonry concerns in the area disliked me for it, but they were not my concern.

"Same plus ten," I said. "I'm feeling magnanimous."

"There's a first time for everything. Anybody else on the crew? Old Black?"

"No, Old Black is working full time for the laborers' union now. It's you, me, and Lee Claire."

"Nice," Ralphie said. "Let me know when you're within a week or two of starting and I'll make arrangements."

"I will certainly do that," I said.

"Thank you, Holmes. Kiss the babies," Ralphie said.

Since the day Mae and Bea were born, Ralphie ended each of our conversations with, "Thank you, Holmes," and then, "Kiss the babies." This time he said it, it buckled my knees. Right there in the kitchen. I think it was with gratitude.

LEE CLAIRE

We rented a wood chipper the size of an Abrams tank, the size of a studio apartment. It was the only chipper the rental place had on hand. The rental guy said they could deliver it right away and did we need a quick tutorial. We said, nah, we're good. The rental guy asked, you've used one of these before? We said, plenty.

We'd never laid eyes upon such a beast. I have no idea why we lied about it. A guy thing, I suppose.

The maw of this thing was a four-foot by four-foot square and the roller teeth we were to feed the brush and larger limbs and trunks into were ominous and awesome. The business hole of the chipper was comprised of two horizontally installed rollers with steel pyramid teeth welded on. Hydraulics allowed the rollers to open or close automatically around the size of the material being fed in like a shark eating either a harbor seal or an eel. When the rental company guys dropped it off at Saul's, me and Lee Claire just stood there looking at it, holding the hardhats with face shields that came along with it, and we laughed and laughed. What could possibly go wrong?

Then we got to work chainsawing brush and pine trees. The smell of organic tree material in February was delicious. I felt good.

The ground was soggy but not too bad because Saul's property sat upon a massive vein of ledge granite that diverted meltwater downhill to a small stream at the property line that then funneled it away to the Atlantic, which was only a mile to the east.

I wore shin-high fisherman boots and Lee Claire wore some galoshes he'd found somewhere, the old over-the-shoe affairs with buckles up the front.

We had the chipper for three days. The plan was to cut what we needed to cut on the first two days, make brush piles, and then liquidate those piles on the last day. But after an hour of lopping brush, our curiosity got the better of us and we had to see what sort of effect this looming monster had on tree matter.

First, we figured out how to start it, which was way too easy for a killing machine such as this. There was a simple toggle switch indicating OFF or ON and next to that a big-ass red push button labeled START. A four-year-old could figure it out. I tried not to think of a four-year-old falling into the maw but it was impossible.

The roller teeth came to life rolling, more smooth and more quiet than expected, emitting an ominous hum. I went to the nearest brush pile and grabbed a pine limb maybe two inches in diameter. I stood at the mouth and looked to Lee. He was by far the more mechanically inclined between the two of us. He motioned for me to put on my hardhat and earmuff hearing protection things, which I did. I fed the limb into the maw and with a barely audible *whuff* it turned the limb into a light mint-colored mist that puffed out of the exit funnel and rained softly to the ground.

Lee Claire's face registered awe, glee, and some kind of strange hunger. He went and grabbed a much larger limb that was maybe six inches in girth and fed it. I found myself backing away from the beast.

The sound of the limb being misted was undeniably musical. It lasted only a moment, this note, this chord, and was followed by a cloud of pine chips and the smell of car freshener. Lee's face crinkled into laughter and he shut the machine down by punching the red START button. I pulled the muffs from my head. "*Sweet Jesus!*" Lee hollered, his voice echoing now that the beast was quiet. "*This is going to be amazing!!*"

I was not about to stand there and argue with him. I was somehow elated that this gentle jazz musician had a primal core. This *was* going to be amazing. Grinning, I looked up toward the Eagle's Nest, the third-story window where I knew Saul's writing office was. Sure enough, he was up there watching. He gave a thumbs up and then disappeared behind a curtain.

"Here's what we have to do," Lee Claire said. "We have to cut everything to a different series of lengths and see what notes we can get out of them."

"You heard that too?" I said.

"Of course."

"That was an A, right?"

Lee gave me a quizzical look. "You heard A?"

"I think so. What did you hear?"

"I thought I heard a flat. How did you come up with an A?"

I thought about it for a second and told him, "I heard the opening chord for 'Won't Get Fooled Again.'"

Lee just looked at me. Then he said, "OK. I get that." This was a huge victory for me, to get Lee Claire to agree with me on anything musical. "So, tomorrow I'll bring my digital recorder and we get as many variations as possible. Then we can cut and paste them together later into a fucking opera, or whatever."

This is precisely why I'd called Lee Claire. Why we began this huge job in New Hampshire February. Here was inspiration. Here was Inspiration and Fun. Here was Inspiration and Fun and Hope.

"We have to give this monster a name," Lee Claire said.

"Grendel?"

"Grendel," Lee said, "yes."

"Did you see Saul up in the Eagle's Nest?" I asked.

"No," Lee Claire said. "Did he have his rifle?"

"He was unarmed," I said. "He looked pleased."

Cutting and clearing trees and brush is exhausting. But we hit it. We established a nice rhythm to the sound of the chainsaw. Nine hours that first day working right into the early darkness and we thought we got the majority of the clearing accomplished. But at the end of the day, Saul came out to survey. He decided he liked what he saw, but he wanted more. He wanted a dozen of the more mature pines to go.

The second day, the pines went. My arms felt like cooked pasta from day-long chainsaw vibration. My back screamed from being held in a cutting position for two straight days. I loved every minute.

After the second day of work, Lee Claire and I retired to the bar. I could barely lift the glass to my lips, my arms were so spent. But the more we lifted, the easier it became.

Lee told me about his latest installation: He'd recently gotten very deeply into recreational ping pong (as opposed to professional). He told me he was drawn to the sound of paddle upon ball. The more he played the deeper he fell into that sound.

His idea was to record multiple games of ping pong. He recorded dozens of games with all the stops and starts and variations of volume and speed of ball upon table upon paddle.

He asked the individuals playing the recorded games to be as nonverbal as possible. This turned out to be impossible, but when he played the recording back, Lee Claire decided he liked the grunts of effort and exclamations and trash talk of the participants.

He recorded forty or so games and then edited them onto a half dozen recordings to be played on a half dozen different playback systems—laptops and tape players. Lee altered some of the ping pong recordings a little bit, throwing a small amount of echo onto them, delaying or increasing or decreasing the volume, but just slightly from one minute to the next so that the listener may hear it or may not or may think there was wrong with themselves. He said the sound was simultaneously comforting and disorienting.

He then set up twenty-one speakers in the gallery, twenty-one being the number of points it takes to win a game of ping pong, and then played the recordings in a repeating loop. When an individual entered the gallery, he or she entered a room with six ping pong tables set up and ready to go with paddles and balls provided. The visitor was encouraged to play ping pong while listening to ping pong. Beer was served. There was the obligatory gallery cheese plate. There were chairs provided and blindfolds for folks who wished only to sit and listen or sit and listen in complete darkness.

I just nodded my head. "Where do you come up with this stuff?" I said.

Lee took a swallow of his drink, a big one, and said, "Ping pong. It's all right there."

On the third day, Lee Claire brought his tiny digital recorder and fashioned a padded box for it made from an empty twelve-pack cardboard and an old t-shirt from behind my truck seat that I used to check oil levels in the Silverado. He duct-taped the box to the fender of Grendel so that either of us could hit RECORD before feeding a limb into the teeth and then "off" when done. The padded box was to try and eliminate extraneous vibratory sounds. We wanted purity of notes. Purity of tree meat and metal.

In the first hour of the third day, we tried to string different notes together as an attempt to compose something like music there at the site, but it became clear we'd never finish the actual job we were being paid for at the rate we were going while composing and discussing musical moods. So we decided to simply record one of each different genre of limb and trunk material and then cobble something together at our leisure.

Over the first two days we had made upward of thirty separate piles of brush and limb over the two-acre area. By noon of the third day, we'd managed to drag and chip only ten piles. I told Lee we'd either have to pick up the pace or pay another day's rental on Grendel, four hundred bucks, which could otherwise be going directly into our pockets. "Then let's pick up the pace," he said, sweating hard in the February midday.

We hauled and liquefied the last piles in the illumination of the Silverado's headlights. We were dopey with fatigue but we got it done. The pile of mulchy woodchips we'd created was a small organic mountain six feet deep and twenty feet in diameter.

Afterward, we sat in the cab of the truck, filthy, blistered, pine-sapped, scratched and bleeding but alive and done. We shook hands because it felt like an accomplishment. Too tired to drink, I drove him into Portsmouth and dropped him at the Button Factory artist lofts where he had his illegal flop. We did not discuss what was next. We didn't discuss anything. The day was a Zen recipe of chop wood/carry water, too perfect to dissect.

HOLMES

The hallucinations.
    Are hallucinations just extra vivid memories?
    Can he touch a memory? Feel a memory's hand in his own. Smell a memory's hair? Fall asleep next to a memory?
    He did not know for sure but he did not think so.
    The hallucinations.

MAE

February, Serious Farm, 2:15 a.m., snowing:
    When being read to at bedtime, which was every bedtime, the girls would drift off quickly, sometimes not even a page deep into whatever book we were exploring. Seven times out of ten I would drift off for a bit, lying next to them in their shared bed,

their warmth and their rhythmic breathing lulling me under even on summer evenings at eight with light still in the sky. I would drift off for a half hour and then blink awake, happy, and gently peel a daughter's arm from my belly where she'd placed it while falling asleep.

On a rare occasion, Mae did not fall asleep before or at the same time as her sister. On this rare occasion, she would whisper to me about our plans for the coming weekend. Is Grammy coming tomorrow? Yes, she is. Are we going to the beach? Yes, we are. Are we going back to Mom's tomorrow or the next day? The next day.

One night, when Mae could not fall asleep, she began to cry, very quietly, tears running down her cheek. Sometimes I get scared, she said, and I don't know why. Me too, I said, wiping her tears. Really, Daddy? Yes, I said, sometimes. And then we fell asleep together holding hands.

BETTE

She was impossibly flat.

There was a bed, and a head, her tiny head, and proportionally enormous tubes coming out of her face, her mouth, her nose. There was no discernible outline of a body. Way down there at the end of the bed may have been the hint of some tenting, her feet. Bette was a six-footer and those feet tents were in the approximate correct distance from her head but there was nothing in between. I thought I saw my mother licking at the gigantic hose coming out of her gaping mouth.

"Where her torso at?" I asked Andy as we stood there looking down at our mother. The flatness frightened me. I had the urge to hold my brother's hand, but that would have been weird.

"Not here," he said.

"Storage?" I asked.
"Rapture?" he asked.
"Rapture?" I asked, "without head or feet?"
"I don't know," he said.

The ICU is an interesting setup. This one was configured like a wheel with the nurses' station being the hub and the partitioned cubicles where the patients lay in their beds the spokes. I think there were eight or so spokes and they were all full on this winter's day. The partitioned cubicles were filled to the gills with machines making breathing sounds along with cartoonish beepings and boopings. We stood there looking down.

"Hey. Andy." A voice filtered through the hospital noises, through the cloth curtain partitioning the cubicles. I looked at Andy.

"Did somebody just say your name?"

"You heard that too?"

"I did," I said, and pointed at my ears indicating my newish hearing aids.

"Over here. Andy." I could see by the look on his face that the last thing my brother wanted to deal with was anything at all. But Portsmouth is a small town and one never knows when one might hear one's name being called at the least opportune time or place.

Andy peeked around the curtain and made an effort at a smile. "Eddie," he said, and took the two steps into the next-door cubicle, hand out for a handshake. Just hearing the name Eddie made me cringe or recoil a little.

I knew Eddie too but not too well. He was a college acquaintance of Andy's. I insinuated myself over in his cubical and smiled at Eddie, shook hands, and then looked down at the hospital bed. There was certainly a body in this one. Huge. Mostly belly, it seemed. Belly and then a head with identical tubation to Bette's stuck into and coming out of the face.

"That your mom next door?" Eddie asked. "I saw her name on the roster at the nurses' station."

"Yup," Andy said. "Who's this?" He nodded down at the belly in the bed.

"Dad," he said. "Heart," he said. "So, did they tell you what your mom did last night?" Andy and I looked at each other. Last night? What could she have possibly done last night?

According to Eddie, Bette had somehow managed to extubate herself the evening before. Yanked her breathing tube right out of her throat. If you've never seen one of those things, they're pretty long.

It would take one seriously concerted yank to get it out.

All of the ICU nurses were talking about it, Eddie said, and evidently not caring who heard. Eddie chuckled throughout his narration. When he finished, we shook hands again and wished him and his dad luck. I crossed over into Bette's cubicle while Andy made a beeline to the nurses' station. I hadn't noticed before that there were cloth strips tied to the bedrail and leading up under the bed sheets. They had Bette tied down.

Over at the nurses' station I heard my brother identifying himself, calmly, and calmly asking the nurse sitting at command control, "Is there anything of interest going on with my mother that we might need to know?" The nurse stared at her computer screen, noncommittal, nonverbal. Just then the main door to the ICU vacuum swished open and who should saunter through but the European surgeon who, post-surgery, had proclaimed his experience with Bette a *nightmare!*

Time was becoming a mash-up of sorts. There had been a pre-surgery consult where the Italian surgeon had promised to make Bette good as new. There was the post-surgery consult where the Italian surgeon had proclaimed Bette's heart muscle to be a *nightmare!!* I may have been part of these consults. Maybe not. Maybe Andy had just briefed me on them. I think I may have been there. The *nightmare* part. I remember that. The surgeon coming into the waiting room, blood on his scrubs, funny hat, and telling Andy and me, pretty sure me, *what a nightmare!* I remember a pregnant pause and then my brother and I bursting into laughter. We appreciate inappropriate honesty. We find it hilarious.

"Ah," he said, when he saw us standing there. "Ah, so. We go talk someplace else, yes?"

He hustled us out of the ICU, past the waiting room and into his office. It was micro and windowless. It reminded me of the offices at Mayhem. The doc went behind his desk, sat, and realized we had no place to sit. He stood.

"So," he said. "Concerns. You have concerns." He did not give us the opportunity to acknowledge or express concerns real or nonexistent. "The second surgery was success."

We, me and Andy, responded with silence. "Very success," he said.

He looked at us, first at Andy and then me, and then back. Finally, Andy cracked this awkward moment by making things more awkward. "What second surgery?"

The doctor's eyes widened. Then they narrowed. "Second surgery," he said, "for leak."

What can one do sometimes but laugh? Almost in harmony my brother and I laughed. The surgeon smiled along, maybe getting used to our senses of humor, not sure how or where this discussion might be headed.

"What leak?" Andy asked, smiling.

"Three leak," the surgeon said. "Three of six bypass leak. I fixed her up good."

"Nobody told us about a leak. Or three leak," I said.

The doctor's eyes widened and then narrowed. "Nobody tell?"

I looked at my brother. He shook his head. The air was thick in this small office with confusion and a sense that several balls had been dropped. Then came a knock on the office door. It was right against my back, the door, so I turned and opened it a crack, expecting a nurse or an administrator come to straighten all of this confusion out. It was not one of those. It was my older brother, Sam.

"Sam," I said.

"Sam," Andy said.

"Sam," the doctor said. "We tell Sam about leak. About second surgery."

"What's happening?" Sam asked, easing his way into the small office.

"Bette sprung a leak, apparently," Andy said.

"Three leak," I said.

"All fix," the doctor said.

"I know," Sam said.

"You know?" Andy said.

"That's what I said."

"Someone called you?" I asked.

"How else would I know?" Sam said.

"You didn't think to let us know?" Andy asked.

"I thought about it," Sam said.

There wasn't much more to discuss regarding the second surgery except the doctor, Dr. Frisco, his name tag indicated, said, "All fix."

"Apparently Bette de-tubated herself sometime in the night," Sam said, to us, the doctor.

"We heard that too," Andy said. Turning to Dr. Frisco, he said, "We assumed that's what you wanted to discuss. The de-tubation."

Dr. Frisco said, "What is de-tubation? No sucha thing. There is extubation. Patient cannot extubate. Impossible." And then Dr. Frisco came out from behind his desk and squeezed between us, us brothers in this very small office.

"Be right back," he said, and squeezed out of his office. We stood there for a second, my brother and me.

"What nationality is he?" Andy asked.

"Italian," Sam said. We stood, nodding. We stood for a minute, the three of us thinking our own thoughts and waiting for the return of Frisco.

After another minute I said, "Why the fuck are we standing in here like sardines?"

"Sardines don't stand," Sam said, "they lie." If my brother Sam sounds a little like an ass, it's only because he is.

I opened the door to the office and slipped out into the hallway. Two of my three brothers standing cheek by jowl was a rarity and supremely uncomfortable. I couldn't remember the last time we had been in such proximity. Probably in the back seat of a station wagon headed somewhere not of our choosing. It felt the same right now, headed somewhere not of our choosing.

* * *

"Your mama," Dr. Frisco began, "your mama has got some kinda personality, hey?" We all nodded like bobbleheads. "She did it all right. She extubate herself. She gotta the strong will to live."

"Or die," I countered. "Who yanks out their own tubation?"

"Not many," he answered. "None, in fact. That was a pretty odd, what she did. But we through the worst. She gonna be good as new. We fatten her up. Good to go."

We were all back in the ICU now, a circle of male vultures looking down at Bette. Dr. Frisco pep-talked us about how well Bette was doing and how well she was going to continue to do. We listened as we watched Bette licking at her airway tube, obvious now, that even in her deeply medicated state, she was trying to disgorge the thing from her throat and lungs. We stood, my brothers and me, looking down at our mother's bodiless head struggling, struggling for a way out.

HOLMES

Some of the hallucinations were very pleasant.

BEA

It was summer and the days were long. The girls were maybe nine years old. We'd spent the day playing variations of softball on Serious Lawn with its knolls and valleys and impossibly lush grass. I could not understand why this ridiculous two-acre lawn was so green. I never watered it. All I did was mow it weekly and it looked like center field at Fenway. We played pickle and I threw batting practice, having graduated from underhand tosses to overhand whiffleball curves and knucklers. The girls were getting good, no longer running in any random direction after making contact. Understanding first base, second, etc.

We ate our baked fish on the upstairs deck, the sun still high in the sky. It was too pretty out to plug in a VCR movie inside and too early for reading in bed so I asked the girls if they'd like to have a camp fire.

With the girls in the back of the Silverado, we rode out to my bone pile of stones and tossed a couple dozen smallish fieldstone into the bed. We made a fire ring in a hollow of the back yard in the long shadows of the pines at the edge of Serious Yard. We collected dry wood from the barn, old two-by-fours and kindling from the low parts of the pines. I showed the girls how to set the kindling and the dry wood in a teepee shape with plenty of space for O_2 to do its thing. Before sparking it off, I went into the barn and fetched the boombox we kept near the hot tub. "Moondance" by Van Morrison was already plattered up, so I kept it in there.

The fire did not hold Mae's interest and she went to the edges of Serious Field to collect wildflowers and milkweed. Bea sat close to me on the cooling lawn. Bea leaned on me and then lay with her head in my lap, me stroking her hair. When "Caravan" came on, she sat up and took my hand. "Will you dance with me, Daddy?"

She'd never asked to dance with me before. We weren't really a dancing family. But of course I'm going to dance with my daughter Bea on a summer's evening. She led me through a series of spins and pirouettes and solemn bowing to one another and then we sang the exuberant "La La La La's" of this gypsy song.

Only hours earlier she had wept and begged to not have to come to Serious Farm for the weekend. She wept and it broke my heart to insist she come.

And now we danced. I told myself to remember the dance. I told myself to remember this dance for as long as I live.

So far so good.

BETTE

I drove straight past Serious Farm on my way back from a day of hospicing in and around Scarborough and went through Dover, over to 16 and down the Spaulding Turnpike on to the Portsmouth traffic circle. Portsmouth Hospital used to be downtown, across the street from South Playgrounds where I'd spent a ridiculous amount of time playing hoop. Now the hospital was ten times its original size and sitting on landfilled swamp just off the traffic circle within handy proximity to the state liquor store.

Bette was now on the cardiac rehab wing, rehabbing, supposedly.

By all reports she was a suck-worthy patient, arguing her way out of the gentle exercises designed to get the heart patient up and moving and arguing her way into benzodiazepines. Bette loved her some Klonopin.

When I walked into her room I was surprised to see there was a gathering, of sorts. Brothers Sam and Andy were there along with the tiniest of tiny doctors I'd ever laid eyes upon; not that I'd laid eyes upon hundreds of tiny doctors, but this woman was small. If she were at the Rochester Fair and wanting to board the tilt-a-whirl, she'd have been turned away because she was not You Must Be This Tall.

And Bette, sitting up in bed, big grin, blue eyes blazing and clear, presenting at this moment like the Bette of yore. Maybe this gathering was a good news sort of thing. Only, standing there, all of us, except grinning Bette, nobody spoke. We just eyeballed one another like a spaghetti western, an Ennio Morricone composition playing in my head.

Until at last, "Halloo," the diminutive MD spoke. "Halloo." Another doctor with another thick foreign accent. "Hallooo, I am Dr. Chamframary. I yam the floor doctor on these day. And you must be the Holmes." Portsmouth Hospital was a regular Doctors Without Borders. She extended her little tiny hand and we shook on it. "Yes," I said.

"So? What? What's on the agenda you all?" I asked because it seemed evident that *something* other than a routine doctor's visit was going on. Dr. Chamframary began to speak, thought better of it, and stopped, dropping her eyes to her baby feet. My elder brother Sam and younger brother Andy just looked at me. Bette continued beaming, creepily. "OK!" I said, "what?"

Brother Sam has a sonorous voice. Sonorous to the point of inaudible, a bass rumble only certain species of earthworm can hear. He began to speak. Put him in a conversation with Bojean and it would be a mixture of sighs and stifled belches. He tried out a few lines that I could not discern. He saw that he was not getting through and let me have it, loud and clear, "Your mother," he said, "has made the decision to die."

I waited for more, but there was no more. I scanned the room, again. Now everyone was smiling. So I smiled. *"I've got pnuemonia!"* Bette hollered. *"It's an old woman's best friend!!"* Bette had been having difficulties modulating her volumes over the past year or so. Nobody was sure what that was about. Even her friends coming for a visit would ask later, "Why does Bette yell?" "We don't know, sometimes she just yells." And it wasn't as if what she was yelling was particularly in need of emphasis. She could be talking about the Crusades and then suddenly let us know, *"I've got broccoli in the fridge!!"*

I must have looked puzzled because Andy took over, thankfully. "Yeah, so it turns out Mom's got a pretty nasty pneumonia cooking. Sam and I happened to get here thirty minutes ago and Bette here and Dr. Chamframary were talking." Chamframary still hadn't looked up, as if she'd been caught with her hand in the opioids jar. "Dr. Chamframary started intravenous antibiotics, but Bette wants them pulled. She says she's had enough. Well, she's had enough of this bullshit is what she actually said." I looked over from Andy to Bette who was still grinning from ear to ear.

"True!" Bette said.

I looked back to the standing room trio, the tall and the small. "And you all think this is a good idea?" My brothers shrugged, in harmony. I looked to little Chamframary, and I could not believe my eyes when she also shrugged.

"Wait. Wait! Wait . . ." I felt a surge of panic coming over my transom. This didn't feel right. Like I'd just walked into one of my own nightmares. I was not remotely prepared for this. I walked over towards my mother, found a metal folding chair, and dragged it with me. I sat down. I had no plan.

"Wait a minute."

And then it all let loose. I was openly weeping. Projectile crying. I had no control. I was embarrassed but could not gather myself. "Can you just wait a second?" I don't even know whom I was talking to.

Bette stopped smiling. It would have been a good time for one of us to reach out, my mother and me, to reach out for the other's hand, or put a hand upon a shoulder, anything tactile, but we Jensens don't know how to go about such things, so we were there, me in my chair sobbing and Bette in her bed, a mother watching her grown son falling apart, her son processing his mother opting for death. I knew enough about pneumonia that she would be gone by Monday without medicine.

"I just . . . hang on. I'll be with you in a second . . ." I was sort of hiccupping now. Ridiculous. I knew about enough about pneumonia to understand that the effects of the infection are brutal and can produce horrific hallucinations and general disassociation. I'd had it when I was twelve and remember the horrors of the fever-induced trip like it was last week.

It also makes you feel so overwhelmingly sick that you wish you were dead, even at age twelve. But antibiotics work quickly and the psychically depressing elements of the illness can switch out fast. Within hours of being shot up with antibiotics, the patient can feel nearly normal again, nearly normal and wondering whether the last several hours of bad pneumonia terrors really happened.

"Mom. Mom." I almost said "Mommy," but saved myself. "I, we, respect what you're going through. And we respect your wishes, I promise. I promise. But can you please, please do me a favor?"

"If I can," she said, modulated, looking at me with her mother eyes rather than crazy Bette ones.

"I, I think I need twenty-four hours to wrap my head around this. Can you? Do you think you can give the medicine another twenty-four hours to see how you feel? This time tomorrow, if you still want to stop the antibiotics, then OK. But right now, I can't, I just can't, my head. I'm sorry . . ." and the tears returned, copious, down my face, but without the sobbing.

"Sure," Bette said, as if I'd just asked to borrow two bucks for a coffee. More silence in the room.

"You were fairly adamant five minutes ago," sonorous Sam said, sounding almost annoyed.

"I was," Bette said, "and I am. But I think it's reasonable. To let Holmes, and you boys too, take a day to think about it. An extra day won't kill me." The good doctor Chamframary laughed, a little squeak, and excused herself after checking the various lines of liquid dripping into Bette's stick figure arm.

"What is she?" I asked.

"A doctor," Sam said.

"No, what kind of name is Chamframary?"

"She's Indian," Andy said. "From India."

"That's probably racist," I said.

"She certainly is short, isn't she???" Bette hollered.

"I wonder if any American doctors work here," I said.

"That's what I was thinking!!"

Walking to the elevator after visiting with Bette for another half hour, I asked my brothers, "Was that a cheap trick? The crying?"

With no hesitation and confirming my love for my brothers, as if I needed it, they said, in harmony, "No."

As different as we are, my brothers and me, as non-emotional, however constipated, I had never questioned their loyalty or, yes, their love. It made me want to cry again, but I choked it off.

*   *   *

In twenty-four hours Bette said she felt better and reported that she no longer wished to die. She thanked me for the intervention. I was pleased, my brothers were pleased, and Mom's friends were pleased.

Turns out she was bullshitting the lot of us.

She lived another eight months. I believe now, all these years after her death, that she made the sacrifice of living for her family. For me. Because we asked. I asked.

But her sacrifice was far from beneficent. She made us pay. Made us pay with her anger and her stubborn refusal to consider peace, to consider a peaceful departure. We'd stolen her peace. I'd stolen her peace. I'd stolen her control and she didn't like it.

So, yeah. Those last horrific two hundred some-odd-days of Bette's life? That was pretty much my fault.

LEE CLAIRE

The February thaw did not last, of course. We were hit with a succession of snow storms back to back to back, which left us with fifty-two inches of snow on the ground. In between the Nor'easters, Lee Claire drove up to Serious Farm one Saturday with his digital recorder and his laptop. We were going to try and piece together the Grendel symphony. He brought his tools, his imagination, and I provided a handle of Dewar's and a bag of ice.

Before we got into the creation of the woodchip soundscape, we sat at the kitchen table and shot the shit. I didn't know much about Lee Claire: where he grew up, did he have siblings, Mom and Dad still together, why he was wasting his time and talent on Little Carrot's strange vanity project called Clown.

On the latter, he said, "I don't know. I really get a kick out of being part of you guys and trying to help as every song we play fights for its life. The just barely hanging on produces a really interesting sound quality. You can hear the desperation and the panic. I like it."

I hadn't thought of our efforts that way, but he was right. Even though we wrote our own material that were comprised of the most rudimentary chord structures, it was a crapshoot as to whether we'd get to the end without a massive trainwreck. The sound of a train wrecking before it actually wrecks. Interesting.

I asked one question about his family, whether his mom and dad were still married, and Lee Claire answered. I asked a follow-up and Lee Claire really started talking. I was fiddling with his handheld digital recording device, accidently on purpose activated record, and could not figure out how to de-activate record. I let the device sit in my lap as Lee Claire spoke. It went like this:

HJ: Tell me about your mom and dad's divorce. How old were you?
LC: I was four. It happened very suddenly and with me not knowing anything about it.
HJ: Do you have any recollections of it at all?
LC: Nope. I just remember my dad was gone one day and I was alone in the house with my mom.
HJ: Do you remember the chronology of your dad getting re-married?
LC: Yeah. I went to pre-school, daycare, in Hudson (New Hampshire) and I became friends with a kid a year younger than me. I was in the kindergarten and he was in the nursery school. And we started hanging out and sleeping over each other's houses.

And his mom became my stepmom.

And so my dad and she just started to connect because of bringing us to each other's houses and that turned into a relationship.

HJ: What was the custody arrangement between your mom and dad when they divorced?

LC: It was joint custody. And I think that mostly meant it was kind of fluid and they could communicate it out. It wasn't a strict schedule.

HJ: What was your impression of how that went during that period before your dad got re-married?

LC: I can't say that I understood it or anything, but there certainly weren't court battles or anything like that. It seems like it just flowed. I was also at that time spending time . . . I remember spending every Friday at my grandparents' house, my dad's parents, and that was one regular thing that I remember.
For the most part I was living with my dad. And I remember spending those Fridays with my grandparents, and I remember spending time at my mom's apartment, but I couldn't tell you if it was a regular schedule or not.

HJ: How did it go from one day you coming home and your dad being gone? It sounds like your primary residence was with him?

LC: It was. Initially what happened . . . well, I was told as an adult that . . . I was told years later, I guess I wasn't an adult yet, that my mom had an affair. And my father caught my mom in bed with another man. And he went and stayed for a period of time with his parents, who lived right up the road from where we lived. It was all the same land. So he did that in the immediate aftermath. So I lived in the house with my mom and I remember a strange man showed up and that was my mom's lover, whom she married and was married to for twenty years.

So it was a sequence of events.

But I think my mom and dad worked something out where it was like, alright, look, we're not going to be together, we have Lee, who's going to live where?

HJ: You're an only child?

LC: Yeah. So I think they made an agreement where my dad would live in the house with me and Mom would get an apartment and they'd work out the custody.

HJ: How long was it before your dad was with your stepmom-to-be?

LC: You mean after my parents split up?

HJ: Yeah.

LC: Not that long. Maybe a couple of years. I think I was eight when they got married.

HJ: So there was a four-year period before they got married?

LC: Yeah. I remember my father dating a little bit. I remember meeting a couple of women. I just think of it now, I mean, my dad was a twenty-five-, twenty-six-year-old guy. He's going on a date with a woman and he wants to introduce her to his son. But (Stepmom) was the only one that ever stuck.

I don't know how long they dated before she moved in. She moved in with her two kids, for a while, I can't say how long, and then I remember them saying they were going to get married.

HJ: So between your mom and dad's split up, there's a four-year period. Where probably, I'm guessing, you went from essentially without memory to having memories of this stuff?

LC: Yeah. Definitely memories of this house with my dad and memories in this place with my mom and stepdad. Very few memories of my parents together.

HJ: That's pretty young. How old were you when your mom and her boyfriend got married?

LC: I was nine or ten.

HJ: OK, they waited five years. And after they got married, they were married for twenty years?

LC: Yeah.

HJ: Do you recall when things went from being apparently pretty fluid in the arrangements between Mom and Dad to not?

LC: Um. I remember hearing the conversation my stepmom and dad were having of how it was very important to my stepmother that the custody become full custody—that my father have full custody.

HJ: You remember hearing conversations about that?

LC: Yeah. Yeah.

HJ: What were your impressions about your stepmom that you remember when she first became part of your family?

LC: (extremely long pause) I remember one thing that I thought was odd, and that was even before they lived together. I remember spending a day at her house. And I remember playing outside with some neighborhood kids and she was inside cleaning and I wanted to just hang out in the house. And I remember she wouldn't let me hang out in the house. She thought I should be outside playing with the kids. It sounds reasonable, but I remember as a kid just wanting to hang out with the adults. I guess that was just some kind of a disconnect for me.

There were a lot of different stimuli at the time. Her two kids, my friend, my childhood buddy from daycare, is now my brother. And there's an older brother. And it was *loud*. I remember the whole situation turning really *loud*. And I didn't like that.

Just the whole culture of it, you know, this family,

this large Italian family. I grew up with just me and my parents, just this very quiet, tight-knit, sort of New England thing and then there's all these people around, arguing and my two stepbrothers constantly fighting—ah—so it was just a different thing that was hard for me to deal with. My father tells an anecdote about when I was a little kid when they first moved in and how it used to be so peaceful in the house, and now I have to fight for my cereal in the morning.

I remember feeling alienated from my dad.

It was like I couldn't hang out with my dad anymore. Just because there's more people in the house and what it turned into was, as I got older and things got stranger, more complex, I was being deliberately kept away from any sort of time with my dad.

HJ: Your dad?

LC: Yeah.

HJ: Now, as an adult, can you think of any rationale as to why that might have been?

LC: I think it was just so all communication was filtered through the party that needs to be aware of everything. And needs to feel secure.

HJ: The party being your stepmom?

LC: Yeah. I remember another time early on my father—my dad and stepmother—had some people over for drinks at the house, and that happened extremely rarely. But my dad invited his best friend from childhood, who lived *right* down the street. He obviously had been there through the whole thing with my mom, you know, old friend of my dad's and his wife, my mom. And a couple of people I don't really remember, but I just remember being in the kitchen getting something from the fridge and my dad's friend was getting a beer and he said, "How's your mom doing?" And that was it. After that, my stepmom overheard and that guy never *ever* came to the house again. Was not allowed. So just a simple question like that—the idea that relationships could be maintained—was very bad.

HJ: Do you have any recollection as to how this was accomplished? This alienation of your father in your own home? How you were kept apart? Any recollection of how this was done?

LC: I think it was just the logistics of scheduling: who's going to bring or drop people off at this and that and there was just no alone time. You could feel this suspicion, and like, we're in a room or in his office and I'd go up there and two seconds later she's there. It was just like, this presence.

HJ: Surveillance almost?

LC: Yeah.

HJ: Do you think your dad was aware of it at the time?

LC: I think so. This really culminated in . . . she was never gone. She was always in the house.

HJ: Did she work?

LC: She used to work when we were younger, but my father, we started our own business, we never had a lot of money, but the one first thing he arranged was that she didn't have to work anymore. But early on she worked.

One time, she was gone for a week, maybe visiting her family or something. It was rare. But my father took me aside this day when we were alone in the house and said that he was going to leave her. And he said he thought that she had a lot of problems. And he just wanted to prepare me that this was going to happen.

He told me that and I went to—it was my mom's weekend—when I came back and walked in the house, the first thing that happened was (stepmom) came up to me, she said, "So I heard your father told you he was going to leave me." And, ah, he never left her.

HJ: Let's talk about how things changed regarding the fluidity of the custody agreement between your mom and dad.

LC: Very quickly—it was one of those things where (Stepmom) was saying, "Well, I have this arrangement with my ex, which is how we do it. You have to do it this way."

And her ex was not in the picture. He saw his boys, like, once a year, maybe. Just not around.

So, I think she convinced my dad it should be that way and it was a court-ordered, legal process.

HJ: Convinced your dad, you think, that it was better that your mom not be involved in order for it to be like her situation with her ex?

LC: I think. I mean, I don't know what her rationale was. I bet it had to do with the idea of equality. She always talked about treating us three boys the same. I can just imagine that the idea of my mom saying "Can I have Lee tomorrow," something off the cuff, would just feel disruptive maybe.

There wasn't any other scheduling because (the stepbrothers) never went anywhere. This was their family and I had this other family. How she convinced him of that, I'm not sure.

HJ: Did your dad and stepmom take legal action to make this a permanent legal deal?

LC: Totally!

HJ: What did they do?

LC: They went to court. This was the beginning of countless court battles. Always in and out of court to, ah, do this to the schedule, change the schedule, everything went through the courts, they were always in court. I think it was basically my stepmom trying to give my mom less time, or my mom trying to get more time or just fight for her time. I remember it being whittled down—it was Friday after school to Monday. Then Friday after 6 p.m., and then Friday after 9 p.m. and then be back by Sunday at six. Just ridiculous little things, like hours on a spread sheet. Incredible.

HJ: How long did the court battle go on for?

LC: They went on until I was in college. It seems like the beginning of the court appearances coincided with my stepmom and dad getting married. This whole idea of "we're a family now we're a married couple."

HJ: Do you remember any adults in these situations giving you any kind of an explanation as to what was going on with the court stuff? Or was it left up to you to try and figure out what was happening?

LC: I knew that it was about visitation. My mom never talked about it, really. But my stepmom was always, *"You can't be spending so much time over there. It's disruptive to what we're doing."* And what came out of my stepmother's mouth about my mom, you know, my mom was a whore. You know, horrible things. And just like, my mom was a fucking dreg of society and I needed to not be there because it was going to fuck me up.

HJ: And that kind of information, coming from your stepmom, started right at the time of her and Dad's marriage?

LC: Yeah.

HJ: And kept up?

LC: Yeah. It just got worse.

HJ: Do you recall your feelings when you heard this stuff?

LC: Yeah. (Long pause) It didn't feel good. It was embarrassing and sad because I didn't know if I should believe it or not. I certainly didn't want to believe it, but, why . . . I wasn't really in a position to imagine anybody making something like that up. My dad never contradicted. He probably should have opened his mouth at some point, do *something*, but he definitely couldn't have defended my mother to me in front of (Stepmom).

HJ: There would have been consequences?

LC: Definitely. I do remember one early thing: there were therapists. This was a new thing. There was no therapy when my parents split up. We just did our thing.

But when Stepmom came in, there was a string of therapists. We would go, the three of us boys would go and do play therapy together. And we'd get comfortable with one and, oh, this person doesn't know what they're doing, and we'd get another person.

But I remember at one point, going to a therapist with my mother. It was a guy. We sat down and I remember, uh, him asking me if I was afraid of my mother and . . .

HJ: Your mom was there?

LC: She was right there, and I just started to cry because I remember not feeling like I was afraid of my mother but being *told* I was afraid of my mother. And I just didn't know what to do.

And you're afraid to tell your mother you don't want to see her this weekend. Being told "You can't be afraid of her; you have to tell her that you don't want to go visit her anymore." But I *wanted* to go with her.

HJ: Say that again.

LC: My stepmother would tell me that I needed to stop being afraid to tell my mother that I didn't want to go with her. "Why are you so afraid of her? If you tell your mother that you're not going to see her anymore on weekends then you can have that gold chain."

Like, little things that we boys wanted when we reached a certain age, we would be allowed to get. Like the gold chain. That was like, at thirteen. My little brother got one, but, it's like, I can't get one until I tell my mother that I'm just not going to visit her anymore.

HJ: Do you think that your mother was aware of what was going on?

LC: (Exhale) Probably not until, like, the stuff . . . she wasn't aware of the stuff that was being said to me. She was definitely aware there was a severe personality conflict between her and this woman, between Mom's husband and this woman. A lot of the actual shouting matches and just awkward, horrible behavior was between Mom's husband and my stepmom—the two new parties to the picture.

HJ: So your mom's husband would confront Stepmom?

LC: He would confront her, hell yeah. I mean, he hated her. And his thing was, I think, he was just defending his wife and her son. Just not being able to stand by silently, like my dad. But seeing his wife hurt by not being able to see her kid and just wanting to do something about it.

There was a break in. My dad and stepmother's house was burglarized and it was presented to me as, there's no other possible scenario but (Mom's husband) did it. Mom's husband broke into the house. And evidenced by the fact that only (stepmom's) shit was taken. And to this day, I don't know. Do I think (Mom's husband) was capable of doing something like that? I do. Do I see (stepmom) as capable of doing something like that, just to blame him? Shit, I don't know. But shit like that . . . I don't know if I should be talking about all of this crap . . .

HJ: Go for it.

LC: My mom showed up to pick me up on a visitation day, and I don't know if this is one of those scenarios where I called and said I didn't want to go and she didn't believe me and just showed up at the house anyway and was like, "Look, you want to come with me?" And (Stepmom) called the cops and they put my mom in handcuffs and she's just bawling, looking at me through the door. (Exhale) Who in their right mind would think any of this shit was beneficial to a kid?

HJ: You've mentioned that if there were any form of backlash from your mom toward your stepmom or toward the visitation arrangement that there would be subsequent backlash to you. Can you describe what you were talking about?

LC: Punishment.

HJ: What kind of backlash are we talking about? Just your mom or her husband questioning or pushing for more time?

LC: Yeah. Just any kind of confrontation. A phone conversation, any kind of contact led to real conflict.

HJ: Any kind of contact?

LC: Any kind of contact between the adults. Mostly between the steps—my stepmom and my mom's husband was like war. If they met each other on the street it was like a gang fight.

There could be a conversation between my dad and my mom—adult conversation—but the abuse my father would take for talking to my mom . . . that wasn't an option either.

HJ: So on the occasion when there would be confrontation or conflict between the steps or between your mom and stepmom, you would be overtly punished?

LC: Yeah, sometimes, yeah. Like spend the evening in my room or just verbal abuse.

HJ: With rationale behind it? A "because?" You're being punished because? Usually when a parent reprimands a child, the child needs to know why. I know we're not talking about standard parenting here, but still, would she say why you were being punished? Or would she make something up?

LC: It was just kind of like, "You're not supposed to do that."

HJ: But you didn't do anything.

LC: I wasn't supposed to call my mom on the phone.

HJ: Holy fuck. So if she got wind that you picked up the phone to call Mom . . .

LC: Oh yeah, that's not allowed. I remember there was like two weeks I had to spend in my room for . . . I wasn't allowed to have friends over at my mom's house. I could go visit my mom, but I couldn't see any of my school friends over there. But that was the only way I could see my school friends because I wasn't allowed to have school friends at my house until I told my mom I didn't want to go visit her.

HJ: Do you remember how (Stepmom) would word this?

LC: It was like a maturity thing. Like, "Until you're mature enough to tell your mom you don't want to visit her, like a little baby, a little mamma's boy, you're not going to get these things." It was like, "Spoiled, spoiled mamma's boy."

HJ: Because you wanted to see her?

LC: Yeah, and as I got older, it was, yeah, I wanted to see my mom, but not because I was like a little kid and I needed my mom. My mom respected who I was becoming and wanted me to participate in the things I wanted to participate in at that age, like sports and hanging out with my friends.

HJ: Your mom would support that?

LC: Yeah, she would sacrifice her time. I remember—I felt really bad about this but—my mom had me every other Monday and my friend asked, "Do you want to come over after school?" And I wanted to go so badly. Mom came to pick me up and I begged her to just bring me over immediately to my buddy's house after school and she did it. I remember her crying a little bit when she let me out of the car and my friend was like, "You made your mom cry." And I was like, yeah. So she, you know, she *got* it. She wasn't going to be, like—"No, this is *my* time."

HJ: Do you remember how old you were when you started to question the soundness of this parenting coming from your stepmom?

LC: Yeah, it was definitely like eighth grade: thirteen, fourteen.

HJ: Do you remember what that felt like or what dawned on you? Can you tell me how that manifested?

LC: It was like a new family emerged during that time, during adolescence, like a peer group. Just like a temporary thing, but it's very potent when you're that age. And I was being *kept* from that. I wasn't allowed to engage in that. I couldn't go to friends' houses. I couldn't play sports. And it made no sense to me. And I wanted to fight for that.

HJ: Were you able to verbalize that with anybody? With your dad or friends? Did you have any kind of outlet where someone would listen to you and say, "Yeah, this isn't kosher?"

LC: Yeah, my friends definitely thought it was weird and I remember some of my friends' parents—I don't remember what they said so much, but they would help me. They knew my situation. They knew I could visit when I was with my mom. They would understand when we were, like, driving—I'm in their car and we're driving by my house and how I might have to duck down so as not to be seen.

HJ: Was any adult able to articulate to you that this wasn't your fault? Did anyone recognize it for what it was? Did you know the term "parental alienation" before we ever started talking?

LC: No.

HJ: Did you have any kind of term for it in your head?

LC: Abjectly fucked. I just thought it was the insecurity of one person just let loose. The parental alienation that I felt was just one aspect of the manipulation of a whole network of people. Like, my father, as an adult, is still alienated from *his* mother because of my stepmom. Still. She's probably going to die and he won't talk to her.

HJ: Let's jump to . . . you're becoming aware that something is a little bit off, at thirteen. How did this culminate? How did you resolve this?

LC: Well, I just up and ran away one day. And I remember feeling like things were boiling. I was sixteen at this point. And really, really chafing. I was, like, madly in love with the girl next door, and I had been my whole life. And it was completely innocent. You know, we rode the same bus and we'd talk and it was just everything I could hope for.

But, if I, if my stepmom knew, I then wasn't allowed to sit down with her because she was a little whore.

HJ: She said that?

LC: Oh yeah, oh yeah. And "whore" couldn't be more of a wrong word to use to apply to this girl, a complete innocent.

HJ: Did you make the correlation between what you're hearing about your girlfriend and your mom? I mean, you *knew* your girlfriend . . .

LC: Yeah, yeah. I guess I hadn't done that, maybe. But this day, I just remember, you know, at sixteen, "No, you can't play any sports," um, "You can't get your driver's license." I couldn't enter driver's ed until I stopped seeing my mom.

HJ: Fuck!

LC: Yeah. You know, all of this stuff is getting a little bigger. No sleeping over at friends' houses until I stop seeing my mother. Um. But this one day, I remember my girlfriend and I talked at the bus stop for like, half an hour. Just standing there talking to each other. And I remember walking home and knowing—just thinking—if I get hell for this today, I'm out. I'm not taking this shit anymore. And I went down to the basement to play Nintendo and she comes down. "You're hanging out with that little whore." Then something else, and then, "your mother," and, "Don't let the door hit you in the ass on the way out. Go live with your mother because this is just about the perfect timing. You're sixteen and your whore mother, it's just about time she's going to want to suck your dick."

And I said, "*You* can suck my dick."

And she slapped me. And I pushed her. And I got on my bike and I rode to the grocery store and I called my mother at work and she came and picked me up and was there in ten minutes. And that was *it*.

(The sound of tapping) Ah, it's a good story.

HJ: It's a horrible story. This is child abuse. There's no way around it.

LC: It's like there's a child's mind in an adult who's pulling all the strings.

HJ: Your relationship with your mom and dad now. OK? You're thirty-eight.

LC: Yeah. I've had some time to absorb things. Heal. The day I left, I didn't see my dad for two years.

HJ: You're an adult now; your dad is still married to your stepmom. Have you ever had the desire or opportunity to say anything to her about any of this?

LC: Desire? Yeah. But I don't think I'd be able to get anything out. I certainly wouldn't be given this sort of space to talk. She still accepts no blame for anything. It's still everybody else who's fucked up. And that's just the way it's going to be.

I still think that leaving was, hands down, the best thing I ever did. If I didn't leave that day, things would be completely different.

* * *

We sat there. The only sound for several minutes was ice cubes clinking against the last glass of scotch. I don't know what Lee Claire was thinking. I was thinking about Mae and Bea and how it must be nearly impossible to come to the farm or to see me at all. I was thinking how completely impossible it must be for them to tell me why.

One time I asked a psychologist friend of mine what he guessed might be going on at Mae's and Bea's house. He said, "You don't want to know."

BETTE

Sending Bette back to her and our beloved home from the hospital under the care and feeding of her elder sister, Auntie NaNa, would fall under the category of Noble Failure.

NaNa tried to make it work and could not. Bette tried to make it work and she could not. We, the family, tried to do our best to make it work, but we could not. NaNa hung on for three weeks, which in itself was laudable, but we, their family, spent more time refereeing their squabbles than enjoying Bette's convalescence in the comfort of her home. It was bizarre to sit and listen to the preteen intensity and illogic spilling from the thin lips of these Wisconsin-raised octogenarians.

Auntie NaNa arrived from the wintery Midwest with the vitriol for her younger sib packed in her baggage along with her night clothes, unders, overs, slippers, creams, powders, housecoats, and nips.

Over the decades, the sisters got together regularly for travel and family reunions and each time each one declared it would be the last. They seemed to despise one another and yet could not resist the pull of blood. They would make their plans, books their flights, rent their cars and assume their positions; Bette behind the wheel and NaNa misinterpreting foreign roadmaps, and they'd pick up their indignations from where they'd dropped them at their last go round.

It was funny, their dynamic. Kind of. Most times.

This time, not. Auntie NaNa was in it to win, and Bette, this winter, was sadly depleted, though she had the strength and the wit to throw the occasional haymaker and make her sister cry. But NaNa would recover and pepper her little sister with jabs: lefts, rights and combinations. At three weeks, we had to call it. A TKO for NaNa.

And the convalescence concept, with or without NaNa's ragging, was something Bette wanted no part of. Instead of engaging in the minimal amount of prescribed physical therapy—arm lifts, leg lifts, walking a few steps across the room every now and then—she preferred to sit in her rapidly funkifying easy chair, in her underwear, and keep an all-day watch on her bird feeder. Not to identify and revel in the late-winter visitation of the hardy chickadee, the warbler, the whatever, but to rage at the marauding squirrels, Ahab-esque, the squirrels who took her legs years previous.

Visits to Bette's house were brutal. The sisters were like two children waiting for parents to return home so they could rat one another out for their unfair and cruel treatment of one another: NaNa barely out of sight in the living room, but well within hearing range because both sisters shouted the shouts of the hard of hearing, with her 4 p.m. nightcap of zinfandel or sherry in a cup, and Bette half naked in her chair, oblivious to the snowfall of dead skin upon her armrests, the headrest and the footrest. Bette was afflicted with full-body dandruff and she was flaking away before our eyes.

While the visits with the sisters were painful, they could also be hilarious theater. Before NaNa's victorious retreat to the land of multiple lakes and mountains of cheese, she would prepare meals for her sister and for us, if we gave enough notice. The meals were a '50s mélange of cocktail sides or other offerings from a bygone era: fruit cocktail from a can and softboiled eggs served any time of day. Sometimes Cream of Wheat. Lunch and dinner were interchangeable, cold offerings, ice cream scoops of cottage cheese with Thousand Island dressing drizzle; tuna fish salad, also scooped into a ball and served in a bowl atop single lettuce leaf to be spooned or knifed onto saltines presented in a circle upon a plate; rolled cold cuts such as olive loaf, bologna, or liverwurst, rolled and run through with toothpick; Philadelphia cream cheese butter-knifed into celery stalk concaves and adorned with green olive; cubed Wisconsin cheese, yellow and white. Sweet wine available at all hours. Stovetop chocolate pudding from a box made with whole milk and served warm. The slow stir of the Jello product was the only time the range top came into use. The oven was employed only for pulled-from-a-tube crescent rolls.

NaNa would lay out her spreads and then disappear back into her living room refuge, sip, and then back in before Bette or visitors were half finished to begin bussing plates and bringing them to the sink to clatter, wash, and sigh, as we finished eating.

I had talked my friend Lee Claire, one inebriated Saturday late afternoon, into coming with me for a visit and the promised NaNa feast was produced. Lee told me as we left the house, stunned by the performance art of a meal and pink pink wine, that he would remember that meal for as long as he lived. He was truly in drunken awe as I once again made a still-daylight DUI run to drop him home and then on up to Serious Farm. I could not tell if these were the best days ever or the worst.

With NaNa gone, back to Wisconsin, we had no choice but to move Bette literally a quarter mile down the road to the nursing home/rehab facility that we all used to joke about being all of our ultimate destinies and destination. And while the home was convenient and friendly and covered by Social Security and actually run by a friend of mine, it was really nothing more than a benzo-dispensing holding tank and wall of smell I've yet to cleanse from my olfactory memory nodules these long years past.

The odor of this facility was a bouillabaisse of ultra-strength industrial cleansing products, human ammonia, institutional kitchen waft, and despair. The smell surprised the visitor every time. By the time the visit was over, the visitor had become somewhat acclimated and perhaps even convinced themselves that theirs was an overreaction. It was not. The next visit proved it so.

Bette never mentioned the smell, but she mentioned pretty much every other negative aspect of nursing home life. Somehow, Bette had dredged up either a long suppressed or recently sprouted racism. She identified caregivers by their color rather than their names. It wasn't a hateful racism, but a racism all the same. She hated the Yellow (Chinese) girl in charge of her physical therapy. She assumed the Black (African American) nurse's aide was withholding meds. The Brown (Indian) doctor would not give her permission to drive, and who the hell did he think he was? I myself was surprised and impressed by the diversity in this New Hampshire institution. Bette's only relief from her angst came in the form of Xanax and Klonopin, and she still hated it all, only softer and with slurred speech. Brother Andy pointed out one day as we watched our mother babble herself to sleep, "I think our mom has a little benzo problem."

The days of winter clawed along with blackboard screeching, bleeding fingernails toward a spring season that for once held minimal joy, promise, or promiscuity. I needed a jolt, any sort of jolt.

SAUL

The months of New England spring were about as you'd figure, weatherwise. The apple trees at Serious Farm blossomed gloriously on a Tuesday, only to be snowed upon that Thursday. Driveway puddles ice-crusted at 5:30 a.m. breeding mosquitoes by noon. Mud season in middle

Maine made back roads to hospice patients impassable for the common man.

The Silverado 4x4 with its eight gallons to the mile was the only driving option in the spring. The Red Sox began another soap opera summer with the sting of curse no longer hovering after blessed 2004. My weeks were circles of hospice Monday through Thursday, working ten-hour days in order to have Fridays off for stonework down to Saul's. Each day was a circle of leave the farm and return to the farm at dark, tired either emotionally, or physically, or both. Each day, the circles varied in radius but ended where they began, lying on my daughters' bed staring at the local nine or staring at the glow stars I'd adhered to the ceiling above the little girls' bed in the shape of the only constellations I know: Orion, dippers, Cassiopeia. As spring deepened, I took Zen solace in mowing my ridiculous two-acre lawn twice weekly because the straight lines comforted me and the sweat flushed the system and made sleep possible, though I was well into my twelfth year of four hours per night. It was an existence. And on my once-per-week visit with Bette, she would inevitably make the false observation, in her beautiful misery, that "Goddam it, this will never end!" And I would tell her again, "No, Mom. It will."

On a Sunday in May, I decided to work at Saul's alone. The massive rebuild of the machine-assisted retaining wall was nearly done, leave the capping and the chinking. The capstones I'd set aside were large but manageable by hand. They were wide and long and thin, weighing maybe between 150 pounds for the smalls and 400 for the bigs. I could roll these up the two-by-twelve plank I used as a ramp for this purpose alone into the back of the Silverado. I could then maneuver the truck close enough to the wall and then plank the capstones from the bed onto the wall and then bar them into the position they would occupy for the rest of my life, at the least, given that Saul or another owner did not become restless and have it moved again. Planking a four-hundred-pound long and wide and flat stone into a truck bed and then from truck bed up to the top of a six-foot-tall wall, by hand, is physically difficult. And probably dangerous when working alone. This was the point of this Sunday. At 2 p.m., with legs wobbly, arms throbbed, and mud-streaked clothes top to bottom, Saul came outside holding a cold Coors Light for me and a bottled water for him. His timing, as usual, impeccable. I was done.

I asked how the writing was going and he filled me in. He asked me how I was doing and I filled him in. When he asked for my mother I had to laugh as they were, in their one and only meet, nemeses, sort of. I'd invited Saul to Bette's house along with a dozen close others to meet Mae and Bea for the first time. They were months old and my friends had yet to lay eyes upon the beauties. At a point in the afternoon I noticed Bette and Saul paired off and Bette speaking without smiling or laughing. Saul wore a serene smile and interjected only occasionally. Later, when the guests had gone and Bette was helping me feed the girls, she mentioned that my friend Saul certainly was racist. I laughed, but did not engage. Of course I could not wait to call Saul and ask him, "What the hell happened, Bette thinks you're a racist." From the Eagles Nest, Saul said, "Tell Bette, she might be right. I might be racist. But tell her I also have a hundred more Black friends than she does." Boom.

I told her. For once she did not knee jerk an answer. She'd been cornered.

"How's Bette?" Saul asked, sipping on his water and looking tired.

I thought about it for a second and said, "She's dying."
Saul didn't flinch. "Any time soon?"

"Yes," I said. "Pretty soon." As I looked at Saul, and he looked back at me, I thought, "You're not looking so great yourself."

I circled back to the farm, watched three innings, and fell asleep on top of the quilt Bette had made for the girls. It was not yet dark outside and the stick-on stars glowed in the dark without me until I woke up, for the day, at one thirty.

BETTE

The pneumonia returned. The old woman's best friend had come around again.

We found out later, after she was gone, that Bette had called her sister NaNa two days before she told any of us that she was feeling poorly. She called NaNa to tell her the pneumonia was back and that it was time to say goodbye. I wish I'd been a fly on the line for that call. I could not picture those sisters being kind to one another. But I am so often wrong.

This time, this pneumonia, we, my brothers and me, we knew what to do. What not to do.

Plus, because we hadn't picked up on her drift the first time, this time Bette made it abundantly clear that this particular setback would be the last. She was absolutely refusing antibiotics.

We asked the nurse to summon the floor doctor and twenty minutes later, all of us, including Bette, including the doctor, were flummoxed when our own tiny little Dr. Chamframary entered into our solemn gathering. We sat staring at her with awkward smiles and she stared back. Finally, my brother's spouse Midge laughed, breaking the ice jam. "Hi!" she said, "remember us?"

"I remember," the good doctor said, with no apparent judgment. And she really did remember. It was not necessary to give her Bette's back story, nor to explain why everyone in this room was ready for Bette to die. Chamframary fetched the necessary paperwork from the nurses' station. Bette signed. An all too familiar DNR notification was tacked to Bette's whiteboard. The doctor told us she would have to speak with her supervisor to greenlight the withholding of antibiotics.

Bette squinted at the doctor and said, "You mean I have to get permission to die?" The doctor chuckled and said, "Pretty much." This was it. In three or four days' time, Bette would most certainly be off and away. So strange.

Bette said, in regard to hospital protocol around granting permission to expire, "Jesus Christ on a crutch." She looked at her watch.

When the orders to withhold curative measures came back, there was not much to do. The nurse asked Bette if she was comfortable and our mother looked around the room for tacit permission to go ahead and request a nice cool drink of morphine and/or Ativan. "Am I comfortable?" she asked Andy. Andy, who was the most evangelical in his opposition to Bette's beloved benzos.

"You look a little uncomfortable," he said. The nurse went away and came back with a fat syringe of something and goosed it into Bette's IV. Her relief was immediate and her words turned to sticky farina paste, slurred like a sorority girl at a day party. Bette's blue eyes scanned the room and for the first time in a year I saw her old amused self in there.

I tracked down a hospital social worker and we agreed to bring an independent hospice service on board to administer to Bette's comfort and death. Most hospitals were still mostly stingy around palliative concepts. There were educated people walking these cleaning product halls who thought it imprudent to flirt with nascent addiction in the soon-to-be dead.

The normal course of pneumonia would give us, the family, time for private words with our departing matriarch, as well as time to alert close friends of Bette's if she chose to take audience. She should have lasted a minimum of three days.

Bette had other plans.

Eyes blinking sleepy morphine lids half mast, eyes closed and then eyes wide open to scan the room, a smile for everyone or herself, maybe not quite believing she was here at last at death's welcome mat, watching her with bemused interest because I knew her well and having a certain sense of what she might be thinking, bemused, I had no recollection of her eyes ever being this blue, startling blue as she lay dying.

Chuckling to herself, Bette, in her happy morphine comfort. We should have had two or three or four days to come and have our private moment if we wished, to hold a desiccated hand if we could force ourselves, to give thanks and profess love though the likelihood of these intimacies was slim. We, with our Jensen blood, found these intimacies near impossible with our Midwestern corn-stalk-in-autumn sensibilities. We had time, two or three or four days, to come back and awkwardly grin our way through this long anticipated parting. Each with our struggle of what should or could be said to one another. This assembly here in this beeping machine room of wire and tubes, would disassemble and strategize our own speeches or non-speeches to our fearless, peerless leader. Our goodbyes. This closing out of the only familial system we'd known. This ending of the Bette Age. The Bette Era. The only era we'd known.

I was sitting in a chair at the bedside, very workmanlike, very familiar to my hospice work and watching as the assembly of sons and spouses murmured and avoided eye contact with one another and checked watches and cell phones. They left, somehow. I don't recall what promises were made for future visits, for we'll-see-you-in-the-morning, for get-some-rest, for well-that's-that-I guess. I was sitting in a chair at bedside watching the faces of the sons and spouses, and I saw a giddy reflection of smart people understanding that this was a moment. This was a moment that would not be repeated. People, yes. People will continue to die. But Bette? Really? Are we really saying goodbye to this one? As they left, first Sam with hunched shoulders, looking angry, looking impatient, and then Andy and his spouse Midge with cheerful, we-shall-bring-treats-on-the-morrow, and I thought I felt the spirit of Amos also there and leaving tearfully, for he truly was the youngest of the sons, and though he spent his life farthest in miles from his mother, he needed her the most. Grown men losing their mother and lost in how on Earth to feel about it. As I watched them leave, the spirit of my brother Amos the last to leave, I felt a touch. I felt a poking at my hand, a bird wing flitting, the cold nose of a pet hamster probing. I looked down at my hand and saw that Bette had snaked her long-fingered hand out from under her dying sheets and was searching. I was confused.

"I'm trying to hold your hand," she said.

I laughed and took her hand up. A bit awkwardly, the hand holding found its way into the soul grip. It felt like holding a cold feather. She was looking at our hands, not at me, and she said, "You were the loves of my life." I was very aware of her use of the past tense. I was very aware that this may have been the bravest thing she ever had to say to anyone.

I didn't have any place special to go. The bar would have been too cliché. The farm too lonely. I did not trust myself to go speak with friends: with Little Carrot, with Lee Claire, with Ralphie Boy. I was afraid to cry right now.

Too cliché. I left the hospital telling Bette I'd be back and I drove the Silverado absently toward Rye, toward Bette's house, toward the beach. It was just driving home as I had done countless times. Early-summer, late-afternoon light crashed the windshield. It should have been late fall, muted, grey and isolated down by the harbor. It should have been raining or spitting snow. I drove roads that I'd bicycled as a kid, ran as an athlete, drove as an adult. Green canopy of mature hardwoods should have been bare and cold with watery sunlight from a retreating winter sun. I felt hollow. Middle emptied. Center punched and removed. She was really going to leave.

I drove around with the radio on, radio off, window down, window up. I drove past the golf course where I worked summers with my father. I headed inland past stone walls I'd built sometime in the last two decades, the decades now not a concern. This era was ending. As all eras must.

I found myself pulling into Saul's driveway and shutting the truck down. It rattled on, coughing hard with some sort of post-exhaust issue. Here at Saul's, I considered working for a while. I had my tool bucket in the bed of the truck, work gloves behind the front seat. My entire wardrobe for the most part is stonework worthy. I considered working but only got as far as walking to the enormous boulder retaining wall, climbing the face and perching on top, gazing into Saul's lovely ledged woods. It should be snowing. I sat and listened to the leaves snick one another in the deepening afternoon breeze. I could hear them snicking. My back to the big brick house of Saul, I sat, and after thirty vacant minutes twisted my neck the limited radius it could manage and looked up to the Eagle's Nest, the aerie. Saul stood there, holding back the curtains and looking out. He was not looking at me. He too was scanning his woods.

I turned back to gazing and raised my right arm high, fist clenched, black power. The power of black.

When the sun settled fully into the treetops I got behind the wheel and headed back to the hospital.

She was shrieking. No. Bellowing. Both. Her door open to the hallway and just shrieking. She said, "Oh my God Oh my God Oh my God." In her hospital room, alone, stick figure arms flailing toward the heavens, the ceiling of her hospital room. Business as usual as RNs cruised past the open door headed to other tasks and unconcerned regarding shrieks, bellows, flails. White sneakers padding, business as usual. Taking a flailing hand. "Mom, Mom, it's ok. Are you OK? Mom it's me." Blue eyes snapping to, wild, focused now. "Holmes! Thank God, it's Holmes." Bette hadn't been much of a God guy for many years. She was now. And me too. Dear God. Help us. Help her.

She desperately wanted me to get her out of bed. And go where? "Let's go. Let's get out of here." Pulling herself into sitting, pulling on my arm, bird feather fingers clutching, pulling, desperately.

Me helping her into a sitting position, helping. She wasn't kidding around. "I don't know, Mom, you're pretty sick."

"So what?" she demanded.

"True." So what, indeed. So I put my arm behind her bones, her back bones and helped her get her legs, I lowered her cage bars and I lifted her poor little legs, her long feet. I saw her suddenly as a sick child, sweet, helpless, night gown bunched, diaper, and bed smelly, she was bed smelly. I got her sitting up and with no real plan took her elbow and was about to lift her to standing. We were going now. Just going. Let's get out of here.

"What are you doing?" said a nurse from the hallway. This she noticed. This helping of my mother. Shrieks? Nothing. This she noticed.

"What are *you* doing?" I said, angry. "I'm helping my mother. What are *you* doing?"

She ignored me and powered into the room, taking Bette's wrist, the wrist I was not holding. Tug-o-war? Wishbone? Make a wish. She ignored me and ignored Bette, just holding the bone wrist and looking out into the hallway for, what, help? Backup? Where was this urgency when Bette was shrieking to the heavens? "I'm in charge here," she said, to no one.

"OK, Haig," I said. "Calm down." I asked the nurse, "What is she scheduled for, for anxiety?" Suddenly, I was authority. The authority the nurse was desperately seeking in this unscheduled moment.

"I'll have to check."

"Could you please?" She took off toward the nurse's station.

"Goddammit," Bette said, and I could swear there was a small smirk, "this bullshit will never end." The nurse came back fairly quickly, back with a syringe. "She's scheduled for Ativan."

"Cool," I said. "How often can she have it?"

"PRN," the nurse said.

"She was PRN as . . ." I almost said "PRN as fuck" but held up, ". . . she was pretty seriously PRN when I got here." I sat down now, next to my mother on the bed and put my arm around her sparrow shoulders. She laid her very warm head upon my left arm. It was as intimate a moment as I could ever have wished. I felt like a father. I felt like a son. I felt full. I felt hollowed. Cored. Here was my lifelong core, giving in sweetly, laying her tired head upon my left arm. Here was my center in full-blown terminal agitation and me not knowing it at the moment, me only looking at the blue eyes of my mother as her blue eyes searched the room for things I could not see.

The Ativan hit Bette like a cartoon pillow. She softened and allowed me to lay her back into her bed. She allowed me to straighten her bedclothes and smooth the sheets around her. She allowed me to place the sheet and the hospital blanket on her body and bring them up to her poor whiskered chin. The blue was leaving her eyes as the lids fluttered. She was whispering something. I leaned in to listen and she was whispering, "No opiates. No opiates allowed."

"It's okay, Mom. You can have whatever you want." I sat with her until ten thirty or so. I nodded off along with my mother. I felt as peaceful as I had in a long, long time. When I got up to leave, she was snoring softly, her toothless mouth open, her hearing aids still in.

I'd just entered deep sleep back at the farm when my phone rang. It was just after midnight. "Your mother did die," is what I heard. I also heard myself say, "Oh no!" and immediately thought, what an odd thing to say. My legs, my poor skinny legs, were dangling over the bed's edge. Your mother did die. *Let's go*, I thought. *Let's get out of here.*

I drove back to Portsmouth. I entered the hospital and went up to Bette's floor. I said hello to the nurses at the nurse's station and thanked them for calling. They asked how they could help. Call the funeral home? Anyone we can call?

Can I just sit with her for a while?

Of course.

I sat with Bette through the night. Some sort of gringo shiva. I removed her hearing aids and tried to close her mouth. Her mouth didn't want to close. I sat with her until dawn and then some. Finally, early morning, I wandered out of her room and realized this was the longest visit I'd had with Bette in well over a year. This brutal year that was pretty much all my fault.

* * *

Mae and Bea were dropped off ten minutes before the service and picked up immediately after. It was a good service. We asked friends who had been gifted over the years with a Bette quilt to bring them so we could decorate the funeral home with Bette's work. There had to be at least fifty. I had no idea she'd made so many. People spoke. I spoke. Mae and Bea stared at me throughout. Bette had smart and well-spoken friends so the platitudes were smart and well spoken. I don't remember any of them. I remember Little Carrot's eulogy, though. He got up and said, with a straight face, "When I was hungry, she fed me. When I needed shelter, she sheltered me. Jesus Christ. Mother Theresa. Bette Jensen." And then he sat down. People laughed in delight. People cried. Bette lay there in her box. My daughters stared at me.

After the service, after some drinks, I drove to Bette's house and went inside. I stood there in her kitchen where I'd stood as a child and as a man. I stood in her kitchen where my father took his last breath. I sat down in Bette's reading chair because I felt sort of faint. Where are you? Pretty sure I said it out loud.

Where are you guys?

HOLMES

Seven days a week became a thing.

The ridiculous two-acre lawn at Serious Farm was expanded to a more ridiculous three-acre lawn and mowing it became a thing. The Magic Trail he'd cut for the kids was reopened and keeping it open became a thing.

The vegetable garden at Serious Farm became a thing.

Absolute insomnia, a thing.

Chasing skirt became a thing.

Things such as listed and others that previously were not things became things. Scotch became a thing. Tramadol.

Seven days a week. No days off from things.

Certain truths were revealed:

Love hurts.

Of the many truths and the many hurts revealed during his hospice experience, the hardest truth Holmes saw was the sixty-year love affair interrupted by death. The ideal loves destroyed by the inevitable and natural leave taking.

Working with a group of recent widows and a widower—ratio seven widows, one widower—he witnessed pain beyond comprehension.

How can this be, they asked, the remainders?

What do I do now, they begged, the left behinds?

This is too much to bear, they stated.

Married at sixteen. Parents at seventeen. Grandparents at forty. Great-grands at sixty. Thick. Thin. Better. Worse. Sickness. Health. Love prevailing throughout. Playing by the rules. Respect. Compromise. Passion. Dispassion. Economic ups. Economic downs. Doubts. Certainties. Hirings and firings. Fears. Comforts. Seasons following seasons steady. And then it's over? Like that? A chest cold turns to pneumonia? A pancreatic cell mutates overnight and six weeks later she's gone? My love? The love? What do I do now? This is too much to bear.

These widows, this widower. Holmes sat and he listened. Holmes sat and he watched. Their crushed spirits crushed him sometimes. Other times not. This is natural. This is inevitable. Love will crush you. Love will kill you.

No thank you.

If this be love, then no thank you. Broken heart disease? No thanks. This epidemic? No thank you. Join up for this? Voluntarily? No thank you. This textbook love? No thank you. No thanks.

But one loves, does one not? How does one opt out on Love? How does one turn the heart to stone?

It's tricky.

Seven days a week became a thing.

Part of the seven days a week was dating women like it was his job. Theater. Expensive dinners. Jewelry. Sex.

Holmes began to garden at night by spotlight and some nights the light of the moon and the stars and sometimes by braille in the complete darkness.

Fireflies, by the hundreds, hovering his fields just above grass levels, lighting, procreating, kept him company.

Even in farm country, the night is never completely black, or at least not for long as 2 a.m. cars on the way home from closing times slithered along Route 9 and caught Holmes on his knees in their headlights. On his knees weeding. Praying, in his fashion.

The factory through the trees humming third shift through the pines threw an eerie light like smoke through the limbs and cast shadows sometimes and sometimes not. Night, deep night, was a subtle world. Red eyes watched from the grasses: foxes, woodchucks, raccoons, coyote maybe. Maybe bear. Maybe moose.

Even mostly deaf with hearing devices removed at night, he could hear owls cruising above, the owls wondering about these new nocturnal movements below. What's he doing out here in our night? Music sometimes from extension cord boombox, not too loud, most times playing the sleepytime ambient choices—The Brian Eno, The Enya, the Bach at Bedtime—leftover CDs from the daddy days to help coax anxious offspring back to the Land of Nod.

Holmes seldom saw that land of late.

Sometimes working the garden with night noises only: crickets, tree toads, bog frog, occasional scream of hunters, the fisher cats, maybe the whirr of UFOs, but too focused on gardening to look up and see.

Bette had never been a God Guy until quite late.

Her son had never really been a God Guy or a Garden Guy.

People changes.

Summer lasted long.

At the first smear of dawn he would head inside to wash garden dirt from knees and nails and change into hospice clothes, which day by day were becoming indistinguishable from stonework and gardening clothes. The good ladies at hospice may have noticed. They may not have noticed. What they noticed was of no concern to Holmes.

Not caring became a thing.

SAUL

I tore down Saul's existing wall by myself.

I was afraid of the things, the observations that might escape my mind and my mouth for either Lee or Ralphie to hear if they were working next to me. I tore down Saul's existing wall and kept up a steady stream of chatter to my Self.

One stone at a time. One stone on this side of the wall-to-be, one stone on the other. Judging each stone, one by one. This is a good stone, remember this one. This stone is no good, use it for fill. How do people voluntarily fall in love? Don't they know what's coming? Is it voluntary? Seems sometimes like there is no choice in the matter. Seems sometimes a biological imperative. What about free will? There's no fucking free will.

Saul's voice behind me. "Who are you talking to, Ace?"

"The dead."

"You okay?"

"Sure," I said. "You?"

"Seeing as how there's no fucking free will, I suppose I'm fine." Saul looked like shit. There clearly was something wrong with him. Or maybe I was hanging around with too many sick and dying people. Learning to die lessons.

Two weeks in, I was nearly done breaking down Saul's existing wall. He was paying me a shit ton of money to do this thing and I could easily afford to have the eighty additional tons of stone I'd need to make it grand delivered in pallets and plastic wrap, but I was considering hauling the eighty tons, a half-ton at a time at a time from Mr. Austin's place in North Berwick. For old time's sake. 160 trips up. 160 trips back. Chop wood. Carry water.

I felt I had all the time in the world. I felt the compulsion to work myself to dust, but this project wasn't strictly about me and my wants. My needs. Saul most likely wanted this thing done sometime before the decade's end.

Saul had paid me a deposit of $40K, about half of the estimated cost. It was the most money I'd ever had in my account at one time.

Bette's house sold quickly. I stayed out of that action, Andy and Andy's spouse Midge handling all of it with finesse, honesty, and professionalism. More money on the way.

I'd always wondered if having a little money would feel different in some way.

It didn't. I didn't matter. It would soon be gone most likely.

It felt a little bloody, this money, so I found a pair of toothless Mainers in my hospice travels to install metal roofing upon Serious House and Serious Barn. It was way overdue and perhaps too late for Serious Barn as it had been leaking heavily for two or three years now. The water damage in one sector of Barn was pretty bad. I way overpaid for the roofing but was pleased to see that both Mainers were sporting dentures by the end of the job and they were pleased to show them to me. Their new teeth were a ray of hope for me, for them, for our planet. For love.

You may think I am kidding.

KAT

Be strong. I will help you.
She wrote on a Post-it.
She with the tattoo on her forearm, three arrowheads in a vertical row, pointing downward to her hand. Reminding her to work. Reminding her to create, every day.
For a while, the formula worked. I tried to be strong. Her love helped me. It was real enough, that love. And then, as it must, love was not enough. And as it failed, as it must, and I asked her to say it, say she loved me, she could not. Would not.
Kat.
For many months, she was hope.
And then hope was gone. Even hope was gone.

HOLMES

One of the women, one of the women Holmes was sleeping with, said that driving around alone was not good for him.

She would ask where he was going and he'd say, for a drive. In her bed, or his, she would make a face of disappointment as Holmes got up at 4 a.m. and she'd say, this woman, "This is not a good thing."

Holmes agreed with her and left.

The boys were being nice to him: Little Carrot booking silly gigs. Tiny rooms. Birthday parties of friends. Backyard cookouts. Candle Shoppe grand openings. Open mics. Gigs for the two of them and sometimes the band. Sometimes two in a week. He knew the boys were being nice to him. It helped.

It didn't help.

Ralphie Boy showing up regularly to Saul's to help and be company. Lee Claire on time at the Pic n Pay on the weekend mornings in the late summer to head over to Saul's.

Somehow it was late summer.

Now we were installing a bluestone patio off the back of Saul's house, Saul adding little jobs. Saul continuing to put money into Holmes' account. Holmes putting money in the boys' accounts. Holmes could not account for this. For what Saul was doing.

What was he doing?

Ralphie and Lee both proficient at laying down the bluestone, sometimes Holmes just watched, with his coffee, with his truck radio, August skies lovely, sun filtering through the already morphing foliage, the green becoming deeper as summer grew old. Saul's wife Patti feeding them all lunch sometimes, Saul upstairs sometimes taking a break from writing and watching the whole affair from his Eagle's Nest.

This was like family to Holmes. These days were precious, he knew. Even in his confusion regarding love, regarding the end of love, just watching sometimes, just watching his good friends working, his body so tired. His mind.

On the weekdays for hospice, driving from Maine house to Maine house, having given up on the Volvo and using the truck exclusively. Fuck the Volvo.

On a particular Thursday morning, Holmes was in the parking lot of the hospice office, readying himself to go inside and sit through at least two hours of Interdisciplinary

Team Meeting. His phone rang and he heard it. Patti calling, as she did these days, to let Holmes know what Saul was thinking and wishing to have addressed over the weekend. The patio was near completion and Holmes was waiting for the green light to begin work in earnest on the Great Wall of Saul.

"Patti," Holmes said.

"Hi Holmes." Her voice was as cheerful as always, crystalline, Chicago.

"What have you got for me?"

"Holmes," she said, her voice changed.

Holmes knew he did not want to hear what was next. He just knew, but there was no place to run. "Holmes, he's in Boston." Holmes said nothing, waiting.

"He's at Mass General." Waiting.

"He didn't tell anyone, Holmes. Only me and the kids, I swear. He's so stubborn."

Holmes could hear his own breathing and he could hear Patti's as well. He felt himself getting angry. "He's in the ICU. Holmes, he's not coming back."

It was stage IV leukemia, she said, chronic lymphocytic leukemia to be precise. A result of being sprayed with Agent Orange forty-five years ago in a far-off circumstance. He's intubated. In a coma. She was telling him this. Her voice different, but telling him this. He felt himself getting angry. *You motherfucker.*

"Do I have time to see him?" he asked. "Is it okay if I go see him?"

Yes.

Yes, he could go see Saul.

"Holmes," Patti said. "The last thing he said before they ventilated him was to be sure and have the wall finished." Holmes said nothing. It didn't make sense. The last thing? *That* was the last thing he said? "I don't think we can, Holmes."

"I understand. Why did he keep making up stuff for me to do, Patti?"

"He admired you, Holmes."

"Admired?"

"He said it time and again, about you. He said, 'He didn't run.' He said you could have just given up on your kids and run, but you didn't. He wanted to help you somehow."

"He did," Holmes said. "You have no idea."

Herbie and now Saul. Herbie had told Holmes his story of being exposed to atomic radiation as a seventeen-year-old Army guy. He and his company sat in the desert and watched as atomic bombs were exploded right over there. They were given goggles. That's how he got his melanoma and his 100 percent disability rating from the government.

Saul. Agent fucking Orange.

For love of country.

Motherfuckers.

Holmes got off the phone with Patti and called Lee Claire. "What're you doing?"

"Recording ping pong balls against this brick wall."

"Got time to go visit Saul?"

"Visit?"

"He's dying, apparently. Already dead. Something."

"What?"

"This is fucking ridiculous," Holmes said.

Without giving it much thought at all, Holmes walked into the hospice building and went straight to the office of his newly hired team supervisor, Victoria. "I need the day off," he said.

"Sure, can you do IDT first?"

"I cannot."

"OK."

"Also, I have to give you my two-week notice." Victoria came out from behind her desk and hugged Holmes. She knew. They all knew Holmes was on borrowed time here. They knew the symptoms of grief.

Holmes' hearing aids fed back like Jimi Hendrix as he laid his head on Victoria's shoulder. They both laughed at the mild absurdity and he left.

Holmes never did give them their two weeks. He was done.

When Holmes and Lee Claire got back from Boston, from visiting the life-supported Saul, Holmes began to clear out Serious Farm.

He was done.

KAT

Have you ever set things in motion and at some point, deep into that motion you wonder, how did this motion?

Your feet are moving, one step, two?

You are lifting, moving things around?

You have a plan but you don't know how?

Your thoughts come in fragments?

You feel OK overall?

But know something is desperately wrong.

Something.

Something has to change. Something has to give.

Move?

Move or perish?

Have you ever felt these things? No?

I rented a dumpster. One of those gigantic forty-yard units you see parked on streets sometimes for kitchen rehab projects or adding a dormer and the neighborhood peoples begin to use it for their own hard-to-dump items like paint cans or a frayed wingback chair. I rented one of those and began to fill it up.

The idea of the fire started in the barn as I sat in my own frayed wingback chair affair, origins unknown, it was here, this chair, when I bought the place. Stunned and doped, me. Tired to my soul. But not too tired to think about my inherited chair and think, *This motherfucker would burn. Would burn good.* I looked around at the posts, the beams. *This barn would burn.*

I sat looking around. I looked out to the ridiculously large lawn and the insect traffic like rush hour in the fading summer. How were there not multiple mid-air collisions? Who or what was controlling this air traffic? Maybe there were collisions and the sounds too small to detect. I looked up at the posts and the beams of Serious Barn as so many times before when dreaming of turning this structure into a dwelling with stone fireplace and balconies.

My eyes found the giant green dragon Santa had lugged along for Mae and Bea on some Christmas ago. I mean giant.

The dragon, six feet long, was perched on a crossbeam, seven feet off the barn floor, keeping an eye on things. "I believe your work is done here," I told the dragon. We never named the dragon. The girls never really took to it.

I lurched out of the chair and pulled the creature from its beam perch and then dragged him by one nylon wing across ridiculous Serious Lawn and over to Serious Burn Pile.

I should just burn it all. All that will burn. Or melt.

Standing next to Serious Pile, one fist still holding dragon wing, I counted four Christmas tree skeletons within. Four years at least since the last Serious Burn.

We were overdue. Pile was comprised of brush, larger tree trunk, roots, carpentry remains, the usual combustibles.

Serious Pile was about to be comprised of much, much more including hot tub, stereo equipment (a mistake), plastic swim pool, baby cribs (two), baby clothes, spare doors pulled from Serious crannies, beds, bed frames, head and footboards, chests of drawers, end tables, coffee tables, vinyl records (a mistake), garden hoses, barn furniture where rock and rollers rested, fiberglass insulation; anything that would burn or melt.

Serious Burn Pile grew large over three zombie days. I didn't believe the fire would be hot enough to melt major appliances down so I tossed them in the dumpster. Little Carrot showed up on day three, unannounced, and watched me dragging my stove across the dirt driveway towards the dumpster.

"What are you doing?"

"Give me a hand," I said, sweating heavily.

"Are you OK?"

"Sure," I said. "How are you?"

"That's a perfectly good stove," Little Carrot pointed out. "What's going on here?"

"I'm not sure." I said. "I think I'm moving."

"Still," he said, "that's a perfectly good stove."

I filled the forty yards quickly with unfixable chainsaws, perfectly good pry bars, a freezer unit, washer/dryer, fifty-gallon drum, large metal buckets full of unidentifiable metal parts, heavy, which sat untouched as part of the purchase of Serious Farm fifteen years previous, dead generator, living generator, tool boxes full of tools, three used-up computer towers and monitors and cables; all by myself, hoisting or rolling larger items up wooden plank into the back of the Silverado and from the Silverado into the forty yarder.

I end-over-ended the dead hot tub from the barn down to Serious Burn Pile. I would maybe pluck the partially melted hot tub motor from Serious Ashes after Serious Burn and toss it into the forty yarder. Maybe not.

I dragged Serious Leather Sofa from the house on out to SBP. I wondered what burning leather would smell like. I might sift through ashes for sofa springs and toss them into the forty yarder. Probably not.

I had a pretty good idea I would not. I worked each day and night well into the late innings of Red Sox games. Summer was dying and the hose were still in it. Like night gardening, I labored by spotlight and night vision. I did not give the coming garden crop of corn, peppers, and squashes a second thought. That phase, whatever that phase was, was done.

I emptied room after Serious room. Eight rooms in all. I created a Craigslist ad on the laptop I did not toss looking for a renter and within one day found one. She asked to keep one bed with frame, a green sofa, white window curtains, microwave, and the antique mirror in Serious Foyer.

"Sure," I said.

"Can I have them?"

"Sure."

All with hollowed dispassion. All in something close to fugue state. There, working and sweating. Not there. Lugging. Dragging. Unsentimental, until day three with echoes now echoing in the house, I took pliers and began removing finish nails from walls that had hung Serious Art. I could not bring myself to burn Serious Art so I stored Serious Art in the attic (not a mistake). These were pieces made by friends. It would have been blasphemous to burn or toss or give back. I had no time to give back.

With each pulled nail I would putty up the holes. Many nails and much putty. Finally, I came to Serious Staircase where three nails sat embedded in the woodwork waist high. The three nails were in a horizontal row, none higher, none lower than the other. The three nails were where our

Christmas stockings—Bea. Mae. Dad—were hung yearly with care. For fourteen years. I sat on the bare hardwood floors, the rugs and the runners all out in Serious Pile, pliers in hand, staring at three finish nails.

Shit just got real.

Pulling them hurt like stigmata but I did not cry. I was done crying.

On the morning of day four after Saul died, I sent a text to Kat and no one else.

WHAT R U DOING TONITE

WHATS UP, she may or may not have answered.

BURNING SERIOUS

WHEN

TONITE

OK

She may or may not have driven up in her white VW Vanagon. She may or may not have navigated the pitted driveway.

I assumed I would pour my heart out to her. I assumed I would purge and beg and make jokes and try to take her hand which she would not allow. I assumed I would pour my heart out, but the only thing I poured out was kerosene, ring around the rosie. Before setting kitchen match to, I grabbed the green dragon, whom I'd set to the side, and climbed Serious Pile to place him cherry on top. I faced him away from Serious Farm so he would not have to look. He may have had fond memories, I don't know. They couldn't have been too fond; we'd never even given the dragon a name.

Standing now at the foot of Serious Burn Pile, kitchen match ready, the Pile appeared to be half the size of Serious Barn, which is a big barn.

"Here goes," I said to Kat, who may or may not have been standing uncomfortably, a comfortable distance from Serious Pile and from me.

I assumed I would pour my heart out but there was no heart to pour, it seemed.

Serious burned very well, and for a long time in colors of the Northern Lights: blue-green, green-blue, blue, lilac, straight purple with horrible sulfur-smelling smoke mixed with regular sweet wood smoke. This toxic burn was illegal as all get out, and I considered briefly Kat's lung health but not mine. Kat's lungs, which may have been breathing there at the farm. The more I thought about it, the more I thought she wasn't probably there.

It burned good and for a long, long time. I barely moved watching and had nothing at all to say. Kat, who may or may not have been there, said okay and was gone. Serious Pile burned on with occasional small explosions of greenish flame, burned on well past the bottom of the ninth. I sat down in the wet grass. "Sometimes," I said to Kat's van as it bumped away on Serious Driveway, "sometimes things just don't work out the way we might have hoped."

"That's OK," I said. "That's OK."

That night, fire burning like the dickens outside, I texted M and B to let them know I was leaving and that I loved them. I also wrote them letters on a notebook page and walked the letters to Serious Mailbox, old school. I had serious doubts that those letters would ever reach them. For one reason or another.

I packed four twenty-gallon plastic tubs with some clothes that I would take with me and walked the remainders out to the burn. I slept for a bit in my sleeping bag on the remaining bed that the new tenant wished to keep. Before dawn I rolled up my sleeping bag and carried it with the four tubs outside to the Silverado.

With the fire still burning, I bumped my way down Serious Driveway for what may or may not have been the last time. Halfway down the driveway, I stopped and turned off the truck. I pulled the keys from the ignition and removed the Volvo key from the keyring. I walked back to where that poor miserable thing sat and put the key in the ignition. "Good luck to you," said. "It wasn't your fault."

Leaving things behind for someone else to deal with: Volvo, half-melted sofa springs and hot tub motor, memories. Learning to die lessons.

By noon I was crossing the Tappan Zee Bridge and headed southwest toward the Shenandoah Mountains, which were the Blue Ridge Mountains, which were the Great Smoky Mountains.

By 2 a.m. of day seven after Saul had died and twenty hours after leaving the fire burning at Serious Farm, I was checking into the Red Roof Inn off Johnnie Dodds Boulevard in Mount Pleasant, South Carolina. As I sat by the pool at 3 a.m. drinking a cold beer, I realized that somewhere in this migration I had missed Saul's funeral. I was fairly certain he would understand.

By 4 p.m. of day eight after Saul died, I had an apartment in Mount Pleasant and had traded the Silverado for a Mini Cooper. There went a chunk of Saul's or Bette's money.

By 2 p.m. of day nine after Saul died, I had a job with a hospice that I would start in one week, and by 4 p.m. of day eight after Saul died, I started to walk a lot. I parked the mini on Anson Street downtown and walked toward the Battery. I walked laps around Charleston peninsula and walked until my back hurt like eight days of stonework and my feet bled through socks like Curt Schilling. I slept on my apartment floor in my sleeping bag and had back spasms through the night. These spasms would keep me company nearly nightly for two years after Saul died.

GHOSTS

The ghosts only came around in certain parts of town. Their's was not a daytime or nighttime thing. Their's was a location situation.

The first apartment I found was in Mount Pleasant. No ghosts over there. My second apartment was on James Island. No ghosts there either.

When I finally moved downtown, I had company. It's one of the reasons I finally moved downtown. I enjoyed the company. Very much.

I never actually saw the regular ghosts, I don't think, but I heard them talking. They spoke to me and they talked among themselves. It was a pleasant and reassuring thing, the voices, the conversations.

Maybe I saw them.

Many times, when I was walking South of Broad, I would see movement from the corner of my eye. At first, I didn't consider ghosts. Mostly I assumed citizenry. Or wildlifery. But when I turned to look there would be no one, no thing. Sometimes, and with no good reason, I thought it was my children walking to catch up with me. Sometimes that feeling was so real and the image in my periphery so clear that I would be brutally disappointed when I could not find them, my children.

My Mount Pleasant apartment was spartan, as was the apartment complex. Just some barracks-looking structures jammed between Johnnie Dodds and Coleman Boulevards. It was a no-bedroom affair, a studio on the second floor with windows to the parking lot. It was fine. It was walking distance to a Trader Joe's and to a Kickin' Chicken establishment with plentiful televisions for the consumption of professional sports. It was October, and the Red Sox had recently collapsed from playoff contention in a controversy involving fried chicken and six-packs of beer in the clubhouse. The New England Patriotics were making fools of the National Football League every single Sunday. I spent some quality time at the Kickin' Chicken, made some acquaintances, ate some wings.

The ghosts wanted no part of Mount Pleasant. Or, not this part of Mount Pleasant. There was a section of town called Old Village, which was architecturally interesting with mansions, gorgeous Gothic or antebellum maybe mansions, pillars, porches, side-by-each with smaller ranch styles and bungalows. Ancient and enormous live oaks lined the streets, which seemed a good place for spirits to matriculate. I didn't spend enough time in Old Village to pick up on that telepathy. I could walk for hours South of Broad downtown and remain a non-threat to the locals, as wandering tourism was a given down there. I had the feeling of eyes upon me, the eyes of the living, on my occasional turn through Old Village streets.

In my Mount Pleasant apartment, I had a mattress I bought and the plastic crate/boxes I'd brought along. I wasn't ready for furniture. Mattress, two pillows, reading lamp, frying pan, fork, knife, spoon, saucepan, coffee maker. Not much later, a chair and a bizarre looking bookcase/desk combo thing I found at a Re:Store on lower King Street.

I found a job right away with a hospice. Charleston County and South Carolina in general were lousy with hospices. Hospi? Probably as many hospi as Starbucks. It was a death and dying free-for-all down here. The state laws in South Carolina allowed for rampant hospice competition while Maine and New Hampshire only signed off on X amount. Anyway, if you had a pulse and an MSW you could find work. But in my case, not for long.

Each evening, each gorgeous October evening, air thick and sweet, temps in the seventies, I would drive over the Ravenel Bridge spanning the Cooper River, park somewhere for free (it didn't take me long to scout out the free spots, like on the side street down by the Harris Teeter which for some reason had no *Parking forbidden* signs or parking meters) and then begin my nightly haunting of these conflicted streets.

Conflicted because I truly felt the push and shove between the living and the dead. The living, arrogantly assuming ownership. The dead, knowing better.

Also conflicted by the eternal debate regarding the inherent goodness or evil of mankind. There was evidence of both soaked into these cobblestones.

My back was so bad that in the nascent days of my parading, I would have to stop at benches or low walls and rest for a while. Sometimes, the pain was a dull ache, always on my righthand side, and other times a knife stab that would stop me in my tracks with a spasm of electricity that may have presented as something epileptic to anyone who may have noticed. When a spasm hit, I was afraid to move—couldn't move. I'd stand straight up and down waiting for it to subside, for the shock to dissipate, before stepping gingerly to the nearest place where I could sit down and regather myself.

It was during the aftershocks of these seizures that I became certain that the ghosts were here and the ghosts were benign. Their presence would slow down from whatever commute or chore they were committed to and sit with me. Sometimes only one presence. Sometimes several. And when I could finally move again, they would walk with me until certain I was okay.

I listened carefully while riding out the pain because I felt there was some sort of dialogue being attempted. Usually I heard the comforting voices when I was at the peak of pain. Pretty clear voices it seemed. And if they were not articulating actual words in English, they were emitting sympathetic frequencies—an "Oh," or a "Hmmm."

Of genuine concern. But when the spasm would begin its retreat, and I could think beyond the pain and try to really listen, the voices stopped.

In the nascent days, I could only walk a mile or two before exhaustion. Holding one's self rigid against actual pain or the anticipation is hard physical labor. As a result of this ongoing labor, I was sleeping very well. Unlike those difficult nights at Serious Farm, I was sleeping very well. At least once a night I'd jolt awake due to a spasm but would quickly change my position on my mattress and fall back into deep and very dreamy sleep.

I dreamed of everything and everyone. The living and the dead. The dreams and my Charleston reality were becoming hard to differentiate. I liked it.

My days were filled with genteel visits into the homes of Charleston County African-American families that were trusting enough of this governmental institution (hospice) to willingly open their doors. Tidy homes almost always and gracious hosts offering a cold drink on a hot day, which was nearly all of the days. My days were filled with listening to living history and asking questions about family stories all the way back to the slave days because this was so foreign to me and fascinating. The most gracious hosts imaginable and willing to answer my naïve questions about race relations and their perspectives on history, which was so different from my public education.

Once entering into the home of a white family on James Island inhabited by a husband and wife taking care of the wife's dying mother. The husband son-in-law opening the front door to me and staring a hole in my Maine license plates. Once inside he began to aggressively present his perspective on the War of Aggression. He had Civil War artifacts hung upon his wood-paneled walls. The longer he spoke the more agitated he became. The son-in-law walked me over to a framed document on the wall, which looked like some sort of certificate.

"What do you think of that?" he said.

"What is it?" I said.

"It's Confederate currency."

"Oh."

"Does that have any meaning to you whatsoever?" he demanded.

I thought on it a bit. It really didn't have any meaning whatsoever. This came out of my mouth: "Keep hope alive?"

Son-in-law wasn't sure if I was poking fun or not. Neither was I. I desperately wanted out of this house, never getting a chance to speak with the dying patient. I made a mental note to register my truck in South Carolina as quickly as possible. I had no desire to re-fight this war. Or any war. Ever again.

A few weeks later, one of our hospice nurses informed me that Son-in-law had been arrested for strangling, but not to death, his mother-in-law with one of her own soiled diapers.

At the end of my working days I would walk. This routine kept me satisfied well past the Christmas holidays. On Christmas Day, I went out for a day's long walk and while walking received a text from a friend asking how my Christmas Day was unfolding. "What are you up to?" he texted.

I texted back, "Walking. Taking opioids. More walking."

He texted back, "You know, church wouldn't kill you."

Winter walking in Charleston was like late-spring walking in Maine. Sometimes a little chill in the air but most times a nice neutral high fifties to low sixties air temperature. Spring in Charleston arrived in mid-February with parked cars becoming coated with the pollen from the foreign-looking species of pine trees. Sometimes, when a breeze moved the trees, the pollen looked like a green fog.

I never actively sought out the ghosts. I tried to just let them do their thing. Open to their company but trying not to be disappointed if they failed to walk with me.

It seems I walked every evening for at least a year.

And then there was the novelty of walking the beaches all through the winter months. It's not that it was impossible to walk Jenness Beach in Rye, New Hampshire, in January. Not impossible but damned cold with winds blasting in from the Isles of Shoals to freeze one's eyelids shut.

There were two wonderful walking beaches nearby. There was Sullivan's Island, which was nearest my apartment in Mount Pleasant, and there was Folly Beach down past James Island, which had a bit more commerce near its sands. The commerce didn't interest me all that much. Taco Boy did not call out to me, nor the t-shirt shops.

Sullivan's had a lone strip of restaurants and bars but was mostly blocks of very expensive homes built upon stilts. The beach was wide even during high tide and so much longer than any beach I'd strolled in New England. The Atlantic here was warm enough to pad barefoot through even in December. The water was murky but active with wildlife activities such as dolphins popping up and out only fifteen yards offshore. Pelicans divebombed the smaller fishes. Skates skimmed just up to the water's edge looking for something—something to do, something to eat. Once I stood barefoot looking down at a skate gently flapping its wings in only two inches of water and filtering that seawater through its geometric gills, which looked like the stripes sewn on a military shirt. I watched for a while and made up various rationales for what it might be doing so close to shore. I am no oceanographer. I am no fishophile. I watched for a while and then moved on to continue my walk.

When I returned I saw the skate washed up on the flat sand, dead. That skate had come this close to shore to expire. A good a reason as any to come close to shore. I wondered if this was normal end-of-life behavior for a skate but then imagined all of the skate corpses littering the beach if that were so.

Perhaps checking out the shore was on this particular skate's bucket list. Like a woman from Ohio with a dying wish to finally visit one of the oceans.

Who knows?

Winter was barely winter. I found a little restaurant and bar downtown called Fuel. It was a gas station converted with gas pump décor and the garage doors remaining garage doors. The place was called Fuel. Get it?

Fuel had a wonderful outdoor seating area with tables for dining and patio furniture for drinking and watching the enormous flatscreen TV mounted up high. For my entire nine-year stay in Charleston, I never got over the novelty of watching the Patriotics outdoors in January. Sometimes it dipped below 50 degrees, at which time Fuel would break out the tree-like propane heaters. These heaters were so efficient that one would break into a sweat while sitting stock still and drinking dollar-fifty PBRs. Folk here were just not comfortable unless they were sweating, I guess.

When I finally moved downtown after two years of circling it, I wound up two blocks from Fuel, down by the hospitals.

These fun discoveries, nothing seismic in importance, but fun, the walking, the ghosts, the beaches. These discoveries added up, one upon the next, until I felt delight fairly often. I would lay on my mattress before falling asleep and feel delight. That was the whole idea behind moving here. To remember delight. To rediscover happy. To recall if I were an inherently optimistic-type human or a perpetual bummer like I'd become upon Serious Farm.

There was still some sunshine in there. Inside.

Of course, I missed my daughters, but there was nothing left to do. I'd grieved. Hard. And would always. But for now, I was Kübler-Rossing acceptance. To a degree. All of the other stages visited regularly: the anger, the anger that I could not figure a way to combat the hole that I'd been pigeoned in as a Less Than, as The Other, as unworthy to be an acceptable father to my very own daughters.

But I could no longer live there, in anger. I'd been outsmarted, plain and simple. Not a huge achievement, to outsmart me, but it stung, nonetheless.

The denial came around from time to time, still. Of course I will see my girls again. Of course we will be fine. Despite all data indicating the opposite, I assumed these truths to be self-evident.

There was the bargaining, the ongoing notions that if I came up with just the right sort of appeal to the girls and to their mother, all would be forgiven—whatever I needed to be forgiven for. For being me.

And the depression, the sadness. I was walking my sadness into a pulp that could be scraped off the bottom of my boots like the poop that it is.

* * *

There is a building at the eastern terminus of Broad Street. It is the Old Exchange and Provost Dungeon. I walked by this building often but never went in. Most days there were employees out on the front stoop dressed in Colonial garb, which was a way of beckoning tourists to come in and learn. There was also a cunning little liquor store across the alley from the Old Exchange. I went in there plenty.

Often, on my walks, I would keep pace with the horse-drawn carriages which were all over the place. There were the carriages and there were the work crews in pickup trucks cleaning up the massive dumpings of the horse part of the arrangement.

The drivers of these carriage were also often dressed in Colonial outfits and they stood as they drove while orating various aspects of Charleston history. I would keep pace to get chunks of free history. The Old Exchange used to be the outer wall of Charleston, with the Cooper River lapping its foundation. Landfill extended landfall a few more hundred feet out into the river over the years, propping up some of the peninsula's most expensive real estate. The Exchange and the Dungeon were taken over by the British at some point before we kicked their asses. They used the dungeon to dungeon American loyalists. Part of me wanted to have a look at the dungeons. In time I would.

The drivers of the carriages also pointed out that massive parties were held in the upstairs of the Old Exchange, and that George Washington himself got his drink on at this location after the Revolution had been won. Or lost. Depending. It seems that over the years I'd visited or even slept in multiple locations along the Eastern Seaboard where George Washington had done one thing or another. I'd never felt the thrill of proximity or a brush with greatness by these visits. Not like I felt when I visited Ernest Hemingway's home in Key West. When I got to peek into Hem's upstairs carriage house where he did some of his writing, I got chills like malaria.

Most times, on my walks, I just made up my own history of Charleston.

On the curvy and cobbled section of Church Street I would watch an elderly couple walking arm-in-arm, he in tweed and bowtie, she in chiffon and neck fur, stepping up the front entrance steps of their discreet eighteen-million-dollar home, and decide on my own that their great-granddaddy or daddies (or perhaps just granddaddies. It wasn't that long ago!) made obscene profits on the backs of kidnapped men, women, and children. As they closed the four-inch-thick oaken doors behind them I would whisper at their backs: "What did you do?"

It wasn't that long ago. Fortunes acquired in the early 1800s may easily be squandered or just as easily compounded.

At Halloween, Black families brought their children trick-or-treating here South of Broad. Was this some sort of tradition? The only night where people who were clearly not tourists and clearly not white were allowed to come and get some? Smiling maids handing out goodies to smiling children tonight but catch your ass here tomorrow . . .

Making stuff up. I was just making stuff up. In time perhaps I could stop this fictionalizing of Southern life and learn to just be and just let them be.

This was a necessary learning process, learning to let them be. To let all things be.

Back at my apartment I began to revisit the absurdist heroes—the Kafka, the Camus, the Kierkegaard, the Vonnegut. These heroes who understood the folly of attempting to assign order to a universe with no apparent order.

I made smiling acquaintance with the librarians at the downtown library on Calhoun. I doubt they paid any attention to what the citizens were checking out, but, if they did, the nice ladies there may have assumed *that boy going through some shit*. In time, I would get to know these library ladies well as we, as a community, used the library as a meeting place to process tragedy. Them volunteering their space for the community to meet. Me volunteering my experience and relative expertise with grief and loss. There was tragedy to come.

And through this first year in Charleston, my first year in Charleston, full of ghosts and painful solitary ambulation and fabricated histories regarding mankind's greatest sin of the buying and selling of human beings, I felt great!

If not great, then a hell of lot better than before I got here.

*　*　*

The Southern outlook on death and dying was significantly different than that of southern Maine. I came to call it the Lowcountry Panic.

The outlook initially caught my attention with one of my first hospice visits when the seventy-three-year-old son of a ninety-three-year-old mother opened his door to me and demanded I explain to him how this could possibly be.

"I can't lose my mama!!!"

I thought, to myself for once, *What did you think was going to happen?*

When I got back to the office and relayed this poor guy's seeming surprise that his very old and very sick (she'd been living with thyroid cancer for three years) mother was nearing the end of the line, one of my RNs said, "Everybody down here wants to go to heaven. But nobody wants to die."

And the African-American families had an interesting approach to dying. While they were always gracious hosts to us into their homes, they did not wish to talk about death. They understood completely what was happening but would not speak of it and preferred that we, the hospice team, did not speak of it either. So we worked around it.

When I asked a Black colleague about this she said, "We believe in miracles."

I thought, to myself, these good folks down here need some learning to die lessons.

*　*　*

There is a green space downtown called Washington Square. Not a particularly original name. It sits between Broad Street and Chalmers, which is severely cobbled. It features a ring of benches, an obelisk, and mighty, mighty live oaks with accompanying dangly moss. In the middle of the square is a replica of the Washington Monument, and off from the center a little is a smallish statue of George himself. There is a brick wall on the eastern edge of the square dedicated to a cat named Pierre Beauregard who was a loser.

It would become reflex over the years to whisper "loser" each time I passed a monument to sedition. A reflex like making a moo sound every time I see a cow. No exceptions. I would sit here often, inside the Washington Square.

I would sit here often over the years as the live oaks provided good shade in the summer and a sense of privacy and a little foreboding at night. This was a safe part of town, not much danger of being approached or assaulted here. I was probably the most dangerous lurker of Washington Square and it should be evident by now that I am no danger at all.

After crisscrossing the streets of downtown, Washington Square was a good place to rest and to see or feel which of the sprites were about.

It was my second September in Charleston and my walks were becoming semi-epic in length and breadth. My brother Andy and my sister-in-law had come to visit in this first year. They'd come in April when all was abloom and ablossom. I was eager to show them the sights and the sounds of downtown, so I walked them hard. I have a hardy family, fairly fit and nearly always eager to explore. After giving them the basic peninsula prowl they were both ready to get back to their hotel. They seemed whooped.

Out of curiosity, I came back into town that night in my truck just to get an idea from the odometer of how far I'd force-marched them. Turned out to be about 5.5 miles give or take. The next day at dinner I apologized.

From the restaurant on King Street called Prohibition, I walked Andy and Midge to Washington Square. It was a little over a mile, it felt, and fairly close to their hotel. I wanted them to experience the calming electricity of the place and see if maybe, just maybe, they might feel, see, or hear my ghost friends.

It was a little past sundown when we entered the park. The three of us sat on a bench and took in the night air, the night sounds. It was still very warm in September and the cicadas were still shrieking. I loved the sound of the tree insects in South Carolina. I'm assuming they were cicadas. They could have been anything. Maybe even frogs.

We sat and were quiet. Midge finally said, "I get it.

"I get why you're here, Holmes."

I said, "Yes."

"There's something. There's some kind of peace here for you. I can see it in your body, the way you walk is different. You're moving like you used to move, before."

"Before . . . ?" my brother said.

"The Troubles," Midge said.

"I think that one's been taken," I said. "But we can borrow it. It fits."

"Any word? From the girls?" Midge asked.

"Nope."

So we sat in silence. Across the square, on the opposite side of the ring of benches, a man sat smoking a cigarette. He caught my eye mainly because of the way he sat, legs crossed, slightly slouched, working the cigarette with obvious relish. There was something about him but I didn't want to stare. I thought he looked somewhat familiar but couldn't be sure. His face was not clear to me in the dusk and the weak lamplight. I thought he might have glanced our way a couple of times. Not so much a glance as side-eye peek. We were the only people in the square, so he may have been out people watching and we were the only people. He got up to leave before we did and exited the square onto East Bay Street. I caught a bit of his profile and he definitely looked familiar.

* * *

Walking Sullivan's Island one afternoon, with the hospice day behind me, this day punctuated by me helping one of our nurses bandage up a sweet old lady's exterior melanoma tumors (they were dangling on the outside of her skin like meaty, veiny crabapples), I decide to try and run a little.

I used to run fairly regularly. At first to train for sports and then just because I like to run. I wasn't particularly fast. My best time for a 10k was just over forty minutes. I liked to run on the hottest of the New England summer days. When I was truly young and stupid, I would stick a marijuana cigarette in my sock and then smoke it at around mile three of a six-mile run. I'm not sure what I was trying to prove. Maybe nothing. Maybe I just liked running and just liked getting high. Why not combine the two?

But as I got deeper into my stonemasonry career, running just became too much of a chore. I'd still do it, but only to get my heart rate up every once in a while. My legs at the end of a stonework day were log cabins. My back a constant nag. I'd long since given up on weed, but it might actually have helped with my calcifying body.

In the last two years before moving to Charleston, I didn't run at all. My discs were just too damaged and could no longer do their shock-absorbing job. I bought an elliptical machine for the farm, but felt like an idiot spinning in place while looking out the window. It was better than no cardio exercise at all, but not much.

I assumed my running days were over forever. But this one October day on Sullivan's Island I decided to try. Down near the water on the packed sand I took a few tentative stabs at a trot. I covered maybe a half-mile before shutting it down. My lungs felt like bricks and I assumed I would pay with spasms that night in my sleep.

Perhaps all of the walking I'd been doing was helping my back, I'm not sure, but for whatever reason, my back did not seize in the night.

* * *

In late October, close to Halloween, I found myself sitting in Washington Square Park long after dark. It must have been close to midnight. There were few pedestrians out. The only bar even close to the park was the Blind Tiger on Broad Street. I heard nothing from over that way. The Tiger was not a bar overly populated by the Woo Girls from the College of Charleston. Woo Girls could be heard on upper King Street ululating in their cups like exotic birds calling out before nesting for the night.

I sat listening to the tree frogs sing.

I was learning to be in the moment.

At the moment it was soft October winds and tree frogs.

And then it was a guy wandering into the square.

I could tell right away that it was the same guy who had been sitting smoking a cigarette a month or so ago when I was with Andy and Midge. I couldn't see his face, only his dark shadow and outline in the backlit midnight. I couldn't tell what he could see of me, if anything at all. I was on a bench and I think mostly shadowed. I'm not sure why I considered this except I wanted to get a look at this guy without him noticing I was taking a good look at him. I know I knew him. The thing about getting older is that you've done some things, been some places, lived in various states, and met a large number of people. Some people leave lasting impressions and some leave no impression at all. Some of those lasting impressions come from people you've only met once and for only a moment. Some people you might have called a friend at some point are utterly forgotten. Sometimes it is difficult to place where or how various people have transected our own paths and why.

I definitely knew this guy.

He sat down at the same bench he'd taken a month ago. He fished in his shirt pocket for his smokes and lit up. Once again, he was in the shadows but I could tell a little bit more about him because I was able to focus on him completely. He appeared to be in his mid to late twenties. He was about six feet tall and about 170 pounds. He wore khakis and a t-shirt. He appeared to be in pretty good shape, his arms muscular and his shoulders fairly wide. He wore what appeared to be a non-ironic flat-top haircut. This aspect gave me the shivers as I continued to try and recall how I knew this man. I have not run across that many people that I could recall who wore flat-top haircuts. I was getting a very strange feeling. Not afraid, just . . . uneasy. Uneasy but more than just a little curious.

Again, I felt like this guy was very cautiously looking over at my quadrant of the park. I hoped I wasn't being too obvious in my efforts to observe him. I didn't want any trouble of any sort. I didn't know if possibly Washington Square was a pickup spot for cruising gay men like down at the Battery.

We sat there, the only two people in the square, for more than thirty minutes. He smoked one leisurely cigarette after another. The manner in which he smoked convinced me beyond a doubt that I knew him. I don't know why I didn't just go over and say hello.

Finally, I got up to do just that. This was the South. Saying hello to strangers was no big deal. As I walked toward him he watched me come, his face completely obscured by shadow, the glow of his cigarette tip alive in the darkness. As I got within ten feet of his bench, the guy casually tossed his butt to the sidewalk and crushed it out with his boot. He was wearing work boots.

When I stopped in front of him and was sharing his shadow I could see his face clearly. He did indeed appear to be twenty-five years old or so. His flat-topped hair was dark brown, almost black. He had brown eyes and a long, straight distinctive nose. He was a handsome man. I knew who he was all right.

"Hi," I said.

"Hey," he said.

I didn't stop. I just kept walking toward Chalmers Street. My truck was parked over by the Teeter Harris.

The last time I'd seen this guy he was sitting in a mulberry tree outside my bedroom window. The last time I'd seen him he'd been dead for a week. The last time I saw my father he was dead and in a mulberry tree in his bathrobe smoking a Benson and Hedges. The last time I saw my father I'd asked him one too many questions and he'd disappeared, disappointed, into the mystic.

This time he was in his twenties, thirty years younger than me, on a bench in Charleston, South Carolina. He was still smoking what I assumed were Benson and Hedges. He didn't try to stop me as I walked past him in the direction my truck.

* * *

My second Charleston Christmas came and went. I visited the Marion Square Christmas Vortex pretty much every night in the two weeks leading up to Christmas. The two doormen I'd met at the Francis Marion Hotel three years ago were no longer working there, at least not as doormen.

I'd been fired by my first hospice for noncompliance or insubordination or something. What happened was I'd told an administrator to leave me alone when she'd tried to strongarm me into doing more comprehensive and more time-sensitive documentation. I got hired by another hospice within a week and within two months the same thing happened. I didn't like documentation. I didn't like administrators. It was suggested I had anger issues.

Imagine that.

* * *

"Do you know who I am?"
"Of course," he said.
"Who?"
"You're Holmes," he said.
"But you haven't even had me yet."
"Yeah we did."
"How old were you when I was born?"
"Twenty-four."
"How old are you now?"
"I'm not."

Then he got up from his bench and walked off toward Broad Street.

* * *

I was up to running two miles every other day. My back was holding up pretty well. I was unemployed for a while so I joined a gym. By now I'd moved from my studio apartment in Mount Pleasant to a one-bedroom on James Island. I moved into one of those apartment complexes with a clubhouse, a mini-gym, and a pretty nice swimming pool. There was a post office-type area to pick up and drop off one's mail. The complex advertised community get-togethers, of which I did not partake. I was not anti-get-together and actually planned on attending the Mardi Gras replication, but then forgot to go.

The mini-gym was no good. It was too small. More than one person in there felt really wrong for some reason. If the other person was hogging one of the two machines in there you were kind of screwed. It did have one of those abdominal contraptions with the two armrests and a backrest where you hoisted yourself up into the air, using the armrests to support your weight and then working those abs by bringing your knees up to your chest. Does that make sense? I started what became a nine-year habit of abdominal or core work in that weird little one-person gym on James Island.

There was a Gold's Gym within walking distance of the apartment complex. It was just down past the Walmart on Folly Road. Next to the Gold's Gym was a King Street Grill, which was neither on King Street nor a Grill. But it replaced the Kickin' Chicken for professional sports viewing. James Island was okay.

One day, driving aimlessly on 17 through West Ashley, I pulled into a Mini Cooper dealership. I swapped out the Silverado for a used turbo Mini. The salesman initially tried to sell me a convertible. After test-driving it I told the salesman that I was already doubtful about my sexuality and did he have something in a hard top. He sold me on the turbo even though I had no idea what turbo was. It sounded pretty manly, though.

I called my brother Mac the motorhead after I got the Mini back to the complex to have him help me explain what I had just done. He said, "Nice! A street legal go-cart made by BMW. How fast have you gotten it up to?"

I told him, "About thirty-five so far."

"Take it out on the highway and goose it. I think you'll be surprised."

That night I rolled onto 526 after dark and got it up to 125 mph. I *was* surprised. I was also surprised by how loud it was. The next day I called Mac and asked him about the splattering sound coming from the muffler. He told me I'd probably paid extra for that. He said loud mufflers are a thing.

"A good thing?"

"Just a thing," he said.

I said, "Aren't loud mufflers a self-canceling phrase?" He chuckled.

Gold's Gym became a thing. I wasn't trying to pump up. I very gently did half-situps and used all of the multiple abdominal machines they had there. It was awkward initially as I had to teach myself how to use these machines. Learn to use them without hurting myself. I knew nothing about the science of core strength. I just felt like doing situps. In fairly short order I was doing hundreds per visit. I ended each gym visit with at least an hour on an elliptical machine. Gold's Gym had a room dedicated to cardio machines and the room was a *movie theatre!* You never knew what feature they would be playing on any given day, but it was easy to get lost in even a horrible movie for an hour or sometimes considerably more while grinding away like a hamster on an expensive machine designed to go nowhere. My thought process was it would do no good to have a fully repaired core if the heart muscle was garbage.

I guess I wanted to live.

None of this was well thought out. It was just a thing. The James Island experience didn't last long. I knew I needed to end up downtown.

* * *

My first encounter with Bernard was ominous. I'd seen him around. He was a street guy, maybe in his mid-thirties to early forties. He was extremely Black and built like a Greek statue notion of manhood. He was often shirtless on hot days and his physique was such that the logical conclusion was that he spent many hours in the gymnasium. He was ripped. He wore a James Harden beard. Cutoff shorts. I often saw him panhandling gregariously on lower King

Street. He seemed to know a lot of the locals and he seemed to have a way with the tourists.

The first time I came face-to-face with him scared me a little. The second time scared me even more. But then we became friends. I think we became friends. I'll never know how he would have defined our relationship.

I was walking along Cannon Street, which at the time was still somewhat sketchy, for me, a white guy. It was pre-gentrification and the houses were mostly falling apart. There were a couple of obvious crackhouses and drug-dealing corners. A couple brave entrepreneurs had opened businesses down there: a tapas restaurant not too far from King Street, a skateboard shop, and a bakery. I was walking along probably looking for *for rent* possibilities, or maybe just ambling. Bernard was sitting in the shade of a bus stop kiosk thing with his bike next to him. He was shirtless and spread out, his arms akimbo resting on the bench top. He wasn't quite six feet tall, but he had an insanely disproportionate wingspan. As I walked by the bus stop he yelled at me: "Hi!"

I thought I answered appropriately. I said hi back at him but it must have come out as a dismissive grunt because Bernard stood up quickly and mimicked a dismissive grunt followed by, "What's your problem, mister?"

I've navigated enough city streets to know better than to engage with this sort of zero-sum conversation. I just kept walking. I just kept walking but made a mental note to avoid this cat if possible. He gave off a very schizophrenic vibe.

The next time I met Bernard he was barreling down King Street on his bike headed south in the direction of Marion Square and I was headed north in the direction of no-particular-place-to-go. I saw him coming and then looked away. Eye contact with the afflicted is a city street no-no.

Too late. He pulled up right in front of me and again, loudly, said, "Hi!"

I could have kept walking but was glad I didn't. This time I countered his "hi" with an equally audible "hi."

Bernard smiled an impressively winning smile and put out his right hand. I shook his meathook and as I suspected might be the case, he did not let go. It was okay. This time he was giving off a very friendly vibe. "What do you do?" he asked.

"I'm a counselor," I said, "mental health."

"You're a doctor!"

"No, I'm . . ." Bernard dismounted and leaned his bike against a building on King Street.

"OK, Doctor. You'll appreciate this . . ." Bernard let go of my hand and began to knead the muscles in the back of my neck. I almost involuntarily smiled but also wondered what the actual fuck.

"Damn," he said, "you one uptight motherfucker."

"It's a problem," I said.

"All right now, Doctor. First thing the most important thing. You gotta trust me. Just relax. Trust me."

"Okay," I said with zero trust in my inflection.

"Seriously," Bernard said, "relax." He then pivoted so that he was behind me and put me into some sort of a full nelson situation.

"I was an athletic trainer for a while," he said. "I have a unique skill set. Now *relax*, goddammit!"

It had come to this: I was about to be strangled by a crazy street dude in broad daylight on King Street in Charleston, South Carolina. Oddly enough, my reaction to this realization was, *Why not*?

From behind me, in a not-so-vaguely homoerotic fashion, Bernard told me to take a deep breath and then relax my whole body. I did as I was told except for the relax my body part. He then thrust his pelvis into my lower back and slowly bent me backward until I heard a very loud pop.

He set me back down and then held me for a bit because he knew he'd wobbled me. Then he let me go and came around to face me. "How you feel?"

"Alive," I said. "Pretty good."

"Imagine how good you'd feel if you could relax a little. You tight."

"It's an ongoing thing," I said. "It's not you." He stood looking at me. He had beautiful eyes, long lashes. "It's partly you," I said.

Bernard laughed and said, "I like you, Doctor." He never did tell me his name, but I learned it not too much later on. He was somewhat a legend on the peninsula. "I like you. Now. I'm in need of twenty-seven dollars and forty-three cents in order to pay off a debt as well as buy me some breakfast. Can you help me out?"

I knew I didn't have exact change. I pulled my wallet and all I had in there was a ten. "I've got ten," I said.

"That's a excellent start," Bernard said. I gave him the bill and he shook my hand again. He remounted his mountain bike and said, "Stay loose. I'll see you around Doc."

And I did see him. Quite often. Each time we ran into one another he would hop off his bike and perform one of his chiropractic moves in exchange for whatever money I had on me at the moment. He was indeed very skilled, but after a while I felt brave enough to tell him, "You know what? I appreciate the adjustments but I'd rather enter into a new arrangement."

"What kinds?" he asked.

"I'll still try to help you out when I can, but in exchange I'd rather you tell me your story."

"My story?"

"Yes."

"A'ight," he said.

It took my remaining seven years in Charleston to receive my end of the deal. He was a distracted storyteller.

* * *

There is a feeling, a feeling something like danger or conspiracy when one is out on the street at midnight and the church bells ring. It is a flipping of the time continuum from all-is-well to things-could-potentially-get-strange. There is a saying that nothing good happens after midnight. I'm not so sure about that. Good and bad are such subjective notions. I can think of a few dozen good things that have happened to me after midnight right off the top of my head. On the other hand, I've had more than a few dozen odd things happen after midnight that most likely would not have happened otherwise. I'm pretty sure it was Richard Pryor who made this midnight observation. He would know.

On a sticky May evening in my third year in Charleston, I found myself just entering Washington Square Park when the midnight bells bonged. It had been over a year that I'd said hello to my twenty-five-year-old father. Either he had not returned since then or we had just missed one another in the interim. I never missed a week of cruising the park. I don't know that I was specifically looking for Dad, but probably.

This midnight night in May in Charleston he was standing, smoking, leaning against the main gate to the square that opened onto Broad Street. There was no one else in the square. It occurred to me that except for the first time I'd seen my dad here, the time I was with Andy and Midge, our meetups had no witnesses. That could mean something, in the long term, when trying to assess my own mental health. No witnesses. If a ghost appears in the night and there is no one there to hear it, does it make a boo? But I was there.

"Boo," I said to my father.

"Funny," he said.

"What's new?" I asked.

"Not much," he said. "You know, the usual."

After a moment's silence, we laughed pretty hard at that one. The usual. When the laughter died down to a chuckle I said, "So you're aware of how unusual this is?"

"It's weirding me out," he said, "completely."

"So, what are we supposed to be doing?" I asked. "Is there some sort of chore you are beholden to? Some sort of chore I'm beholden to? This can't just be a random occurrence, right?"

"You got me, kid."

"And that," I said. "In your present form, you're less than half my age. And what is your present form? You look pretty solid. What would happen if I tried to touch you?"

"No idea."

"Are you ectoplasmic? Mist? Meat?"

"I honestly don't know," my father said. "I'm new at this."

"But you've been dead for thirty some odd years."

"So?"

"So, it seems you've had some time to settle into . . . this."

"You seem to be rather preoccupied with the notion of time. And age. Those things don't really matter so much."

"Don't matter where you are?"

"Don't matter anywhere."

My dad and I never really had the opportunity to have an adult conversation regarding metaphysics or quantum physics or the notions of time or age. I was ready to concede his point that time and age really don't matter much, on any plane, when he asked me, "How old are you?"

"I'm fifty-four, Dad." I held my breath a little at this, not knowing if he recognized the significance of fifty-four to me. That my dad was fifty-four when he died.

"Fifty-four? Hey, that's how old I was when . . ."

"I know. So, you remember that?"

"Of-course I remember that. It was a pretty significant day, as I recall."

"It was," I said. "I think about it all the time."

"You do?"

"Yes. You are greatly missed, Dad."

"I am?" I just looked at him. He really had no idea how profound his early exit was to his family. To me.

"Yup."

"Let's go for a walk," he said.

He took off toward Broad Street and the Ashley River. The Blind Tiger was quiet with only a couple bar patrons nursing drinks in the front window. Dad led me straight to the Old Exchange building. He didn't speak and he didn't smoke. He walked with a vigor, but he always did walk with a vigor, even in his old age that was my present age. I wondered if I walked with a vigor.

Dad marched right up the steps to the front door of the Exchange, taking the set of steps to our right. He reached out his right hand and opened the front door. It wasn't locked. Not for him anyway. He didn't do the ectoplasmic ooze through the solid walls like movie ghosts do. He just turned the door handle and led me in.

There were a few low lights burning in the lobby of the Exchange and I wondered if Dad needed light to see where he was going. So, I asked him.

"Of course I need light, how else would I see?"

"I have no idea," I said. "I have no idea how any of this works."

"There's not much to it," he said, but did not explain any further.

Dad walked along a carpeted hallway to a stairwell that led down. He was taking me down into the Provost Dungeon part of the building. Thankfully, there were some lights remaining on in the stairwell and some low light coming up from below. He led me past the museum displays of mannequins in manacles depicting prisoners held in this ancient prison. He led me through the incredible brick archways that held up the entirety of this gigantic and ancient building. I'd seen archways like these in buildings in Prague and those buildings were significantly older than this one. They knew how to build a building back in the day.

He walked me past the displays and into a corridor which was blocked by a very thick-looking black-painted door with the iron ring door handle treatment. I didn't know if this was the original door hardware or an affect the museum people had installed for dramatic effect. Whatever, it worked. The door handle.

My dad pulled on the ring towards himself and the door quietly and smoothly opened. More low light from this corridor. I was half expecting those firey torchy stick things planted in the brick walls but there were electric lights running every thirty feet or so along the arched ceiling.

We walked.

It felt like we were headed in the direction we'd just come from. If we weren't, then we must have been in a tunnel under the Cooper River, or maybe walking parallel to East Bay Street. This was an interesting feature, this underground tunnel taking us somewhere into the Charleston peninsula. I'd never heard tell of this thing and I wondered what function it served throughout the Chuck's varied and violent history.

My Dad led the way but only a step ahead of me. The tunnel was dry and the air was comfortable. We walked for quite a while, not speaking but not at all uncomfortable in each other's company. I assumed my father would show me what he intended to show me soon enough, or tell me what he wanted to tell me. For the time being I was just enjoying the hell out of this most unlikely circumstance. I always did feel comfortable with my father, the little time I got to spend with him. I seemed to be his designated work helper back when he was on shore and alive. If there was some painting to be done, he had me help. If there was a tree to be taken down he taught me how to operate the chainsaw. If the TV antenna needed fixing up on the roof, he sent me up there. I loved it. I loved being his helper. He may have had roles for my other brothers, I'm not sure. But I really did feel special when he'd tap me on the shoulder and say, "C'mon." That meant we had a chore to bang out.

And I knew this wasn't normal, walking a tunnel beneath Charleston with the young ghost of my father. I knew this could all very well be my imagination at work, but it most certainly felt real. I dragged my fingers along the brick wall of this tunnel and red dust adhered to my hands, got under my fingernails. I wasn't worried about the power going out and losing our way down here because my father was leading the way. I felt utterly safe, which was probably the best thing a father can do for his kid.

Eventually, finally, he stopped. I wasn't wearing a watch this evening but it felt as though we'd been walking for well over an hour. My Dad stopped at another black-painted door with another iron ring door handle.

"Here we are," he said. "End of the line."

"OK," I said.

"That's it?" he said. "OK?"

My father was now looking directly at me. His hands were in the pockets of his chinos. His eyes were neither young nor old, they were just my father's brown eyes. He patted his t-shirt pocket, looking for a cigarette but decided to not.

"I don't think I'm going to be seeing you for a while," he said. "So now is the time."

For the first time since seeing him in Washington Square some months ago I felt afraid. Not of the whole paranormal thing. This felt good. This felt normal.

"Why?" I said.

My dad looked at me patiently. His twenty-some-odd-year-old ghost self. "There's not a lot of why. You know that, right?"

"I do. I guess I do."

"I don't have answers, Holmes. There are no rules, no protocols. I really don't know how any of this works." My dad was talking to me.

"I know it's been hard for you."

"It was hard for you," I said.

"Yes," he said. "It's hard. It's hard for everyone. It's hard for your daughters. It's hard for their mother. But I think you understand as well as anyone that there is love."

I stood looking at my father. This may have been the only time I'd ever heard him use the word love. I could feel that time was running out. I was not going to be seeing my father again for some time. I started to talk.

"You were loved, Dad. I don't know why we didn't say it, any of us. Why we couldn't. None of us.

"I don't know if you have any idea how much influence you had on us. I don't know what went wrong with you and Bette. I don't know what your marriage was like. She wouldn't talk about it. But there was an enormous hole after you died. We miss you. Badly."

I wasn't about to pull the crying trick that I'd done with Bette when she so badly wanted to leave, but I was having a hard time not.

"You are loved, Dad. You were a good man, here on Earth. I knew that when you were alive, but it's even more clear in the years you've been gone. You were solid. You were honest."

"Okay," he said. "I've got to go, but I want you to listen to yourself right now. I don't know how things will turn out with Mae and Bea. I don't. But I want you to listen to yourself. Listen carefully."

"Okay," I said, "I think I understand what you're saying. But tell me, what was the point of this tunnel trek? Did this really happen?"

"Just go topside," he said. "Things are going to get interesting."

"Did this really happen?"

My dad, my dad's ghost, my imagination, my psychosis, said, "Fucked if I know."

My father reached out his right hand. I reached out as well. The handshake was the same. The same as when he would come into my high school locker room after a game and shake my hand and then leave. The same as the last time I ever saw him alive. It was strong. It was as real as the day is long. We shook hands like always and then he turned to go back the way we'd come. My dad looked over his shoulder at me and, smiling, took a hard right and vanished into or through the bricks of the tunnel wall.

"No, you didn't," I hollered, laughing.

I heard him laughing from somewhere and then I heard nothing but my own breathing.

I stood there for a while, beneath Charleston. Then I pulled on the iron ring door handle, which opened to a set of stone steps. I went up until I came to a metal door. I opened that and found myself in a parking garage. I walked toward the first opening onto the street and found myself at the corner of President and Cannon, right down the block from Fuel. The cicadas, the frogs were singing, or screaming from their hideouts. I found myself staring at a mint greenhouse with a *for rent* sign planted out front.

* * *

I was able to get myself moved in downtown within the month. I had to pay some penalties at the apartment complex over on James Island, and the douchebag property manager of the mint house downtown demanded first, last, and a ridiculous security deposit that we both knew he would never give back. But it was worth it.

It was the bottom floor of a two-story house. The first floor of the house was eight feet above sidewalk level, which came in handy during rainstorms and flooding, but that only happened twenty to thirty times a year. The apartment had ten-foot ceilings and a trio of French doors opening out to a narrow deck/veranda situation, which I envisioned roosting upon and listening to Red Sox games on the internet radio.

The house was a well-crafted classic Charleston almost railroad style with built in bookcases and whitewashed wainscoting all around. Ceiling fans. It was a two-bedroom affair with the larger bedroom being close to grand with its own bathroom and floor-to-ceiling windows looking out at the brick alley between the mint house and the brick dwelling next door. The brick dwelling next door was covered in flowering vines that I think was jasmine. There was a tree growing in the alley that I found out was a loquat tree with orange loquats hanging like Halloween lanterns all throughout the branches. The jasmine and the loquat leaves made it seem as though this urban and lopsided house was planted in a rainforest somewhere when I sat on my veranda or looked out the grand bedroom window.

Speaking of rain, the roof of the house was metal, and when downpours came it was a pleasing percussion. The second bedroom was small and strange with a ladder leading to a tiny sleeping loft. The second bedroom was accessed by moving through the kitchen and through an almost hatch-sized doorway. It had a submarine-style bathroom and shower. It was tucked away, hidden and I preferred it over the grand. I moved into that bedroom after a month of sleeping in the grand and feeling like I was on a raft at sea. I loved this house and would remain here for the rest of my decade in Charleston.

I passed a very pleasant first year in the mint house. Mostly pleasant. I got fired from my second hospice job, once again crossing the wrong white woman administrator. Not worth even relaying the details or thinking about. But I did think I'd had enough of hospice work. I'd learned enough about death. I'd learned enough about dying. I was intent upon living for a while.

I got a job working with the US Navy as a suicide prevention guy. Pretty much the opposite of hospice. I worked with the young enlisted and had a ball doing it. I didn't have to wear long-sleeved shirts in summer to cover my tattoos, as the Navy pretty much invented tattoos. I didn't have to swallow my foul language usage. I learned it was nearly impossible to get fired from a government job. It felt like I was settling in for the long haul. Why not?

The Red Sox rebounded from their last-place finish the year before and found themselves very surprisingly in the playoffs and then the World Serious my first October downtown. Fuel was a fun place to watch games on the TV, with its outdoor and dog-friendly patio, but there was a sports bar down Cannon and up on King Street called the Beerwerks that was specifically Bostoncentric.

As in any bar, there were some knowledgeable folks to talk to and some flaming idiots. Since I had no TV of my own at home, I sometimes had to sit stone-faced and nonresponsive if I happened to land upon a stool next to an idiot. The friendly and hardball-savvy strangers I met, both locals and tourists, made up for the occasional knucklehead sandwich.

Initially that October, I spent time in a variety of bars as the Sox plowed their way through the tournament. I watched them bounce the Joe Maddon Rays and then the Tigers of Detroit somehow scratching runs against a historically tough pitching staff of Justin Verlander and Max Scherzer. Big Papi once again sold what remained of his soul to the Devil and came through with an otherworldly clutch grand slam into the Fenway bullpen as Torii Hunter tumbles over the bullpen wall and police rejoice, arms raised in partisan joy. I walked from bar to bar on King Street, sometimes not even going in and only watching an inning or two from the street doorways. Bartenders I knew, waving hello. Most of my Charleston friends were of the service industries: bartenders, baristas, doormen, bike taxi persons.

I watched as we matched up World Serious against the old friend St. Louis Cardinals. We'd seen them before in 2004 when the Curse of the Bambino was broken and in 1967 with the hellacious Bob Gibson and a motherfucker named Curt Flood. I remember this. My dad and I, him with his smoke and his Budweiser, me running home from school to catch the end of these day games. We sat there, sad, Dad and me, when we lost in seven games. I cried for sad Yaz, for Rico Petrocelli, for George Scott. I believe my dad may have been crying inside.

Now, up three games to two against these latter-day Cardinals, I squeezed into madhouse Beerwerks, wanting to be with people, even people I did not know. I found a wobbly round table, the tall kind built for barstool chairs, the tabletop already wet and sticky with something—humidity or beer or nacho cheese. I had my ratty ballcap B and my left forearm tattooed B, which stands for Bea but is of the same Red Sox font, so I felt good.

There were two seats at this table, the only two seats remaining even before first pitch and the bartender, Dave, a Buffalo, New York, hockey player, without asking, came out from behind the bar to set a cold Bud in front of me.

"Feeling it?" he asks.

"Feeling it," I said.

A guy around my age stood looking around, a little lost. I nudged his elbow and pointed at the empty stool at my table. He said, "You sure?"

Turns out this guy was originally from Claremont, New Hampshire. He left that gray little town a long, long time ago for Texas. He was in town for some sort of accountant's convention and was staying at one of the new hotels just down King Street from the Beerwerks. He saw all the Boston gear and decided to come on in.

We talked about the Red Sox and the inevitable dad thing that could not be avoided when talking about the Red Sox. He said the only time his father ever called him, ever, after leaving home, was in October 2004, at midnight, after the curse had been dispelled. And he hasn't talked to him since.

"Is your dad still in Claremont?"

"Oh," my new buddy said, "he died. As fathers will."

No matter where I watched these games this October, I was accompanied by the silhouette ghost of my father as he and I watched together. Whether parked in a bar or standing in a barroom doorway, he was there, just barely within my peripheral, cigarette glowing, watching and saying nothing. I don't know why he was no longer talking to me. I didn't tell my new buddy about it.

All through this October, I texted during games with my brothers Holy Mackerel and Andy and a guy named Chuck who somehow got linked into the group. We made stupid and obvious observations, semi-sexist comments, recalled recollections of shenanigans past, that sort of thing.

They texted me throughout this Game Six, as the Sox took the early lead and the Cardinals looked forlorn, done. A kid standing to watch the game used our table to hold his drinks and made sparing comments, but was intensely involved. In the eighth inning, he went up to the bar and came back with a tray holding nine shots of Fireball. He placed three in front of my buddy, three in front of me, and three for himself.

"Three outs to win this thing," he said. With each out, we drank. When our closer Uehara got the first out on a week grounder, we grimly toasted and drank up.

And then, after the Uehara strikeout of the final overmatched Red Bird, the Beerwerks went bathouse with drunk student transplants who had obviously learned the game in front of New England television sets and on New England Little League and softball fields.

The kid who bought the shots looked at us, dazed, shook our hands and wandered into the meat of the fray. I watched the ensuing scrum with a smile and a pretty good buzz. My phone lit up and I assumed it was my brothers or Chuck with final comments.

The face of my phone read, BEA. I had not heard a word from either of my daughters in many weeks. My beautiful and intelligent and sweet seventeen-year-old daughter Bea sent a text at the stroke of midnight. All in caps: DAD WE DID IT.

I pulled my ratty Sox hat down over my eyes, showed the text to my new Claremont buddy. He saw my tears and he hid his own eyes by looking down but he'd been crying too. Men are funny. We shook hands and I hit the bricks for the slow walk home through these gorgeous haunted Charleston streets. I was not alone. Red Sox Nation both dead and alive was out for a hoot and a bray.

DAD WE DID IT

* * *

That January I received an email from the College of Charleston admissions office. It asked me to provide proof of South Carolina residency. Weird. I could either mail or email an image of a South Carolina driver's license or utility bill or pay stub. Or I could stop by the admissions office with same. I had all three, but what the fuck? At some point I'd looked into whether C of C had a doctoral social work program, but they didn't even have a master's. This was strange. Normally I would ignore what most likely was some sort of computer error or misguided marketing ploy, but something told me to follow up.

I went to the admissions office and they had no record of an email being sent to me. When I told the student working the admissions front desk that I'd been asked to produce evidence of residency, she said, "Oh, you want to go over to the bursar's office. There's an office in there that handles in-state and out-of-state matters. It's on Calhoun Street, right next to the Chapel Theatre."

The Chapel Theatre. Where Bojean and I had watched *Endgame* unfold. Where I learned to hate/love Samuel Beckett.

"I know where that is," I said. "Thank you."

I walked over to the building and was able to see the proper administrator right away. I told her my business, the request for in-state residence evidence and she began tapping away at her keyboard.

"Right," she said, reading her screen and holding a hand out for my paperwork.

I held the paperwork in my own hand but did not hand it over. "What is this for?" I asked. "To my knowledge I have no connection to you folks at all. I'm just a citizen. Already went to college."

The pretty administrator lady read more from her screen and told me, "We have two pending applications for admission. One from Mae T and one from Bea T. They're both applying for in-state tuition due to their father, Holmes Jensen, being a resident of South Carolina for over two years."

My jaw must have unhinged.

"Do you know these applicants?"

"Yuh."

"Are you Holmes Jensen?"

"Yuh."

"Your daughters?"

"Yes."

"Are you okay?"

"Can I look at your screen?" I asked.

"Of course." The nice lady swiveled her computer screen around so I could look at it. It was just as she said, the girls had submitted applications for in-state tuition to the College of Charleston.

"Does this mean they've already applied here?"

She reached her hand to pivot her screen back but didn't grab it as I was still staring, dumbstruck, thunderstruck, gobsmacked, unbelieving in what I was reading. "I'm fairly sure," she said. I let her take the screen back.

The wonderful lady clicked a few more keystrokes and read. "Yes," she said. "They applied in November and were accepted in early December." She read on. "From Massachusetts. Lexington school system. Excellent grades. Top-notch applicants. We accepted them immediately."

My jaw had not returned to its upright position. I handed the amazing lady my proof of residency and she got up to make copies. She made copies, handed my stuff back to me and sat back down. "That should do it," she said. "Have the girls decided on C of C?"

"No idea," I said. "This is the first I've heard of it."

* * *

I did not believe any of it. Even when I received texts from both girls in late August letting me know they were halfway to Chuck in mom's minivan.

We're staying overnight in Gettysburg, Bea wrote. *Gonna tour the battlefield in the morning. We should be in Charleston kinda late tomorrow. We have a hotel for tomorrow but don't move into the dorms until this weekend. Think me and Mae can crash with you until then? We can stash our stuff in the dorm but can't move in until Saturday.*

I didn't believe it.

Of course, I typed. Not believing.

It felt like a trap. Or a dream. Or a dream of a trap.

August in Charleston is a swelter. To me, a wonderful swelter. I walked even more than usual throughout the heated months of May and June and July and then August. I spent even more time in the gym working on my core. I ran. I sweated through six shirts a day. Six sets of underwear. I wore flip flops everywhere except work. I walked the beaches of Sullivan's Island. I walked the beaches of Folly. I made a couple trips to the Isle of Palms to go walking. I walked the public access beaches at Kiawah Island.

I didn't believe it.

I didn't believe it even when they banged on my door on a Wednesday morning, on foot, with backpacks. I opened the door and there they were . . . smiling, really smiling. Hugging me. Smiling. "Daddy!! Can you believe this?"

No.

I looked past my beautiful daughters to President Street and to the corner of Cannon.

"She's gone. She dropped us off."

I didn't believe it. My PTSD hot blood on high alert.

"Come in! Come in! Are you trying to cool off the whole outdoors? Come in!"

For the longest time I just looked at them. And they looked at me.

None of us believed it.

I'd set up two futons in the grand bedroom. I'd put out clean towels in the grand bathroom. I'd cleaned the bathroom. The whole place. They looked around. "Dad, your apartment is beautiful!"

They put their backpacks in the grand bedroom and came and sat on the sofa in the living room. I sat in the black leather easy chair. Mae was holding something behind her back.

"Watchu got there, kid?" I asked.

Mae revealed a bottle of a quite shitty brand of tequila.

"Jesus," I said.

"What time is it?" I said.

"How old are you?" I said.

"I think I have three shot glasses," I said.

* * *

Freshman year was a blur of joy. For me. I'm assuming the girls were having a good time. We settled into a quasi-routine of them coming over to my place once a week or every other week for dinner. They said they missed my cooking. I didn't believe it. But there they were, banging back pasta with bolognaise. Shoveling chili. Choking down baked chicken. I even made them omelets with their initials on top made from American cheese.

We listened to the good old artists on the Craigslist stereo system: the Beatles, the Ramones, the Ry Cooder, the David Lindley. They were into country music at the time so they introduced me to the Luke Bryan and many other amazingly forgettable others. I drove them to Charlotte, North Carolina, to a mega-gathering of country fans come to see an all-star lineup of country mega-stars, none of which I could remember except for Luke Bryan for some reason. I dropped them at the gate and watched them get swallowed by the crowd of Daisy Dukes and sleeveless denim shirts and boots boots boots. When I picked them up four hours later, they were a little tipsy from shared moonshine and happy. They were so happy.

So was I.

During freshman year I would run into one or the other of them randomly at Kudu or on Marion Square. Bea's apartment was on Elizabeth Street in a part of town called Ansonborough. It was just on the east side of Marion Square and a gorgeous part of town. Mae lived closer to me on Ashley. Both apartments may have been the nicest they may ever live in. Of course they and their roommates were not fastidious housekeepers and whenever I visited their respective homes I did my best to keep my mouth shut about the clutter. They were women now. They'd figure it out. Or not. Eventually.

We met up often to have happy hour half-priced sushi at O-ku on King Street. Mae and Bea would get dressed up for it. They were beautiful young women. I took them to the every-Wednesday outdoor barn jam in Awendaw. We sat on benches under canopies of Spanish moss sipping our BYOBs and checking out the local talent.

We had house concerts at my place. Little Carrot flew in to visit and we'd do a quick set along with other musicians I'd met. M and B would bring ten of their friends and I'd take it in. Ear to ear. I couldn't believe it. This was a miracle. Nothing less than a miracle and I will never forget it, ever.

Life had taken a turn for the way better. I looked for my dad on my walks during freshman year so I could tell him about this turn and see if there was any way I could introduce him, somehow, to my beautiful children. I hit Washington Park on the regular and at all hours but did not run into him.

The girls decided to stay in town for summer. I warned them about the heat but they seemed to be as smitten by 99 percent humidity as I was. They got jobs as hostesses, Mae at Fuel and Bea at Hall's Chop House on King. I continued to try and prevent sailors from offing themselves. I was actually having some luck at that endeavor.

This was an enchanted summer. An enchanted year.

One evening in mid-June, I was in my loft/bunk thing reading. The AC was pumping and I'd hung a little mini-fan from the ceiling to keep the air moving up there near the ceiling. My phone began to buzz with activity. Heavy activity. Before I could even pick it up to look at who was calling or texting it had gone off at least six times.

The first text was from Mae . . . *Where are you?*

The next text was from Mae . . . *Is Bea at your place?*

Before I could answer the texts Mae called. She was crying. "Where are you?"

"I'm home . . . Mae, what's going on?"

"Have you heard from Bea?" Mae was nearly in hysterics.

"Mae, slow down. What's happening?"

"There's a massacre, Dad!"

I held the phone between my shoulder and ear as I climbed down the ladder from my loft and then ran to the living room and the veranda. I could hear sirens now.

"It's right in Bea's neighborhood. There's a bunch of people shot, Dad." Mae was no longer crying but sounded close to hyperventilating.

"Are you home, Mae?"

"Yes."

"I'll be there in two minutes. Stay on the line." I stepped into my flip flops and ran down the eight concrete steps to the sidewalk and began to sprint to Mae's. Not even ten feet down Cannon, someone started running with me, next to me.

Bernard.

"What the fuck happening, Doctor?"

"My kid says there's a bad shooting down Calhoun by the library. Mae, are you there," I said, speaking into the phone.

"Here."

"I'm one minute away. You dressed?"

"Yes."

I turned to Bernard. "My other kid lives right there, I have to get over there."

"A'ight, Dad. Be cool. I'm with you."

Mae was waiting on her porch. Her face registered fear like I'd never seen. *Sometimes I'm afraid and I don't know why.* She gave me a quick hug when Bernard and I climbed her steps. I introduced her to Bernard.

"I know Bernard," she said.

"This your kid, Doctor?"

My mind didn't have the bandwidth at the moment to try and figure out how these two knew each other.

Bernard was now standing next to Mae. "Sis is fine. She got nothin' to do wif what happening over there. Right?"

"I don't think so," Mae said, "but she won't answer her phone. I'm fucking freaking out."

By now there were helicopters criss-crossing the sky over by Marion Square. Sirens upon sirens. We were standing a block from MUSC and it seems that every ambulance they owned was ripping out of their staging areas.

"We gotta go," I said to both Mae and Bernard. "We'll go on foot. They'll never let us through down there in the car."

We weren't ten running steps up Ashley when Mae's phone went off. She looked at it and looked like she was trying to strangle it, her eyes nearly popping out of her head. "WHERE THE FUCK ARE YOU!!!" And then she started to sob and shake. She could barely keep the phone to her ear.

I reached my hand out and surprisingly Mae gave her phone over to me.

"Bea?"

"Dad?"

"Yes."

"What's going on? Is Mae OK? What's happening?"

"Bea, where are you?"

"I'm at Folly. There's shit reception here."

"Mae's OK. We were worried about you."

"We can see at least four helicopters over downtown. What's happening?"

"I'm not sure. Mae thinks there's been a shooting down by your neighborhood."

There was a short silence on Bea's end and then she said, "I'm getting a Facebook feed now. Holy shit, Dad, it says someone went into the Mother Emanuel Church and shot a bunch of people."

"Oh no." I glanced at Bernard.

"It says the shooter got away. He's out there somewhere. They're looking for him."

"OK. You say you're seeing that on Facebook?"

"Yes."

Mae did some furious thumb typing and pulled up her Facebook feed. It was as Bea said. A mass shooting, Mother Emanuel AME Church on Calhoun, confirmed deaths, numbers unknown at this time, young white male shooter, whereabouts unknown, massive manhunt underway, shelter in place.

"Bea, come home if you can. My place. I don't think there's any way you'll be able to get back to your house tonight."

"Okay, Dad."

"If they're not letting cars back onto the peninsula, find a hotel and wait until tomorrow. You have a credit card?"

"Yes."

"Why do you have a credit card?"

"What?"

"Never mind. Get to my place if you can. It's far enough away from the church that maybe you can make it."

Twenty minutes later, Bea and her roommate were in my living room with me and Mae and Bernard. The girls' eyes were glued to their phones and my eyes were glued to my girls. I was thinking, a lot.

"OK," I said, "listen." The girls looked up. "This is important. First, don't even worry about the guy, the shooter. They're going to find him." The girls had been in a half panic wondering if the shooter might be somewhere nearby.

"They're going to catch him. He's nowhere around here, OK." The girls just looked at me, eyes adrenaline open and clear.

"Here's the thing . . . it might get very ugly around here." I looked at Bernard, who was sitting at the dining table, looking at the floor. Baltimore was still furious over the killing of Freddy Gray. Ferguson, Missouri, was still on fire over Michael Brown.

"Do not, under any circumstances go out by yourselves. Hear me? I'd rather you not go out at all for a while."

The girls nodded.

"I don't know if C of C will cancel classes or what, but if you go out, you go out in a group. Understand? Do not go out at night. Not for a while."

The girls just looked at me. Bernard picked his head up and looked at me. "Mr. Bernard," I said. "Do you concur?"

"I concur, Doctor."

"I think we should all crash here tonight and maybe tomorrow too. Maybe longer."

The girls nodded, saying nothing.

"You too, Bernard."

Bernard then stood up. He walked over to where I was sitting on the sofa. I stood up. Bernard reached out his right hand and we shook on it. "I'm good, Doctor." He then looked at the girls in the room and told them, "I'm out there. I'm witchu. Some shit start, I'll be there. Look for my face."

Bernard turned back to me. "Take care of these ladies. I have an eye on them too."

I believed him.

Bernard headed for the door and I felt better knowing he was out there. I did believe that he would somehow watch out for Mae and Bea. I hoped that my dad was out there, doing the same.

I thought to myself, *This place is going to burn.*

* * *

This place did not burn.

What is the opposite of burn?

The shooter was caught the following day. A skinny idiot. I won't even talk any more about him. He doesn't deserve an ounce of energy thinking about him. What deserves consideration, is what happened after. What happened after was my first true indication of forward human emotional evolution.

Less than twenty-four hours after killing nine African-American members of the Mother Emanuel congregation, he was caught and arraigned. Until that time the peninsula held a profoundly uneasy quiet, waiting.

At the arraignment, family members of the murdered congregation stood before the video image of the shooter and forgave him. Forgave him.

They forgave him.

That forgiveness changed everything immediately. For me. I don't know if Charleston was changed. I don't know if Charleston is simply a different place on the planet, but the weeks following this horror made an impression on me that will never be altered. I saw a miracle and now I believe in miracles.

The place did not burn. After the shooter was caught and his ideology was revealed, the communities came out and the communities came together. Initially, it was the return of customers to the King Street commerce. But it was different. People on the sidewalks talking, quietly in twos, threes, and fours. Students suspending their boisterous skylarking. Not all of them, of course, but most. For me it was sitting down at Kudu where a window seat facing southeast gave a clear view across Marion Square to the Mother Emanuel steeple. My friend Josh, the owner of Kudu, came and sat with me and we talked.

"You okay?" he asked.

"I don't know. You?"

"Same," he said, "I was here. I saw all of it. Or, the aftermath." Josh is a giant of a man. A North Carolinian in his early thirties, a Division II college power forward. He was looking at his giant hands and they were trembling a little.

He said, "Yesterday I saw a most incredible thing. A van pulled up right in front here and a group of six Black folks got out and headed over to the square. One had a bullhorn thing and one was carrying a stepladder, so I decided to go see what they were up to.

"There was already a gathering at the square, I don't think it was planned or organized. It was just a couple hundred people standing around, talking. I'd say half black, half white. Those folks from the van put themselves right in the center and started in. I'm not sure if they were from around here or not. Not sure who they were affiliated with, but they started in. I don't blame 'em.

"No justice, no peace. I don't blame 'em. We got to organize and fight back, I don't blame them one bit. This racism, they said, has gone on too long in this city and we must fight back *by any means necessary.*"

"Holy shit," I said.

"Yeah, holy shit."

"I hadn't heard about this."

"No, you didn't. But you gotta hear this." Josh took a deep breath to compose himself. "It started real quiet. I wasn't sure where it was coming from at first, but it started somewhere in the crowd." Josh's head was hanging, I could barely hear him.

"It started real quiet, but not for long. It was 'Amazing Grace,' Holmes. The crowd started singing 'Amazing Grace' and it sounded really good. Ever been to a Black church service, Holmes?"

"I have," I said.

"The singing at a Black church service is something. I don't know about all of 'em, but the ones I've been to . . . damn. Harmonies. Sweet voices."

"Yes," I said.

"That damn crowd in Marion Square took up 'Amazing Grace' like I've never heard it. Sweet and low, but clear as a damn bell at midnight." Josh stopped there. He put his giant palm over his face, his eyes.

I waited for a minute and had to ask, "So what happened?"

Josh looked across the table at me and then out the window to Marion Square. "Here's what happened," he said. "The group from the van? They joined in. They started singing too. The guy with the bullhorn up on the stepladder? He climbed down and joined the crowd."

I think my mouth was open, mouth breathing.

"Charleston sang those folks right off the stage. They sang all the verses. When the 'Amazing Grace' was done, that was it. Whatever sort of protest those folks had in mind, and I don't blame them one bit, but whatever they had in mind changed to something else. Jesus, look at my arm."

Josh held his giant arm out across the table and his hairs were on end.

* * *

There were two weeks of funerals. We learned through the media all about the lives of the people who were murdered. From the Reverend Pinckney, who was leading the Bible study group that night, to the young man who told the shooter *You don't have to do this* before he was killed. The shooter intentionally left two survivors to tell the story with the aim of starting a race war. We read all about it. We all talked about it in hushed voices.

People came. From all over the country, maybe the world. People came to witness the funerals and to bear witness to this miracle that was unfolding. People came by the tens of thousands and as a congregation formed a chain of hands across the Ravenel Bridge.

My daughters and their friends were part of this chain. My daughters and their friends went to the memorials.

At my work, I asked my colleague Mrs. B for a moment of her time. We sat in her small office and closed the door.

"I don't understand," I told Mrs. B. "I don't understand this forgiveness. Can you explain this to me?"

Mrs. B was born and raised in the lowcountry, South Carolina. She said, "It's simple, Mr. Holmes. I, personally, will not jeopardize my relationship with Jesus with any act of hatred. Not ever. I can't speak for anyone but myself, but I do not believe I am alone in this."

"But this," I said, "what happened . . . it's too horrible. It's too blatant."

"It's been blatant, Mr. Holmes. Ain't nobody trying to hide anything."

I could only look at her. Her beautiful face. Her beautiful eyes. Her beautiful heart.

"You know the story, Mr. Holmes. I see you every day preaching to your students. Darkness cannot drive out darkness, only light can do that. Hate cannot drive out hate, only love can do that.

"I see you every day, Mr. Holmes. You couch it in your Yankee humor and your Yankee make-believe hard. But we can see it, even if you don't.

"You came here for a reason, to Charleston. I think you know that. I know that. I saw your pain when you talked about your daughters when you first started here. And now look. It's a long journey and the future is uncertain, but you came here for a reason. Now, I know you are not a church man, and I know Jesus is not your cup of tea, but you came here for some sort of a reason."

* * *

On June 25 I stood in line for two hours to pay respects to Pastor Pinckney, the good pastor who welcomed the white face into his Bible study and communed over Scriptures for one hour before he was gunned down. Pastor Pinckney's wake.

I stood alone in the crowd, not the only white face but a minority. I stood side-by-side with a Black man of my age who stood alone as well. He wore a red polo shirt and daddy jeans and Nike hightops and somehow managed to not sweat through the polo in the time we stood in the June 25 heat. We stood side-by-side, not speaking but for a quick hello, and we inched forward toward the basement door of Mother Emanuel. We'd joined the line on Elizabeth Street and as we reached Calhoun we saw the crowds and the media. We watched as a lone and familiar figure wandered up Calhoun from East Bay, an elderly Black man alone until he reached the media and he was quickly surrounded, no one talking to him, only lights and cameras filming his solitary walk up the street. Jesse Jackson looking old and tired and completely baffled. He looked lost and alone.

We, me and red polo, were within thirty feet of the church door, but when Jesse Jackson arrived and someone took him by the elbow and led him inside, we stalled.

I turned to red polo and said, "Jesse."

Red polo said, "Mmm hmm."

I said, "He spoke at my college graduation."

Red polo looked at me now, my face, and said with a smile, "Didn't know the reverend was as old as that."

I chuckled.

Red polo asked, "Do you recall what he spoke about at your college graduation?"

"Not really," I said. "All I remember from the all of it was that his speech had absolutely nothing to do with us graduating seniors, our lives, or our futures. It was a political speech. The only part I remember is when he said something about 'the paralysis of analysis.' That's it. I may have been a little high at the time."

Red polo laughed. "Paralysis of analysis," he said. "Pretty good. I'll have to remember that one next time the wife gets into my binness."

We stalled. Jesse fucked us up. We stood for another hour without moving, sweating. Paralysis indeed. I gave up and walked the mile home. I didn't check the interweb to see what Jesse had to say, if anything. I hope he didn't say anything because the people of Charleston are doing the talking on this one and I hoped the nation was listening. Charleston was speaking for itself. Quietly and with dignity. Accommodating the media with sound bites but not providing the glorious Ferguson flames at sunset. Just boring dignity and respect for one another. Faith and dignity don't show up well on the TV/iPhone screen. I hoped we'd continue to disappoint.

On June 26 I took the day off from work to attend the funeral of Pastor Pinckney because our president was going to attend and because something I could not quite comprehend was happening here in Charleston. I felt the need to understand. To try and understand. And to be a part of rather than as usual, an observer.

So, I tried. Wore a tie and everything. Took off walking at 8 a.m. for a 1:45 p.m. funeral, arrived at relative destination, soaked. I cut diagonally from where I live to the TD Bank Arena, thinking for some reason that there would be maybe a line of early risers but that I would waltz in, find a seat in the AC'd facility, and chill for, oh, five hours, gladly, to see what the best president of my lifetime had to say about the status of mankind in 2015.

I cut through an alley to Meeting Street where there was a pretty big crowd waiting, media, and a cop. I nodded toward the line, twenty across and a hundred or so deep and said, "I'm guessing that's the line to get in?"

Cop said, "No, those are the ministers. The line is that way." he pointed north up Meeting Street.

"Okay. Thanks."

I started up Meeting and crossed Calhoun and the line kept going four blocks up to John where it turned up toward King. The line was four across the sidewalk. I figured, as I walked, there were five rows of four every ten feet, so, twenty dressed up folks, sweating, every ten feet. The line was a half mile anyway. A half mile is, what?, 2,600ish feet? 2,600 divided by 10 = 260 units. 260 units x 20 people = 5,200 people not counting the ministers. TD Bank Arena capacity is 5,100. I wasn't getting in. I walked the little over a mile back to my place, past the well-dressed in line, past the latecomers to be shocked by the numbers ahead of them, entered my house, soaked to the skin, even my tie drenched. I stripped and showered and went to lie on the sofa, not even 9 a.m., but I was tired. So I sat at home instead of joining in, because there was no room for me. That's okay. I will read and rest and write and think about what I've witnessed this week in Charleston.

That evening, the evening of June 26 in Charleston, South Carolina, Mae and Bea came around. I'd promised to cook for them and they arrived early. I was asleep on my sofa after watching the greatest president of my life lay it out. I watched him breaking into "Amazing Grace" and lay it out, just like my neighbors on Marion Square, singing down hatred. I lay on my sofa, not moving, barely breathing, air conditioning humming, and I fell asleep with dreams. It seems most of my dreams of the last two decades have been about daughters Mae and Bea. I dreamed of them before they were born. I dreamed of them trying to soothe me. I dreamed of trying to find them. Two decades of dreams and on this day I dreamed of them again. I did not hear the knock on the door as I dreamed and also I cannot hear. They came in as they have their own keys. Of course they have their own keys. I sat up, blinking.

The girls sat in chairs, across the room, looking at me. Bea told me she had attended an AME church meeting the night before with a friend.

"*How was it?*"

Bea only shook her head.

Mae looked at her hands.

"*Do you guys recognize what is happening here?*"

Both of my beautiful daughters looked over at me. Over. Not up. Not down. They looked over at me and nodded.

"*What?*" *I asked.*

"*What do you think?*"

"*What are you seeing?*"

My beautiful daughters.

Mae looked at Bea. Bea looked at Mae and then at her father. "*Can love really fix this?*" *she asked.*

END

Epilogue

On June 29, an email in my inbox:
You keep popping into my head. It actually started a few days before the shooting and now I'm done ignoring it.
How are you?
You didn't ask, but this is what I think about us. We know how to be the same kind of silly when we are happy. And to question absolutely everything even when we probably shouldn't. And somehow keep our hearts open, even through tragedy. Yeah, that's me looking for connection, but it's also damn true, and I'll believe in it, cause even though my memory sucks and yours is way better, I so fondly remember your happy little jigs and songs. They represent something much much larger for me than you can ever imagine. And I remember stuff like seeing your breath outside in the dead of winter, blending and disappearing with mine. And wanting to study you and understand you and feel the way your crows' feet must feel when you smile. They feel wise don't they? And for whatever reason that makes me feel pretty good and pretty hopeful about life. So thank you for that.
Memories of you.
Bojean

I wrote back:
Dear Bojean
I bought a Cadillac.
It is one quiet ride.

About the Author

Dean Ludington received his Bachelor of Arts degree in Journalism from the University of Rhode Island in 1979. He worked briefly in the newspaper business before being introduced to and captivated by stonemasonry. Ludington wrote a how-not-to book entitled *Stoned; Immaculate* at some point in the late 1980s. The book remains unpublished so far. He enrolled in the Master of Social Work program at the University of New England in 2006 and received his clinical license in 2009.

Dean Ludington is the son of a submarine sailor and librarian. Both are deceased but leave behind a passion for travel and learning.